ELICIT

Eagle Elite Book 4

by

Rachel Van Dyken

Elicit
by Rachel Van Dyken
www.rachelvandykenauthor.com

To my husband
This book series wouldn't be where it is without you.
You started it all when you said, "You know thirty miles
from us an ex-mafia hit man was arrested after being in
hiding for twenty years by pretending to be a farmer…
write that. I'd read that."
Love you so much!

Elicit: To evoke or draw out (a response or an answer or a fact) from someone in reaction to one's own actions or questions. Existence: A corrupt heart elicits in an hour all that is bad in us.

PROLOGUE

Tex

RAGE CONSUMED ME as I looked around the building. A sea of familiar faces stared right through me. It was as if the past twenty-five years of my life had held no meaning at all.

Had I been nothing to them?

Nothing but a joke.

The reality of my situation hit me full force, I stifled a groan as I fought to suck in long, even breaths of the stale dusty air.

"It is your choice." The voice said in an even steady tone, piercing the air with its finality.

"Wrong." I stared at the cement floor; the muted color of grey was stained with spots of blood. "If I really had a choice, I would have chosen to die in the womb. I would have drowned myself when I was three. I would have shot myself when I had the chance. You've given me no damn choice, and you know it."

"You do not fear death?" The voice mocked.

Slowly, I raised my head, locked eyes with Mo, and whispered, "It's life. Life scares the hell out of me."

1

A single tear fell from her chin, and in that moment I knew what I had to do. After all, life was about choices. And I was about to make mine. Without hesitation, I grabbed the gun from the waistband at my back, pointed it at Mo and pulled the trigger.

With a gasp she fell to the ground. A bullet grazed my shoulder as I knelt taking time to reach for the semiautomatic on the concrete. When I stood, I let loose a string of ammo; the sound of it hitting cement, brick, bodies, chairs, and anything else in the line of fire filled me with more peace than I'd had in a lifetime of war.

I stalked towards him, the man I was going to kill, the man who had made me feel like my existence meant nothing. I held the gun to his chest and squeezed the trigger one last time. When he collapsed in front of me, it was with a smile on his face, his eyes still open in amusement.

Chaos reigned around me and then suddenly, everything stopped.

When I turned it was to see at least twenty dead, and Nixon staring at me like he didn't know me at all—but maybe he never had. And wasn't that a bitch?

He took a step forward his hand in the air. "Tex—"

"No," I said, smirking. "Not Tex. To you?" I pointed the gun and pulled the trigger. "I'm the *Cappo*."

Part One: A Rise to Power
CHAPTER ONE

Two weeks before the incident...

Tex

"No! No! Stop!" Mo tossed and turned in her sleep, her arms flying around the bed as if she was trying to punch someone—though really she was only landing blows to the air.

With a sigh I grabbed her fists as gently as I could and whispered in her ear, my lips damn near shaking with the need to caress hers, to make her feel better "Mo, you were dreaming."

Her long lashes blinked against her skin a few times, possibly clearing out the images that had just haunted her rest. "Sorry." Her glance fell to my hands as they held her wrists midair, and she jerked away from me and moved to the side of the bed. "It was just a bad dream."

My touch had once comforted her. She used to crave it; at least I thought she had. It had always been about me and Mo. We were a team, a dysfunctional one, but a team's a team right?

"It's okay," I lied. It was absolutely not okay that she wanted nothing to do with me, that she was scared of me, that she was pregnant and I'd done everything within my power to make it easy on her—even when every day it was harder on me. "Just go back to sleep, and things will look better in the morning."

But they wouldn't. She knew it. I knew it. Hell, everyone who knew us and our family knew it. Things never looked better in the morning.

Actually, I preferred night. Not because I actually enjoyed sleeping—hell if I didn't need sleep I wouldn't do it. Too many images ran through my mind, pictures of death, blood, more death. But the real messed up part? I wasn't haunted by the dreams like Mo was—no I was the exact opposite. Death inspired me, it drove me, it motivated me. Hell, I was the one you'd least expect. Chase even had problems doing some of the dirty work.

But me?

I was the worst type of person.

Because I craved blood like a drug.

I craved death. I craved war. I craved it like an addict. And I loathed the days of peace because they reminded me that I was basically an orphan. Unwanted by my family, unloved. And now? Unwanted by the girl I'd sworn to love for the rest of my life.

So, sugarplums? Santa? Unicorns? Sheep? Nah, that shit didn't fit in my dreams.

It never had.

Mo moved away from me pulling the covers up around her frail body. She'd been losing so much weight it was ridiculous. Weren't you supposed to gain weight when you were pregnant? It stung that she didn't want me to go to her doctor's appointment with her. Apparently he'd said she was stressed. Right, like I could do anything to help that. I was doing everything within my power to fix things—to fix us—to fix her—to fix the family. Nothing worked.

Nothing ever. Freaking. Worked.

Being with Mo wasn't just my peace, it was like I'd finally found someone that got me, someone who understood who I was, even when I chose not to reveal my whole self to her. One look, and I knew she knew. All the shit that went on in my head, but she didn't pester me, didn't make me explain anything, just loved me as I was. And now, it was gone. I was gone. There was literally nothing left.

My role was no longer fulfilling its purpose. I'd known it for a while now, without wanting to admit it. But the signs were clear.

It was time to take my place. Time to bring the nightmare to life, to wake the beast, to be what I was born to be.

Vito Campisi's son.

CHAPTER TWO

Dreams are believed to be 1/60th prophecy.

Mo

I'D HAD THE SAME damn dream for the past three nights in a row. Small details changed. One time I was out in an open field, the next I was in an abandoned warehouse. And the most recent one? I was in Tex's car. The dream started off normal, Tex and I would be laughing and joking around, and then all of a sudden a gunshot would ring out into the night sky and I would find blood on my fingertips.

When I asked Tex for help, he shook his head and laughed.

He said I deserved it.

And I always woke up with the feeling that I actually did. I deserved it. I groaned and reached for my phone to check the time. It was only seven in the morning. Tex and I had been away from the family for four days. They'd freaked when we left everyone in Vegas, but I wasn't exactly in the best emotional state to be partying it up and putting on a good face. I didn't exactly possess that talent like my brother did. People could always read my emotions. Thankfully, Tex knew that my face was one of my tells, so he hightailed me out of Vegas and back to Chicago. Though, he'd been so freaked about my news he'd forgotten to tell everyone where we went.

So naturally they assumed we were dead.

Because when you work for the Mafia? Yeah, that's just a normal assumption. I mean if Nixon was missing I wouldn't call the cops. I'd call the family to order and start torturing people to find his whereabouts. We always assume death before life.

Sucks, but it's the truth.

"Hey!" Tex knocked on the bedroom door. "You ready for breakfast in a bit? The plane landed a few minutes ago so we should probably—"

"—get ready." I forced a smile. "Sure thing. Just give me a minute."

Tex didn't move from his spot in the doorway. His eyes drank me in; he always stared at me like that. Like a man who could never get his fill. I used to love it. Now it just made me feel guilty and sick to my stomach.

I wished it were possible to emotionally survive off memories. Because if it was, I'd survive off all of ours together.

"Hey Mo, you ready to go or... well damn me." Tex walked into the room, his face went completely hard. "Mo you look..."

"Sorry. "I blushed tucking my hair behind my ears. "New swimsuit for the summer. You like?" I pressed my hands against my hips then did a little twirl. I'd always wanted a white bikini but my dad had forbidden it—until now. He was dead and I could wear whatever the hell I wanted. Within reason, which is exactly what Nixon had said when he saw me ordering things off the Victoria's Secret website.

"Like? Freaking love. "Tex shut the door behind him and walked slowly towards me, his eyes focusing in on my hips, then my stomach, and finally settling on my breasts. When he reached out, it wasn't to gently touch my skin, or caress me lovingly. No, that wasn't Tex. He didn't do gentle; he did hard, demanding,

7

possessive—all Alpha, no apologies.

So when he grabbed my body and pulled me against him, I expected his fingers to move to the strings holding my top up, instead he cupped my face and whispered across my lips. "I've never seen anything so beautiful in my entire life."

Heat invaded my cheeks. "It's just a suit."

His eyes hardened. "Mo, listen to what I'm about to say. Nothing is just a suit on you. You don't just wear jeans, you don't just wear a damn t-shirt. Everything you put on your body is so mother effing beautiful that I don't know whether I should hide you somewhere so no one else can enjoy the pleasure of looking at you, or just take you so you know exactly who you belong to."

I shivered in his arms.

"And just in case there was ever a question." His hands moved from my face down to the strings holding my bottoms together. With a slight tug, they fell to the ground. "You. Are. Mine." I blinked in surprise as his fingers gently worked the strings of the top until it joined the bottoms on the floor. "Now look at yourself, and tell me you don't see perfection. Tell me you don't see..." He walked me to the mirror and moved my hair, kissing my neck and moving to my shoulder. "...how freaking beautiful you are."

Insecure, I averted my eyes.

Tex reached around my body and gripped my chin, forcing me to look at myself. "Fine, if you can't see it for yourself, look into my eyes. Look at my face. This is the face of a man totally undone. You don't just do this to me. "He slid his body against mine so I could feel the evidence of his desire. "You make me want to never leave this room. Ever. You're beauty is something to be cherished. Never deny it, not to me, not after seeing you like this." Slowly, he turned my body so that I was facing him. Every hard plane of his body screamed as it pressed against mine, waiting for release. Instead of doing what I imagined Tex would do, he kissed me softly on the mouth and stepped back, even though I knew it was painful for him to do so. "Now, put on some clothes we're going to be late for dinner."

I was naked, I wanted him, and he was leaving? "But—"

"Our time will come, Mo." He winked. "You're still a freshman this year and Nixon would freaking murder me if he even knew I was in here with you, let alone with you naked and giving me those demanding eyes. Believe me, I'm so aroused I can't see straight, but right now, you're under Nixon's protection. I want you—but only if he doesn't shoot me before I get to have you." With another wink he walked out of the room softly shutting the door behind him. And so began the first of many times where Tex chose not to sleep with me. Instead, he seduced me with his words, his looks, his touches—I was damned before I even had a choice.

Tex motioned for the bathroom, the movement jolting me out of the sensual memory. "Can you manage on your own or... ?" He scratched his head and crossed his chest with his arms.

I laughed. "I'm only four weeks, Tex. I think I can walk to the bathroom without face planting."

"Sure." His eyes narrowed. "If you're sure."

"Tex," I snapped. "Look, I appreciate the help but just... stop." *Stop making me feel guilty. Stop looking at me like I'm damaged! Just stop! Look at me like you used to. Like you promised you always would!* I suddenly wanted to shatter every mirror in the room. I was stuck at the lowest of the low, and I couldn't even tell him the truth.

A muscle twitched in his jaw as he took two large steps towards me. "No. I won't just stop because you say you're fine. I've never done this before. I don't know what the hell I'm doing okay? I may be an ass but I'm worried about you, so excuse me for asking you every damn second of the day if you can handle things. *I'm* having problems handling things, and it's not my body going through this, alright? So if I ask you every half second how you're doing, don't be a bitch, Mo. Alright? Besides..." He stepped back and exhaled another curse. "Right now I'm your best bet, after all the kid isn't even mine and I'm taking credit for it."

Tears stung behind my eyes, and emotion thickened in

the back of my throat as I tried to find my voice. "Tex, I'm sorry. I just—"

"Whatever. Yell if you need me. I'll go start the coffee." He slammed the door behind him, leaving me in silence.

Maybe that was the reason for my nightmares. In all my life, the Tex I knew would never slam a door in my face. He wouldn't raise his voice, he would never—and I do mean *never*—approach me with as much as a raised octave to his tone.

But now? It seemed my entire existence infuriated him. He wasn't the same man I'd known my whole life—which begged the question, was he ever who I thought he was? Or just who I wanted him to be? Who we as a family needed him to be?

War has a way of changing people... but with Tex, the thought lingered, *what if he's been just waiting to strike?*

What if...

We invited the enemy in our very own home.

Only to be infiltrated from the inside out.

Things had been brought to my attention over the last three weeks, disturbing things... if they were true. I chewed my lower lip in deep thought.

"Mo!" Tex yelled from the other side of the door. "Thirty minutes, get moving, you want to look your best."

I saluted the door with my middle finger and made my way into the bathroom. My reflection killed me. It really did. Because on the outside I looked the same. Dark silky hair that fell to my mid-back, bright blue eyes, a sharp feminine jaw, high cheekbones, and olive skin that I'm pretty sure every girl would kill for—just hopefully not kill me for. Sad, that the thought actually entered my head. Then again I'd had a lot of threats to my life within the past few weeks, just more secrets to hide from everyone.

I lifted my shirt and patted my flat stomach. What would it be like to bring a child into a family of war instead of peace?

What child of mine, or even Tex's for that matter, would have a shot in hell with the information I'd just learned? Was it even fair to bring innocence into our blood-stained hands?

I shook my head and tried to snap out of it. Nixon would be expecting his sister, the typical smart-ass, sarcastic, slightly narcissistic pain in his ass. And right now I was acting like Eeyore. "Snap out of it, Mo." I took a few soothing breaths and turned on the shower.

Time to put on a show.

Time to fool them all.

Again.

CHAPTER THREE

Blood is always telling. It holds the key to our existence. It holds your life and eventually your death.

Tex

I GRIPPED THE COFFEE CUP so hard my hand hurt. The scalding burn of the liquid through the porcelain was the only thing that made me feel better. Great, I was officially turning into a masochist. Hell, maybe I'd always been one. I'd have to be to keep going back to Mo and praying that things would be different.

But every damn time it was the same.

She offered me a piece.

When I wanted it all.

And then she'd gone and cheated, not that I was really able to stand on a soap box about that one, considering I'd cheated first. But still, I had cheated one time to acquire some information, not because I actually enjoyed getting smothered by someone who smelled like cheap perfume and wore red lipstick on the outside of her lips. I shuddered and took another sip of coffee. The second time I'd cheated I'd done it purposely, to piss Mo off. Better than break her heart. At least if she was pissed, she could shoot me and get it over with, but that had been a gargantuan error, you know because I was still freaking obsessed with her and all. Right, good move Tex, just make her hate you enough to go and sleep with some effing bastard stupid enough to get her pregnant. Shit. Had she even checked for STDs? How did I even broach that conversation with her? Shuddering, I took another long sip of coffee. Thankfully, I'd made it strong. Hell, I probably should have added whiskey to it—Nixon would need it.

We would all need it after shit went down.

I checked my phone just as Mo came breezing into the kitchen. That's what she did. She breezed. She never did something so common as walking. It would be impossible for her. Every movement was fluid, purposeful, graceful. It was distracting as hell when the person you were in love with, moved like some sort of goddess out of a mythological tale.

She was my Aphrodite.

My Athena.

I freaking worshipped that woman.

But our relationship was like the nerd of the class trying to date the popular girl, I think in essence, she felt sorry for me. Then again, I'd never let her know the real me, so maybe it was my fault.

"Tex?" Mo approached, tilting her head to the side. Black hair swirled across her shoulders. "Did you hear what I said?"

Nope, too busy being distracted by those hips. "Sorry I was just thinking about what I was going to say."

Mo's eyebrows drew together. "Just stick to the story, right?"

"Right," I repeated. Damn, she didn't even realize that with every look she pulled another string, I was like a puppet, and I hated that analogy because I'd felt like a puppet my whole life. "I'll just say we're in love."

Mo nodded slowly, her eyes filling with tears.

"And that I messed up." My teeth clenched. "That I'm so

freaking in love with you I didn't use a condom? Is that what you want me to say? Help me out because I really don't think that's a good plan, Mo. Not if you want me to live in the foreseeable future."

Mo rolled her eyes, the tears turning into amusement. "Well, maybe don't use the word condom."

"Right." I offered a smile. "How about I tell Nixon that I wanted to beat him at *something*, so I decided to get his twin sister knocked up?"

At that Mo laughed out loud.

"You what?" A voice roared from the door.

I closed my eyes and hung my head as Mo's face froze into a smile in front of me. Right, in love. Happy about baby. Happy, happy, happy. Shoot me in the mother effing face.

I turned and opened my arms. "Friends! You're home!"

"What. The. Hell. Did you just say?" Nixon roared, throwing his bag so hard against the countertop it skidded off and collided with one of the chairs nearly sending it through the window. His hands barreled into tight fists as he stomped towards me.

"Friends?" I offered backing up so that Mo was behind me. If Nixon pulled out a gun I'd take the bullet. She knew that, I knew that, Nixon most likely knew that, which probably meant the odds were I was getting shot in a few seconds.

Nixon grabbed me by the shirt and pushed me against the countertop. The hard granite bit into my back making me momentarily wince. He pushed harder; my skin was going to get rubbed raw if he kept doing that. I pushed back a bit to give us some space. We were pretty matched for height and strength. I could have fought back, but I owed him this. He couldn't beat up the guy who actually did get his sister pregnant so he might as well use me as the punching bag. Ha! Story of my life. The freaking Abandonato punching bag. Fantastic.

"What did you do?" Nixon's voice damn near shattered

the windows as he slammed my body against the counter again. The granite scratched against my back for the third time, the sharp slice of pain in the small of my back telling me the skin had been pierced. Yeah, I was going to start bleeding all over the floor any second.

"Nothing," Mo answered for me. I peered around Nixon and glared at her. It was my fight not hers, because she'd made it mine, so she needed to stay the hell out of it and let me protect her.

"Wouldn't really call getting you pregnant nothing, Mo, but to each his own." The minute my lips formed a smile, I received a bunch in the jaw, then another. My bottom lip was sliced by my own teeth causing the blood to start trailing down my chin.

"Nixon stop!" Mo wailed. "Please!"

The metallic taste of blood filled my mouth. With a jerk Nixon released me. I grabbed a nearby towel and wiped my face.

Chase walked into the kitchen, hands raised. "Nixon, calm down."

Yeah, not something you say to the boss.

Nixon turned his rage-filled eyes on Chase and pulled out his gun. "Stay out of this."

"Nixon!" Trace pushed Chase out of the way and moved in front of the gun that was aimed for Chase's heart. Aw, family drama. "Put the gun down! Let them talk."

"Trace..." Nixon's jaw flexed, his teeth ground together. "Stay the hell out of it."

"No." She crossed her arms. "Not until you put the gun away." Swear his ice blue eyes turned the exact color of Hell, flashing completely black before he waived the gun around.

"Does no one listen to me anymore?" Nixon looked around the room. "If I want to shoot Chase in the face for defending Tex, I'll do it. If I want to shoot Tex because he touched my sister, I'll do it. I'm the boss. Rules don't apply, and right now I'm jet lagged and a bit pissed off that that jackass—" He pointed the gun at me, just in case there was any confusion as to which jackass he was referring to. "—basically just admitted to getting my sister pregnant." As if remembering about the fight to begin with, Nixon let out a groan low in his throat and moved towards me again. This time the gun was homed in like a beacon to my head. "Tell me she isn't pregnant. Tell me you did not just ruin my sister's life. Tell me, Tex. Tell me."

I eyed the gun. "Are you really going to kill the father of your soon-to-be niece or nephew?"

Nixon hesitated, his eyes narrowing. "I didn't say I was going to kill you. I could shoot you, and you'd still be perfectly fine, maybe walk with a limp but then again that would be a reminder not to do stupid shit. Don't you think, Tex?"

I'd known Nixon my whole life.

He wasn't bluffing.

I nodded my consent and braced for impact. "Go ahead."

His teeth clenched as he gripped my shirt with his free hand and pressed the barrel of the gun to my shoulder. "Don't mind if I do."

The shot rang out like a bomb going off in the kitchen.

The impact burned like hell. The bullet lodging somewhere between my clavicle and my deltoid.

Everyone started screaming at once.

But I held Nixon's gaze.

I didn't blink. I didn't yell. I made no sound whatsoever. I was a hit man. Hit men didn't cry. Made men didn't cry. The only remaining descendent to the *Cappo*? Did not cry.

Liquid started staining my shirt and dripping down my chest onto my stomach as I waited for Nixon to say something—anything. I probably needed to stop the bleeding before I passed out.

"Clean yourself up." Nixon shoved a towel in my hands. "Meet me in the living room in fifteen." He slammed the gun on the counter and grabbed Chase by the arm. "Get the bullet out and pull some morphine from the stash, but don't give him too much. I want him to feel every damn punch."

As Nixon walked out of the room I did what I'd always done in the family to alleviate tension; I made a joke. "Welcome home Nixon!"

Mo groaned into her hands next to me while Chase gently grabbed my arm and ripped my shirt open so he could look at the wound. "Tex, your humor isn't helping the situation, not this time."

"Made Trace laugh." I pointed with my good arm.

Chase looked behind him and shrugged. "She doesn't count, she laughs at commercials and butterflies." He turned back to me and froze.

I smiled as Trace held the gun to his back. "You were saying, Chase?"

"Damn this family's violent," Mil said from her corner near the door. "But seriously Trace, put the gun down. I want my husband to live so he can get me knocked up some day." She winked.

Chase paled.

"Mil," I babbled, nodding like a bobblehead hit man. "Have I told you how much I love you? Cause I do, I really do."

Mil rolled her eyes. "You're getting blood on the hardwood, rock star. Let Chase clean you and drug you. Trace and I will make the popcorn and grab the whiskey."

CHAPTER FOUR

Lies are almost impossible to repeat backwards because whatever you're lying about didn't really take place making it so your brain creates no memory to pull from.

Mo

CHASE TOOK TEX out of the room, most likely to shield us from the cursing that would take place once he pulled the bullet out of Tex's shoulder. I shuddered. My fault. Everything was my fault.

One stupid choice.

One moment of weakness.

"What's wrong dolce ragazza?" He took my hand in his and kissed my open palm. *"Your face isn't normally so sad."*

I shrugged. *"Oh you know, the life of a Mafia princess, lots of drama and broken crowns."*

His face fell, I'd always thought of him as some tragic hero. The way his features were framed made him look like a soldier or hero from King Arthur's Court or something. He always acted that way too. Like he was a hero. Too bad I knew all his secrets. I looked up into his eyes again. Definitely too bad, because he was gorgeous.

"Sit," he ordered. *"Drink."*

"Drinking won't help," I said dryly. "Believe me."

"Wine." He scooted the bottle closer. "It always helps, no?"

"Yes."

"No?" He teased and winked. "Seriously Monroe, you need to take better care of yourself."

"Right, I'll just schedule that pedicure when I get home. Happy?" I pushed a wine glass towards him. Everyone else was in bed, but I was awake. Awake, and oh so blatantly aware that Tex had brought home another girl.

I heard her moans.

I heard her screams.

And then they turned into mine when I finally couldn't take it anymore and got the hell out of the house.

The only place I knew I could go that was actually safe belonged to my family. It was one of our many investments. A fancy bar and grill a few miles away from the house in one of the nicer subdivisions. I knew some of our men would be there blowing off steam. They'd recognize me, and if anyone tried anything, they would shoot them first and ask questions later.

I hadn't expected him to be there, however. He rarely went out in public.

And that was when it hit me.

"Nixon sent you, didn't he?" I licked my lips and stared at the red liquid as he filled my glass.

He didn't answer right away, instead his strong hand reached for the stem of the glass, his fingers wrapping around it, caressing the smooth surface for a minute. "And if he did?"

I shrugged.

He leaned closer until I could smell the warm swirling scent of honey and whiskey on his breath. "And if he didn't?"

"Then..." My voice shook. "That means you've been following me? Like a stalker?"

"Stalker." He laughed and leaned back. "I like the sound of that. Stalker of the Abandonato family gem."

I rolled my eyes.

19

"What?" he whispered, tucking my hair behind my ear. "Don't tell me... you think I'm full of shit." His lips grazed the same ear. "When really, I've been watching you your whole life. Always close. Always ready to attack. Always ready, ready for the time..."

"The time?" I sucked in a breath. "For what time?"

He pulled back, his eyes snapping to my mouth. "For the time when you finally say my name—when you finally need me."

"And that time is now?"

"That time was six months ago." His voice dropped lower. "But I'm a patient man."

And that was it. He released his hold on me, his sensual gaze took in the people around us, and then he pointed to my glass. "Drink, Monroe. We have much to discuss."

"Mo? Everyone's in the living room waiting. I figured..." Trace's voice trailed off. "Well, I figured you'd want to make sure Nixon doesn't kill him."

"Right." I nodded. "Be right there."

With shaking hands, I pulled out my phone and sent one simple text.

Me: It's done.

He replied back immediately.

G: Good. I knew I could count on you do get the job done. You're an Abandonato after all. For what it's worth... thank you.

Me: Don't mention it.

CHAPTER FIVE

Getting shot hurts. The end.

Tex

I LICKED MY LIPS, and winced as I tried to stand to my full height. This was going to hurt. That much was true. Just shooting me wasn't going to appease Nixon. Had the positions been switched—I would have done the same, possibly worse, because I was a possessive son of a bitch, and I loved Mo with my whole heart. Well, at least the heart that wasn't in Hell for all the crimes I'd committed.

"The truth." Nixon paced in front of me. "All of it, I need to hear it."

Mo swayed into the room, her face pale. I offered a wink of encouragement. I had this, I had *her*. I wouldn't let her down.

"I love her." I nodded. "I made a mistake. Mistakes happen. Condoms don't protect one hundred percent and—"

"Please—" Nixon lifted his hand in the air "—spare me a sex-ed lesson. Pretty sure you're the last person who should be giving advice on safe sex."

The room fell into a tense silence. My voice cracked.

"Well, that's basically everything. Don't tell me you weren't aware of our... extracurricular activities."

Nixon's eyebrows shot up, swear they almost went through his forehead. "That's what you think I'm upset about?"

Next to me, Chase groaned and took a step out of the line of fire.

Nixon let out a laugh that was anything but amused. "You son of a bitch. I should just end your life right now. Tell me not to do it, Chase."

Chase didn't say anything. Bastard.

I glared to my right. Chase kept his face impassive. Great. I officially had no fans. Even Mil and Trace were silent. *Thanks Mo, really, so awesome to be hated by the only family I've ever known because I'm protecting you and some prick's unborn child.* Felt good. It was all good. Totally what I deserved. After all, I was a Campisi; we freaking breed mayhem.

"You," Nixon spat, "were in bed with two girls, not one, two." His nostrils flared. "Not less than three weeks ago. So yeah, sorry if I'm a bit pissed that you were screwing my sister while you were screwing every whore within a fifty mile radius!" His fist went flying, hitting me square in the stomach. I hunched over and puked as he hit me again and again.

Unable to hold myself up anymore, I collapsed onto the floor, holding my stomach so that I wouldn't puke again.

"Enough," Mo said quietly. "Nixon. Enough."

"It will never," he said in a hoarse yell, "be enough. Never. Do you hear me?" He lunged for me again but was stopped by Chase, because apparently he wasn't as heartless as I'd first assumed.

"Walk away, Nixon." Chase grabbed Nixon by the shoulders and directed him towards the door. But Nixon, wasn't having any of that, he fought against Chase so hard you'd think I'd actually killed Mo rather than getting her pregnant. There were worse things in the world, weren't there? I mean, didn't we face death every day?

"Nixon." Mo cleared her throat; her voice seemed shaky. Damn it, she was afraid of her own brother. "Tex didn't do anything wrong. He simply gave me what I asked for."

Say what?

Wow good to know the story changed from something totally believable to mass insanity—I was as sure as dead.

"What do you mean?" The anger had faded slightly from Nixon's voice.

Mo shrugged. "I missed him. We slept together. Once, for old time's sake. That's all it took. It's not Tex's fault I seduced him."

Yeah I would have loved to be a part of that seduction. Freaking loved it. Too bad it didn't happen, because Mo was a dirty little liar.

"I basically attacked him." She looked down at her feet. Was she blushing? Seriously? "He didn't really have a choice but to appease me—and we all know Tex, he doesn't choose himself. He always chooses me, every single time, to a fault. I'm his weakness." Something about the way she said it didn't settle with me. Because if she knew that, others knew, which meant I was a giant-ass chicken walking down the middle of a road directly into oncoming semis.

Damn her. I hated that of all the weaknesses in the world—hers was the one I couldn't shake. The one I couldn't overcome. I would never conquer my love for her. Ever. I could die tomorrow, and her name would be the last thing to cross my lips.

"That true?" Nixon directed the question towards me. Mo's gaze was intense, as if she was praying I wouldn't take the higher road and say *no man, it's my fault, I messed up.* Instead, feeling like a jackass, I nodded my head.

Nixon put the gun down and shoved his hands in his pockets. "You'll do the right thing, still. Right, Tex?"

The right thing? My head snapped to attention. Even

Chase looked confused, his eyes pinched together causing a line to form on his forehead.

I looked at Mo for help. Realization must have dawned, because her face went white as a sheet before she launched herself into Nixon's arms. "No! Nixon, no you can't make us!"

"Chase," Nixon barked, "make the arrangements."

"Uh?" I raised my hand. "For my funeral? Is that what we're discussing? Kind of in the dark, man."

"Maybe to you." Swear Nixon's eyes were dripping black as they pierced through mine. "But some may call it a celebration."

"What?" I repeated. "The hell. Is going on?"

"Do the right thing." Nixon popped his knuckles. "Unplanned pregnancy out of wed-lock."

My mind did the calculations.

And apparently two plus two really does equal four.

And I was screwed.

I wondered how bad it would be... to marry someone who you loved with so much of your soul that it hurt to breathe. Only to know that you're her second choice. Or maybe not even a choice in the first place. Just a happy replacement until something better came along.

I wasn't so sure I could live with that.

And suddenly I felt like Chase did all those months ago. When he was in love with Trace, when I couldn't understand why the hell he was acting like such a hormonal woman over his feelings when we had bigger things to worry about.

But that's love.

It makes you feel.

"Don't," I whispered. "Please Nixon, anything but this."

He tilted his head, his eyes narrowing as he examined my face. "Thought you loved her?"

"I do." My answer was quick. Confident. "But she doesn't feel the same way about me."

"Then she should have thought about that before she

24

jumped into your bed, don't you think?" He sidestepped me and started barking instructions to Chase about the marriage. Words like, tonight, make it fast, and hurry were not ones I ever wanted associated with what should have been the most important day of my life.

The most special day of hers.

I looked down at her flat stomach again. My eyes wishing they could peer at the tiny soul that had been created. I was protecting the innocent.

Even if that made me the guilty.

I was doing the right thing.

Even though I was pretty sure I was traveling down a road I would never be free from, to a destination that would feel a hell of a lot like constant torture.

Would I lay down everything I was? Everything I had to offer, to protect someone who didn't give two shits about me?

I stared at her face.

The one I dreamt of every night.

Yeah. I would offer her everything. And in return take nothing. Story of my life.

I give.

They take.

I give some more.

They take it all.

CHAPTER SIX

Hearts weren't meant to be broken.

Mo

"ARE YOU MAD?" My voice cracked. I might as well have yelled, the room had been so silent. Tex wasn't speaking to me. He wasn't speaking to anyone. The light had officially died from his eyes ever since earlier that afternoon, and it was all my fault. It wasn't intentional. I'd do anything to protect my family. Anything.

Even if it meant damning both of us in the process.

"Am I mad?" Tex repeated, his muscles rippling across his arms as he flexed his hands and then made a fist with his right, punching the bed lightly. "No, not mad. Mad would mean I was crazy, nuts. Madness assumes the person is one step away from insanity. I think what you're asking is, am I angry, and more importantly is said anger directed at you?"

"That was a really long explanation." I tucked my feet under myself and leaned against his muscled shoulder. Everything about him was larger than life. From his body to the way he spoke. Tex didn't do small. He did big. He moved his hands when he talked as if he was preaching at a Baptist church. He laughed like it might be the last time he did so. He made love… well he made love like he believed in it, like there was nothing in the world he'd rather be doing than spending time pleasuring me, exploring me; he made me feel special. And in the end, that had been my downfall with him.

I was owned by him.

No longer me.

I'd gotten kind of lost in his bigness, so I'd backed off. It helped that I'd had a good excuse; he'd cheated. Though, later on, one of the men told me the truth. He'd done it to get information about Mil's family. Would have been nice to know it at the time, but I was too damn upset to say anything. Upset with him, upset with me.

And scared.

Yeah. I was really, really scared.

Terrified.

And I couldn't even tell him why.

"For what it's worth…" I shuddered. "I'm sorry."

"Do you love me?" he asked.

My entire body seized. *Did he just ask what I think he did?*

"Mo? Do you love me? It's a simple question. And no I don't mean love me like the way you love Chase or Nixon. Do you love me? Do I own your soul? Your heart? Do you love me? Forget all the shit that went down with other girls, forget getting pregnant. It's just you and me. Do you love me?"

Breath got caught in my throat. It was like my lungs weren't working. I tried to answer him, really. My mouth was open and everything. I couldn't lie. I couldn't lie! Please God, don't make me lie. In that moment I wished for death. Anything would be better than doing what I had to do.

"I've been watching you for months. I think it's time to play my cards." He leaned forward. *"Just how important is protecting your family? Would you die for them? All of them? Go to the ends of the earth to save them?"*

"Yes," I slurred. *"What did you put in my drink?"*

"Just a little... concoction. Believe me, it won't hurt. It will just make things, a lot less painful and allow us to keep a close eye on you." Something sharp hit my arm, I looked down. Why was I bleeding? What was that? A needle the size of something I'd only ever seen on TV poked through me and something pushed into my wrist. I screamed in pain.

He held out the glass. "Drink."

I drank.

I had no choice.

"Do you know who he is?" he asked and then laughed. "Of course you do. Everyone does now that the Cappo has been killed. See? See how I'm already laying out my cards on the table? Now, let me tell you how this is going to work..."

"No." I whispered into his chest. When he tensed I slid up his body and whispered in his ear, "Volpe."

Tex's eyes immediately flew to mine. A bit of understanding dawned, but it was enough. He'd put me in an impossible position. But in that moment I could at least offer him hope.

Because things weren't at all what they seemed.

And by using my word—the one I used to scream when I was little, when Nixon was trapped in the torture box my dad built, when I was locked in my room—Tex knew exactly that.

A war was coming.

And he was the target.

He just didn't know it yet.

CHAPTER SEVEN

Impossible: Also known as trying not to love the person who holds your heart.

Tex

VOLPE MEANT FOX in Italian. Mo had a fascination with foxes with she was little. Okay, so maybe it was more of a fixation. She liked their tails. At any rate, it was the word Nixon told her to use when she was either afraid or something was suspiciously wrong.

It was the one word I knew she would never use.

Unless she truly meant it.

The only problem. Was she afraid of me? Of the situation? Or was she suspicious that things weren't as they seemed?

I didn't have time to think any further.

A knock sounded at the door, and then Nixon burst through. "It's time, grab your shit."

"Wow, good afternoon to you too." I sang.

"It's nine in the morning." His eyes scanned the room. "Let's go get the ceremony over with."

"Just like that." I whispered under my breath.

"Did you say something?" Nixon asked, his voice even, his eyes blazing with fury.

"Nah, man." I rose from the chair in the corner. I'd been drinking by myself in that chair, sitting at the stupid courthouse just waiting for someone to tell me it was time. "Just thinking about how excited I am to be your brother-in-law."

Take that bitch.

Nixon scowled and held the door open for me. "Please, I'm already going to have nightmares after today. Don't make it worse."

"You're going to be an uncle."

"Tex."

"That was me making it better," I snapped. "Because regardless of how you feel about me right now or even about Mo, there's a child, okay? A child that has our blood." I pushed against Nixon's chest. "Our blood. Our family. We protect our family."

Nixon hung his head, licking his lips. "You're right."

"I know." I gripped Nixon's shoulders. "Don't make it worse than it is. You've had your fun, you shot me in the shoulder, beat the shit out of me, and made me bleed. You've taken out your anger, and you've let me take responsibility. So for the love of God, can we please, just hug it out and be friends again? Because I'm scared as hell, and I can't do this alone."

Nixon nodded and then grabbed my face with both of his hands and kissed each cheek. "Welcome to the family, brother."

"Now I finally get a family." I joked.

Nixon didn't laugh, instead his eyes softened. Oh, hell no, the last thing I needed was for him to feel sorry that I was an orphan.

I gripped his shirt and jerked him close to me so that our heads almost knocked. "Look at me like that again, and I'll get your sister pregnant again just for the hell of it."

"You son of a bitch!" Nixon knocked his head against mine sending me sailing back against the wall. Oh, look, a candlestick just got impaled into my shoulder. Damn it!

"Too soon?" I winced.

"Tex," Nixon roared just as the door to the room opened.

"Boys?" Trace peeked her head around the door. "Everything okay? Everyone... alive?"

"Sad she has to ask that, huh Nixon?" I winked.

"Mother loving son of a—"

"Nixon." Trace grit her teeth. "Leave it."

And just like that, Nixon did. I never imagined I'd see the day where bad ass Nixon Abandonato would be shut up by a woman. But miraculously, he put his gun away, thank God, and walked over to Trace, softly pulling her into his arms.

Jealousy surged through me from every angle.

I looked down, immediately ashamed.

"Let's go." Trace's clear voice rang out. "The family's waiting."

Numbly, I followed them down the hall and into the small room where the justice of the peace was waiting.

Mo was standing as stiff as a board in front of the room.

I wanted to weep. And I wasn't a guy who let emotion take a hold of me that often; I was more of a believer in emotion being a weakness.

But she was so pretty.

Not beautiful, pretty.

Like something my ma would have told me not to touch when I was little, something so precious that I couldn't play with it. Instead, it would be set far away from my grubby little hands. I wasn't allowed to touch, but I could stare all I want. I could memorize the lines of the object, I could visualize what it would be like to be with it, I could even want it, love it, obsess over it.

But I could never, ever possess it.

I took purposeful steps towards Mo and gently grabbed her hand, clenching it in mine.

Yes, her choices might be the reason we ended up in this position. But I'd started the chaos. It wasn't her fault she didn't know when to get off the train. Because the thing about going over a hundred miles an hour all day every day? Eventually you forget you actually had a destination in the first place.

You forget to get off.

And that was all on me.

I'd put us there because of my job.

And I'd kept her there out of selfishness.

Never realizing I was damning us both to a marriage of something worse than convenience. Unrequited love—because I'd love her until my dying breath, but Mo? It was entirely possible by marrying her, I was keeping her from loving someone else, from being what she should have been, what she was good enough to be.

I was keeping her in the family.

The one place she swore to me she wanted to escape.

Welcome to the Mafia, blood in, well isn't that just shitty part, there is no freaking out.

CHAPTER EIGHT

Words bring both life and death.

Mo

SHAKING, I PUSHED the wedding band that I hadn't even chosen onto Tex's finger and repeated the vows. My voice was hollow as I promised to spend the rest of my life with him, in sickness and in health. I wanted to collapse under the pressure, the weight, the fear.

When it was Tex's turn, I looked up.

I shouldn't have, because his eyes, those green eyes framed by perfect long, dark lashes gazed into mine and I was lost in a sea of desire. It hit me so hard it was difficult to breathe. Gasping was all I seemed to be doing, taking in huge gulps of air only to remind myself I had to actually exhale too.

He'd loved me once.

Would he ever love me again?

Forgive me?

Even though he was looking at me like he wanted me, I knew the truth, I'd driven a wall between us. I wasn't sure if Tex wanted to scale it—I wasn't sure I deserved to have him try.

Protect him. At all costs, protect those you love.

That was my mantra, the one my ma had taught me when I was little. And God, I was trying, trying so hard.

"…in sickness and in health, for as long as we both shall live." Tex finished, his voice cracking in the end as my fingers trembled in his hand.

"By the power vested in me, I now pronounce you Mr. and Mrs. Vito Niscio Campisi Jr."

Tex visibly winced at the sound of his name—his real name, the one his father had given him, his very dead father. The one he'd shot not three weeks ago.

I gave him a reassuring smile.

It did nothing but turn his eyes to ice.

"You may now kiss your bride!"

Everyone clapped awkwardly while Tex stepped closer to me, tugging my body against his. Slowly, he leaned down and kissed me briefly on the cheek before stepping back.

My body screamed with the injustice of it! Not even a real kiss on my wedding day? Not that I deserved it, but it was Tex. The final nail in the coffin had been smacked into the wood. Tex never did things like that. He was the peacemaker, he was the one that made me feel like everything was going to be okay. He was my constant.

And I'd hurt him.

I would have fallen into hysterics right then, had I not turned around and seen *his* face.

Swaying, I stopped walking in time to gather myself, but it was too late, he was already walking towards us.

"I think congratulations are in order." He grinned then pumped Tex's hand. After a brief exchange he tilted his head in my direction and grinned that devastating grin. "And Mo, looking as beautiful as ever."

"Th-thanks." I stepped closer to Tex.

"Thanks for coming, Sergio. "Nixon hit him on the back. "You're family, you should be here."

Sergio's crystal blue eyes cut straight to me. "There's no place I'd rather be than where I am right now."

I sucked in all the air I could, and forgot to exhale… only this time, it ended up with me collapsing to the floor.

CHAPTER NINE

Truth always finds a way out…

Tex

"WHAT THE HELL!" I grabbed Mo's body right before it crashed against the floor. "Mo? Mo!" I shook her and then pulled her into my chest. "Baby, talk to me…" Panicked, I kissed her mouth, urging her to wake up.

Her lips moved against mine as she let out a moan and then jolted back.

If I was being honest, it kind of scared the hell out of me—I hated not knowing what to do in this situation.

"Mo?" Sergio's voice was laced with concern as he leaned down next to me and slowly touched her face. It was such an intimate caress that I was momentarily dumbfounded.

And then, like someone hitting me in the chest with a freaking two by four, I staggered back, nearly landing on my ass.

"YOU!" Had Mo not been in my arms I would have shot him. I didn't give a rat's ass that we were in City Hall. I'd go to prison. Gladly.

Sergio's brows furrowed together in confusion. "Me,

what?"

"You did this!"

His face paled. "I did not cause her to faint!"

"Not that!"

"Tex." Nixon put his hand on my shoulder. "It's been a long day and..."

Mo stirred. "Tex, sorry... I just, so hot..."

"Can you sit up?" I asked in the gentlest voice I could manage, which just so happened to sound gruff and irritated.

"Yeah, yeah, I can, um, I can get up." Mo struggled a bit as I helped her to her feet.

Chase came up behind us with Mil. Everyone was hovering, and I was sick of it.

"Guys, give her some space." I kept my eyes locked on Sergio's. The bastard had no right to be staring at what was mine. I stepped around Mo so I was directly in front of him. With a grunt and a curse, he stumbled back.

"I'm fine guys, really, I'm fi—"

The sound of glass shattering pierced the air. I covered Mo with my body and looked up just in time to see Chase grunt and then fall to the floor followed by the Judge who'd just married us. Only there was no getting up for him.

He'd been shot in the head.

"Chase!" Tracey and Mil yelled at the same time, while he held up his hand from the ground with a thumbs-up.

"Get the girls out!" Nixon roared grabbing me by the collar of my shirt. Mo tripped as I pulled her to her feet. Trace and Mil kept their heads covered as they ran towards the door. Sergio pulled out his cell phone and followed me out then started barking orders in Italian to his men.

Well at least he'd brought backup.

Then again, why the hell would he need it?

Police filed down the hall just as Nixon and Chase emerged. They were both smiling and laughing like they'd just gotten wasted at a party.

"Split up." Nixon growled, the smile fell from Chase's lips as he winced.

Mil ran up to him.

"I said..." Nixon's voice lowered. "...split up, I've got Chase. Girls you go with Tex and Sergio, we've got this. Make the calls." He pointed his free hand to Sergio. "Get one of your men in here to look at the cameras."

An officer ran up to us. "Sir?" He directed his sir to Nixon who sighed and pinched the bridge of his nose. "Let the Chief know we were getting married. After the ceremony two shots rang out, silencer." He tugged at Chase's shirt.

I pushed his hands away. "Let me." With a rip, the shirt weakened under my grasp. The bullet had lodged in his left shoulder. "Aw, we're bullet twins."

"Not. The. Time." Sweat poured down Chase's face.

I winced. "Sorry, been there, lived through that." As carefully as I could, I pushed against the skin surrounding the wound. "Yeah, it's lodged in there pretty good. From the looks of it, shooter probably used a rifle, possibly an MK12."

"Son of a bitch, that hurts." Chase leaned heavier onto Nixon.

I tried not to smile, but it was the best damn part of my day seeing someone else get shot. Not because I wanted Chase to die but because I could at least focus on something other than Mo and the fact that Sergio had touched her in a way that was too familiar, as if he'd touched her in that way before—repeatedly.

"We'll let you know what we find." The officer patted Nixon on the shoulder and walked back into the room.

"Well." I sighed looking around at the guys. "Clearly we don't know how to do normal weddings."

Everyone fell into comfortable laughter as we walked out of the building. The girls were probably halfway home by now and freaking out if I knew them at all.

"Nixon!" The same officer came running down the stairs,

his chest heaving. "The papers…" He bent over and blew out a gutful of air. "The ones signed by the Judge…"

"Yes?" Nixon said impatiently.

"They're fake." He handed them over to us. "I'll make copies and send them through the usual associates but, the wedding today? It wasn't real."

My mind whirled with possibilities. Was the Judge in someone's pocket other than ours? How the hell did that happen in our own city?

"Thanks." Nixon nodded. "Once we have the papers, we'll take it from there, understand?"

"Yes sir, of course sir. I'll let the Chief know."

"Well." Nixon cursed and kicked the wheel of his Range Rover. "Will life ever be boring?"

"Bleeding." Chase panted. "In case you guys were, oh I don't know, worried? Concerned? I mean, right flesh wound considering almost dying a few weeks ago, I got it, but it burns like hell and I really, really need to make sure Mil isn't at the house ripping the curtains from the windows in a shitstorm of emotion because you sent her away, Nixon."

At that Nixon laughed. "When is Mil not pissed, Chase?"

Chase smirked. "Don't you worry about that."

"Disgusting," I muttered.

"Says the soon-to-be father." Nixon said dryly.

I glared in Sergio's direction and answered, "Right. Soon-to-be… *father*."

If he was bluffing about anything he didn't have any tells. Instead, he simply met my stare with one of his own.

One that told me.

I wasn't getting shit.

CHAPTER TEN

Dogs can smell fear… so can people.

Mo

MY HANDS WOULDN'T stop shaking. I blamed it on the shooting. Since when have I ever been terrified of getting shot at? Never. I'd been around this life since as far back as I could remember.

Funny, how it wasn't the violence that caused me to tremble.

But *him*.

I wanted wine so badly it wasn't even funny. Irritated, I followed the girls into the kitchen and waited for the guys to get home.

It was a tie between who I wanted to strangle first. Mil was stringing so many curses together it was hard to decipher if she was upset at the situation or at Chase. Trace spent her time soothing Mil while giving me the, "Are you okay?" eyes.

After about ten minutes the doors burst open, and the guys barreled in. Chase stumbled a bit as Tex helped him into one of the chairs.

My husband, God it still sounded wrong, ran out of the

room to grab our kit while Nixon tore the rest of Chase's shirt away from his body.

"Mil." Chase clenched his teeth. "I'm fine!"

"You bastard!" She punched him in his good arm. "Stop taking bullets!"

"Right." Chase snorted and lifted his head to the ceiling, closing his eyes. "Because it was a choice!"

"Well!" Mil huffed. "Damn it, Chase, just try not to get shot every two weeks. It's irritating as hell!"

"You're irritating as hell!" he fired back.

"Good one, must be losing your touch with all that blood loss."

"Mil," he warned, then his eyes flashed as her breathing increased.

"Could you guys not eye screw each other right now?" Nixon swore and ran his fingers through his messy hair. "It's going to be hard enough to get Chase to sit still Mil, so if you could stop making it so that he wants to do you on the kitchen table, we'd all really appreciate that."

Mil flushed and crossed her arms over her chest. "Sorry."

"No you aren't." Chase leaned forward and winked

She licked her lips.

I groaned into my hands. The last thing I needed was to see how ridiculously happy they were.

"Whoa!" Tex walked back into the room. "I leave and things get *more* tense?" He snorted and put his hands on his hips. "That's a first."

"Everyone!" Nixon held up his hands. "One thing at a time. Tex, keep your head out of your ass, pull the bullet out while I deal with the fake marriage contracts and murder. Sergio, can you—"

"I'll sew him up." Sergio nodded. "Just another one of my many talents." He winked at Trace and Mil. "I'm really good with my hands." He turned his head slightly, briefly making eye contact with me before going over to the kitchen sink and turning on the water to wash up.

The girls' mouths dropped open.

"Oh please," Chase grumbled, sweat starting to pour down his face, most likely from the pain.

"Tex," Sergio ordered, his voice slightly accented, which I knew from experience happened only when he was under stress and not paying attention to his annunciation. "Could you grab the scalpel?"

"I hate this part." Chase squeezed his eyes shut.

Mil gripped his arm.

Nixon was pacing back and forth, yelling into his phone, but all I was focused on was Sergio as he very carefully made an incision next to the wound and began working.

He was an artist.

Since when had he become a surgeon?

"I'm older than you guys," he answered without looking up. "In case you haven't noticed that my balls actually descended."

Tex rolled his eyes.

"And…" Sergio made another incision. "…I actually graduated at the top of my class and went to two years of medical school."

"Was that before or after your parents went to prison?" Tex sang out with a forced smile lifting his lips. "I mean, just curious about the timeline and all."

"Hmm…" Sergio placed the scalpel on the table and grabbed the tweezers. "Let me think. It was probably after *your* parents disowned you and before you killed your father. Yeah, how's that for a timeline?" His voice was so smooth that if you weren't listening you'd think he delivered a compliment instead of an insult.

Tex's jaw twitched.

"Not now, Tex." Chase winced and cursed violently under his breath, half in Italian half in English. "Not while he has tweezers in my skin. Damn, that burns."

Sergio smiled with his lips but his eyes remained viciously cold and emotionless. "Almost done."

"How old are you?" Mil asked, still not taking her eyes off of Chase.

"Old," Tex answered for him.

After a few seconds Sergio lifted his head and looked directly at me. "Old enough."

The room got really tense.

"Twenty-eight." Tex swore. "It's not like he's an elder or anything. Damn, Sergio, could you be any slower?"

Sergio smirked, slightly lifting his head to the side to give me a knowing look. "I like to take my time with things."

My stomach fluttered and then clenched.

"All good things..." Sergio squeezed the tweezers together and pulled slowly out of the wound. "Come with time." When he dropped the bullet onto the table he lifted his eyes for a second time and met mine.

I didn't look away.

Because I couldn't.

I was hiding so much. And Sergio knew that—he knew everything.

When I finally broke away from his gaze, it was to meet Tex's. He was furious, but what was worse? He was suspicious. And the last thing I needed was to put him back in the line of fire after all the things I'd done to keep him out of it.

"Thanks." Chase exhaled as Sergio wrapped his shoulder.

"Of course." Sergio grinned.

"Tex!" Nixon yelled from the other room, "Get in here. Now."

When Tex didn't move, Sergio took it upon himself to make things worse. Damn him. "Run along, foot soldier, go see what the boss wants."

With a snarl, Tex walked by Sergio nearly knocking him over in the process, which to be honest wouldn't be hard because again, Tex was huge; at least six-foot four and Sergio, though not small by any means was only around six one.

Chase let out a low whistle. "Damn, Sergio, who pissed in your Cheerios this morning, huh?"

Sergio watched Tex walk down the hall then turned his full smile on everyone. "Off day."

Now that the drama was over, I just wanted to lie down, preferably without Tex giving me crazy eyes or Sergio being suggestive. Slowly, I rose from my seat, and tried to walk away.

"Mo…" Sergio's smooth voice interrupted my escape. The room was quiet, so everyone had heard, it wasn't like I could run away and say I didn't hear him.

"Yes?" I turned.

"A minute?"

"Sure." I crossed my arms.

His smile grew, making his features come alive. He'd always looked like he'd just walked off the cover of GQ photo shoot, dark straight hair, aristocratic nose, a side smile that melted people on the spot, and lush lips that made promises no girl should ever, ever, take seriously. "Over here."

Gently, he grabbed my elbow and led me down the hall and around the corner, where Nixon's room was. Far away from the office where Tex and Nixon were currently yelling.

I swallowed convulsively when he pressed me against the wall and leaned into me, his forehead touching mine. "Talk to me."

"No." I licked my lips and averted my eyes.

"Mo…" He tilted my chin towards him. His breath was warm, inviting. "You used to tell me everything."

"That was when we were friends."

Damn his smile! "And we aren't friends anymore?"

"Really?" I spat. "Do friends treat each other like this? Hmm?"

Sergio's eyes darkened as he leaned in and brushed his

lips against mine. "Hell, no." His voice was thick with desire. "I highly doubt I should treat my friends or associates for that matter, the way in which I want to treat you."

I tried to fight the pull.

But it was impossible.

I didn't love Sergio, not like I loved Tex.

But he'd picked up Tex's pieces when I was in desperate need of someone to clean up the mess.

And he'd given me the one thing I'd been craving for years.

Purpose.

"Afraid all your friends will find out?" he whispered against my lips. "Afraid of all the little lies?" He licked my lower lip then tugged it with his teeth. "Which lie, Mo? Which one are you most afraid of?" His hand moved to my neck as he slowly massaged the knots out.

I swallowed and pulled back, my heart slammed against my chest. "All of them, Sergio. I'm afraid of all of them."

A loud clamoring sounded to my right and then in a blur, Tex's fist went sailing by my face landing a perfect blow to Sergio's jaw. He staggered backwards, his body slamming against the wall behind him as he finally slumped to the ground, disoriented as hell.

Tex grabbed my hand and jerked me towards the master bedroom. He flung me inside, and the door banged shut behind him. I looked up just in time to see his hands reach for my body as he forcefully pushed me against that same door and then slammed his mouth over mine, his tongue not asking permission to enter into my mouth but doing it with such force, such fluidity that I let out gasp and finally a moan.

He didn't kiss like Sergio.

He didn't kiss like anyone I'd ever known.

My body arched towards Tex as he ran his tongue along the seam of my lips. He drew my bottom lip into his mouth with his teeth, then pulled back and plowed his fist into the door directly above my head. To the sound of cracking wood, I jumped a foot and skittered away as he barked, "Mine!" Then nearly took the door off the hinges as he pulled it open and stalked down the hall towards Sergio, who was now just getting up off the floor.

It would have probably hurt less had Tex shot him.

Sergio smirked as Tex made his way down the hall, his footsteps damn near breaking through the hardwood floors as he stomped.

"*You—*" He pointed at Sergio. "—will not touch her."

"Hmm…" Sergio winked in my direction. And the man officially had a death wish. "Shouldn't that be up to her? Who am I to deny her if she asks?"

"She won't," Tex clipped. "Believe me."

"But if she does?"

"She won't." Tex's voice dripped with hatred, his hands shook at his sides. "Where do you get off coming into my house, touching my woman—?"

"Actually—" Sergio's smile grew "It's Nixon's house, and last I heard, she wasn't your woman… at least not legally. Funny, does the son of the dead *Cappo* suddenly think he belongs? After all these years?"

Tex's face paled.

It was a liver shot.

A kidney shot.

A low blow.

Because I knew that deep down Tex never felt like he belonged, like he fit in.

"So maybe it's your turn to listen." Sergio pushed at Tex's chest. "You have no one. Nobody. Your real family doesn't know what to do with you, and your new family's forced to claim you. And you're pissed because I kissed a girl I happen to like? Damn, boy, you may as well have peed on her. Would have been more subtle. But here's the thing, while your eyes drip with hatred, while you direct every single ounce of strength towards strangling the life from me, maybe you should pause and ask yourself. If she's really yours, why the hell was she kissing me back?"

I gasped, covering my mouth with my hands as shame washed over me.

Tex sucked in a large breath, like he'd just gotten sucker punched and wasn't able to exhale.

"Good talk." Sergio smirked. "Now, if Nixon isn't busy, I should probably go help, you know, since we're actually family."

With that, Sergio pushed past Tex and stalked down the hall.

Leaving me in a tense silence with Tex.

"Tex, I—"

Tex held up his hand. "Save it."

"But you don't understand. I think if I explained—"

He let out a bark of laughter. "Explained what exactly? Hmm, Mo?" He moved towards me, his eyes full of hurt. "How bad it sucks that while I'm pissed as hell that you put me in this position—I still wish it was really my child you were carrying? How now that I've seen you and Sergio together, all I keep wondering is what type of bastard doesn't take responsibility for his actions? Or how about this? I've been on my knees, bleeding out, apologizing, falling all over myself, willing to go to the depths of Hell and back for you, and you thank me by kissing that asshole, only a few feet away from me? Right okay, sure, you have the floor. Please, Monroe, go ahead, try to *explain*."

I opened my mouth. " I—" Nothing but a garbled, cracking noise came out, making me sound more guilty than ever.

I had nothing. His assumptions worked because they were so far from the truth—when I agreed to do what I was doing, I hadn't known the cost. All I could focus on was keeping Tex safe, keeping the family safe.

But I'd had no idea what it would cost me.

In a way Sergio had made it too easy for me to keep lying, to keep everyone in the dark.

"You're right," I whispered. "I'm sorry. You have to know how sorry I am." I begged him with my eyes.

He looked away as if too disgusted to even make eye contact. "I'm going out, don't know when I'll be back."

"Tex!" I gripped his arm. "It isn't safe!"

"Safe?" he snarled then threw his head back and laughed. "Right, and you're so worried about my safety?" His eyes narrowed in on my hand. "Let go, Mo. I'm serious."

I knew he wouldn't hurt me, but I was still terrified as I watched the muscles in his arm twist and expand; he was barely in control of himself.

"No." My voice quivered.

He cursed and pried my hand away from his arm. "Do me a favor."

"Anything."

"Stop it." His voice was hoarse. "Stop pretending to care, Mo. I can't... I just..." He shook his head. "I can't do this, whatever this—back and forth thing is. I can't do it. Hell, if you want Sergio go to Sergio. Apparently we aren't even legally married."

"What?" *Oh no, no, no, no, that was the deal!*

He shrugged. "You're free. Don't get me wrong, I'm a sucker for punishment, so I'll still do whatever it takes, but this, whatever this is between us—" He pressed his lips together. "It's done."

The jackhammer in my chest squeezed my lungs, making it impossible to breathe, as though he literally reached inside me, wrapped his hands around my heart and squeezed until every last drop of blood pulsed out of it.

CHAPTER ELEVEN

Drinking the memory of someone away? Doesn't work.

Tex

THE DOOR SLAMMED behind me as I went to the garage and got into the Range Rover. The engine growled to life, and I peeled out of the driveway. What really sucked? I was making my getaway in Nixon's SUV. Sure, I had my pick of any of the cars at his house. But the truth of the matter was this.

They were his cars.

His house.

Could I afford my own shit?

Hell, yeah, I could. But what was the point? What was the point of anything? I buy an expensive-ass car for what purpose?

I pushed down on the accelerator once I got onto the main road, the car increasing its speed until I was going around a hundred.

My phone rang.

"What?" I barked into it.

"Tex!" Nixon's voice was sharp. "What the hell man? We have shit to do."

"You have shit to do. I have shit to forget." I pressed end and slammed the phone on the dash as I accelerated even more.

I passed car after car, the speed doing nothing to make me feel better about the sinking feeling in my stomach, or even about the ache in my heart.

Finished—I was finished with her. A man can only take so much and I'd just hit my limit. Visions of Sergio's hands on her body, his mouth touching her lips, and the simple truth that she was given every opportunity to push him away.

Rather than hold him close.

With a curse, I pulled into the parking lot of Slim, one of the bars I frequented. It was a hole in the wall biker bar that had seen better days, but it was mine. Pathetic. The one thing I owned in this universe and it was a shitty bar.

I liked having my own space to interrogate, and it just so happened that alcohol came in handy when needing to clean up blood, well that and the loud music. Swear, it would make a grown man cry to know how many people lost their lives, their freaking souls in that back room.

I turned off the car and walked purposefully through the front doors with every instinct on high alert—too high if you asked me—I sauntered over to the bar and slammed my hand onto it.

Marco took one look at me and slid a bottle of Jack in my direction. "Rough night?"

I snorted and took a pull directly from the bottle. "Try rough existence."

"Need me to—"

"No." I waved him off. I already knew where he was going with his question. He would ask if I needed him to take care of something, I'd either answer yes and slip him the name and address of that certain something, or I'd say no and we'd pretend like he didn't ask me in the first place.

Being the Abandonatos redheaded step child did have its

perks. It meant I got to do things my way every damn time—as long as I got the job done.

"You need anything else, let me know." Marco slapped the counter a few times with his dishtowel and went over to his next customer.

"So," a sultry voice said from behind me. "It's been a while."

"And it's going to be a lot longer too," I said without turning around. "Go to Hell."

"Ouch, wearing our bitch pants tonight, are we?" Nails dug into my back. I could only imagine the slut thought it would be erotic, when really all I could focus on was the fact that I could peel each perfectly painted nail from her fingers without even blinking.

Yeah, I was in a dark place if I was thinking of hurting a woman.

I'd slept with her once and didn't even know her name, just that she frequented my bar and was easy.

"Go away." I took another swig.

"Fine." She pulled her hand back leaving me alone again.

Within ten minutes I'd had my fair share of the bottle, but not enough for me to forget Mo or what she looked like in someone else's arms. Damn it!

The house phone rang above the noise.

Marco answered and then eyed me across the bar and rolled his eyes then made a shooting motion with his hand. Bastard probably had an assignment from Frank. Oh right, another fun fact? I completed contracts from all three families.

So I might not belong anywhere, but at least I was rich as hell and damn good at what I did.

The bar fell silent. Curious, I looked up at the door.

Three men walked in.

One had a cane, but it wasn't for walking, more like whacking if you get me, and not the good kind. The guys flanking him looked like they'd just got done doing steroids and needed a place to release all their tension. Their shoulders were huge, and they were at least a head taller than the rest of the group. The man in the middle paused, his eyes scanning the crowd before falling on me.

A smile curved his lips as he started walking towards the bar.

Well, shit. Either I was dying or he was, and honest moment? I didn't care which way the tables turned. How sick was that? I needed a damn heart transplant, that's what I needed. Maybe if I had a new one, the old one would stop hurting so much.

"We finally meet." The man said pulling out a stool next to me.

"Right," I snickered. "I've been waiting for years to meet you too. Tell me what's Mom look like? Do I have her eyes? I've been dying to see my true family, gosh darn it this is the best day of my life. Can I call you Dad?"

The guy motioned to Marco for a drink. "You... are a smart ass."

"Aw..." I slapped him on the back earning me a grunt from the other two men who took a step towards us but stopped when the man held up his hand. "Thanks. That's like the nicest thing anyone's said to me all day, and I'll let you in on a little secret, I was having a kick ass hair day so I had all kinds of compliments."

"Clever." The man chuckled and ordered a whiskey on the rocks.

"My hair?" I joked, trying to throw him off balance. "Thanks man, I mean I don't swing that way, but I may make an exception if you keep complimenting me like that."

"Tell me..." He still wasn't looking at me, but his side profile gave me all the information I knew. Long scar from his left ear to his nose, like someone had slashed his cheek. Salt and pepper hair, a fit body, probably around five ten and one seventy five. His fingernails were clean, meaning he wasn't a made man—most likely he ordered things to be done—and his posture screamed control. Slight accent? I needed to listen harder.

"Tell you what?" I smiled willing him to look at me so I could look into his eyes and see into his soul. That's what I did. I read souls. Not in a creepy way but in a way that made me damn good at what I did. One look into someone's eyes and I knew... unfortunately it only worked with would-be killers. With Mo? Clueless.

My instincts were always off with her, always had been, always would be.

"Do you truly enjoy this little act?"

"What act?"

"This." The man finally turned and pointed at my smile. "And do you think you could fool me, of all people?"

"Well, considering I don't really know who you are," I said with a shrug "I guess you have your answer, and honestly..." I leaned forward so I was inches from his face. "I don't give a flying rat's ass what you like or don't like, take it or leave it."

"You should."

"I should... what? Hmm, Grandpa?"

"You're funny. "He chuckled throwing back his drink. "And you should... care that is."

"Give me one good reason." I let my knife fall into my hands from my sleeve and hovered over his femoral artery, ready to cut within seconds.

"Only a very desperate or very stupid man would kill me. Which are you, I wonder?"

Taken aback that he even knew I had the knife hovering near his leg, I pulled back and answered honestly, "A little of both."

"This time next month—" He finished his drink. "You'll be dead."

"Cool, you telling me ahead of time so I can plan my

funeral, or do you just like giving people good news?"

His cold grey eyes looked me up and down. "I expected you to be smaller. Your father, he was a small man."

"Probably why I killed him. I hate small men. How tall are you?"

"Again, clever act. It would work on anyone but me..."

"Because you're stupid or... ?"

He leaned forward, the knife dug into his thigh but he didn't wince. Instead, he chuckled. "Don't you think your uncle should know these things?"

"Uncle? Wow." I laughed. "That's rich. My family finally claims me after I kill the *Cappo*. Nice, let me guess I'm next on the hit list."

"Funny that you didn't even know..." The man tilted his head. "Or maybe just sad?"

"Know what?" I kept my smile firmly in place even though I was so curious I itched to torture him so I could find out.

"Your family... the ones you've been protecting? They've ordered a hit on you worth ten million."

At that I laughed.

"You're a loose end." My Uncle smirked. "And we hate loose ends."

"So, I'm a wanted man? Cool, maybe they'll get my picture right this time when they send that text around. Last time they had my hair so freaking dark, well, I mean, to be fair the lighting was horrible and—"

"Listen to me." He sneered. "And listen very carefully." His breath smelled like rum. "Kill or be killed. Those are your two options. Be who you were born to be and The Abandonatos, The Alferos? They will kill you. But, if you decide to disappear, then I'll pretend this little conversation didn't exist."

"So." I laughed to cover my intense irritation, also knowing it would piss him off, possibly giving me more insight into his character. "Let me get this straight. You want me to be a good little boy, stay put, not talk, and not claim my birthright. If I do all that, not only will my own family hunt me down, but my adopted family will as well, leaving me basically without anything? Am I right?"

"Yes."

"Awesome, so here's the thing." I moved my knife lower and made a slice, cutting through his pants then covering the cut with my right hand. With my left hand I grabbed one of the limes from the bar and crushed it, allowing the drips to fall into the cut.

He winced and tried to move out of my grip but I had at least fifty pounds on him, so it was pointless.

"I have no family. Never have. Never will. So when you threaten me, come at me with something bigger than that. Come to me when you're ready to kill me, not when you want to threaten me, because next time I see your shit-eating face…" I dropped more of the acidic fruit onto his cut. "I won't just slice you here." I chuckled. "I'll slice you everywhere Uncle, but I'll keep you alive when I do it, and it won't be fruit but actual acid I drip into each wound until you beg for death. I have no family. And by the looks of it, you like it that way, because it gives you adequate time to take over as *Cappo*, but this is where I want you to listen very carefully."

His entire face was filled with rage.

I leaned forward like I was going to kiss his cheek, give him the respect he deserved, and instead I whispered in his ear, "The next *Cappo* has to be strong enough not to piss his pants when someone a third of his age makes threats. I don't just own the families here in the U.S., and if you push me, I *will* step up and I *will* own the Campisi clan. I'll cheerfully take my place and make you look like the little, pathetic bitch that you are. So if we're done here, why don't you run along, hmm?"

I reared back and slapped him on the face twice, then

motioned for his two men to come help him up.

"You're a stupid, stupid boy," my uncle spat.

"Hey, I think there's a song with that title in it!" I chuckled loudly, so pissed off that I was ready to pull my gun on him. "We're done here. Oh, and next time you step into my bar it better be with a bomb chained to your chest. Or I'll kill you." I smiled viciously. "*Capiche?*"

Chapter Twelve

How do you miss someone who's turning into a stranger before your
very eyes?

Mo

ACCORDING TO THE CLOCK next to my night stand, it was nearing two am and Tex still wasn't back. I'd texted him a dozen times and even tried calling. Ridiculous! Was I really worried about a man that knew about five hundred unique ways to kill a person? I mean seriously. It was Tex. He was the guy that smiled while he pulled the trigger. But still, he was weak. He was weak, and I'd made him that way, and when he left he was in bad shape.

I shivered.

Nixon was pissed at me too; actually it seemed everyone was pissed at me. We had a dead body, a marriage that wasn't actually legal, and more questions than answers. The horrible part was that when Nixon asked me if I knew anything, I straight up lied to his face.

Sergio had been in there.

He'd watched me lie.

He'd let me, the bastard. But he was doing his part too,

both of us were. I just wish it wasn't so damn hard to do the right thing. I'd always believed that if you chose others over yourself, you were rewarded, never once did I understand the extraordinary sacrifice it was, when you were asked to be selfless. My chest ached.

I reached across the bed and grabbed Tex's pillow, holding it close to my chest, inhaling his scent like he was my drug. He'd been the only constant thing in my life, and I didn't want to live in a world where he wasn't annoying the hell out of me, where he wasn't trying to crack a joke in order to make me laugh when all I wanted to do was cry.

The sound of a door slamming jolted me from my pity party. Tex! He was home. I just needed to see that he was okay. I just wanted to know he wasn't bleeding or dying.

Quietly, I padded to the bedroom door and reached for the knob, only to have it pulled open. I staggered back and gaped.

Tex stood there, shirt off, swaying on his feet.

Drunk as hell.

"Mo." He said my name like a curse, like he reserved it for the darkest pits of Hell. "Why can't I be done with you? Why?" He pushed past me and stumbled on to the bed. "I can't quit..." He shuddered, his voice muffled by the pillow. "I can't quit seeing you when I close my eyes. I hate you so much, but not as much as I love you. I could never hate you as much as I love you. It's impossible... believe me." Tex sighed and rolled over, his fists balling as he hit the pillow. "I try every day."

Stunned, I could only stand and wait for him to say something else.

Instead he fell into a fitful sleep and started snoring.

With a sigh, I shut the door, walked over to the bed, and pulled the blankets over his muscled body. My heart was beating so loudly I was afraid it would wake him up. I wasn't sure if I was upset over what he'd said or hopeful that the hate hadn't taken over just yet, meaning there was room for forgiveness, right?

He stretched his hands above his head and then curled an arm underneath the pillow, making his bicep bulge to epic proportions. I gasped. He was too beautiful for his own good and the crazy part? He didn't even know it. He'd always felt different than Nixon and Chase because his coloring was lighter. Instead of having dark hair he had light brown hair with pieces of red sewn through, almost like highlights. His eyes were a crazy deep blue, not a light blue but a dark blue, like an ocean storm. When he was pissed, he could seriously give Poseidon a run for his money in the angry god look.

Sighing, I pushed his hair away from his forehead and leaned down to kiss his cheek. The minute my lips graze his skin, he grabbed my hand and had me flipped on my back, pressing my hips against the mattress. Tex hovered over me, his eyes blazing.

"I don't want to want you," he ground out slowly "I don't want..." His chest heaved.

"Tex..." I cupped his face, warm tears sliding down my cheeks. "You should sleep."

"No time for sleep." He moved off me anyways and laid his head on my shoulder. "No time for sleep when you're about to die."

I froze. "You're dying?"

"Ten million." He sighed. "Insulting."

With that he fell asleep.

And I stayed up the rest of the night wondering if every sacrifice I'd made had been in vain, because they were still after him.

CHAPTER THIRTEEN

We're only as strong as our boss is to other bosses. Period.

Sergio

"SO?" I ASKED throwing my keys onto the table and reaching for a bottle of water.

"Ten million." The voice said in a bored tone.

I stared down at my phone and kept staring. Ten million? It had to be a joke? How insulting, not only to the rest of the families but to Tex himself. Only ten million? Ten million did not get us results. Blood. Maybe. Death? Absolutely. But results? Ones we needed in order to move on to the next step of the plan? It wouldn't happen and it needed to happen; otherwise, they would all die.

I would die.

There would be nothing left.

A cleansing was coming.

And I was doing everything I could to keep it from happening, but that's the thing about not existing—about being a ghost. Interfere too much? And people start to talk.

Nixon might as well have been a detective with as many questions as he was firing at me. Why did I really go to the wedding? Why was I at his house? Why was I helping when I usually stay behind the scenes? What did I have to gain?

I sighed, feeling more ancient then my twenty-eight years and glanced at my phone. "Fine, we wait until it's higher."

"But—"

"That's all." I hit end. My screen immediately turned into the picture I'd kept of Mo. The one and only picture I'd snuck when she wasn't looking which, when I thought about it, wasn't the most romantic thing in the world.

But it was all I had.

One picture.

One night.

The end.

Funny, because she'd told me as much—but I hadn't believed her. I'd never experienced that type of attraction to another person. An attraction that's so strong that you end up doing stupid things.

Like planning for the future.

Mafia rule number one? Don't plan, it's rare to experience a happy ending.

Ten million. The number may as well have been written on my forehead. Damn, they were going to have to do better than that.

I had two choices.

Let the chips fall.

Or maneuver each chip for my own purpose—for the family, for Mo, for blood.

The problem? I wouldn't come out looking like the hero, but the villain. In fact, I was pretty sure that if I took that step... if I stopped hiding in the shadows, I'd end up shot.

Dead.

Buried.

I looked back down at my phone, my heart hammering in my chest. If I did nothing, she was as good as dead, they all were. It would only be a matter of time before things came to a head. Maybe not this month, maybe not next month—hell, it could be a year before things progressed.

But again, the ending was always the same.

"Mo," I whispered touching the screen with my fingers, caressing the glass because the last time I touched her face, she'd pulled away, taking my heart with her.

The only time she'd given in to me—given in to *us*, was because she was angry at him.

I was her best defense then.

I was her best defense now.

"Damn it. "I closed my eyes and allowed myself a brief moment to imagine what freedom would be like. I could run away, knowing that each step I took was stained with the blood of my family.

Of the girl I've loved since I was five.

So, with shaking hands, I lifted the phone, dialed Nixon's number and said the words I never thought I'd utter again.

"What?" Nixon barked into the phone. "Everything good on your end?"

"I'm in."

"Sergio..."

"I'll lock up everything tonight, meet you at the house, stay as long as you need... time to retire the ghost, brother."

Nixon cursed, the phone went silent for a minute. "You do this, you make yourself a target. You've been in hiding for a reason, Sergio."

"Let me worry about it." My stomach clenched. "I'm back, get ready, a shit storm's coming and I'm pretty sure the wind's blowing straight from Sicily."

"Right." Nixon sighed. "I'll be waiting at the house."

"Okay." I pressed end, slowly dropping my phone to the counter. It rang, once, twice, three times.

I answered on the fourth, not bothering to say hello.

A voice rasped in my ear, "I will come for you. I promised I would if you ever showed your face again."

"Fine." I barked as dread filled my stomach. Damn I worked way too hard to protect a family who hated me so much. "What's the worst that could happen, Pops? I get shot?" No sooner had the words left my mouth, then the mirror in front of me shattered falling to the ground in slices of discarded glass. A second gunshot rang out, ripping the leather from the couch.

I sighed, bored with his games already. And funny, they'd just begun. "Tell Don that his shot is off by a half inch, I'm still standing. Oh, and next time you shoot at me, at least hit something worth shooting. I hate wasting ammo. So should you, considering I have all the family money and you have, what? Five dollars to your name? Then again, that's what happens when you make a deal with the feds. Tell Ma hi. Oh, and Pops?"

My father cursed wildly on the other end. "*Do* not call me that!"

"Good to hear from you." I grinned and ended the conversation. Yeah, I'd made my choice, it was probably the wrong one, but hell, at least it would be entertaining.

The house was silent as I locked up, setting the security cameras so I could monitor what went on in my absence. I grabbed the keys to my BMW coupe and felt nothing.

No remorse.

No fear.

But perhaps... I looked down at my phone, a bit of regret.

Regret because she wasn't mine to protect. But I was going to do it anyway. Regret because I was going to make her life hell by trying to prove to her that I could be good for her.

After all, she didn't even realize that Tex was already a dead man, regardless of whether the planned worked or not.

He would always be a Campisi.

CHAPTER FOURTEEN

Expectations are always greater than we realize.

Tex

SUNLIGHT STREAMED THROUGH the curtains, damn near frying me to death and not making my headache any better. Cursing, I rolled to my side, trying to figure out where the pounding was coming from and who I had to shoot to make it stop. I officially had a hangover from hell. As I rubbed my eyes, I glanced at the night stand. A glass of water was waiting along with two painkillers.

Mo wasn't in the bed with me anymore. Not that I blamed her. Lying next to her was torture anyway. Feeling the curves of her body. Even when I was too drunk to do anything about it? Sheer hell. Swear, I almost grabbed my gun and ended myself right then and there. But Mo had given me such a loving look, and though I pretended to pass out. She'd touched my face.

Damn we were bad for each other.

Like an addiction we couldn't quit. I wanted to put her on the shelf and walk away, but that's the thing about perfection. The sinner in you wants it so desperately, hoping it will make all the dark go away, that instead of walking away, like you should, you take it, you stare at it, and you devour it until there's nothing left. I wondered if Mo realized how much I was doing that to her… how I used sex with her as a way to make myself feel whole, less tarnished.

Groaning, I rose to my feet, popped the pills in my mouth and slowly made my way towards the door.

I opened it softly and glanced down the hall.

Sergio was standing in the kitchen talking to Nixon in hushed tones. Mo was in the corner eating cereal, her eyes about as big as the Cheerios she was trying to choke down. Great, someone probably died.

Cursing, I stomped down the hall, fighting the urge to ram my body into Sergio's causing him massive blood loss, and grabbed a bowl from the cupboard.

"Someone's not a morning person," Sergio said in low clipped tones. The fact that the bastard was still speaking with his slight accent, which frankly made him sound like a giant ass, didn't help matters.

"Yeah, well…" I stretched my arms above my head. "I had these weird nightmares where I was holding a really sharp knife to someone's neck and then all of a sudden he'd piss his pants. I never did see the guy's face, though he screamed like a bitch, had a slight accent, six-foot one, with the tattoo of a cross on his left hand."

Sergio rolled his eyes.

Nixon glared at me.

Mo coughed next to me.

"What?" I shrugged. "I can't share my hopes and dreams with you guys?" I poured the cereal into my bowl. "Some family."

"Ten million," Sergio said smoothly. "Makes you feel like less of a man, doesn't it? To think, that's the price of your measly little life. Hell, last year a made man went down for twelve."

"It's too early for me to kill you." I yawned and poured some milk into my cereal.

"You think I would let you?" Sergio chuckled, sounding amused as hell.

"I think you'd have no choice." I chomped down on a bite of cereal, the crunch the only sound in the kitchen except for Nixon's teeth clicking against his lip ring. For whatever reason, he knew this was my battle not his. "And ten million is still ten million. Think of all the surgeries you can pay for after I rearrange that pretty face, hmm?" I pointed my spoon at him. "Now it doesn't sound so bad."

Sergio smirked, his eyes roamed from me to Mo and then back to me. "It's cute really... how you can't really take a hint. All brawn no brains, isn't that what people say?"

"Girls." Chase walked into the room and yawned. "Stop fighting or Mil's gonna come out here with a gun. The woman's exhausted, let her sleep."

"Maybe if you didn't keep her up all night..." I laughed.

Chase held up his hand. "So dehydrated taking a piss was like trying to find water in the Sahara."

"Details I didn't need to know," Nixon piped up. "Ever."

"You guys always talk about your women like this?" Sergio asked looking around the room.

"Actually," Mo said with a sigh, "this is tame."

I grinned. "Sharing is caring."

"No wonder people keep trying to kill you guys off... no respect." Sergio tilted his head at Nixon. "So, are we in agreement?"

"About the no respect?" Nixon crossed his arms.

"About me staying at the house."

"Whoa, whoa, whoa!" I pushed out my chair and rose to my feet, my hands clenching at my side. "What the hell, Nixon!"

"Yeah." Nixon broke eye contact with me and shook Sergio's hand. "But the rules apply to you just as much as they apply to Tex or any single guy. Lay a hand on my sister without her permission and I cut it off."

"You didn't cut off Tex's hand." Sergio pointed out, a smug grin plastered across his shit-eating face.

"No." I rolled my eyes. "He just shot me at point blank range. But hey, maybe you'll get lucky and get to choose when the time comes!"

Sergio threw his head back and laughed.

I pulled up the sleeve of my shirt showing him my wound.

He stopped laughing.

Nixon crossed his arms. "We understand each other?"

Sergio whistled. "Damn Nixon, you're a scary son of a bitch, you know that?"

"First compliment of the day." Nixon shrugged and gave me a pointed look. "Tex, we need to talk."

"*Dun, dun, dun.*" Chase sang.

I smacked him on the back of the head and followed Nixon into his office, wishing like hell I knew what had crawled up his ass and taken root. The man never spoke to a member of the Elect away from the other members. Meaning, I was in deep shit. Fantastic.

I pasted a grin on my face and took a seat on one of the leather chairs, propping my hands behind my head, trying to look relaxed when really, I was bit worried he was going to shoot me again.

"The marriage—" Nixon licked his lips and pulled out a few sheets of paper. "—wasn't made legal." He handed the forged documents over to me. "On top of that it was never filed. Sergio's already forged new documents that have been filed with the state." His eyes flickered down to the floor. "Now that I've thought about things... I don't know if it's in Mo's best interest to marry you regardless of what you did to her."

The room started going black. I tried to remain calm.

What exactly was he saying?

"But—" Nixon paced in front of me, his fingers tapping against his thighs as he walked back and forth across the dark wood floor. "—it's probably in your best interest to be tied to us. Ten million," he said with a smirk. "Tell me you didn't laugh when you heard it."

"My ass off." I gave him the answer he wanted, when really I'd been more hurt than anything. "Not that it matters, they won't get me. Nobody can touch me."

"Just because you're a Campisi doesn't mean nobody can touch you. Which is why I want you guys to pretend to be married… as far as everyone knows, it's real. The documents will be filed, protecting both of you, but in the end, it gives Mo an out once all this dies down."

"An out?" I repeated.

Nixon pinched the bridge of his nose and licked his lips staring at the door. "Love. At least give her a chance to find someone to love… someone who won't rip her heart out, stomp on it, then try to put it back together again. She deserves that."

"And I can't give her that?"

Nixon studied me. "I don't know, can you?"

Nightmares flooded my vision… blood, death, death, and more death. And then there was Mo, the only perfect thing in my life. The only constant.

I studied Nixon right back.

He was nervous.

Upset.

Fidgety.

He never fidgeted.

And he always made eye contact, but he kept blinking and looking at the floor, then back at the door, then back at the floor. Finally, he leaned back and touched his face again.

He was freaking crumbling right in front of me.

"You're stuck," I said softly. "Protect me or protect Mo."

"Right." Nixon shuddered. "Unite you guys and..."

"You can say it." My heart dropped to my stomach. "It's not like I don't know what you're thinking right now."

"And what's that?" Nixon's jaw cracked.

"You can't trust me," I whispered. "Not anymore that is. Regardless of Mo being pregnant... you can't trust me because I'm a Campisi, and eventually it will be time to take my place... in Hell." My hands started to shake. "And damn if you don't want me to take Mo along for the ride. Hell, I don't want to take her along for the ride, but I would, because I'm a selfish bastard."

"She's innocent." Nixon shook his head. "Can you honestly say that you can love her? Protect her from that existence? From that bloodline? In the end, would you choose The Family over her?"

We both knew the answer.

Because as much as we loved our women.

We always chose what was best for the family. It's what a boss did.

It's what the *Cappo* did.

If it was my men stuck in a warehouse full of enemies or Mo at home with a gun to her head.

I'd sacrifice her to save them.

Because a family is only as strong as the boss—and if the boss is weak, the family crumbles.

"I see," I finally managed to say. My voice was low, hoarse from the emotion I was trying to hold inside, or maybe it was just the anger coursing through my body making me want to punch something—that something being Nixon. "Anything else, *boss*?"

"Stay alive." Nixon's eyebrows shot up as he gave me a stiff nod "And maybe... things will turn out, you never know."

"Right." I ground my teeth together. "And maybe one day butterflies will take over the world and replace guns."

As I tried to walk by Nixon, he gripped my arm and said in a low voice, "Never lose hope that things will one day be different."

I snorted and jerked my arm out of his grip. "The difference between me and you… I lost hope the day I was born. I don't believe in hope. Life and death."

"And love?" Nixon angled his head, his eyes digging as if trying to look into my soul.

"It's a once in a life time thing. You get one chance, and if you screw it up, rarely does the boat come back around again."

CHAPTER FIFTEEN

Nobody ever said protecting others at your own expense was easy.

Mo

"WELL, THAT WAS FUN." Chase elbowed me and offered a sympathetic smile. If the guy was trying to keep me from sobbing in my bowl of Cheerios, he was doing a really crappy job. "Smile, Mo."

I offered a creepy tooth-filled smile.

Chase winced. "Maybe next time, huh sexy?"

I rolled my eyes and placed my elbows on the table. Chase was either the worst brother in the world or the best. Ever since we'd found out how messed up our blood lines really were, meaning our family tree freaking pretzled together, I'd thought of him as more of a brother than a cousin.

"Things will get better." He sighed, patting my head.

"Just…" I waved him off. "No more talking."

"Talking helps… it's like free therapy." He stole a bite of my Cheerios. I stared him down.

He took another bite.

"Chase!" I snapped irritated. "Get your own damn Cheerios!"

He took another huge bite; milk ran down his chin. "See, made you react. You can thank me later."

"For putting me in a pissy mood?" I argued.

Chase got up and gave my shoulders a quick squeeze. "Why don't you go do something normal today, Mo? Take the girls, go shopping or something. After all, you're a married woman now. Hell, go spend some of Tex's millions, he's good for it. In fact, the more I think about it the happier I get. Go to Victoria's Secret, prance around in front of him then, say something like 'no touching.' Man, the guy would shit himself."

"Wow," Tex grumbled walking into the room. "Teaching my wife ways to torture me. Thanks Chase, but she does that by just breathing the same air and refusing to make eye contact with me."

"Whoa." Chase held up his hands. "Shit just got tense. I'm out, but remember what I said, Mo." He winked and punched Tex in the shoulder before walking out of the room.

Tex stared at me, his deep blue eyes swirling with anger. I took a tentative step back, trying to protect myself.

"Do you really think I would hurt you?" he asked in a low voice.

I shrugged. "You've been slamming a lot of doors."

A smile appeared then disappeared. "Yeah well the doors deserve it."

"Because?"

"Easy." He took a step towards me. "They block my view of you, and my number one obsession is your safety."

Air whooshed out of my lungs. "R-right."

"Go shopping."

"What?" My head jerked to attention. "Are you serious?"

"I never joke about clothes." Tex smirked, humor returning to his eyes. "Or wine. You know this about me, Mo."

I smiled back at him, feeling a bit lighter in the chest.

He took another step; we were close enough to touch.

Exhaling, he reached out and tilted my chin towards him. His touch burned me, creating a need so possessive that my entire body started to shake.

"Shop, relax, take the girls," he whispered. "Enjoy yourself and know that I'll be here when you get back."

"But—"

"Mo." Tex's grip tightened on my chin. "I'll send some men with you. You'll be fine. Safe. And I'll be here taking care of business."

His eyes flickered to my lips. Before I could stop myself, I kissed him. Our mouths collided. Tex lifted me into the air, growling as his hands slid into my hair giving it a little tug so that he could kiss down my neck. When his mouth found mine again, he broke off the kiss with a curse, taking a step away, his chest heaving.

"I'm sorry," I murmured, mouth swollen and eyes filling with tears. "I know you hate me."

Tex's eyes hardened as he placed his hands on his hips and looked away. "I could never hate you as much as I love you. That type of hate? That depth of hate? Doesn't exist, baby, believe me, I search for it every night that you lay next to me and I refuse to touch you. I crave it every minute of every day when I see your beautiful face." He swallowed. "Go get the girls, you're wasting daylight. I don't want you out after dark." With that, he stomped off.

And I fought the urge to run after him.

To tell him I loved him too.

To explain everything to him.

But telling him the truth would solidify his death. So I kept my mouth shut and sent a text.

Me: Talked with Nixon this morning. Marriage is a go. Looks real. Forged. We good?

G: Good work, Mo. I knew I could count on you... don't make me regret doing this your way. He has the protection of the Abandonato family, it's a start.

Me: That's good, right?

G: If it was bad, you'd know it by the bullet sized hole in your husband's forehead. I'll text you when I need you.

Shopping proved to be more fun than I imagined. First off, apparently Mil hadn't had any alone time since being married. Not that Chase minded, or Mil for that matter, but she was excited to have some freedom.

It wasn't lost on me that we were walking around the downtown area of Chicago with a newly minted Mafia boss on one side and the wife of one of the most powerful Mafia families ever... on the other.

Which left me.

Fake wife to the would-be *Cappo*. Awesome. If anyone was going to get shot, pretty sure it would be me first, them second. Then again, we took Vinnie and Lou with us.

Apparently they'd gotten drunk on the job a few weeks back so this was their way of repaying Nixon for not keeping a sharp eye.

Vinnie was our cousin and had a tendency to screw up, but he was a kick-ass shot and found great joy in all types of violence, so shopping? You might as well tell him you were replacing his penis with a flower.

And Lou, well he was one of my favorite associates. He always dressed nice, smelled nice, but he had a real serious problem with playing nice. Let's just say it wasn't in his nature to be patient. He shot first, asked questions later—if he remembered to ask questions at all. So he was like a mini-me version of Tex.

"This is nice." Trace took a sip of coffee and threw on her sunglasses. "I haven't gone shopping since Nixon bought me that Prada backpack."

"Ah..." I nodded. "The day of reckoning also known as

the day the college kids tried to rough up my brother's love interest."

"You make us sound like a movie." Trace rolled her eyes. "Star-crossed lovers or something like that."

"Admit it," Mil piped up. "After everything that's gone down in the last year—we'd be like prime time."

"Like Scandal." I nodded. "Only better."

"Bite your tongue!" Trace scolded and then laughed. She had a serious addiction to nighttime television.

"So, you guys wanna stop anywhere else?" I asked while we walked by Victoria's Secret. The guys were a few feet behind us.

Trace looked up at the sign above the door. "Let's go in here. You did just get married."

"By force." I held up my hand. "So it's not like Tex is going to be touching me or anything." I said the last part in a grumbling tone because honestly, I would do anything, short of ending up in prison, for the guy to kiss me again. To kiss me like he wanted me.

Mil and Trace shared a look before Mil pushed me towards the door. "He's still a guy, Mo, believe me—" She tilted her head. "—all you need are a few... temptations. Besides, what could it hurt?"

"Oh I don't know." I sang as they dragged me in. "My pride, my heart, my unborn child, my—"

Mil held up her hand and rolled her eyes. "I get it. Now stop being a baby and let us whore you up."

"Oh goody." I clapped my hands together in fake excitement. "That's just what I need to do, look like one of Tex's whores."

Trace pinched me in the arm.

"Ouch!" I rubbed the spot. "What was that for?"

Trace glared.

Mil answered for her. "Your head's in your ass, but that's okay. If there's anything I'm good at, it's pulling heads out of asses and setting things to right again. Take Chase for example..."

"Chase?" I repeated, as we walked further into the store, past the PINK section and into the lacy section that I had no business being in. "And just how did you help him?"

"Easy." Mil shrugged and gave us a sly smile. "I offered my temple of a body, and now he's too exhausted to be a jackass. Problem solved." She laughed and then shrugged as if to say what else can ya do?

Trace threw her head back and laughed, giving Mil a high five.

I fought a smile and turned away from them.

Vinnie and Lou made their way into the store. Vinnie shook his head in disgust while Lou thumbed a nightgown with strings. It was meant to be sexy. He looked horrified; clearly complicated clothing messed with his head.

"This." Mil tapped me on the shoulder and shoved a few hangers of lingerie into my arms. "Go try on."

"How did you even—?"

"Go!" Mil stomped her foot. "And when he can't keep his hands off of you, I expect a 'thank you, Mil.'"

"You fit in too well." Trace nodded. "I'm glad you're keeping Chase and not giving up on him."

"Takes work." Mil winked and rubbed her hands together. "But who am I to shy away from work?"

"Just call it sex," I grumbled stomping past them. "No more code words!"

I slammed the door behind me and stared at my reflection in the mirror. Every moment I'd spent with Tex... it had always been simple. We slept together, we talked, we laughed. I'd never actually tried seducing him. If he said no? Or if he made fun of me, or worse yet, was disgusted, I wasn't sure my already fragile heart could handle it.

"Hurry up!" Mil banged on the door.

Cursing, I tossed my purse onto the floor and fumbled

with the first lacy thing I saw. It was a black, completely see-through and had a halter top that tied around the neck leaving the entire back open. I wasn't a prude by any means, but I felt more naked in that dressing room than I'd ever felt in my entire life.

"How's it look?" Trace called.

"Good?" I said it like a question.

"You have a kick ass body. "Mil snorted. "Of course it looks good!"

I quickly tried on the rest of the things. I knew if I didn't I'd be forced to let the girls in just so they made sure I followed through. I only had intentions to buy one of the outfits.

But Mil wasn't having it. The minute I came out of the dressing room, she pulled everything from my arms and pointed at one of the cushioned black chairs, then went to the cash register.

"I think," I huffed and blew a strand of hair from my face, "I like Mil in *small* doses."

Trace laughed and sat in the chair next to me. "She's awesome though."

"Right. She's also screwing Chase's brains out, and he didn't really have a ton to begin with. Should we worry?"

"Nah." Trace shrugged and leaned back, closing her eyes for a moment. Her cheeks were flushed; she looked happy, relaxed. "We'll just buy him more protein bars and Gatorade. He'll power through."

Mil joined us a few minutes later wearing a sneaky grin on her face.

"What did you do?" I groaned.

"What?" she asked innocently. "I may have thrown a few… products in with the clothes, but to be fair they were on sale and honestly nothing would make me happier than you driving Tex to drink. Just think, bringing the *Cappo* to his knees."

"He's not the *Cappo*," I said defensively, then realized I'd jumped to his defense perhaps a bit too quickly.

"Um, yeah." Mil nodded, her eyes narrowing. "He is. Trust me, I don't know what Nixon's been telling you guys, but my family's been chomping at the bit for the announcement, meaning only one thing. That little hit of ten million? It's going to double if he doesn't make a choice."

"Why does he have to choose?" I asked. "I mean we don't need a *Cappo*! And his family doesn't even like him." I seriously wanted to break something. I hated that he was getting pushed into that position. Tex was strong but only as strong as he allowed himself to be. I was afraid for him. Afraid for us.

"Family is blood," Mil explained slowly. "It won't matter if he suddenly converts to Judaism and refuses to step on spiders because he believes they have souls. The truth is, they need to know where he stands."

"And if he stands against them?" I whispered. "What then?"

Mil fell silent.

Vinnie and Lou opened the doors to the store. The wind gusted, hitting me square in the face. I took a deep breath and looked down the street. "Shit."

"What?" Mil paused, reaching into her purse. "What is it?"

Trace reached behind her back and gave Vinnie a thumbs down.

Three men in suits climbed out of a black SUV as if in slow motion. They took their time sauntering towards us. A few people on the street stopped to gawk and then hurried into stores, slamming the doors behind them. A kid on a bike nearly collided with a telephone pole before high tailing it in the opposite direction. Mil stood in front of me. I tried to move her but she wouldn't budge. In this little scenario she was a bit more important, being a boss and all, but I knew not to argue with her, at least not now.

The man in the middle was almost bald; he had a walking cane and a slight limp, and he looked pissed. I didn't recognize him—that was until he came within a few feet of us. He had stormy blue eyes, just like Tex's.

Not. Good.

They wouldn't do anything out in the open, but that didn't mean I was feeling the urge to break out into song and dance.

"Mrs. Campisi, is it?" The man offered a predatory grin that sent chills along my spine. I hated it when people smiled like that. Why smile when you want the world to know how pissed off it makes you?

"Sir," Vinnie said smoothly. "Please step aside. We don't want any trouble. The girls are having a relaxing day shopping."

"Relaxing," the man repeated as the two men accompanying him, the ones who looked like Italian sumo wrestlers snickered. "I haven't relaxed since the day I was born."

"Maybe you should get a pedicure," I said through clenched teeth. "Those work wonders for me when it's that time of the month…"

"Or…" Mil shrugged. "I could always shoot you, relieve some of that tension between your eyes. In fact, it would be my pleasure, much quicker than botox."

"De Lange." The guy snorted. "You disgust me."

Mil grinned. "Good, I'd hate to attract you. God, you look older than sin. How's the leg? Skiing accident?"

The girl had a mouth on her; no wonder Chase was enamored.

"You…" He nodded to me. "You are Campisi's wife, are you not?"

"I'm carrying his child." I shrugged. "What does that tell you?"

"I have a message for him."

"So say it," I snapped. "And tell your lap dogs to stop staring at my chest before I stab them in the throat."

The two men shared a laugh while I let my knife slide down my leather jacket and held it up between my fingers.

"I wasn't kidding."

They stopped laughing.

The man held up his hand, it was covered with rings, manicured, hardly the type of hands of a grunt worker. "I want to meet with him. I'll tell him anything he wants to know about the family. No guns. No men. Just the two of us, having a nice little chat. Uncle to nephew."

Trace sucked in a breath next to me, while I narrowed my eyes harder. "You must not value your life."

"Why do you say that?"

"He could rip you to shreds with his bare hands."

"Not—" The man sneered. "—if I cut them off first."

"What? With your teeth?" Mil snorted. "Is that all? We're kind of busy."

"That's all." He nodded to us and took a step back.

In a flash something sharp hit me in the thigh; I staggered back against Trace as blood started seeping through my jeans. The sharp pain turned into a burn that radiated through my leg. I could feel the wetness of blood start pouring down from whatever damage he'd caused.

He looked at the wound and grinned. "Sorry, it slipped, consider yourself warned."

"Thanks." I answered, my breath coming in gasps. I threw my knife directly at his friend's right thigh. It impaled itself beautifully.

Muttering a string of vulgar curses, the guy stumbled backwards.

But Tex's uncle didn't flinch, simply stared me down and then finally threw his head back and laughed. "Well done... once I kill your husband, I may just take you for myself. I could use a little… spunk."

"Run along, old man," Mil spat. "She may not shoot you, but I have a loaded gun and I get really trigger happy when I'm not able to use it."

He nodded, still smiling and sauntered off.

"You okay?" Trace gripped my arms while Vinnie tried to lift me into his.

"I'm fine." My teeth began to chatter. "Nothing like getting shot after going shopping for lingerie. Think God's trying to tell me something?"

"Yeah." Mil reached for her cell. "Have more sex because you never know when you're going to get shot, where the hell did the gunshot come from anyway? Must have had a silencer, I heard nothing, saw nothing." Mil swore as she dialed a number.

"You calling Nixon?" Trace asked, trying to steady me.

"No, I'm calling Chase." Mil placed the phone in her ear. "I'll let *him* tell Nixon."

Trace sighed. "Good call."

They were talking like one of us getting shot was a normal occurrence, maybe for the guys, but for us? Not so much. In fact I'd only ever been shot once and the pain hadn't been this extreme, not at all. The burning continued, radiating up my leg and into my hip. I clenched my teeth as their voices started getting more and more quiet. My ears felt fuzzy along with my body, the pain was still there but it felt like it was spreading everywhere and all I needed to do was close my eyes and everything would be alright. Unable to hold out any longer, a hoarse whimper escaped through my lips.

"She's losing a lot of blood." Vinnie clenched his teeth and tried to elevate my leg while keeping me in his arms, I clung to him tightly. "We need to get back to the house now."

"Why so much… blood?" A numbness took over, replacing the pain, making me thankful.

"I'm not a doctor." Vinnie's voice shook.

"Vin?" Trace asked. "What aren't you telling us?"

"It's close to her femoral artery."

Why did they sound like they were talking under water?

"How close?" Trace asked, her voice sounded hollow, dark spots started invading my vision.

"Oh God!" Trace gasped, and then everything went black.

CHAPTER SIXTEEN

Too much damn information, not enough action.

Tex

I PINCHED THE BRIDGE of my nose while Nixon continued talking. Sergio and Chase were on the couch looking through a series of surveillance tapes around our local businesses while I tried to fight the urge to punch Nixon in the face. Granted, he was just trying to fill us in, but did Sergio have to be present? His every heartbeat insulted the shit out of me and I was itching—*itching* to end it.

"So—" Nixon popped his knuckles. "—Tex."

My head snapped up. "What?"

"Ten million, and by the looks of it, you have your old family wanting to know who's side you're going to pick whereas your new family—"

"Us." Chase winked.

I rolled my eyes.

Nixon chuckled. "Right, your new family offers protection, so at this point, the ball's kind of in your court. Do you want to make a statement? Or do you want to lay low for a while?"

"When has laying low ever helped anyone?" Sergio pointed out. "As far as I'm concerned, laying low means he's hiding. Why the hell would a man hide?"

"Why indeed?" I repeated. "Statement. I'll make a statement." I didn't fill them in on the actual statement I'd made the day before with my uncle, but that was fine. I could cause a fuss, get the attention away from the Abandonatos. I owed them that much at least.

Nixon looked down at his phone. "Hey Trace what's—"

His entire face paled.

Chase made eye contact with me.

And then I heard screaming on the other end while Nixon's damn hand shook with rage, his eyes narrowing more and more. I half expected a vein to pop in his forehead. "Hurry." He hung up and shook his head slowly in my direction, his nostrils flaring with anger. "It's Mo."

"What's Mo?" I stood, my hands on hips, ready to take action, ready to kill any bastard who'd dared to lay a hand on her.

"She's been shot." Nixon cursed and threw his phone against the couch.

"Is it always like this?" Sergio whistled.

"Shut the hell up before I shoot you in the face," I roared, charging towards Sergio.

"Whoa!" Chase moved in front of Sergio just in time for me to pull out my gun and aim it at his chest.

"Shit," Chase muttered. "Put it away, Tex, we've got bigger problems apparently."

"She was shot in the leg." Nixon said his hand firmly gripping my shoulder. "Lots of blood we need—"

"I'm calling in a favor." I snapped and quickly dialed the De Lange's second in command. He'd once been a surgeon and wouldn't blink twice if I asked him to come in and perform emergency surgery.

"What?" He barked into the phone.

"I need you. Nixon's house. Now."

"And if I don't come?"

"Then I'll hunt you down, and you'll really wish you would have…"

"On my way." He snickered and ended the phone call.

Nixon sighed. "You sure you want the De Lange's involved?"

"News flash, Nixon," I growled. "The whole damn Mafia was already involved the minute you protected me in Vegas, the minute Mo said she was pregnant. We have the strongest family in Italy posting on Craigslist for my damn head! Adding in the De Lange's does nothing. Just invites more people to my funeral."

"You're not dying." Chase sighed.

"Right." I nodded, but I knew it was the opposite of true. I'd die… my death was as certain as my love for Mo. It might as well have been written across my forehead.

My love for her would kill me.

Because in the end. When I chose the Campisi family.

It would be at her expense.

And I'd ask Nixon to kill me for it.

Only then could I keep her safe… only then would my word be trusted.

"Nixon!" Trace yelled running into the house.

In a blur Vinnie brought Mo in and laid her across the kitchen table.

"Shit!" I raced to her side. "Chase get the morphine."

Mo's eyes fluttered open and then rolled to the back of her head as she started convulsing.

"We're going to need blood." Sergio started cutting away her jeans with scissors.

My mind whirled. "Use mine, use my blood."

"You have to be a match." With one final rip Sergio pulled the jeans from her left leg, blood spewed from the wound.

"We are!" I roared. "Chase!"

Chase tossed me the morphine.

"Needles, we need to draw blood, grab an IV."

"We doing this here?" Chase closed his eyes, muttering under his breath before running back into the storage room where we kept weapons and drugs—the good kind.

My hands shook as I cradled Mo's pale face. "Baby, can you hear me?"

She moaned.

Nixon slammed his hand into the wall as more blood poured from her leg. "Stop the bleeding, damn it!"

"I'm trying!" Sergio yelled right back, his hands covered in my wife's blood. Red, a color that used to comfort me, bring me peace, was finally bringing me death.

"No." I shook my head and kissed Mo's face. "No, you gotta fight, baby! Okay? You have to fight!" There was so much blood it was impossible to tell where the wound even was.

"Needles." Chase threw them at me; I caught them midair and grabbed the rubber band, tightening it with my mouth as I wrapped it around my bicep. The sting of the needle was nothing compared to the horror I witnessed in front of me.

"You better hope to God you have enough blood to give her before you pass out too." Sergio didn't bother putting on gloves as he shot Mo with morphine directly into her thigh.

"God's never been on my side," I mumbled, as I watched the blood pull from my body into the needle.

"Well, you better hope He is now." Sergio moved his hands to Mo's chest. "Because she's losing consciousness, she's lost too much blood."

"Mo!" I yelled as Sergio leaned down and pressed his ear against her mouth. He cursed as he whispered something in her ear. She moaned and shook her head, her eyes opened and then closed again.

I swear I stepped outside my body and watched my soul start to crumble into thin air. "God, I'll do anything to save her. Take me instead, take the evil, purge the evil, leave the angels where they belong." I continued pulling, pulling vial after vial of blood, my knees shaking as weakness took hold. Finally Nixon put his hand on my arm and whispered for me to stop. Damn, I was going to bleed myself dry for that woman if I had to.

Minutes ticked by, they may as well have been hours. The De Langes finally burst through the door. Stephen took one look at Mo and jumped into action, his hands moving across her wound as if he already had the injury memorized. He sighed in relief at the wound. "It's not her femoral artery but a large vein was hit, she'll be fine." He pressed his hands tighter against her leg, "Sore, but fine. If we don't' stop the bleeding she'll die, but I imagine you guys already knew that." Swearing, he removed one hand and reached for the forceps. "I need someone with steady hands."

I moved to his side. "Tell me what to do."

"Okay," he said pressing my hands against her actual wound. "I need to remove the bullet but it's going to keep bleeding so I need you to keep your hands pressed against this every time I remove my hands, the minute I pull the bullet you press against the wound as hard as you can manage without breaking her leg. Think you can do that?"

"Yeah." I croaked. "I can do that."

His hands moved so fast it was almost a blur. Within ten minutes she was breathing normal again, the bleeding had all but stopped but my hands? They were frozen in that spot, terrified that if I moved even an inch, if I even breathed wrong, it would end her life.

"Sergio." Stephen coughed. "Need those hands of yours, sew her up."

Sergio moved forward, hands trembling as he took the needle and thread and began sewing everything closed.

"You can remove your hands now, Tex." Stephen's voice was rough, exhausted.

Nodding, I pulled my hands free. They were coated in her blood. It may as well have been mine—if she died, I would die too. There was nothing else to it. No other option.

"Thank you," I said hoarsely.

Stephen sighed and looked around the room. "You guys are in some deep shit, you know that right?"

"Where is she?" Luca burst into the room followed by six men and of course Frank Alfero, Trace's, Grandpa, and boss to the Alfero family.

"Aw, a reunion." I grimaced. "Nice."

"Mo?" Luca moved to the table. "Who is responsible for this?"

Everyone fell silent. Blood was everywhere.

Finally Trace answered. "Tex's Uncle."

"Alfonso Campisi?" Luca said in a horrified voice, his face getting redder by the second.

"So much for that vacation." Frank pulled out his cell phone.

"Wait!" Nixon held out his hand. "What are you doing?"

"I think it's time…" Frank's hands had a slight tremble to them as he put the phone to his ear. "Call to order."

The room fell silent again while Frank closed his eyes and whispered, "Not just our family—we need all of them. Now."

"All of them?" Nixon and I shouted.

Luca held up his hand.

"Twenty four hours." Frank sighed. "We meet here. It is time for the arms to come together."

"Please tell me he's not doing what I think he's freaking doing." Nixon pushed against Luca's chest. But Luca didn't move.

"What?" Luca spat. "Get a hold of yourself son. We rise together, we fall together. You die, we eventually die, it is the only choice."

"What is?" I asked, apparently the only one brave enough to do so.

"He's calling a commission," Nixon said in a hollow voice. "The first since eighty five... the first since the old bosses returned to Sicily."

"Meaning..." I swallowed. "The FBI is going to have a freaking field day."

"I'd pay to be at the airport." Chase nodded. "Freaking pay for someone to record that shit."

"Campisi better hope Mo lives," Luca said quietly. "Otherwise, there will be no need for a meeting at all."

"What makes you say that?" Trace asked while Frank hung up the phone.

"Tex..." Luca nodded in my direction. "She dies, you have my permission, from one family to another. One blood to the next." He approached me slowly then kissed each of my cheeks. "My blessing—you may cleanse the line, son. And I'll help you do it."

"Damn it." Nixon slammed his hand against the counter top.

"Regardless." I looked around the room. "We're going to war."

"Yes." Frank took a step towards me and put his hand on my shoulder. "I believe we are."

Chapter Nineteen

They say that each time you go under the knife, you never come back the same as before you went under.

Mo

THE LAST THING I remembered was pain, severe pain, and so much blood that I ended up passing out after Sergio whispered in my ear that Tex needed me. At least I think he whispered that. I may have dreamed it up all things considered. I still felt pain, but it was more of a heaviness in my chest, like I was paralyzed, unable to move. Panicking, I tried to wiggle free but couldn't budge.

Open your eyes! I tried. Then I moaned and tried a second time.

"Mo, shhh." Tex. I'd recognize that voice anymore. It was the same voice that told me to fight, the one that called me baby. God, I'd missed that voice. It seemed now when he talked to me every word was clipped, filled with rage, at what I did, at the situation, at me. I fought tears. Fought and failed as they slid down my cheeks.

"Open your eyes, baby."

I sniffled and then slowly, my eyes opened, they took a

while to adjust to the darkness of the room — my room, the one I had been sharing with Tex. I blinked a few times, embarrassed that I'd been silently crying.

Tex sighed, his rough fingers slowly wiping the tears from my cheeks. His mouth descended, first kissing my forehead, and then hovering over my lips, asking for permission. Waiting to see if I'd turn away or lean forward.

It took every ounce of strength I possessed to move — but I was able to do it, I mean to the naked eye it probably looked like I blinked, but Tex saw. And that was all that mattered.

His mouth touched mine, softly, his tongue caressing my lips then slowly entering. It was the most tender kiss I could ever remember him giving me, like he was afraid that I would break.

"Are you in pain?" he murmured against my lips.

I shook my head, then found my voice and said hoarsely, "No."

"Do you remember what happened?"

My eyebrows drew together. Blood. I'd been shot. But who was it? What bastard would dare? My entire body trembled.

"It's okay, shh." Tex wrapped his body around mine, pulling me into the cocoon of his warmth. "He's already dead."

"You killed him?"

"Not yet." Tex's teeth ground together. "But I imagine I'll have a few volunteers when the time comes. We'll tag team it."

"Sounds fun."

"Like hunting a deer." Tex chuckled. "We'll spray paint a giant-ass target on his back and then fight for first shot."

"Me." Shivers rocked me. "I get first shot."

"Aw, baby, I was always going to give you first shot, but I figured you'd want to wound him before we set him loose in the field."

"Knives to both thighs or maybe just snapping his

Achilles in half so that he can't run? Yeah that sounds good."

Tex froze behind me.

"What?" I shivered again, cuddling closer to him, my back pressed so tightly against his chest I could feel his heartbeat.

"Nothing," he choked out. "I just hate that I'm that freaking turned on by talks of violence."

"It's the knives." I swallowed. "Guys like sharp things."

"Guys like big things." Tex ran his hand down my left arm, his fingertips dancing against my skin. "Shiny things too. Ones with dark hair, and bright eyes. Things that have dirty little mouths and kick ass habits toward gory acts of violence."

"Hey that's me," I teased.

"How are you really feeling?"

I sighed and closed my eyes. "Tired. Upset. Irritated."

"I can get more drugs—"

"No." I cleared my throat. "They make my body feel heavy."

"I may have fallen asleep on your chest, my head's kind of heavy on account that it's filled with so much knowledge."

I laughed. It felt so good that the giggling almost turned into full on sobbing. Tex hadn't joked with me in a year.

A freaking year.

And he was being his old self.

Funny, the gentle giant with killer instincts.

"Knowledge huh?" I prodded leaning into his warm body. "You sure about that?"

"Oh I'm positive." Tex nodded. "What else would be in there to make it so heavy?"

"You want me to answer that or just leave it?"

Tex smirked and leaned in. "Is that your way of asking if I want you to taunt and tease me or are you just looking for an excuse to run your fingers through my hair?"

"Guilty?" I said a bit breathless.

He laughed again. My gut clenched.

I hated that it wouldn't last long.

I knew the clock was ticking—I wasn't sure if his good mood would leave as soon as I was healthy or if I was just being gifted with his smiles now because he was so terrified I was going to die.

With a grunt, I managed to turn on my side, I needed to look at his face—gain courage by reminding myself why I loved him.

"Tex?" I whispered, unable to tangle my legs with him because one was so huge it was probably its own planet, I managed to lay my head against his chest for a brief second before concentrating on his full lips.

"What?" His voice was ragged, his breathing came out in spurts like he was running a race and losing every second he didn't suck in enough air.

"Kiss me again."

"Mo—" His dark blue eyes heated to black within seconds. "This can't change anything. I'm not—"

"So it changes nothing." I shrugged, even though my heart screamed *this changes everything!*

"I won't stop." He leveled me with his glare, then his lips formed a sensual smile. "I don't think I have it in me. Thank God the bullet only hit a vein making you bleed like crazy, but any closer to your artery and you could have died—*would* have died."

"So." I tugged his lower lip with my teeth. "Make it all better?"

"Damn it, Mo." Tex reached for my arms bracing his body above mine. "You're injured!"

"Fine." I sighed, right like I ever gave up that easily. "Do me a favor then?"

"Anything," he vowed his hands cupping my face with such tenderness I almost burst into tears.

"Did they bring my shopping bags in?"

"Yeah, why?" His eyes narrowed.

"Get them for me?" I asked innocently.

With a shrug he got off the bed and walked over to the first bag, I lifted up on my elbows. "Not that one."

He lifted the pink Victoria's Secret bag into the air.

"That one." I suddenly felt nervous. "I bought some new PJ's. Grab them?"

Tex brought the bag over to the bed and started rummaging through the tissue. His hands froze.

He looked away, then back down at the bag, then away. With a curse he wiped his face with his hands and just continued to stare.

"Well?" I urged.

"Those..." His voice was a mere growl. "...are not pajamas."

"Of course they are!" I argued with a triumphant grin "The sales lady told me so."

He took a steadying breath, closing his eyes as he pressed his hands on either side of the bed, next to my feet.

"So?" I licked my lips. "Help me put one on?"

"Hell, no." He tossed the bag onto the floor. "Why would I put something on you that I'm just going to rip off within two seconds?"

"And you know how I hate it when you ruin new clothes."

He threw his head back and laughed. God I missed that sound. "Right, I would hate to ruin anything for the Mafia princess. What type of husband would I be if I ruined all your clothes?"

"What type of husband would you be if you didn't give your wife what she needed?"

"Oh, so now you need me for my body?" Tex grumbled, still in good humor.

"No." I gripped his t-shirt and pulled him closer. "I just want you for sex."

"Damn, can we put this in writing?" He teased, his

mouth nipping mine.

"If it makes you feel better." I gasped as his hands moved underneath my t-shirt inching up my sensitive skin.

"But—" His hands stopped. "Mo, I'm serious. This can't change anything. I'm still upset."

"So pretend you aren't..." My voice shook. "Pretend for five damn minutes that your hate doesn't match your love. Pretend you don't have ten mil on your head. Pretend I'm not Nixon's sister."

"I can't..." Tex sighed.

He was going to walk away. My body went rigid, waiting for the rejection.

"I mean, five minutes Mo? What the hell? Since when have I only lasted five minutes?" He smirked.

I hit him as hard as I could in the shoulder, which wasn't that hard considering how weak I was.

His mouth met mine. And soon my shirt was on the floor.

He said it changed nothing.

But little did he know—it changed everything.

Because we were about to have unprotected sex.

And I wasn't pregnant.

Not with his child.

Not with anyone else's. Thank God nobody had said anything about the baby, I was lucky they were so worried about me being okay—that they hadn't even thought to ask about a miscarriage.

So yeah, I was changing everything. Playing by my own rules. I'd made this deal with the devil to begin with—and I was going to follow it through.

To save his life, like he saved mine? Yeah, I'd follow through.

CHAPTER EIGHTEEN

*Chasing the devil isn't hell. It's realizing that you're chasing
yourself that's hell.*

Tex

WHAT THE HELL was I thinking? Smooth skin taunted me,
begged me to touch, to caress, to damn near lick from head to
toe and refuse to stop until Mo was so boneless that she could
barely lift her head.

Sex with Mo had always been playful, fun, hot as hell,
but right now? It was scorching. My heart, you know the part
that I still had, scolded me, told me to stop while I was ahead.

But my head?

My body?

Begged and damn near pleaded for me to continue
touching her. She was mine, after all. Not Sergio's, not
Nixon's, not anyone's but mine. She'd always been mine damn
it, and I was going to make sure she never forgot that. It
wasn't even about love... what I was doing was pure need.
Forget love. Did it even fit in our relationship? After the hurt
we'd given each other, I had no idea. But what I did know?

No woman ever responded to my touch like Monroe

Abandonato. In a smooth motion, I lie across her body, careful to keep my weight on my elbows so I could hover.

"Your shirt is still on," Mo said hoarsely.

"Right." I looked down. "Odd, yours came off surprisingly fast for being almost dead a few hours ago."

Mo rolled her eyes. "Right, some barbarian just ripped it from my cold body."

"Not cold," I snapped, my right hand moving down her shoulder, stopping at her strap and then sliding it down her arm. "Hot, very, very hot."

"Are you complimenting my skin?" She arched as I drew slow circles down her stomach and then tugged her other strap down.

"Yes, Mo. That's what I'm doing. I'm complimenting your skin temperature because I'm a player like that, and that's my game."

"Game," she panted as my fingers slid behind her back and unclasped her bra, "needs work."

"Game," I mock repeated, "hasn't even started." With a tug I threw her bra onto the floor and stared my fill. In all my years of living, I would never get used to seeing her naked body in all its glory. Damn, she was topless and it was like staring at the sun—utter perfection that I knew she was allowing me to mar with my hands, taint with my bloodlines, I narrowed my gaze on her stomach.

"You're still so skinny." My thumb caressed her belly button. I hoped the baby inside her, even though it wasn't mine, was okay. I'd asked Stephen and he said when she was feeling better we could run tests, but for the most part if she miscarried, there would be more blood. Her injury had been bloody and if we hadn't stopped the bleeding it could have been more serious—but as it was, she would just be really sore for a while.

"Tex." Mo hissed out a breath. "Are we doing this or are we talking?"

"Oh." I reared back, allowing the thoughts to dissipate. "I'm sorry, are you tired of talking? Need a little more caressing?" I tugged her shorts down and cupped her ass. "A bit more teasing? Nipping? Tugging? Pulling?" I lowered my head to her hipbone, licking around in lazy circles as she arched towards me.

"Damn it, Tex!"

"Aw, baby you know I love it when you scream my name." I chuckled, fanned my breath across her stomach then replaced it with my tongue. Tasting Monroe Abandonato was my number one favorite thing to do in the entire world. Her taste was unique, totally her, and I coveted it more than a sane person should. Then again, I never claimed to be anything but insane so there you have it.

Mo's fingers moved to my shirt, she tried to tug, but she was too weak from blood loss, which again reminded me that I probably shouldn't be trying to seduce her, but my body had other plans. And damn if I didn't want to mark her, brand her, fill her to the hilt and just bask in the fullness of what it was like to be inside her.

"Tex…" Mo dropped her hands from my shirt with a sigh of frustration. "I'm going to need a little help here."

"Say please." I straddled her and slowly lifted my shirt up to my head but didn't pull it completely off yet. "I'm waiting…"

"You're an ass, you know that right?" She wiggled beneath me.

"Keep doing that, I've got all the time in the world. Really, you're not slowly killing me or anything by rubbing against me."

"Take off your shirt!" she said through clenched teeth. "Please."

"Aw, there it is… who taught you manners? Nixon?" I chuckled and could almost imagine that there wasn't a chasm of anger and hurt between us… I imagined a world where I was the father of our child in earnest, where I was the hero, rather than the monster.

When my shirt fell to the floor, Mo's breath hitched. Her dainty hands danced across my rigid stomach, tightening my muscles to painful levels wherever she touched, her fingers slowly, agonizingly, moving up and down.

"This is new," she whispered, her hands hovering over one of my many scars.

"Yeah." I licked my lips. "It's a flesh wound."

She rolled her eyes. "Right, I know all about those."

"Sorry to break it to you but yours is more than a flesh wound there, little tyke. I thought you were dying, and if you want this to continue you'll stop reminding me why I shouldn't be getting you naked."

"Nixon may shoot you."

"Great." I leaned down and kissed her hot mouth. "Then he can get my other shoulder; it was feeling left out anyway."

Monroe laughed against my lips, I couldn't help but follow suit, her hands reached for the zipper of my jeans—and all laughing went straight out the window.

It would take an act of God for the girl to be able to actually strip me of all my clothing, so I stood, yanked off my jeans and waited for her to blush.

She always blushed.

It's part of the reason I loved her so much.

She pretended to be a bad ass, but that was to protect herself... she pretended that sex wasn't a big deal. But I knew it was. To Mo it always was... maybe that's why it stung so much that she would give her body to anyone but me.

I'd taken the girl's virginity.

I'd been the forever guy.

Until I wasn't anything anymore.

"Tex—" Mo held up her hand. I grasped it and lay down next to her.

"We shouldn't do this, Mo." My body was screaming

speak for yourself!

"I know." Mo nodded, her lips trembling as a tear fell down her cheek. "But you've always kissed me when I'm down, and Tex, I'm really—" Her chest heaved with emotion. "Really down right now."

"Alright." I sighed. "An hour... for an hour... only *we* exist. But when that hour's up... to protect you, to protect me, Mo... I'm going to go back to focusing on anger, on hate, because if I don't, I'm pretty sure one or both of our hearts will shatter."

She nodded.

And that's all it took.

I was stupid enough to promise her an hour.

And she was stupid enough to take it.

With tenderness I'd never been able to fully extend towards Mo in the bedroom, I slowly kissed her mouth, savoring her flavor, sucking her lips. If I got an hour, it was going to be a damn good hour.

Her arms wrapped around my neck, pulling me tighter against her. We kissed until my lips hurt, until hers were swollen, and when my mouth was still buzzing with pleasure, I kissed her harder, I kissed away the pain, the memories, the past... and in return gave her everything I was capable of giving.

When our bodies joined it was with such a jolt, that I lost my breath. It had been too damn long. I moved within her, slowly at first, giving her body time to adjust to me, shocked that it needed to in the first place.

And kissed her mouth.

"So good," Mo whispered against my lips. "Harder."

"You're—" I panted. "—injured."

"So?" She hooked her good leg around me. "You were saying?"

"Damn it."

She grinned.

"Think you're funny?" I pumped harder, faster, digging my hands underneath her ass to angle her towards me so that I was hitting one of mine and her favorite places.

Her nails dug into my back.

"Tex!" She found her release, I soon followed, but I kept my eyes open, watching her, loving that look of pure bliss on her face.

I was still inside her when the knock came at the door.

Mo's eyes widened in horror.

"Yeah?" I answered lazily.

"Hey, it's Nixon."

Well shit.

"Is Mo feeling okay? I heard yelling"

"Uh…" I bit my lip to keep from laughing while Mo turned twenty shades of scarlet beneath me. "Yeah she was um, dreaming."

She rolled her eyes.

"Oh okay, can I come in and—"

"No!" I yelled. "I uh, I'll come out, I need to talk to you about something and she's super exhausted." Especially after the hour we'd shared.

"Fine." Nixon's footsteps echoed down the hall.

With a curse I slumped against Mo, then very slowly removed myself from her body and put on my clothes again.

Wordless, I helped her put on her bra, her shirt, her shorts, every article of clothing looked in place. I even pulled her hair back into a ponytail and tied it.

"Tex." Mo's eyes didn't meet mine.

"Yeah?"

"What if an hour wasn't enough?"

How was it possible for someone's heart to be so elated and so broken at the same time? "Then you probably should have thought of that before you jumped into someone else's bed… Today I gave you an hour. A year ago I would have given you an eternity." With that, I stomped out of the room cursing myself as I heard her soft sobs escape her mouth.

It was better this way.

It had to be.

CHAPTER NINETEEN

Everyone has words they hate. The word I hate? Choice. It seemed my whole life was framed around such an innocent word. Innocent. How ironic.

Sergio

MO AND TEX had been in the back bedroom for hours. My hands were still stained from all the blood. I'd stopped trying to wash it off hours ago; it made a good reminder anyway. Blood on the hands.

Especially when my cell phone rang.

"Is it true?"

I sighed into the receiver and walked out to the back yard of Nixon's house. "Is what true?"

"The Commission?"

How much to tell? I was caught between needing to protect the family but also protect my own ass—protect blood.

"It's happening," I whispered. "Not that it makes any difference to you. That wasn't part of our agreement."

"No," he snapped. "But part of our agreement was that you'd give us any useful information."

"*Useful* information," I corrected. "The kind that will help keep the bad guys behind bars and the good ones out free. So excuse me for not exactly thinking of calling you."

"We'll be watching."

"Big Brother always is," I said curtly. "Good day."

I shoved the phone back into my pocket and groaned. When had things gotten so complicated? Stepping out, choosing to help the family seemed like a good idea... but I hadn't calculated what stepping out would do. There was a very serious reason I was a ghost. And it had nothing to do with not wanting to be a part of something big—but everything to do with being watched by the feds. I'd basically painted a target on my back the minute I stepped out of my alleged retirement.

And now, the ones I owed favors to? They were going to come knocking.

With a sigh, I walked back inside just in time to see Mo emerge from the bedroom. She looked... ravaged. Completely and utterly screwed.

I tilted my head. Her face was flushed; her ponytail was even crooked. Amazing, that after everything, Tex still thought he had a fighting chance with the very girl pointing the gun at his back.

In the end... he would choose Campisi.

In the end... she would choose Abandonato.

In the end... there would be bloodshed.

CHAPTER TWENTY

Sex changes everything and nothing all at once.

Mo

"YOU LOOK RESTED," Sergio said in a low voice.

I stumbled against the wall, stupid bum leg, and blinked in his direction. His dark hair was pulled back in a ponytail low on his neck, his blue eyes searching mine as if he could see every damn area Tex had placed his hands.

"I, um…" Scratching my head, I offered a tiny shrug. "I slept a bit. "

"Sure you did." Sergio grinned. It wasn't a happy grin. It was absolutely predatory and pissed. "Did you need help with anything?"

Crap. What I wanted was to spy on Nixon and Tex, but that wasn't happening with Sergio breathing down my neck. "Water would be nice."

Sergio looked me up and down for a few more minutes his eyes hooding as his gaze settled on my lips. "Fine," he snapped. "I'll help you get to the kitchen."

"Oh that's okay I just—"

"Stop arguing Mo, I won't bite you… not with his scent

all over your skin. Not very sporting of me."

I closed my eyes as heat spread across my body.

Sergio wrapped a muscled arm around me and then lifted me off the floor. I had no choice but to lean against him—he always smelled the same, like clean minty spice. It used to comfort me. But now? It made me sick. It reminded me of what I'd done with him. I blamed him when really I should have blamed myself. It was my fault not his.

When we reached the kitchen he placed me on the counter like a little kid and stalked over to the cupboard. "You want ice?"

"Please," I whispered gripping the counter top with my hands like it was my only lifeline.

Sergio gripped the cup in his hands and went over to the freezer, the ice plunked into the glass, making the room feel that much more tense.

"He's going to destroy us all." Sergio's back was to me as he filled the glass with water, his voice was so matter-of-fact and cold I wanted to shiver. "I hope you know that. He's a Campisi, one doesn't just stop being a Campisi."

Deflated, I tried to ignore the truth of Sergio's words. "You're wrong."

"Am I?" He turned around and his eyebrows shot up in surprise. "And what makes you the expert?"

"I just..." I chewed on my thumbnail. "I know his heart. He's good, and what we're doing..."

"What we're doing..." Sergio threw his head back and laughed. "Had nothing to do with you seducing him then screwing with his head, Mo. Absolutely nothing. So what the hell are *you* doing? Because I'm pretty sure the others would like to know as well."

"I'm making it real." I swallowed the tightness in my throat and stretched my hand out for the water.

Sergio sighed and placed the cold glass against my fingertips, not removing his hand but keeping mine trapped against his. "Mo, regardless of how real you make it—you can't save him."

"But the plan was—"

"—marriage." He shrugged simply. "And you still got shot."

"But—"

"Mo." Sergio released the glass and placed his hands on either side of my hips, pressing his body against mine so forcefully I gasped. "He will die."

"No." I shook my head forcefully. "I won't let it happen. They said if we did it this way it would protect him."

"You do realize…" He lifted his head and brushed his knuckles against my cheek. "I will save you before I save him."

"Don't." My lips trembled. "I'm not worth it."

"Let *me* decide your worth Monroe." He took a protective stance in front of me. "And in the end, once this is over, I want you to remember, I was the one that was willing to forgive and forget whereas the one you claim to love—the one you want to save—is going to be dead in a month—for choosing blood."

Cursing, Sergio backed away and stalked out of the kitchen leaving me alone with my thoughts. No longer thirsty, I placed the glass on the counter and tried to get off the countertop. Yeah, that wasn't working very well. My leg wouldn't let me maneuver.

After five minutes of trying not to kill myself. I slumped against my knees and waited for footsteps to come down the hall.

Wonder of all wonders, it wasn't Tex that had come searching for me but Nixon.

"You weren't in bed," he snapped, his cold eyes fierce.

"Right." I sighed. "I was trapped on the countertop."

"Mind telling me how you got there?"

"I flew?"

Nixon grinned. "Smart ass."

"Love you too, brother."

His smile fell; he took a few tentative steps towards me. "Tell me you know it's bad."

I nodded.

"Tell me you know there will be death."

I nodded again.

He cursed and wiped his face with his hands. "Tell me in the end—" His voice shook. "Tell me you'll do what I say."

"I can't." With trembling hands, I wiped away the tears already running down my face. "I still love him."

"I know." Nixon picked me up into his arms and carried me down the hall. "That's the damn problem."

I sighed against Nixon's chest. His tattooed arms were hanging onto me so tight you would have thought I was the most precious thing in the world to him. Then again, we were all we had. Everyone else... dead.

"Mo." Nixon's voice cracked as he placed me on the bed and then sat down on the mattress, his weight causing it to creak. "The Commission, we weren't born yet..."

"The first one." I laid my head on his shoulder. "Did lots of people die?"

"Well." Nixon chuckled. "It wasn't exactly a fiesta."

"Bite your tongue," I scolded. "Sicilians do not have fiestas, we have parties, blood baths, you know, the cool kind."

"Right." He sucked in his lip ring and leaned against his legs. His right foot tapping against the floor, made him appear nervous which, if you knew my brother, was totally out of character.

"Are you okay?"

"That would be a giant-ass no." Nixon's laugh was hollow. "I think she may be pregnant."

"Who?"

His foot stopped tapping. "Who else, genius? Trace."

"Oh." Well that was a bit of a shock. "Why do you think

that?"

"Because I know her, know her body." And there went that foot tapping again. "And it suddenly all makes sense, you know?"

"What does?"

"Blood." Nixon whispered hoarsely. "It makes so much damn sense, Mo. I would do anything—anything for blood."

"Like a vampire?" I joked, punching him in the arm.

"Like a vampire," he echoed, his voice losing its edge. "Mo." He grabbed my hands. "I will always protect you, I'll always protect what's mine, but the choice Tex is going to have to make." He squeezed lightly. "I guess I just need you to understand the pull that blood has on someone's loyalty." His eyes filled with sadness. "Regardless of how he feels for you— you aren't—"

"—blood," I whispered. "So you're saying."

"I'm saying in the end remember who you are." Nixon shrugged. "Remember who he is."

"I'm tired." I faked a yawn.

"Right."

"Oh, and Nixon." I gripped his hand together. "Tell Trace I'm happy for her."

Nixon's eyes narrowed. "Interesting."

"What?"

"I would have thought you would have noticed by now... what with experiencing the same things... similar symptoms and such." He crossed his arms.

"Yeah, well." I shrugged. "Every pregnancy is different."

"Just like life," Nixon added. "Sleep tight Mo."

I nodded, emotions clogging my throat.

Two hours later, a heavy weight descended on my bed and large arms cocooned around my body.

"Tex?" I whispered.

"Yeah?"

"Enemies or lovers right now?"

109

He sighed and kissed my head. "Both, we'll always be both."

And I had my answer.

CHAPTER TWENTY-ONE

Sometimes all you want to do is pull the covers over your head and pray the truth out of existence.

Tex

THE NEXT MORNING came too soon. Sunlight flickered through the dark curtains, landing on my face. My body ached, my bones felt brittle, and I'd lost all feeling in my left arm.

Mo snuggled closer to my body.

My body decided it liked it and pressed against hers.

I told it to stop.

But yeah, it had a mind of its own. Besides, when you fit so perfectly with someone, it's kind of hard not to want to fuse the pieces together. With a sigh, I pried myself away from her, the tingling sensation in my arm reminding me of the loss of her body.

The chat with Nixon the day before hadn't gone well. My uncle had suddenly decided to go off the map. All the Sicilians were currently in flight to the states for The Commission, and he'd disappeared like the bitch he was.

Sergio, aka shit for brains, even tried tracing the cell number and it was disconnected, meaning only one thing, he'd heard about The Commission and he knew what my next move was.

Mother freaking splendid news.

The meeting of the powers wasn't to take place for another week—we needed everyone to get adjusted. And Nixon had cheerfully given Luca and Frank the job of making sure no shots accidently misfired, yeah I didn't envy them.

Mo made a little noise in her sleep and flipped onto her back.

God, she was beautiful.

God, I was an asshole for not telling her that every damn day.

Someone knocked softly on the door then opened it. Trace's head poked through, staring at a calm Mo and then glaring at me.

"Whoa." I held my hands up in innocence. "I was staring at her, not aiming a gun."

"You choose her," Trace whispered. "When it comes to making a choice, you always choose love, screw blood."

"Are you drunk?" I took a few steps towards her.

"No." A tear streamed down her cheek. "I just... you need to know, in the end... your life is about choices, they either make or break you, don't let your past destroy your future."

"And if it already has oh wise one? And by the way this is weird, I haven't even had breakfast, how are you even able to think this early?"

Trace's brown eyes narrowed, with a flip of her dark hair she shrugged. "I'm an Abandonato. I'm always watching."

"Vacation," I muttered. "You should try it—you know away from the boss."

"Tex," Trace snapped. "I'm serious. When the time comes it's not about what Nixon wants, it's what's best for her." With that, she closed the door, leaving me confused as hell and a bit curious as to what she put in her Cheerios to make her so awake at seven a.m.

Damn Nixon had his hands full with that one, always had, always will.

I took one last look at Mo and left the room making my way to the kitchen for some breakfast.

Trace was sitting calmly at the table eating, what do ya know, her Cheerios. Chase was in the process of stealing the box from her fingers while Mil hit him on the head with a newspaper, you know like owners do to their dogs when they piss on their shoes, and Nixon, he was deep in conversation with Sergio, Luca, and Frank.

"Did I sleep in or something?" I yawned gaining everyone's attention.

"Ahh, the beast's awake." Luca smirked.

"Says the trained house cat." I flipped him off. I'd never been afraid of Luca. Hell, if anything, he should be afraid of me, of what I represented.

He ignored my slight to his scariness and shrugged, taking a long sip of his coffee.

I poured myself a cup of coffee and joined everyone in the kitchen. Nixon was the first to speak.

"We'll do it at The Spot."

"The meeting?" I clarified.

Nixon nodded and leaned back in his chair. "We can control the environment there."

"And what exactly are we hoping to accomplish?" I asked.

"What we always aim to accomplish." Frank ran a shaky hand through his silver hair. "Peace."

Just then Chase fell out of his chair on account of Mil pushing him, just as Trace freed the box of Cheerios and made a run for the pantry.

"Can't even control our own breakfast, but world domination and peace, good luck with that." I snickered.

Luca licked his lips, his cold eyes watched me drink my

coffee as though memorizing each movement. "You will help us."

"And if I don't?"

"I'll shoot you." Luca picked a piece of lint off his suit and glanced back at Nixon. "It really is a lovely day. Why don't you take Tracey out for a nice morning walk? We have time to plan later."

"My death," I grumbled.

"What other choice do you have?" A muscle popped in Nixon's jaw. "Either you stand with us or you stand with them. You stand with us, they try to kill you but at least we protect you. You stand with them, they still try to kill you, and in the end we have to."

"And why's that?" I licked my lips. "Why the hell would you have to kill me if I took my rightful place? Because really, that's the only messed up piece to this entire puzzle! I killed my own father, so why shouldn't I take his spot? What makes you, Nixon, any better than me? What makes what I have to do any less damning than what all of you did when you became the head of the family?"

The entire room fell silent.

Even Chase and Mil stopped fighting.

"You truly do not know," Frank finally whispered. "Do you, son?"

I set my coffee onto the table and wiped my face with my hands. "Know, what?"

Frank placed his hand across mine, mumbling a prayer in Italian before whispering, "You have a sister."

The room went red, and then black, and then red again. "What does that have to do with me?"

"Damn near everything." Luca snorted. "I think it's time we adjourn, let Tex savor the fact that he still has some family worth seeking out…"

I was still stunned when Frank put his hand on my shoulder and whispered, "Blood always wins."

Mo.

My sister.

Nixon.

Holy shit.

Choices.

They'd been leaving hints all along.

They were going to make me choose. One look at Nixon said it all—because I knew he would choose Mo every single time—if he'd never met her, he would choose her.

Just like I would choose my sister.

To protect her, I would join the devil.

To protect her, I would fight my friends.

CHAPTER TWENTY-TWO

Being in the Mafia is like playing house. Everything is fine until
someone pulls out a gun.

Mo

BY THE TIME I made it down to breakfast it was more like
lunch. Chase and Mil had left a note that they'd gone out
shooting and Nixon was just getting ready to take Trace to the
grocery store.

Weird.

How normal we all seemed.

But nothing about our family was normal, which I was
reminded of yet again when Nixon strapped ammo to the
inside of his ankle.

"Where's Tex?" I cleared my throat and crossed my arms.

Nixon and Trace shared a tense look.

With a curse Nixon mumbled, "Hell if I care."

Trace smacked him in the shoulder, but he just shook his
head and gently took her arm, leading her out of the house.

"We'll be back this afternoon," Nixon called. "I left plenty
of men and you do still have Tex here with you, so all should
be well, you know, unless he's asked to choose—"

"Nixon!" Trace yelled his name so loud even I was shocked, she never yelled. Ever.

He blushed slightly and ducked his head as they walked out the door. Okay, that was weird.

I poured myself a cup of coffee and grabbed a granola bar from the pantry. It was a really pretty day, no way was I staying inside while everyone else was out doing something. I was sick of being babied, even if I did get shot, it wasn't like I'd almost died or anything.

I ate the granola bar and choked down the coffee, then limped towards the back door.

"Going somewhere?" Sergio asked, peeking out from behind the newspaper.

"Hell." I smiled sweetly. "Care to join me?"

His gaze unwavering he simply answered. "Too late."

I shrugged and shouldered open the door limping across the back yard. The tree, just like everything else, looked harmless.

I'd spent years climbing that tree.

I imagined I was a princess in a tower, just waiting for my prince to come rescue me. It didn't help that Nixon always told me stories about princesses in towers convincing me that I was like the girls in the story—it's kind of how the whole Mafia princess thing came into play. Tex thought it was hilarious and teased me about it relentlessly when we were little.

Yeah, I'd kill to have him tease me right now.

What had I been thinking?

One hour? Was I insane? Delusional?

And, further to the point, was that one hour enough to bond him to me forever? It had to be, because I wasn't so sure he would give me another chance with him. He wore his anger like a shield. Even when we slept, I could feel it coming off of him in waves.

With a sigh I placed my hands on the tree and lifted

myself into the air, my bum leg swinging against the bark. At least it only ached a bit today.

My legs dangled nearly touching the ground.

How pathetic, I couldn't get any higher.

But at least I was alone.

With my thoughts.

I wondered if I would do things differently, if I could go back in time, would I have chosen not to protect Tex? Or would I have gone to Nixon first, asked for his help rather than make a deal with a ghost?

My text alert went off.

G: You tried Mo, and that's all we could ask. In the end... hopefully it will be enough to keep them from killing him. Nobody wants the head to come down on the tail.

Me: We'll have to just keep trying.

G: Yes. We will.

I thought back to that night... closing my eyes as the memories wrapped themselves around me like a choking sensation.

"Mo?" Sergio caught me as I stumbled against him. "Are you alright?"

"Stupid Tex." I grumbled, my words felt heavy in my throat. "I hate him, make me forget him, please, it's only ever been him! I need it to be someone else!" It was after Mil and Chase's wedding and I'd drunk way too much wine, thinking I could drown my sorrows in the glass apparently.

Sergio sighed and pulled me into his arms. "You think I want what isn't mine to take?"

"I know you do!" I pulled back, more like stumbled back and poked him in the chest. "You've always liked me! Admit it!"

Sergio chuckled and held his hands up in the air. "Guilty, but you'll hate yourself and in the end, I'm positive you'll hate me."

"Let me hate you too, then... let me hate you as much as I hate him, as much as I hate me."

"Oh Mo." Sergio pulled me back into his arms and kissed my

forehead. "Fill the world with hate, and all you get is hate. Fill your soul with more hate and it breeds hate. Hate this world needs less of. Love, however, I could do that."

"Don't love me," I spat. "The last person that loved me didn't mean it."

"He did," Sergio whispered. "And you know that."

"Please!" I begged, my voice hoarse. "Please just make love to me."

"What lengths would you go to... to save him?"

"Save him?"

Sergio gently placed me in the chair next to his bed and ran his fingers through his long thick hair. "Tex. What would you do to save him?"

"Anything," I choked. "I would do anything, but why does he need saving?"

"Everyone," came a familiar voice behind me, "should be given a second chance, Monroe. Don't you think?"

I turned and with a gasp promptly passed out.

I jolted awake. Crap, Mafia rule number one, don't fall asleep in a tree unarmed. I stretched my arms above my head.

"What are you doing?" Tex yelled running towards me, fury etched in every plane of his face. Oh yay, another lecture. Like I hadn't been getting that enough, what with Sergio, Nixon, and Tex it was like living under constant parental guidance.

"What's it look like I'm doing?" I closed my eyes again and leaned back.

"Funny you should ask." Tex's voice was closer now; I could almost feel the heat of his body. "Because it looks like you're climbing a tree but we both know you wouldn't be stupid enough to do that, right?"

I blinked my eyes open. "What?"

"One of us is pregnant. News flash, it isn't the one with a penis!"

"So I can't climb trees now? The injustice of it all!" I

challenged, hating how much I loved his stormy blue eyes, and how fiercely protective they looked in that moment.

"Sure you can." He gripped the branch above my head and lifted himself effortlessly next to me. "But for future reference I'd just appreciate it if you'd at least put a net underneath the tree and strap tiny parachutes to your ankles, you know just to be safe."

I opened my mouth to speak but he interrupted me.

"Oh, and when I say tree I mean that one." He pointed to a tiny little tree that was planted next to the house and probably couldn't even support the weight of a bird.

"Are you saying you want me to sit on that tree when I have an itch to climb?"

Tex grinned, his smile reaching the corners of his eyes as he winked and looked back at the tiny tree. "Sure? Why not?"

"And I'm not strapping parachutes to my ankles, weirdo."

"Hmm?" Tex tiled his head and flicked my shoe. "At least they're swollen enough that they may break your fall. So you've got that in your favor."

"My ankles are not swollen, you ass!" It was an impossibility not that he needed to know that.

"Mo, if I was in a shipwreck and holding onto your ankles was my only hope for survival—I'd live."

I cracked a smile then pushed against his muscled chest. "Why are you picking on me? Don't you have spiders to kill and ants to examine with a magnifying glass?"

"Aw, low blow." Tex chuckled. "You had to bring up my childhood torture methods."

"I saved those ants." I sniffed. "No thanks to you."

"Want to know a secret?" Tex asked, looking back at the house and then leaning in until our lips were an inch away.

"Yeah," I whispered. "Tell me."

"I wanted you to save the ants."

"Oh, really?" My eyebrows arched in surprise. "So you

tortured things in order for me to… what?"

"Well, that's easy." Tex shrugged. "You had a weakness for the innocent, if I wanted you to come running, all I needed to do was harm the weak…"

"Evil."

"Necessary," he said with a firm nod. "Especially necessary given I wanted the great princess's attention." He cleared his throat. "So we're in the tree, why?"

"Because I—not we—*I* was thinking."

"Awesome, well can we think somewhere on the ground where I'm not an easy target for would be assassins? I mean it's been twelve hours since I've been shot at. I really don't want to push my luck."

"Aw, where's the bravery? Let's put a target on your back and paint your face red, think that will work?" I laughed.

"Aw, baby, if you want to see me blush all you have to do is ask." Tex said in a gravelly voice, all notes of humor drained from his tone as his eyes drank me in.

I shivered.

"Are you cold?" His eyebrows knit together. "Let's get you inside and I'll find a blanket."

I nodded, hating myself even more. He was treating me like a princess and I wasn't even pregnant—that I knew.

Wow, I never thought I'd be one of those girls, the ones who actually plotted how to get the Mafia boss to slip up and impregnate me so the lie could be true.

Tex jumped out of the tree and turned, holding his hands up to me. I smiled and fell against his chest.

Just as a figure in black stepped out on the back deck, and shot Tex in the leg.

I screamed.

But my scream was silenced by a blunt object hitting my temple. And everything went completely black.

CHAPTER TWENTY-THREE

Blood always tastes metallic but before the metal even enters your consciousness, it tastes forbidding, like you know something's wrong but you're powerless to stop it.

Sergio

SHIT, THAT HURT. I rubbed my head, my temples were pounding. Was I hungover? Wait, it was morning and—

I jolted to my feet and grabbed my gun.

The house was silent.

Quietly, I stepped around the corner into the kitchen, two men were laying on the ground. Blood pooled at their backs. Mother of God, what had happened?

I walked out into the front of the house where a few of our men were normally stationed and cursed.

Dead.

Five of them.

All dead.

Shot in the head. I leaned down to feel each pulse. Nothing. A piece of white paper fluttered on the last man's chest.

Are you listening now? said the note.

"Shit!" I kicked the ground and pulled out my cell. Nixon answered on the first ring.

"What?"

"It's the men—"

"My men?"

"I was knocked out, we've got seven dead."

"Where's Mo?"

His question swamped my body with a chill. I dropped my phone and raced full blast to the back yard, almost tripping on my own feet as I made it to the place where I'd last seen her.

Only to find one of her flip flops on the ground.

And blood right next to it.

I fell to my knees.

They had no idea what they'd just done.

I knew though—I knew who did it, just like Nixon knew, and I knew, in the end the war they'd just started wouldn't just go down in history.

It would freaking define it.

CHAPTER TWENTY-FOUR

Doing anything to save someone isn't really a sacrifice, not if you truly love them.

Tex

"WAKEY, WAKEY." Something slapped me on the face. With a grunt, I tried to open my eyes but the pain was exploding down my leg. Shit, had I been shot? Again?

"I said…" Another kick to my good leg that was, soon to be bad if the bastard kept kicking. "Get the hell up!"

"And?" I blinked my eyes adjusting to the dark room. "Do a little circus dance? I mean—" Another kick this time to my shin. I wheezed. "Damn at least stop tickling me, if you want me to dance just ask, I don't care that—" Three more kicks, well I was going to be lame the rest of my life nothing more to say about that. I'd been tortured many times, always came out with scars but I hated, despised, freaking despised getting kicked, it was… degrading. "Fine, fine."

I tried to rise to my feet, but my left leg was still bleeding, I could feel the warmth seeping through my jeans and my right leg was bruised from my ankle to my hip.

"Tex!" Mo screamed.

What? Why was Mo with me?

The events of the afternoon came crashing down around me like a blanket of rage. With a shout I ran in the direction of her voice but was stopped by another kick to the back of my knees.

"Shit." I fell to the ground. "Stop kicking me!"

"I'll stop kicking you," the heavily accented voice teased, "when you stop irritating me with every breath you take."

"So first—" I moved to my knees and faced the stranger "—you want me to get up and dance? And now you want me to stop breathing? Anyone ever tell you that you have ridiculously high demands?"

"You're mouthy."

"Aw, you staring at my mouth?" I joked, backing away, more like sliding away towards Mo on my legs.

"You will not reach her," the voice mocked. "She's tied up, but never fear she can see you. She will watch everything we do to you."

"At least give her popcorn," I muttered.

"I'll do better." The man's footsteps echoed as he walked towards me, then suddenly the lights flickered on. We were in a basement, no windows, no doors that I could see, and really poor lighting. Mo was to my right chained to a freaking chair, and the man walking towards me was none other than my uncle.

I smiled when he stopped in front of me.

"You think this is funny?" he spat, his eyes damn near popping out of their sockets.

"It's so damn hilarious I'm having hard time not having a case of the giggles." I narrowed in on his gaze, his mouth was tightened in a firm line, his eyes clear but dilated, he was either high or really pissed off. Faint bruising darkened the skin beneath his eyes; he hadn't been sleeping, and by the smell of him he'd possibly been on the run.

"Tell me." I smirked. "You get your invitation to The

Commission?"

His nostrils flared.

"Oh wait, did they send it to my house by accident? My bad, I'm sure they're just confused as to who owns the power to the Campisi clan. If you want I can give them a change of address form or something."

Snarling he backhanded me across the left cheekbone almost ripping apart skin with his giant ass ring.

"You step up, you die." He wiped his hands on a silk cloth he'd pulled from his pocket and snapped his fingers.

The two giant dudes came rushing towards me and lifted me into the air then sat my ass onto the coldest metal chair ever created.

"So." I nodded, allowing them to tie me up. "What is this? You kill me, deliver my head Goliath style, and then what?"

"This?" My uncle smiled. "My son, this is me welcoming you to the family."

"Awesome." I nodded. "So it's like a hazing ceremony. You gonna put some body paint on me? Because I have to say Mo would totally dig that." I winked in her direction. She gave me a watery smile but said nothing. Had to stay strong for her. Had to be steel. Had to live. Had to survive.

"I'm going to cut out your tongue." My Uncle grinned as if amused at the thought. "And then I'm going to send it to your adopted family with a note—along with your girlfriend's fingers."

"Wife," I corrected.

His eyes narrowed. "I stopped the ceremony. She isn't your wife."

"Wow, hate to break it to you, but she is. Check the files, have one of your minions put their computer skills to the test. We. Are. Married. You kill her, you bring down the Abandonatos on your family. Your funeral, just saying."

He examined me for a bit then turned and addressed Mo.

"Where's your ring?"

I gave her a reassuring wink.

"The bastard forgot to get me one on account that we got married in such a rush... I'm pregnant." She glared. "Surprise bitch."

Oh, God I loved that woman.

I knew we were in a dire situation, but damn I wanted to rip her clothes off and kiss her senseless.

"So you?" Uncle turned and angled his head at me. "Would do anything for her?"

"No shit."

"Interesting." He reared back and slapped her across the face so hard she fell to the ground, blood spewed from her mouth.

"Stop!" I yelled. "Hit me, I'll take her punishment. Damn, do you even have a soul? She's pregnant!"

"Proof?" My uncle pulled out a knife. "I could easily slice her from gut to chin and kill the spawn of your seed within her."

Shit, shit, shit, shit.

"You could." I almost vomited. "But again, you're forgetting something very, very important."

"And that's, what?" He laughed.

"She's the boss's sister. And the boss... well let's just say he's best friends with the Nicolasi and Alfero Families. Ain't no way you're getting out of the country alive, shit, they'd all die in order to kill you. You'd be bringing down the four families, including the De Langes, I highly doubt you want to do that."

"Sometimes..." He fingered the knife. "A man is desperate enough to take such chances."

Without any warning he lunged for me and stabbed my thigh with his knife. I didn't yell. I simply stared at him even though my vision was starting to get spotty.

"I will torture you." He gave me an evil smile. "Pray you

survive it."

"Oh, I will," I said hoarsely. "After all, I have an uncle to kill."

CHAPTER TWENTY-FIVE

Losing someone you love isn't the hardest thing in the world. It's watching it happen before your very eyes — that's hard.

Mo

I'D NEVER BEEN in a situation like this before. I'd heard about it, I'd witnessed it, but I'd never lived through it, wasn't so sure I was going to live through it now. Tex was still bleeding from getting shot in the leg, though by the way he had staggered towards me I imagined it wasn't as bad as I first assumed. Not that it mattered since he had a freaking knife sticking out of his shot-up leg at the moment.

"So this is fun." Tex spat out blood onto the cold cement floor, more blood dripped down his chin.

"I agree!" Another slap from his Uncle, followed by laughter. "I'm having the time of my life."

Tex's head fell back against the chair for a moment before he blinked in my direction. Blood caked his entire face, but his gaze was unwavering. I held onto the look he gave me, I cherished it, pulled it close and prayed that God would deliver us from the hell hole we were in. One thing I was hopeful for? That they wouldn't kill us, that they weren't that stupid, but that didn't mean I'd escape with all of my limbs attached to my body.

"Twenty years!" his uncle shouted. "Twenty years I've waited to take my rightful spot, and your father was this close!" He held out his fingers in front of Tex's face. "So very close to naming me his second. He was tired, he was ready to step down, and you go and kill him!"

"Aw, shit man." Tex shook his head. "So you weren't smart enough to get it in writing or something? Pity."

His Uncle screamed and punched him in the gut. Tex gagged as his body convulsed. "I am Alfonso Campisi, and I will be the next in line."

Then he burst out laughing, his head hanging a bit like he didn't have strength to lift it. "Holy shit, you could have totally starred in Gladiator, 'I am Alfonso Campisi!'" His voice mimicked Alfonso's to perfection.

"This—" Alfonso pulled the knife from Tex's thigh. "—is no game."

"Good, I freaking hate Monopoly."

Alfonso lifted the knife into the air. Tex had finally pushed him too far.

"Stop!" I yelled. "Please, just stop!"

The hand holding the knife paused in the middle of the downward stroke as Alfonso looked in my direction. Tex groaned and shook his head at me. The knife impaled itself again into his leg, Tex let out a string of expletives as Alfonso started making his way towards me. I instantly regretted my decision.

"So." He unchained me, then grabbed me by the hair and dragged me towards Tex. "You must love him… with all your heart?"

"Yes," I whispered. "Desperately."

"Then you'll do anything to secure his safety."

Yeah, I already had and looked how that worked out. "Naturally." I lifted my chin and spat in Alfonso's face. "He's ten times the man you'll ever be."

"So now you challenge my manhood?" Alfonso grinned. "How about I take you up on the offer then?"

"Offer?" I squinted as the light above Alfonso's head flickered in my line of vision.

"To save your love..." Alfonso tilted his head and reached out, cupping my chin with his fingers, his thumb caressed my lower lip. "What will you give me?"

"Hell no!" Tex shouted, his voice filled with gravel. "I'd rather die than see her breathe the same air as you."

"That—" Alfonso dropped my chin and sneered at Tex. "—can be arranged."

"Boss!" One of the men was talking on his phone in hushed tones. "Boss!"

"What!" Alfonso roared.

The guard held up the phone. "Problem."

Cursing, Alfonso wiped his hands on the rag from the metal table. "Fine, it will give the couple time to say goodbye."

With a laugh he followed the guard out the door. I slumped against Tex's chair. "What do you need?"

"Well since you're taking orders, a hamburger and fries would be killer." Tex sighed. "Or maybe a milkshake? Yeah I'm changing my order, chocolate milkshake, stat."

"Tex." My voice shook. "I can't joke right now. I can't, not when you're bleeding, not when you could almost die, not—"

"I'm not blood," he said in a hollow voice. "Does it matter to the Abandonato princess what happens to me?"

I awkwardly staggered to my feet and grabbed the rag from the table, wiping his face as I answered, "The same could be said of me, I wiped across his lips, the blood had already started to dry, I'm not blood, what does it matter to the Campisi heir?"

Tex's eyes fluttered closed for a brief second before opening, nailing me to the spot, consuming my very heartbeat, making my pulse do nothing but scream his name. "It matters."

I nodded, touching the rag to the corner of his mouth. "It matters."

I wasn't sure if untying him would get us in more trouble, so I did the next best thing. I leaned down and kissed him.

Our mouths met in a frenzy.

He tasted like blood.

Which meant he was alive.

My Tex was alive.

And he was mine.

CHAPTER TWENTY-SIX

When all hell breaks loose all you can really do is hold on and maybe close your eyes.

Sergio

"START AT THE BEGINNING." Nixon paced in front of me, waving his gun wildly in the air. You know, the gun that he didn't even have a safety on. When it pointed to my face I sighed and leaned back in my chair. We'd been over it for the past hour. Each detail.

And we still had nothing.

"Clearly I was taken from behind," I mumbled, embarrassed that I had been taken at all and horrified that someone was able to even sneak by our men, which made me wonder what the hell type of people the Campisis actually were.

Nixon sat the gun at the table and sat in the chair next to me. "Where would he take them? He wouldn't be stupid enough to kill them."

Luca and Frank remained silent as they stared at the table. Yeah the table wasn't going to help us folks. Then again, maybe they were just getting too old for this shit.

I ran my hands through my hair. "*Mo* they'll let live."

The room fell silent except for the hum of the fridge and the ticking of the Grandfather clock in the hallway.

Chase drummed his fingertips against the table and pulled out his phone. "Does she have her cell?"

"Given my specific skill set, don't you think I've already gone down every possible avenue of her rescue?" I tried to keep my voice even. "She doesn't have her phone, Tex doesn't have his phone, they're gone and the only way we're getting them back is if we wait."

"We are not waiting." Nixon growled.

Trace put her hand on his back and started rubbing. Nixon flexed and unflexed his fist.

"There is no way to track her." I sighed. "I'm sorry, Nixon. We wait. We have to."

"We wait when I say we wait," Nixon yelled.

I held up my hands in surrender. "Fine, you're the boss."

Luca stood abruptly and marched out of the room, cell phone in hand.

"Wayta piss everyone off, Sergio," Chase murmured.

"This isn't my fault!" I shouted. "I was taken from behind!"

"You should have been paying attention!" Nixon roared. "What the hell were you doing! Watching a damn sitcom!"

"She was with Tex!" I jumped up from my chair. "She was safe!"

"She is never safe with Tex." Nixon jabbed his finger in my chest pushing my legs back against the wooden chair. "Never, do you understand? From here on out, you're her freaking shadow. I want to know how many times she tosses in her sleep, I want to know how many eye lashes she loses per hour. When we get her back, not if, but *when* we get her back, her life is more important than yours. Do we have an understanding?"

Rolling my eyes wouldn't be effective, but that's exactly

what I wanted to do. And this was why I hated working for the family. I bit my tongue, allowing myself a few moments of sanity before speaking. "We have an understanding."

"Good." Nixon popped his knuckles and picked up his gun again.

"Put that down before you hurt yourself," Chase whispered then gripped Mil's hand and whispered into her ear, "They'll be fine, Tex is an animal."

"That's the problem," Nixon interjected. "He's an animal I can no longer control."

"You don't know that," Frank piped up. "You know nothing of what happened."

It was true, even the camera system had somehow been overridden so we were literally blind on all fronts. How the hell had they infiltrated so quickly, the thought that it was planned entered my head probably the same time Nixon's cold gaze met mine.

"No." I shook my head. "Tex wouldn't do that."

"Would he?" Nixon whispered. "How else would they be able to infiltrate the house? It's a fortress."

"Nixon—" Trace held out her hands in front of her. "No, we're talking about Tex, your best friend Tex!"

"The world is an ugly place," Nixon spat. "You of all people should know that, Trace. After all, Phoenix was my best friend too, and look how that turned out."

"Enough." Frank entered the room again sliding his phone back into his pocket. "They're fifteen miles south of here."

"What?" We all said in unison.

My eyes narrowed to tiny slits. "How do you know that?"

Luca met Frank's gaze. It was tired; hell they both looked like they needed a vacation. "Oh, Sergio, I know a great many secrets. This one, I just hoped to keep a little longer."

"All good things," Frank whispered.

"They must end," Luca agreed. "Let's go."

CHAPTER TWENTY-SEVEN

The kiss of death — what a way to go.

Tex

KISSING MO WAS EASING the pain. Had I been dying, this was exactly how I wanted to go. With her tight body pressed against mine, with her hot breath tickling my lips, with her tongue teasing every inch of mine until I was ready to go insane.

I wanted to wrap my hands around her, but they were still tied behind me and it wasn't some crazy BDSM shit that had them tied. Nope, just my crazy family. Hell, I'd always envied Nixon and his family. I fought against the zip tie. Yeah, envy officially gone.

"Tex." Mo pressed another lingering kiss to my lips. "I have to tell you something, it doesn't matter anymore because —"

Shots started firing from the outside.

"Get behind me, Mo."

"No!" She crossed her arms. "I'm not using you as a shield!" Her eyes widened in horror.

"I said. Get. Behind. Me. Now."

She looked between me and the door. "Look, if I pull the knife from your thigh you may bleed like a bitch but at least I can get you loose and—"

"Mo!" I wasn't above begging. "Please, for the love of God, just let me do my job, let me protect you, this is all I have, my body as your freaking shield, alright? My soul for yours. That's what I have right now. That's what I'd give to keep you safe, so I'm not asking you, I'm telling you, I'm demanding you get behind me before I He-Man my way out of this binding and rip off my damn hands in the process."

With a stunned expression she hobbled behind me.

"Crouch," I instructed. "I want them to see me first, not you, if shots are fired, at least it won't hit your head."

The shots kept echoing outside the door. Whoever was out there was seriously having a hell of a good time with their semi-automatic.

More shouting and then complete silence.

I counted to three before the footsteps started.

Funny, how counting to three used to be something I was taught when I was little and had a tendency to go all rage-oholic.

Nixon had been the one to teach me to control the rage. He'd always said the most powerful men in the world weren't the ones who were angry but the ones who knew where to direct their anger.

I wanted to be powerful.

So I learned to direct.

I learned to collect the emotions and then use them to my benefit.

So right now, I wasn't scared.

I was pissed.

Beyond pissed.

Livid.

Ready to lose my shit, because Alfonso had taken something precious to me and exposed her to Hell, and I wanted to be the one to send *him* there, I wanted to be the one to end this bloodshed, this battle within my family.

I'd never fit in. I'd never felt complete, I'd always had this lingering feeling that something was missing in my life. Even Mo hadn't been able to fill it, but as I sat in that metal chair and counted to three I thought about my life, about what I wanted it to mean.

And I realized.

For the first time in my life, it had to mean something, not just to Mo, but to my family, to blood.

Nixon, the bastard, was right. I would choose blood because I refused to let things like this happen again. I refused to let Mo get hurt again, so I'd choose the opposite side, the enemy camp, if that meant that she was safe for the rest of her life.

If it meant she could have the baby in a world full of peace rather than war.

I'd choose blood every time.

Without hesitation.

Because the one thing Nixon never warned me about was that you may choose blood, not out of loyalty but out of desperation, out of unyielding love for someone who wasn't blood to begin with. I would choose blood to save the ones who weren't.

The door clicked open.

It was too dark to see the tall hooded figure as it made its way across the cement floor.

The lights were flickering causing an almost eerie effect to the guy's entire body. He was dressed in ripped jeans, a grey hoodie, and had a large ass AR16 strapped to his chest.

"So..." He sighed as if the weight of the world rested on his shoulders. "We meet again."

He pulled the hood down.

And I almost passed out from the shock of it all.

Mo reached for my hand and I whispered the word I

never thought would cross my lips again.

"Phoenix?"

CHAPTER TWENTY-EIGHT

Some people never die.

Mo

SEEING HIM ONLY meant one thing.

I'd failed.

Phoenix eyed me and shook his head just slightly. Well crap, was I supposed to act like I didn't know he was alive? Tex turned to face me just as Phoenix lifted his finger to his lips as if swearing me to silence.

Right.

Hadn't I been doing that the whole time?

Tex glanced between us and hung his head. "Can someone please tell me what the hell is going on?"

"Surprise?" Phoenix offered with a lame lift of his shoulders, he looked like he'd just been to Hell, played ping-pong with the devil, lost, and was sent back to roam the earth miserable and alone.

"Note the laughter." Tex's teeth clenched. "And get me out of these damn zip ties."

"That I can do." Phoenix swung the gun behind him and pulled out a knife then walked around the chair and sliced the bindings—just as Nixon, Luca, Chase, and Frank waltzed in.

"Mo!" Nixon yelled then blindly ran in my direction dropping to his knees beside his best friend. He pulled me into his arms and damn near crunched my spine. "Are you okay? Did they hurt you?"

"No, they didn't hurt me, I'm fine." Holy crap the ball was going to drop any minute now. "Tex protected me, he got the brunt of it, well until this one… um, started shooting up the place."

Luca cursed. "I said to make it quiet."

"There were ten of them, I did it as quietly as I could, boss." Phoenix said through clenched teeth.

And that was the moment I'm pretty sure my brother lost his mind. His fingers dug into my back before he pushed me away and turned.

Slowly, he rose to his feet, leveling his piercing gaze on Phoenix.

I half expected Phoenix to smirk or laugh or say something that would have been typical of his character. Then again, Phoenix wasn't the same anymore. From his now dark hair and battered face he looked like hell, no longer the golden boy, just an empty shell. Almost like he had died, his soul left, and his body stayed.

"What. The. Hell?" Nixon spat. "Luca?"

"Oh shit, there goes the gun." Tex rose to his feet and leaned against the table as Nixon pointed a gun to Luca's face.

Luca sighed and hung his head. "I'm truly getting too old for this. Nixon, put the gun down, in fact, we need to leave before more come. We'll talk at the house."

"We talk now." Nixon yelled shaking the gun in the air.

"Mo's alive," Phoenix said softly. "Tex is alive. Your family…" Phoenix took a step towards Nixon bumping his chest. "…is alive, because of that man." He pointed his finger at Luca without taking his eyes off Nixon. "So I suggest you bury your pride for a few minutes, think logically about what you're aiming to do, and come to the same conclusion I have. We need to leave. Now."

I gasped, putting my hand over my mouth.

Phoenix had never in all his life talked to my brother that way before, I mean, I didn't even boss Nixon around or tell him what he was doing was stupid. That was like asking to get shot.

Nixon continued to stare at Phoenix then slowly lowered his gun and tucked it back into his jeans. Emotion imbued his voice with gravel as he said, "Let's go."

Each step, or in my case hobble, to the car hurt. I had Tex on one side of me, refusing to let go of my hand and Nixon on the other side gripping my right hand so hard I thought he would break it. So basically I was like the little play thing between them, the bone between the two pissed off dogs. Phoenix walked ahead of us, talking in hushed tones with Luca and Frank. I was still trying to appear as shocked as everyone else when really, I wasn't. Not at all.

After all, it was Phoenix who'd come to me and Sergio in the first place.

It was Phoenix who was trying to save Tex.

It was Phoenix, of all people, who was trying to save my family.

Ironic, right?

Clearly our plans had gone awry if he was showing his face, which meant I had to come clean to Tex. I just—I didn't want to, I couldn't. What if he hated me? What if he never kissed me again? Things had just started to get better, well before we got shot at and tortured.

"Get in." Nixon damn near jerked the door from the car and pushed Phoenix inside.

Once we were all in the SUV driving back to the house,

Chase finally spoke up. "So this is cozy."

"Not now, Chase." Nixon growled.

And that was it. That was the entire conversation as Sergio made warning glances in my direction from the rearview mirror. Right, I was to keep quiet, pretty sure I got the message already.

Once the SUV was parked in front of the house and we started piling out, Nixon announced, "Now, we talk, and you." He pushed Phoenix's chest. "Are going to start at the very beginning."

"He won't remember." Luca spoke for Phoenix. "You'll have to ask me."

"And why would I do that?" Nixon turned his glare on Luca.

"Because." Luca's shoulders tensed. "I'm the one who planned it all."

CHAPTER TWENTY-NINE

It may seem like all the Mafia does is fight... but what else is there to do when you have endless power and money—and several families wanting to lead?

Tex

"SO DOES THAT MAKE Luca your doctor and you... Frankenstein?" I asked Phoenix once we got back into the house.

"Ha, ha," Phoenix answered. "You know, you're really not as funny as you used to be."

"Well you're not as sexy as *you* used to be."

"So I've been told." Phoenix grumbled and holy shit did he just blush? Nah, I was reading into things, clearly reading into things, the guy had no conscience.

The minute we walked into the house I crumbled against one of the barstools and just sat. I was bleeding all over the hardwood but didn't really care all that much.

I was more interested in the fact that Chase had just moved behind Phoenix and was currently flexing his knuckles.

It was too late to warn him.

So I watched instead as Chase grabbed Phoenix by the

RACHEL VAN DYKEN

shoulders flipped him around and punched him in the face.

"Ohhhh." I winced. "That'll hurt tomorrow."

"What the hell was that for?" Phoenix yelled from the floor, blood spewing from his mouth.

"For Mil," Chase spat. "That was for Mil."

"Mil?" Phoenix shook his head. "My sister? Why would you care?"

Chase's face paled. "Oh shit."

"Chase!" Mil came barreling down the hall and launched herself into Chase's arms and wrapped her legs around his waist. She kissed him so hard even I wanted to look away— then again the party was just getting started, so you better believe I watched with rapt attention.

Chase kissed her back and slowly pried his wife from his body.

"Mil," Phoenix said from the ground, his tone irritated.

"What?" She looked around and then down. When her eyes locked with his she burst into tears and fell to her knees. "Phoenix? Is it, really you? Are you? What happened? Why are you alive? Not that I'm upset you're alive. You ass!" She punched his shoulder. "How dare you do that to me? I hate you! I hate you!" With a sob she threw herself against his chest and started bawling.

Chase looked completely shell-shocked as he sat at the table and folded his hands over his face. He shook his head a few times before groaning into his palms.

After ten minutes of hysterics, Mil was finally able to talk like a normal human being.

"Mil," Nixon snapped. "Grab Trace and take Mo to the back room, we need to get her cleaned up."

"R-right." Mil sniffled and rose to her feet. "Okay, I can do that, come on Mo." She gripped Mo's hand like a life line and led her out of the room.

Phoenix didn't move from the floor, just shifted to lean his back against the cabinet.

146

At the table, Chase held his head like it weighed a thousand pounds.

And Frank and Luca were pulling out bottles of whiskey like we were going to light our entire house on fire via alcohol.

Nixon took a seat at the table, I jumped down from my stool and joined them, and complete silence followed.

The Elect were together again.

But not really. Two of the pieces were dark, damaged, damned, and broken, and I wasn't so sure we would ever fit back into the mold we'd originally created for ourselves.

Luca sat the bottle in the middle of the table and passed out glasses, while Nixon cleared his throat and whispered, "I think, you should start at the beginning."

CHAPTER THIRTY

All one big happy Mafia family — said no made man ever.

Sergio

"WAIT." PHOENIX HELD up his hands. "First, are you two, dating?" He motioned to Chase a look of pure betrayal on his face.

"Asks the dead man," Chase growled, his eyes dripping with hatred. "No, you ass, we aren't dating."

"Oh." Phoenix breathed a sigh of relief.

"We're married." Chase coughed and looked away.

Phoenix pushed back his chair so hard it flipped backwards. "You're what?"

"Married." Chase grinned shamelessly "As in we promised to be together forever... brother? No? Too soon?"

Phoenix's nostrils flared wide as his face turned an interesting shade of purple.

"Oh, and PS I need your help finding that stupid white horse, I looked everywhere, just tell me already so I can be her hero."

"You—" Phoenix pointed at Chase, his breaths coming in and out like he was running a race. "—are not her hero."

"Well, not to give too many details, but those were her exact words last night." Chase winked.

Phoenix launched himself across the table but was intercepted by Frank. I however, wanted out of the family drama. I had enough going on, thank you very much. Besides, it was only a matter of time before I dropped the bomb on Tex, letting him know it was all a ruse.

Everything with Mo was fake.

And wasn't that horrible?

It would push him to choose what he should have chosen a long time ago. And it would free Mo up to stick with blood—to stick with me.

"Guys." Nixon tilted back the bottle of whiskey and took two giant swallows, his face impassive as if he was drinking water. "First things first. Why are you alive?"

Luca leaned forward. "I think I can answer that."

The room fell silent.

"It was a simple decision, a move of sorts. We almost lost Phoenix three times on account that his heart wasn't being very cooperative. The plan was to inject him with enough potassium chloride to stop his heart for a few brief moments before performing CPR. But the plan was botched when he ran into the line of fire."

Phoenix tensed next to me; his fingers gripped the table for a brief moment before his shoulders sagged. Yeah the guy was a loose cannon; tell me something I don't know.

"Once the body was removed, my men had less than two minutes to revive him and stop his organs from failing." Luca shook his head. "I didn't think we would be able to—"

"Wait." Nixon held up his hand. "Is that why you had a clean-up crew ready the minute everything went down with Anthony?"

"Precisely." Luca nodded. "Frank and I only use the best. We even had a surgeon in one of the vans."

"Frank?" Nixon's eyebrows shot up as we all looked in

his direction.

Frank leaned forward. "It was for the family."

I fought the urge to roll my eyes. Wasn't it always for the family? We needed to start coming up with a better excuse.

"And Sergio." Oh shit, wayta throw me under the bus early Luca. "Made it possible to create a whole new identity for Phoenix, he flew him to Italy to infiltrate Campisi and figure out if the family was indeed crumbling as rumors had said to be true."

"Sergio?" Chase asked.

Now all eyes were on me.

"I did it for family?" I said it more as a question and a joke. Nobody laughed. Well, hell. "It was my job, as a ghost, to protect the information."

"So Phoenix has been in Sicily?" Tex asked. "Doing what? Vacationing while I get shot at?"

"No, you ungrateful ass," Phoenix hissed. "I've been keeping your sister alive." He grabbed a shot of whiskey and threw it back, then slammed the glass onto the counter. "You're welcome."

Tex paled. "Is she okay?"

Phoenix rolled his eyes. "I wouldn't know since I had to save your sorry ass this afternoon, but I left her in capable hands if that's what you're asking."

"Are we going to go get her?" Tex tried to stand.

"Sit." Luca snapped his fingers. "All in due time."

Nixon wiped his face with his hands. "What about Tex?"

"Right here." Tex raised his hand and waved it back and forth. "You don't have to speak about me like I'm not in the room."

"Sorry." Nixon glared. "What about my bastard of a brother-in-law, Tex?"

Luca opened his mouth to speak then made eye contact with me. It was my turn to hurt him, but words were failing me. Tex's eyes searched mine and damn if I hated myself for wanting to thrust the knife deeper.

"It was a set up," Phoenix finally said. "My idea, I'd been hearing rumors about Alfonso wanting to put a number on your head, I figured the best way to keep you safe was to make you like blood, to make you an Abandonato."

"But..." Tex looked between Luca and Phoenix. "Mo's pregnant, I mean, she slept with—"

All eyes turned to me.

Oh, this wasn't going to end well.

Before I could move Tex had launched himself onto my body, his fist coming up to sucker punch me in the face. "You son of a bitch! You got her pregnant! I know you did! I knew it!" Another punch, where a tooth decided to lose itself on behalf of Tex's fist. "Admit it!"

"Stop!" Luca slammed his hand on the table. "It was a lie!"

Tex stopped punching me, blood caked to his fingers and his face as he reared back and looked at everyone in the room, disbelief marring his features. "What do you mean it was a lie?"

"She's not pregnant," I mumbled through a mouthful of blood. "And I didn't sleep with her."

"She's not pregnant." Tex repeated. "She... lied to me?"

"To protect you," Phoenix said smoothly. "She figured the only way Nixon would allow you to marry, especially after the whole Campisi episode was to say there was a baby, though it would be impossible to say it was yours considering..."

Right, considering the last time Mo and Tex had slept together had been months ago.

So she had to lie.

And I was the scapegoat. Not that I didn't make out with her, not that I didn't try to seduce her later and get horribly rejected.

"But—"

"It's no longer important." Frank waved us all off.

Nixon sighed. "Then what is? Where do we go from here?"

"Well." Frank folded his hands on the table and addressed each and every one of us. "Where one plan fails, another one always succeeds. We still aim to bring down the head and Tex, son, you're going to be the one to do it."

CHAPTER THIRTY-ONE

*Lies, lies, and more lies. And just when you think you're done,
you're asked to repeat the process.*

Mo

"ARE YOU SURE you're okay?" Trace asked as she helped clean
me up from our little escapade into Hell. My face was bleeding
a little bit and I had a cut above my left eye, but other than that
I looked awesome compared to Tex.

"Yeah." I licked my dry lips. "I'm fantastic."

"He's alive," Mil muttered for the fiftieth time. "I can't
believe it. Did you guys know?"

I wanted to say no, but found I couldn't even lie to my
friend's face, so I averted my eyes and shrugged.

"Does that make him the boss now? Do I step down?"
Mil paced in front of me. "I mean, what—"

"Mil." I reached out and grabbed her wrist. "He's a ghost
now, he isn't supposed to exist and until he does, people can
never know he's alive, do you get what I'm saying?"

"So you knew." She jerked away from me and crossed
her arms.

I looked guiltily between the two of them. "I found out in

Vegas. I snuck into Sergio's room…"

"Phoenix?" I gasped. "But how are you alive?"

"Modern medicine," he offered, his smile hollow. "Do you want to save him? It's a simple question."

"You shouldn't be here." Sergio took a step around me and handed Phoenix a slip of documents. "Go back to Chicago, keep her safe, and for the love of God don't let anyone see you."

Phoenix took the documents and stuffed them in his jeans. "I can help you, but you're going to have to trust me."

I took a step backwards. "You aren't exactly high on the trust tree, Phoenix."

He chuckled, giving me a glimpse of the dimples girls used to cry over. "Yeah, well I wouldn't trust me either, but know this… I can help. I'll get Luca on board, we can figure it out before it's too late."

"Before what's too late?" I asked desperately.

"Tex is a Campisi," Phoenix stated blandly. "Eventually he will be forced to choose, he's too important of a weapon not to use. And it's time he took his place. Whether that's beside the enemy or the friend—now I guess that's up to you? Just how good of an actress are you, Mo?"

"The best." The lie came swiftly.

"Good." Phoenix exhaled. "Because I have a really bad feeling this isn't going to end well for anyone."

"Then walk away." Sergio grit his teeth. "Leave Mo out of this."

"No." Phoenix licked his lips. "She may be the only one close enough to him to make it work."

Sergio groaned in his hands. "Just this once I'd like to stay out of the Abandonato family drama."

"Why?" Phoenix shrugged. "When it's so damn fun?"

I finished telling the girls what happened in the hotel room, my idea about lying to Tex about the pregnancy. I knew he was loyal, above all of us. God, did I know he was loyal. And I used his love, that precious love he had for me, and turned it into a weapon.

"Does he know?" Trace asked softly.

"No," I whimpered. "I'm afraid to tell him."

"Rip the damn band aid off." Mil nodded. "Otherwise he's going to be pissed and a pissed Tex is not a happy Tex I think we can all agree on that. He's like the anti-Happy Meal."

"Right." I giggled. "With a gun as a toy."

"And spikes on his box," Trace joined in.

A knock on the door jolted us from our talk. "Trace?" It was Nixon.

"Yeah?" She walked to the door.

"A minute." Nixon eyed all of us in the bathroom. "Actually, all of you, in the kitchen, now."

"Has he gotten more demanding as he ages?" I asked aloud. "Or is it me?"

"He should wear more color," Mil added. "I think it would make him happier."

"Trace makes me happy, thank you very much and I'm walking right in front of you, if you girls want to gossip about me, I suggest you text."

"You monitor our phones," I pointed out.

"Aw, shucks I guess that leaves no gossip then. Bummer." Nixon said ahead of me as he wrapped his arm around Trace.

I stuck out my tongue.

"Saw that." Nixon laughed.

I flipped him off.

"Saw that too, c'mon, Mo, be original."

"How about I just punch you?" I asked.

Nixon stopped walking and turned. "I'm trying to decide if being married to Tex has made your comebacks worse or better." He angled his head. "Hmm, worse, I'm going with worse. Now, hurry up."

By the time we made it into the kitchen it looked like a freaking bomb had exploded on the table.

An empty bottle of whiskey sat in the middle. Phoenix cradled his face as purple bruises blossomed across his left cheek and jaw. He kept clenching and unclenching his teeth as if to try to alleviate some of the ache. Tex was leaning heavily on his chair, his breathing ragged. Sergio had the start of a black eye, and Frank and Luca were talking in hushed tones with Chase all the while Phoenix sent him seething glares.

"Tension." Mil nodded. "Fantastic."

"Girls." Nixon cleared his throat. "You should probably know what's been going on." He filled them in on the parts I had left out. When he was done, he looked exhausted.

And I just felt like hell.

I glanced at Tex, hoping, praying a look of understanding would pass between us, water under the bridge, I tried to save his life, that sort of thing.

Instead he looked right through me.

As if I didn't exist.

Anger, I could handle from him.

Indifference?

It was like twisting a knife into my heart and leaving it there, I took a step towards him but was held back by Nixon.

"So." Nixon sighed. "Phoenix is going to be staying here just until The Commission."

All eyes darted to Trace, who had gone suddenly silent.

She licked her lips and walked over to Phoenix and placed her hand on his shoulder.

"Don't." Phoenix said hoarsely. "Whatever your about to say, don't say it. I don't think I could handle it, don't think I want to. I don't deserve your forgiveness or the peace it would bring me. So don't be yourself, Trace. For once in your life be the bitch. Slap me or something, because it would hurt a hell of a lot less than your forgiveness."

Trace nodded as a tear fell down her face.

"I don't have a leg to stand on," Phoenix whispered. "But I'll protect you, all of you." He lifted his head. "With my life.

My word is all I have now. It's my air, it's my soul, it's my heart. All I have to offer is my gun."

"We'll take it." Trace answered for Nixon.

Nixon and Chase nodded while Tex continued to stare at the wall.

I tried to move towards him again and Nixon again pulled me back like I was some sort of child.

"Sleep," Nixon demanded. "Grab a bite to eat and go rest, I know it's only seven but we have a big day of planning ahead of us. And a pissed off Campisi that wants Tex's head."

"Just give it to them, then," Tex mumbled. "It's what you want."

"What I want?" Nixon roared. "Doesn't really matter, now does it, Tex? What I want is peace. What I get is war. What I want is for my sister to be happy. What I get, is *you*," he freaking growled before pulling me tighter against him. "You're going to help us fix this whether you like it or not, then you're going to be the man you were raised to be."

Tex lifted his head. "*That* I can do."

"What do you mean?" I jerked free from Nixon. "What the hell do you mean?"

"Your husband," Nixon said in a cold voice, "is choosing blood."

CHAPTER THIRTY-TWO

The Mafia isn't romantic. Regardless of what people believe, there is nothing romantic about gunshot wounds and death. Only tragedy, yet there is romance in the perfect death, knowing you've died to save others. That's as romantic as we get.

Tex

THE LOOK ON MO'S FACE damn near broke my heart... then again, she'd been breaking my heart only to put it back together then break it again for the past year so why should now be any different? I hated that my number one concern wasn't staying alive—but making sure she was okay. I was freaking bleeding all over the floor and I was worried about the cut above her eye, about her bum leg, and about the fact that I'd just told her to her face that when it came down to it.

I wasn't going to choose her.

But did she know? What that decision cost me? What it would end up giving her? An actual life. A chance at happiness. Probably not, and I sure as hell wasn't going to defend myself, not after finding out that she'd lied to me.

About everything.

Not even pregnant.

A stand-up guy would cringe thinking we'd just had unprotected sex two days ago.

But I wasn't a stand-up guy.

Nope, I was a Campisi, so that evil part of me hoped and prayed I had knocked her up so I could keep her forever.

But the bad guys never get to keep the treasure in the end—they end up cursed, and I suddenly realized why my father had started the rumor in the first place about me being cursed.

I was cursed the minute I took my first breathe of air, because I was already marked with the Campisi blood.

With a sigh, I stood to my feet and promptly collapsed back into the chair. Well that was unfortunate.

Mo took a step forward, this time Nixon didn't block her. Instead, he grabbed Trace and made his way down the hall.

"You need help," Mo murmured, her hand finding mine. I quickly jerked away from her touch. It made me want things.

It made me yearn.

"Tex." Mo put her hands on her hips. "You need the med kit, just... stay."

I sighed.

"Like a dog," Sergio added.

"Yeah well, this dog could still rip your head off so joke around again, really, I dare you."

Sergio rolled his eyes and got up from his chair storming out of the room.

"Is it me or has he gotten more dramatic?" I said dryly.

"Since when are things not dramatic." Chase chuckled then eyed Mil, crooking his finger for her to come over.

For the first time in Mil's existence, she didn't argue. With a sigh she sat on Chase's lap and faced Phoenix.

"So." Phoenix cleared his throat. "Is he good to you?"

"Right here." Chase swore.

"Yeah," Mil sighed dreamily. "The best."

Phoenix nodded.

"And when he misbehaves." Mil twirled a piece of her hair. "I just hold a gun to his man parts, and he suddenly becomes so much more agreeable."

Phoenix burst out laughing while Chase rolled his eyes and said, "Believe it."

"Dude." I shook my head. "That's not cool. No part of that is cool. Mil, not okay."

Mil shrugged. "How else am I supposed to be heard?"

"You use words," Chase said slowly. "And this miraculous thing happens with ears. You know what those are for, don't you? Or are you more familiar with the mouth?"

Mil grinned and licked her lips. "Aw, baby, you want me to answer that in public?"

"Oh, God." Phoenix held up his hands. "No, please no, fine, I get it you guys love each other and..." he coughed. "Share the same... bed."

"Ten bucks says he's going to have nightmares tonight." I nodded.

"I'll take that bet." Frank piped up.

Luca laughed.

"Phoenix?" Frank asked. "A minute of your time?"

"Take it all." Phoenix pushed away from the table. "You own me anyway."

The three of them walked out of the room towards the living room, leaving me alone with the always sexual Chase and Mil, so basically I would have rather been back in that dark room getting punched in the face and shot at.

"Back!" Mo hobbled as fast as her bum leg would take her into the room. With a thud she sat the kit on the table and frowned.

"What?" I asked wincing as the pain was starting to travel up my leg.

"Not here." She sighed. "We need to go to your room I need you to lie down."

Chase chuckled. "If I had a dollar—"

"What?" Mil gave him an I–will-kill-you expression. "Really, I'm dying to know."

"Then..." Chase looked at me helplessly. "I'd only have a dollar?"

"Good answer."

"Shit," he mumbled under his breath.

"Come on." Mil stood. "We'll help you guys take Tex to his room."

"I'm fine." I grumbled standing again only to fall back in my chair.

"Aw, he's like a baby giraffe." Chase clapped. "All wobbly like."

"Can I at least be a baby tiger?" I pleaded. "My pride and all that."

"Baby tigers are so cute." Mil grinned.

"Just kidding. I want to be a baby tarantula."

"Too late." Mil sighed happily. "Baby tiger it is."

Mo hid a smile behind her hand before grabbing the kit. Chase moved to the side of the chair and helped me to my feet. "Try not to like my touch too much, man. Remember I'm married."

"I'll try to keep my penis at bay." I said dryly.

"That's really all I ask." Chase grunted as he helped me walk down the hall. "Well that and keeping it in your pants."

"I can't even walk, I won't rape you, dude."

"One can never be too cautious," Chase sang.

Once we were in my room, Chase dropped me onto the bed. It squeaked under my weight.

"How the hell do you have sex on a bed that makes so much—" Chase's voice drowned out as he looked from me to Mo and back to me. "Right, so, I'm just going to go help Mil clean her guns..."

Mil rolled her eyes. "Because that's what we do in our room at night. Clean guns."

"Thanks, guys." Mo said softly as the door closed behind

them. When she turned and faced me it was with hurt in her eyes and no smile on her face.

A part of me wanted to reach out.

Instead I closed my eyes and whispered, "Well, let's get it over with."

CHAPTER THIRTY-THREE

Giving yourself to someone else is only stupid if they don't take what you offer.

Mo

NOT THE MOST ENCOURAGING words to come out of his mouth but it was a start. I propped open the kit and pulled out the supplies I'd need: Antiseptic, pain killers, tweezers, gauze, wipes.

"Mo, this isn't a hospital you don't need to bandage me up or anything. Really I just want—"

My head jerked up. "What? What do you want?"

His nostrils flared as he looked away and mumbled, "A shower."

My body suddenly went hot and cold all over like it couldn't decide if I liked the idea of helping him in the shower or if I was terrified of what could happen, what that could mean. Then again he could barely walk so it wasn't like he was going to try to seduce me.

"Okay." I nodded. "I can do that."

"Mo—"

"Tex," I snapped. "Let me help okay? It's my fault

anyway."

"Don't," he growled. "Don't for a second blame yourself for my bad blood, do you understand me?"

I turned my back to him and stormed off to the bathroom, flipping on the shower so steam started to billow around my feet. After grabbing a towel and making sure there were no objects in Tex's way. I marched back out of the bathroom and held out my hand. "Let's go."

"Forceful." Tex's crooked grin caused my heart to falter. "You would have made a horrible nurse."

"Or the best," I said. "It's all in how you look at it."

"Right." He gripped my hand and slowly stood. I wrapped his arm around my body helping him carry his own ridiculously muscled weight, and we staggered to the bathroom.

"How are we going to do this?" Tex was out of breath already and sitting on the toilet lid, leaning his head on his hands.

"Um…" I held up my hand and closed the door. "Just one second." I turned around and swore under my breath as I slowly peeled my clothes from my body.

"Mo," Tex croaked. "What the hell are you doing?"

"I'm helping!"

"No." Tex hissed like he was in pain. "You're really not."

Ignoring him, I left my bra on and pulled down my jeans. Bra and underwear were safe, right? Without speaking I started pulling his clothes from his body. First his shirt, or what was left of it since it was so stained with blood. What was once white looked red and horrifying.

He winced when I pulled it over his head.

Damn the man. It would be impossible to get used to the way Tex's muscles freaking hugged his midsection like they were too swollen to do anything else but stick out and be sexy.

Clenching my teeth I moved my hands to his jeans and slowly undid the button. Tex looked away quickly. Right, no eye contact. Like a prostitute. Or did they make eye contact and just not kiss?

Yeah I was so out of my league.

I could do this. I could help.

I slowly unzipped his jeans, the sound turning me on way more than a simple noise should, and whispered, "I need you to lift a bit."

"'K." His voice was barely audible as he pushed against the countertop on each side and lifted his body up so I could slide the jeans off. The minute I slid them past where the shot grazed him, he swore.

"Sorry."

"Not—" he heaved. "—your fault, Mo."

"Boxers." I licked my lips.

His gaze finally met mine. "Boxers?"

"We need to take them off."

He nodded three times before lifting himself up again. I jerked them off as quickly as possible and turned away. The last thing I needed to be doing was attacking him with my eyes while he was injured.

"I'm ready." His deep voice ripped me to shreds, made me want to push him against the wall and demand he love me. Demand he never leave me. Ask him to stay…

"Okay." I turned and looked.

And immediately wished I had never fallen for Tex.

Because no man would ever compare to the broken one in front of me.

My heart beat to fix him. My soul yearned to join him.

"Alright." I saluted. "Just think of me as your grumpy old nurse."

Tex eyed me up and down. "Yeah you look nothing like a grumpy old nurse. In fact, I'd probably purposely walk in the line of fire in order to get patched up by you."

My lungs were paralyzed.

Air didn't come.

Words ceased.

So I nodded as I helped him to his feet and then stepped into the shower with him, leading him to the bench and pointing the shower head towards his body.

"I feel like a child." Tex smiled wide. "Do I look helpless? Be honest, Mo. I can always tell when you're lying. You avert your eyes and put your hands behind your back like your hiding cookies."

"I do not!" I rubbed my hands and put them behind my back without realizing it. Tex pressed his lips together and nodded his head towards me.

"Really? You don't?"

I unleashed my hands and returned his smile. "It all started with that first stolen cookie when I was six."

"Liar." Tex stretched out his legs and winced. "It started when you were five... with the piece of chocolate I told you to steal."

I gasped. "I forgot about that!"

"The girl's got a weakness for the dark side, don't you, Mo? Your grubby little hands stole Nixon's dark chocolate and then you didn't want to have to give it back, so what did you do?"

I folded my arms across my wet chest. "I ate it."

"Not it."

"I ate them."

"How many? I forget?" He chuckled.

"Ten mini candy bars and then I threw up all over my church shoes."

Still laughing Tex reached for the soap. "One of my top ten Mo moments."

"Ten?" I joked. "You have a top ten list?"

"Hell yeah I do." Tex soaped up his body but cringed when he hit the sliced skin on his leg, so I bent down and started slowly cleaning the blood away with a wash rag and the soap.

"So…" My hands moved seamlessly across his leg. "Name a few."

"Hmm…" Tex leaned his head back against the tiled wall. "The day you wore that kick-ass swimsuit."

"The white one?"

"Yeah." Tex's voice lowered. "I wanted you so badly that day but I knew it was too soon, so I waited. Good things come to those who wait they say."

"And did they?" I asked.

"Did they what?"

"Did the good things come?"

Tex was silent for a few seconds then said, "They come and go… like life."

"Another moment?" I moved to his other leg and washed up and down.

"When you smiled."

"What?"

"Each time you smile." Tex shrugged. "It's a new moment, so I always say when you smiled at least that's how I keep track in my brain. Each time you smile is a new moment so I store it and I tell myself that's my favorite one right there."

I smiled.

"See? New moment. Mind blown."

I shook my head and sucked on my bottom lip before moving the soap up his thigh and across his stomach. With a groan he closed his eyes. "Best nurse ever. We should get you a button."

"A button?"

"Yeah a button that says number one nurse or something like that. Put it on all your clothes… good plan, right?"

"Right." I rolled my eyes and continued washing his abs. "So what's number one?"

His eyes flashed open as his Adam's apple bobbed up and down. Water droplets cascaded down his square chin landing on his chiseled chest. "The day you married me."

I slid my hand down as the soap dropped to the tiled ground. "But you were so angry."

"At the circumstances," Tex whispered. "And maybe at you, a bit, but it was the happiest moment of my life, knowing you would never be able to run away from me—from us. Knowing that even if you broke my heart, I still had a ring on my hand saying you it was yours to break and that I probably deserved it in the first place."

My hands moved up his stomach to cup his face. "And now, now are you mad still?"

"Mo." Tex groaned as he gripped my wrists. "What do I keep telling you? I could never hate you as much as I love you."

"Still?" My lower lip trembled.

He sighed. "Still."

"And even though you're choosing blood..."

Tex sighed. "Sometimes a person does what he has to do, to protect those he values the most."

CHAPTER THIRTY-FOUR

Death makes you see things clearly... sometimes that's not a good thing.

Tex

I WOULD HAVE GIVEN damn near anything to be at my full strength, to be able to lift Mo into my arms and whisper promises across her skin. Instead, I was so weak it would be an adventure just trying to get out of the shower. But her skin, it was so pretty, each time the water hit her, it pressed against her flesh and then receded down her face and honestly it was so distracting that I almost had to close my eyes.

"Tex?"

I released her wrists and leaned back so I could cool off. I didn't want her to know that the shower was so hot I was ready to pass out—then again it was probably because my blood was heated to dangerous levels just breathing the same steam as her. "What?"

"For what it's worth... I'm sorry."

"For what..." I repeated. "...it's worth... I'm kind of flattered you value my life as much as you do, Mo. You're the only one who would go out on a limb for me."

"Nixon would, so would Chase," she argued.

"No." I shook my head. "Not anymore, and the sick part is I can't blame them, I mean I have a freaking sister that I've never met and I feel possessive as hell right now over that girl... she could be a raging lunatic and I'm still concerned that she's safe. Blood—"

"—wins." Mo cleared her throat. "Right, I get it. So, should we wash you off?"

"I'm such a dirty boy." I said dryly, my eyebrows shooting up in good humor.

Mo suppressed her laughter with her hand and stood in front of me. "Right, okay so I'm just going to..." She gulped. "Rinse."

"Wash, rinse, repeat," I said in a hoarse voice. "Talk dirty to me, nurse."

"Keep joking like that, and I'll be sure the nurse slips and hurts the patient, *capiche*?"

"Physical pain I can tolerate." I chuckled and then realized what I had said, or what I'd meant by that. Beat me, slaughter me, make me bleed, but break my heart?

And you've just destroyed my reason for living.

Take away Mo?

And you've just wrecked my entire existence.

I cleared my throat. "Are we doing this or not?"

"Yeah." Mo licked her lips and positioned the shower head over my body. I closed my eyes as the warm water cleansed me of all the soap and blood—my sins, however, stayed. And wasn't that a bitch?

Never clean.

"Alright." Mo turned off the shower. "I'm going to grab some towels and dry you off so you don't slip."

"Wow." I folded my arms across my chest to keep warm. "I get toweled off too?"

"Try not to get too excited." Mo winked. "I towel rough."

"I can do rough."

"Not this kind of rough."

"Just don't injure what doesn't like being injured... gentle, you know the meaning of that word don't you?"

"I was always horrible with school, you should know that." Mo called from beyond the door. She returned with two white fluffy towels and tossed one at my face. "You dry the upper half, I dry the lower half."

"Score."

"Keep talking."

"Sorry." I grumbled rubbing my face and hair with the towel and moving down my arms and chest. I stopped briefly to look up since Mo hadn't started but her eyes were trained directly on me. "Uh, this isn't a theatre Mo, if you didn't pay you can't stay, sweetheart."

A blush stained her cheeks before she started vigorously rubbing my legs taking several leg hairs with her, damn it!

"Okay." I pushed her hands away. "That's enough nurse for the day."

"But you're still wet." She pointed at my thighs.

I looked down, she looked up.

It really couldn't have been timed any worse. I'd always prided myself in being able to control my body and my lust, I was easily able to keep myself in check around Nixon especially when I checked out Mo. So why the hell was my body rejecting every sane ounce of logic I threw at it?

"Er..." Mo dropped the towel and looked away. "Um, I'll just, you can finish up and then I'll..." She twisted her hands. "Help you out of the shower and to the bed—to sleep!" I winced as she shouted the last part in my right ear. "Sleep, because you need rest."

"Thanks, Mo." I nodded. "Pretty sure I know what sleep is for."

Her cheeks stained even redder before she walked out of the shower and wrapped a towel around herself. The woman had seen me naked countless times before. Hell, technically we were married, and she was still blushing around me like she'd never seen a man before.

I wanted to remedy that.

Correction, I wanted to be the only guy to remedy that.

With a sigh, I stood on wobbly feet and slowly made my way out of the shower, I was at least able to make it to the counter before I had to stop. Mo quickly grabbed my arm and without saying another word helped me to my bed.

What happened next was probably my fault.

I was suffering blood loss.

So really, she shouldn't have expected anything less of me.

When I fell back on the bed, I took her with me, and ripped her towel off in the process.

"Two hours," I ordered softly in her ear.

"Two?" She squeaked.

"Yeah." My arms tightened around her body. "Please?"

With a defeated sigh she whispered, "Okay."

Part Two: From the Ashes
CHAPTER THIRTY-FIVE

It's best to have failure happen early in life. It wakes up the Phoenix bird in you so you rise above the ashes. –Anne Baxter

Phoenix

THE ANSWER IS NEVER as simple as the question. And when Luca asked me the question, I had no idea what my answer would be. In a million different scenarios I never imagined I'd be back where it all started. When you're a kid you're always told that your choices will haunt you, that they become like blocks you build off of.

My freaking blocks were destroyed.

And I was smothered beneath the rubble, just waiting for death to take me, because honestly? I should be dead.

I wanted to be dead because maybe then this sick feeling in my chest would go away, maybe if I was dead I wouldn't have the nightmares.

Maybe if I was dead, I wouldn't want what I literally had no business wanting.

Life.

"What the hell did you do?" I screamed jerking against the IV and hospital equipment. The hum of instruments made me so sick I puked in the van. "Luca! Answer me damn it!"

"We had an agreement."

"Bull shit!" I roared. "Why! Why can't you just let me die?" The rage that had been my constant companion my whole life was threatening to take over, I looked for a weapon, for anything to end my own life, to go to Hell where I belonged. The shine of a scalpel caught my eye; I snagged it from the table and held it to my throat. "I'll do it! Don't think I won't!"

Luca's eyes took in my shaking hand. "Son, you're story isn't over."

"Who are you to decide that?"

"Who are you?" Luca asked calmly. "I saved your life so you could save more lives — I offer you something better than death."

"Oh yeah?" I hissed. "What's that?" The rage was pounding against my skin screaming to be set free.

"Redemption."

The knife clattered out of my shaking hands, I watched as it banged against the floor of the van and swayed a bit as his words hit me square in the chest.

And just like that, the rage I'd kept inside for so long, broke.

I broke.

And burst into tears.

"I can't — I can't."

"You can." Luca joined me on the gurney. "And you will."

"I have nothing." I whispered.

Luca held out his hand. "You have blood."

"Phoenix? Are you even listening to me right now or are you seriously stupid enough to stare at the wall while I lecture you?" Nixon paced in front of me. Damn it, felt like I'd been sitting in his office for hours. Pictures of me and the rest of the guys lined the walls. They may as well have been years ago, eons. I wasn't that same person, didn't even recognize that face in the picture. It looked so casual, so carefree. I had been anything but that.

I refused to look at the smile on my face.

In fact it made me so damn sick I wanted to puke up every ounce of food I'd had for the past week.

My life had been such a joke.

And now, it was about to get worse.

"Yeah," I whispered and leaned forward. "I'm listening, man, and I'm sorry I kept so much from you, but—"

Nixon's fist came flying so hard that when it hit, I heard bone crack in my jaw before I fell to the ground in a bloody heap.

"That," Nixon spat, "is for being a complete ass to Trace. I'm still not over it, and it's going to take more than you saving my life for me to be completely calm with you two in the same room."

I wiped the blood from my mouth and felt my entire body sag with defeat. "Understood."

"Don't get up." Nixon pushed his boot into my back and pressed me hard against the area rug. "I will end you if you as much as look at her with anything other than indifference. Do you feel me?"

Hell yeah, I felt him; his boot weighed a hundred pounds. "Yes, sir."

"You work for us, you don't work for yourself. You protect us, you protect the girls, and you tell me every damn detail. Yes?"

"Yes, sir."

He removed his boot. I expected a kick to the side. What I got? An outstretched hand. Confused, I took it as he pulled me to my feet.

With a grimace, Nixon pulled me into his arms and hugged me so tight I almost stopped breathing. "Another thing," he said gruffly. "I'm so damn happy to see you."

I collapsed against him, embarrassed that I didn't even have anger as a shield anymore, but defeat, so much damn defeat and regret that I stank of it. I wanted to sob, I wanted to wrap my arms around my ex-best friend and apologize until my voice was hoarse, but the thing about messing up like I did? Leading the life I did? Words mean absolutely nothing. It was like throwing feathers into the wind and hoping they'd make it to China.

Words hold no value when you've used them your whole life to hurt people rather than heal them.

So I had action.

And they were about to see a lot of it.

Nixon released me and pointed to the leather seat across from him.

I sat and leaned forward, suddenly uncomfortable with the tense silence and vulnerable exchange.

"You look like hell." Nixon grinned and leaned back in his chair, his lip ring catching some of the light from the otherwise dark study.

I smirked. "Yeah well, I've been to Hell, seems they don't treat guys like me well down there, so I came back with a few… bumps."

"Your hair's brown, your nose looks like it's been broken four times since I've seen you and you have circles under your eyes bigger than Tex's mouth. What the hell have you been doing?"

I licked my lips. "Oh you know a little of this a little of that." With a shrug I relaxed a bit in my seat. "I've been working for Campisi, couldn't look like a De Lange so let my hair grow all natural and got in a few skirmishes trying to prove my worthiness."

"And Tex's sister?"

I froze.

"Phoenix?"

Swallowing, I licked my lips nervously. "Sorry, yeah, she's… safe."

Just thinking about her made me a nervous wreck. I had

her to thank for the broken nose and dark circles. Woman never slept and tried to kill me the first night I watched over her.

"Name?"

"Bianka." Shit, saying her name made my entire body tight. "But I just call her Bee." She hated that nickname, and what do ya know? That's where broken nose number two came from. I'd learned long ago never to fight a woman, never to make them feel small. So even though it hurt like hell to get the crap beat out of me, I let her hit me, I didn't fight back. Ever. Fighting back brought too many memories... memories that made me feel like the devil himself. So I allowed my nose to break knowing it would hurt a lot less than the sickness in my soul.

Nixon scratched the back of his head. "Well damn, we'll need to meet her."

"Not now," I said quickly. "Not with The Commission coming up, we'll have to keep her in hiding until Alfonso's out of the picture."

"Any idea where he is?"

"No," I said honestly. "But I can find out, I still know some of his men and money makes them talk... a lot. Well money and whiskey which thankfully Luca has in spades, so I usually do pretty well."

"Fine." Nixon's eyes narrowed. "And... with everything else, Mil and Chase and... all of us, I mean, are you handling things alright? Do you need..." He lifted his hands into the air, and looked away. "Do you need to talk to someone?"

I smiled, Nixon was all hard–ass, but it was funny how Trace had helped him in ways he probably didn't even realize. She hadn't made him soft, just... sensitive to things that he normally wouldn't give a shit about. "Nah man, I'm actually good. Luca's been helpful."

"Never thought I'd utter those words until this last year." Nixon swore. "But I get it." He stood. "Alright, get some sleep."

I stood and started making my way to the door then paused and turned. "Nixon?"

"Yeah?"

"Is she happy?"

"Who?"

"Mil."

Nixon slapped me on the back. "So happy I wear ear plugs at night when we stay next door to them at the hotel."

"Too many details," I grumbled.

Laughing, Nixon shrugged. "Hey, you asked."

"I'm glad."

"Me too." His face darkened. "Because if Chase didn't latch on to someone or something soon I was going to shoot him in the face and bury his body in the lake."

"You're joking right?"

Nixon gave me a slight push out the door. "I never threaten someone unless I mean to carry it out. Goodnight, Phoenix."

The door shut in my face.

I stared at the wood, taking time for his veiled threat to sink in. He'd kill me if I did as much as stare at Trace wrong and the sad part was, I would want him to.

"So, how'd that go?" Chase said from the kitchen holding open a bag of Cheetos and devouring them like he'd been on a cleanse for the past two months.

"Awesome."

"I hate the office." Chase shuddered. "Swear he has bodies buried under his chair, one time I asked and he laughed, didn't deny it, that should tell us something right there."

"You talk more than I remember." I eyed the Cheetos and nearly gagged. I hated anything messy. Maybe that was what happens when you die and come back to life, you have these weird quirks you never had before. I used to love junk food, now? I was more of a kale and spinach type of guy and despised anything that was made and not grown. Yeah, I'd gone bat shit crazy. I even hated cake.

"I talk because the sound of my voice makes your sister so damn turned on that she can't see straight." He slid a Cheeto between his front teeth and bit down.

"Bastard." I huffed.

"She called me that last night but I think it was all in good fun."

I clenched my fists.

"Damn." Chase shook his head. "So much control now, I'm not sure whether I should give you a high five or ask you what the hell happened."

"I died that's what happened you ass."

"White horse." Chase snapped his fingers. "Where is it?"

I crossed my arms. "Not telling."

"Dude, do you even realize how bad she wants it? I'm the dream guy I should find it."

"Nah." I went to the fridge and pulled out a bottle of water. "I think I'll let you suffer for a bit, if you're really the dream guy you'll find it without my help."

CHAPTER THIRTY-SIX

Lips that taste of tears, they say are the best for kissing — Unknown

Mo

MY HEART STARTED thumping so fast I half expected Tex to start laughing or crack a joke.

"So we've graduated from one to two?" I said as I breathlessly lay across his chest, my back pressed against his stomach.

"Yeah."

"And then—"

"—I do what I have to do to protect you."

My heart twisted. "You mean you do what the son of a dead Mafia boss does... you do what a guy with a sister to protect does, right Tex?"

He sighed. "Right."

"And that leaves us?"

"With goodbye."

"So this is it then." My voice cracked. "No matter what I say? No matter what I do?"

"Two hours and then you'll never have to worry about hearing my voice on the other end of the phone, Mo."

"What if I want to?" The ceiling fan twirled around in circles ignoring each jab of pain that shot through my chest at Tex's words.

"I won't be calling Mo, not after the two hours, not ever. I won't answer your texts, I won't be available for you. To do this, we have to separate for good."

My teeth clenched. "I'm tired of the men in my life telling me what's best for me."

"Two hours." He ran his hands up and down my arms. "Take it or leave it, but I strongly suggest you take it."

"Because you're going to blow my mind?"

His warm breath tickled my neck as he leaned up and kissed below my ear. "Yeah, something like that."

"Two hours," I repeated and crawled off his battered body and made my way towards the door. When I flipped the lock I knew there was no going back. I would love him as much as my heart was able to love.

And I would give him my heart for safekeeping knowing I would never be able to find someone who loved me as deep and as wide as Tex did. This was it.

Most people don't get moments like the one he was offering me, usually people don't realize they had a moment until it's already gone then they're left to live off the memories.

I had both.

He was giving me both.

Two hours.

I turned just as Tex leaned up on his elbows, his stormy blue eyes beckoning me like a laser beam. Maybe if he wasn't so broken, I wouldn't be so attracted. I'd always been a sucker for wounded animals... so it made sense I'd fall for a guy like Tex, one who never fit in, one who never saw the sheer beauty of the man that he was.

It's why our love made sense.

I was the girl everyone protected from the ugly.

And he was the ugly.

Beauty and the Beast.

"One thing," Tex whispered.

I took a step towards him and paused. "What?"

He closed his eyes briefly before opening them and saying in such a clear voice I swear the universe shook around me. "I love you more than life."

"I—"

"Say it in two hours, use those words as your goodbye, Mo, they'll mean more to both of us."

Nodding, I took the next three steps to the bed and stared—drank him in as his eyes greedily scanned my body. "Mo?"

"Yeah?"

"Let me love you."

My hands shook as I reached out for him. He tugged me back onto the bed, our mouths met in an explosion of emotion. Tex gripped my hair and pulled it free from its rubber band, digging his hands into its depths only to pull again as he tilted my head back and slid his tongue down my neck.

"Open for me," he whispered as his mouth made its way back to mine, his tongue met mine, tasting like whiskey and warmth. He spent at least ten minutes kissing every corner of my face, memorizing it… saying goodbye, and with each kiss my heart both soared and shattered.

This was my last moment with a man I should have had forever with.

My hands dug into his back as I straddled his lap. With a growl Tex threw the remaining towel across the room and unhooked my bra.

"I could worship you like this." His tongue flicked my collarbone as his mouth descended. "I could die like this."

"I will die if you stop."

"Two hours, Mo." Tex chuckled warmly against my chest. "Patience."

"Or we could just set a record? Yeah let's do that." I wiggled in his lap.

"Stop." He braced my hips, exhaling a hiss before his eyes darkened. "You never did take instruction well."

"I play by my own rules and all that." I winked.

"Damn, you're perfect."

I gasped when he lifted me slightly off his lap, the air hitting my stomach briefly before he slid off my remaining underwear. I expected him to lose control, I expected him to do what Tex always did—pleasure me until I cried with need and then take his own.

But this wasn't like other times.

It wasn't like anything I've ever experienced.

His callused hands moved across my hip bone, his eyes trained on my skin. Eyelashes fanned across his cheeks as he stared, inhaling and exhaling, bidding his time.

"So beautiful," he choked, his thumb rubbing across my hip, his fingers digging into my butt as he pulled me closer to him.

I swallowed the emotion in my throat as Tex tilted his head and moved his left hand to the other side of my hip, running his knuckles up and down my rib cage until I moaned.

"So perfect."

"I'm ready for you," I gasped. "I need you."

"Let me, Mo." Tex's hands gripped my sides as he lightly lifted me so that I was fully straddling him and he was lying back against the pillows. "Please let me say goodbye to my favorite parts of you."

"Parts?" I breathed as those wicked hands moved from my hips past my ribs and cupped my breasts. With a moan his head fell back.

Tex groaned. "Yeah Mo, my favorite parts, which basically means every single part of you."

I shivered as he released my breasts, his mouth

descended where his hands had been and with a soft sob he pulled me tight against him. The heat of his body was wreaking havoc on mine. I tried to move against him but he was too strong—so I stayed put, even though I was dying a bit inside.

"Mo." Tex's hot mouth cupped my ear. "I'll never forget what you look like... when I do this." His hands gripped my butt, jerking me abruptly against his arousal.

My head fell back.

"So beautiful." He kissed my exposed neck. "I want to stay like this forever."

"Funny," I murmured. "Because I want a little more than this."

"Patience." He laughed softly.

Yeah, not happening, especially with the way he was kissing my neck, his tongue massaging every soft spot of my skin until my body started shaking. Every kiss brought me to the brink of release, only to be left needing, wanting, desiring, because he would stop, gather himself, and then just stare at me.

"I need you." I cupped his face. "Now."

"Not yet." His thumb caressed my lower lip. "Not until you're begging—not until your sobbing my name. Then and only then will I fill you until all I feel is Mo Abandonato—until all I breathe, is your essence."

CHAPTER THIRTY-SEVEN

You will never know true happiness until you have truly loved, and you will never understand what pain really is, until you have lost it — Anonymous

Tex

MO'S BEAUTIFUL BLUE eyes blinked mischievously back at me. I would miss that look, the one that said she wasn't going to back down from any of my challenges. Her looks were her tell. I could see the love she had for me in her eye—it was why it hurt so badly when she betrayed me, because regardless of her actions and her reasoning—she still loved me.

And I knew it every damn I time I looked at her face.

Loving Mo was my greatest and hardest accomplishment, because loving someone meant that person had the power to use your love against you, and I knew it was only a matter of time before Mo did that. It would be by accident, but it would happen.

It was why we had to say goodbye.

She wouldn't do it on purpose. Mo didn't have that type of mind.

But I did.

I was protecting her from me, and protecting her from herself... a clean break was the only way to keep her safe but selfishly it was the only way to keep me sane.

Every text.

Every phone call.

Every picture.

Would haunt me for the rest of my life.

So once I hunted down Alfonso and killed the sorry son of a bitch, I would find my sister and take control of my family.

And the war between the families would continue because I knew one thing Mo didn't.

The Campisis didn't just want my blood.

They wanted the Abandonatos.

I wished I could go back and forget the words that Luca and Frank said, but the men knew more than anyone else— bad blood gets people killed and the Campisis, though momentarily leaderless, wanted my head and were more than happy to ask for Nixon's and Chase's in the process.

I'd rather die a thousand deaths than put the people who raised me in danger.

"Tex!" Mo wrapped her arms around my neck. "Where'd you go?"

"Right here, sweetheart," I murmured, brushing a kiss across her lips. "I'll always be." I moved my rough hand to her chest and pressed. "Right here."

Her lower lip trembled. "You promise?"

I nodded. "When the nights are dark... when you're alone and afraid... when you're sick at the prospect of dating for the first time, when you're sad..." I shrugged and rubbed my hand across her chest. "Know that a part of me will always be with you."

Tears streamed down her face. "It doesn't have to be like this, Tex."

I wasn't a strong enough man to lie to her face, to tell her everything would be okay when I knew it wouldn't. Hell, I was too weak to tell her I probably wasn't going to survive The Commission in the first place.

"Come on." I gently pulled her off my lap. "I want to show you something."

"Uh." She looked down. "But aren't we—I mean two hours and—"

"What? You afraid of a little adventure?"

"No," she growled. "I just feel—"

I laughed and moved her hands around me, damn her hands felt good. "Yeah, I feel too, but I promise, this will be worth it. Do you trust me?"

Mo released her grip and sighed. "Yes."

"Excellent." I grinned and lifted her gently off me. "We'll have to be really quiet. We're sneaking out of the house."

"We've done that before." She pointed out grabbing one of my white t-shirts and a pair of sweat pants.

"True." I licked my lips and tossed a red t-shirt over my head and pulled up a pair of athletic shorts. I held out my hand. "Everyone should be in their rooms or in the kitchen eating, we'll sneak out back." I winked.

She gripped my hand and nodded.

I grabbed a blanket from the bed and limped alongside her until we were outside by our favorite tree.

With a sigh I spread the blanket on the ground and sat down, she followed, the blanket was big enough to wrap both our bodies in.

"So." Mo exhaled. "You interrupt rocking my world to take me outside under the tree?"

"Yup."

"Because?"

"Because of that." I pointed behind me to the little scratch on the trunk that said Tex and Mo forever.

Mo gripped the front of my shirt as her eyes welled with tears. "I forgot about that."

RACHEL VAN DYKEN

"I never forget," I whispered. "Plus I have a scar from trying to do that when I was five."

Mo chuckled. "We used to come out here after everyone went to bed."

"And I'd tell you to pick a star."

"I picked a different one each time."

"As any smart little girl would." I grinned at the memory. "A new star means a new wish."

"My wish was always the same."

I choked on the emotion clogging my throat, filling my lungs, making me want to scream. "Mine was too."

"Together forever." Mo interlocked her fingers with mine. It's what we'd written under the Mo and Tex forever... I'd just wanted to be by her side when I was little.

"You were my favorite then, Mo. You're my favorite now."

Her head pressed against my chest, the wetness of her tears soaking the front of my shirt.

"So tonight..." My voice was hoarse. "I wanted to make the best of what we're leaving behind—I want to make a new wish on a new star."

"What's the new wish?"

I dug my fingers into her hair and kissed her forehead. "My new wish... is this..." I tilted her chin towards me and kissed her lips. "Be happy Mo. It's all I want in life, your happiness. It's why I live, why I breathe, why I bleed—for your smile. Don't let what has to happen turn you into a person I don't recognize."

"H-how," Mo sobbed. "How can you expect that of me when you're ripping away my reason for being happy?"

I kissed her salty cheeks. "I didn't say it would be easy."

"Which is why we're using the stars."

"Right." I trailed kisses down her neck. "It's why we need the stars."

"Tex." She blinked her clear blue eyes a few times as tears

188

washed down her face and slipped down her chin. "This is my wish." Her lips trembled. "For you to find peace—in a lifetime full of war."

"You're my peace," I admitted with a grim smile.

"So when you're in war—think of me."

Our mouths met in the middle, each of us digging at each other's clothes, pulling them off and tossing them under the tree. I'd always wanted to make love to her under the stars.

I was getting my final wish.

With a groan I pulled off her sweats and hovered over her. "Say it, Mo."

"Now!" she cried, her hands fisting over my back, as her legs wrapped around me, rocking her core towards me. "Tex Campisi, I love you…"

I surged into her with a primal cry, knowing, it would be the last time my name would most likely cross her lips.

Slowly I glided in and out, savoring the feeling of her body contracting around me, wishing things were different but vowing that I would protect her until my last breath.

With a cry, her head fell back as her body shook against mine. I wanted to wait, I wanted to wait because finishing meant we would go back inside.

But I couldn't wait.

Our mouths fused together as I thrust one last time, sending myself over the edge into an explosion that I would remember for the rest of my life.

"Two hours," Mo said sadly against my lips.

"Yeah," I panted. "But if I only had two hours to live—I wouldn't have done anything differently."

She licked her lips and smiled softly. "Me either."

CHAPTER THIRTY-EIGHT

Giving your body to someone — trusting them with it, is a purely selfless act, yet it's strange how selfish it sometimes feels.

Sergio

THAT WAS GOING to end badly. I looked away from the backyard window and cursed.

"You're in a good mood." Phoenix sat down next to me and folded his arms across his chest. "So, what did you need?"

I'd called Phoenix down here to go over the plan. Frank and Luca had already gone to bed and I knew that Phoenix needed the details only I could give him.

"Luca's offering fifty grand to any associate willing to point out where Alfonso's hiding."

"Right." Phoenix leaned back in the chair. "And once I find out where he's hiding, I eliminate him?"

"No." I licked my lips nervously. "You give him this." I slid the envelope across the table and waited while Phoenix picked it up and read the contents.

"No way." He dropped the envelope. "Are you insane? Do you want to die?"

"It's the only way, and you know it."

"To get killed." Phoenix slammed his hand onto the table. "I didn't die, go to Hell and come back again so that you could put the Family in that type of danger."

I swallowed again, waiting for patience to bubble to the surface. I wasn't eighteen. I wasn't an idiot. I knew what had to be done, I also knew, that because of who I worked for, if it wasn't handled... delicately, we'd all go to prison.

"Look." I exhaled. "We'll take care of the rest, but Alfonso needs to get that invitation. He needs to be at The Commission, or the plan fails."

Phoenix's eyes pierced through me. "You're inviting us all to our deaths. Having Alfonso and his men there means a shoot-out, it means our funeral, it means the death of everything I've sacrificed for, and it means the death of Nixon." His voice cracked. "It means the death of Chase." He looked out the windows and paled. "And it means Tex is going to have to be the one to pull the trigger."

"That—" I nodded. "—is exactly what I'm counting on."

Phoenix cursed.

"Get it done." I stood. "Or do I need to remind you, exactly who you work for?"

Without another word, Phoenix grabbed the envelope, stuffed it into his pocket, and stormed down the hall.

I waited a few minutes then texted Frank.

Me: It's done.

Frank: He took the bait?

Me: Yes.

Frank: Good.

Me: You know this could go either way... right?

Frank: Have a little faith in him—we all deserve a second chance... this is his.

CHAPTER THIRTY-NINE

War is the change of kings — John Dryden, King Arthur

Phoenix

I BLINDLY GRABBED a set of keys and slammed the door to the house behind me. When I clicked the unlock button it was the red Ferrari that lit up the garage.

Unfazed, I stomped over to the car, opened the door and started it, completely numb from the inside out. Or maybe not numb, just really pissed off and unsure of how to proceed. Cursing, I peeled out of the garage like the fires of Hell were licking at my damn boots and hit the accelerator once I passed the iron gate.

Guys my age shouldn't be thinking about their friends' deaths.

Guys my age shouldn't be hunting for associates, slipping money into the wrong hands and asking for favors.

Guys my age should be just finishing college, starting their lives, possibly settling down with the right girl or maybe even the wrong one. The point? The life I was living wasn't life, it was absolute Hell on earth and I had no way to get off the carousel as it went round and round taking me with it.

The envelope in my pocket might as well have been burning a hole through me. At the stoplight, I pulled it out and sat it on the passenger seat. A memory washed over me, just another one of the memories I'd been trying desperately to keep away, especially considering what I'd just been asked to do.

"Dude, it's a sports car, you're supposed to go fast." Chase taunted from the front seat while Nixon sat in the back and slapped him across the head.

"Why go fast?" I pointed out. "When going slow means everyone sees you?"

"Man's gotta point." Tex chuckled. "Wave at the ladies, Phoenix."

We were sixteen and thought we were bad asses. Nixon's dad had just bought another sports car and we'd taken off the minute all the men were in their meeting.

"Hot damn," Chase called from the front seat. "This car's like a sexy woman, all curves, no stops."

"Stop turning yourself on," Tex said. "It's weird and please stop making eye contact through the rearview mirror as you grope the leather."

"Ass." Chase threw on his sunglasses and moaned again.

Laughing, I looked back at Nixon. "Think we'll buy cars like this when it's us in charge of the family?"

"Hells yes," Tex answered for Nixon. "You guys are going to be the most bad ass bosses on the planet while Chase and I work hard at pleasing all the women that throw themselves at you."

I rolled my eyes and laughed.

A horn honked in irritation behind me. "Damn it." I hit the accelerator again and sped through the green light, gripping the steering wheel like it was my salvation.

It had been me and Nixon who were next. Chase and Tex had no pressure. Chase was the cousin, Tex the cursed son of a Campisi who wanted nothing to do with him.

How had things gotten so messed up?

I wasn't the same man I was before those gunshots. Death hadn't redeemed me; it had killed every ounce of light and happiness. It was like experiencing my own death over and over again—I couldn't stomach the fact that any of the guys would be in danger.

I slammed my hand on the steering wheel as I pulled the car up to the usual spot where Campisi associates would eat.

Italian.

Of course.

A small Italian café that looked about as daunting as walking up to a bagel shop with a poodle on the front.

I needed to do this.

I had to do this.

What the hell was Frank thinking? Or Luca for that matter?

Cracking my knuckles, I closed my eyes and allowed my brain to go there... what would happen if... ?

Saying nothing to the guys meant their deaths.

Saying something to them meant mine, most likely.

Interfering meant more bloodshed.

Doing nothing meant I hadn't changed.

Doing nothing meant I was still the same Phoenix as before, but like Sergio said, Tex had to pull the trigger.

And in that instant, I knew exactly what I had to do.

With shaking hands I dialed Tex's number, I'd memorized it, knew it by heart.

"Phoenix?" Tex sounded like hell. "What's wrong?"

"I have a plan." I cleared my throat. "But it stays between you and me."

Tex paused. "Does this plan end up getting me killed?"

"Possibly."

"And Mo? She'll be alive when it's over?"

"Maybe. Hopefully. That's the general idea."

"I'm listening."

"I need to make a drop first." I sighed. "Then, you and I

are planning this from the ground up, no mistakes, no telling Mo, no telling Nixon, no sneezing in Chase's direction. It has to appear real."

Tex was silent for a moment then let out a little chuckle. "Phoenix, are we staging a coup?"

And that was why I'd always loved Tex—always trusted him with my life, he was so damn smart it was terrifying.

"Just meet me in an hour, your bar."

"Done."

I hung up the phone and immediately felt the pressure release from my shoulders. Staging a coup? Damn straight we were, only I was pretty sure the monarchy that was about to fall wasn't going to take kindly to what was about to happen.

CHAPTER FORTY

What is the opposite of two? A lonely me, a lonely you. – Richard Wilbur

Mo

"WHO WAS THAT?" I yawned stretching my arms above my head. The last thing I wanted to do was move or try to start putting on my clothes again. That meant we were done.

It meant the end of us.

And I wasn't ready for that, not now, not ever. I just didn't know how to convince him to stay, when I knew logically, it was smarter for him to go.

Tex's gaze darkened as he slowly exhaled and looked at me. "A friend."

"Oh." I looked down at my bare chest and pulled the blanket over me.

"Mo." Tex's swollen lips and tousled hair made me yearn to touch him again, to ask for another five minutes of his kisses of his touch. "I need to go soon."

I hesitated. In a moment I probably should have sobbed my eyes out and thrown my arms around his neck, I hesitated. Because Tex wasn't a typical guy, when I cried it broke his heart, but it was almost like it made him more resolute to do the right thing, like his only job on this planet was to protect each tear as it fell, even if it meant his blood covered those tears in the process.

With a sigh, he reached for his shirt, his back muscles flexing in the shimmering moonlight as he pulled the shirt over his head and slid on his shorts.

A shiver coursed through me.

"You should go back to school." Tex exhaled and rubbed his hands together. "I think it would be... good."

"School?" I repeated. "We're about to say goodbye and your parting words are that I should go to school? Seriously?"

Chuckling, Tex pulled me in for a hug. "We do have ten minutes left."

"I wouldn't know." My eyes narrowed. "I don't wear a watch."

"Irresponsible." He hissed kissing down the right side of my neck. "How will you ever be early if you don't know the time?"

"I've always had you," I said arching my eyebrows and tilting my face towards his.

Our lips met.

"True." Tex breathed me in, nuzzling his nose in my hair. "Eight minutes, Mo."

"Eight minutes where I'd rather time didn't exist." I whispered watching pain roll across his face in a wave. "Kiss me again."

With a soft exhale, he brushed his lips across mine, little feathery strokes that tempted me with promise of something more. He used his tongue to trace the outline of my lips before sliding inside, past my teeth, tasting every inch of me, giving me every inch of himself. Living in the moment, both of us knowing that it would soon be over.

"Seven." I whispered against his mouth.

"Go to school," he urged for a second time. "Make

mistakes, Mo. Get in trouble, let Nixon find you sneaking wine into your backpack. Get sent to the Dean's office, make mistakes," he said again then licked his lips. "Let someone pick up the pieces of your broken heart, let someone fix what I destroyed."

"What if I want to drop out and hermit myself in my room?" I refused to look at him.

"That's not living, Mo." Tex cupped my face. "I have five minutes left with you, do you want me to use it to kiss you or lecture you on why I'm right?"

I grinned as a tear slid down my cheek. "Both."

His smile matched mine. "I forget how much you like being scolded."

"Only if the one scolding has a firm hand."

"Every last inch of me is firm and you know it." Tex tugged me into his lap. "School will distract you, it will give you a better future then guns and war, it will take your focus from tragedy to the future. Please, for me, Mo, please try to do normal."

"Normal." I shook my head. "Not sure I know what that word is."

"Normal," Tex repeated. "Making love to someone under a tree not because you have to say goodbye, but because it's the best way you can think to say hello."

My lower lip quivered.

"Normal." His voice was hoarse. "Marrying the love of your life not because her brother shoots you at point blank range—but because not marrying her would be a fate worse than death."

He was silent then added, "Three minutes."

I clenched his shirt with my hands and fought the urge to sob against his chest.

"Normal." Tex's voice was barely audible. "Going from country to country, traveling all over the world, not because you have a hit on you, but because you want to see the girl you love smile in every country God ever created."

I knew the time was ticking by, it seemed the less time we had the faster it went, I guess that's life.

I was looking at two more minutes, maybe less, with my lover, my friend, and all I could do was clench his shirt in my hands and twist, somehow willing him to stay on the ground rather than get up and walk towards certain death.

"Normal." Tex moved to his feet, helping me up. "Giving the woman you love two hours of your time, because you can't imagine spending your minutes, those precious seconds, any other way."

Tex kissed my mouth hard, nearly bruising my lips before stepping back and kissing my nose.

"Time's up," he said gruffly.

"We're no longer friends." I said it as a statement, not even a question.

"For two hours I was your lover, your friend, your everything." Tex looked away. "For the rest of eternity—I'm now your enemy."

"I hate life."

"Don't." Tex grimaced. "It will be easier to just hate me instead."

"But—"

"We're done here, Mo. Go back inside."

"Tex—"

"I said." His jaw popped. "We're done, now go back inside and go to sleep."

I kept the blanket wrapped around me and grabbed my clothes, a sense of loss washed over me as my feet padded against the cold grass. Each step I took was like trying to run through cement. My heart was beating, but all I felt was pain. A sob escaped my mouth as my feet touched the back deck, I turned around one last time to see his face.

To get my goodbye.

But he was already gone.

As if the Tex I knew had never existed in the first place.

I hung my head and cried. I cried for the boy I knew, the boy that turned into a man. A man who was forced to make a choice, his past or his future. I cried because I knew the Tex I'd loved, the one who'd held me so tenderly in his arms, was never going to come back.

He would have to go all in.

Tex no longer existed.

No, now he was Vito Campisi Jr., and the world was about to feel his rage, I only hoped my family wouldn't be shredded in the process.

CHAPTER FORTY-ONE

It is easier to find men who will volunteer to die, than to find those who are willing to endure pain with patience—Julius Caesar

Tex

I LEFT THE OLD ME with Mo for safekeeping. It was the only way I knew I could get in the car and meet Phoenix. So as I took those few steps towards the front of the house, I allowed myself to grieve the man I had been— And mourn the man I was becoming.

I thought of Mo's smile of how that one tiny thing changed my world from dark to light.

I imagined her lips, her moans, her body, how welcoming she'd always been to me.

And lastly, I thought of her pure heart, her soul, how she was willing to fight demons on my behalf, knowing full well she was defending the very monster she feared.

She was strength.

She was everything.

When I reached the front of the house I turned around and gave it one last glance. I was leaving as Tex, and I'd be returning a Campisi. Whatever Phoenix had to say wasn't going to end well in my favor, but if I could protect her, save her, I'd do anything.

Anything.

"Goodbye, Mo," I whispered into the air and took a deep breath before grabbing the keys to one of the Ducatis and hopping on.

The reign of Alfonso was going to end—and it was going to end by my hand. Alive or dead. Retribution was coming.

With a smirk I took off towards the bar.

By the time I reached my normal watering hole, I was numb, not a good numb either but the type of numb you feel when you know you're about to do something that's irreversible.

The point of no return was officially my theme song.

Each step towards Phoenix meant a step away from Mo.

And I hated that I had the strength and courage to go forward, wished in that second that I was a bit of a coward, willing to steal her away and live in peace on some godforsaken island. Hell, I'd catch fish for the rest of my life with that woman.

But that's the thing parents don't tell kids, teachers candy coat everything, no adult in my life ever prepared me for reality. Nobody ever said that the life you see on TV is rare— bloodshed? That's the norm. The picket fence? That's what you get if you're lucky.

I wasn't lucky.

Never had been, never would be.

The scent of cigarettes hit my nose as I pulled open the door to the establishment. My boots clicked against the floor as I made my way to the bar. It was near empty except for Phoenix.

"Water?" I pointed at his glass. "Please tell me that's

vodka."

Phoenix shrugged. "Sorry to disappoint."

"Admit it." I took a seat on the bar stool. "You found religion or something."

"Nah, just my soul." Phoenix lifted the water to me and nodded. "Now, about our plan."

I held up my hand. "Something tells me one of us needs to be intoxicated for this."

He nodded. "It may be wise to have a bottle of whiskey handy."

I reached behind the bar and grabbed a bottle of Jack Daniels and two shot glasses. "How deep are we going in, Phoenix?"

"You're a Campisi." He stated the obvious. "The question is never how deep, you should know that by now. What you need to know, is how to move the pieces in your favor so strategically that nobody knows you've won until it's already happened."

"I'm shit at chess."

"Bull." Phoenix snorted. "Your IQ makes me feel like a three-year-old sometimes."

I rolled my eyes and took a shot, wincing as the dry liquid poured down my throat, giving me no relief, just a burning sensation of dread in my empty stomach.

"So, let's hear it."

Phoenix drummed his fingertips against the counter top. "You need to send a message."

"To Alfonso?"

"To everyone." Phoenix's eyes flashed. "Not just Alfonso but every damn family at The Commission, word needs to spread so fast that you're freaking trending on Twitter within two seconds, get the picture?"

"Mass murder by Tex Campisi trending on Twitter, right, that would be the day, okay so the only way to do something that… extravagant is either put fireworks in Alfonso's ass or—"

"Kill them," Phoenix snapped. "You have to kill them all."

"All?" I swallowed.

"A cleanse of... sorts." Phoenix shrugged. "Luca, Frank, Nixon, Chase, Mo, Mil..."

Each name he fired off was like a hammer to my head. My blood broiled beneath the surface of my calm-as-hell smile. "A demonstration."

Phoenix's hands shook as he grabbed the bottle and poured himself a shot, only he scooted it to me and nodded. "Blood always wins." He lifted his glass and clinked it with my shot. "Cheers."

CHAPTER FORTY-TWO

People fear death even more than pain. It's strange that they fear death. Life hurts a lot more than death. At the point of death, the pain is over. Yeah, I guess it is a friend. – Jim Morrison

Sergio

MY HEADACHE HAD EVERYTHING to do with the fact that I wouldn't know what choice Phoenix made until it was too late.

"Don't interfere." Luca had instructed, like the freaking Godfather himself. I wasn't an idiot; I knew Luca thought of Phoenix like a son. Really, good for them, they had a life and death bonding moment and now he was trusting Phoenix to be the man he hoped he'd saved, not the one who had died that day.

I wasn't sure who to trust.

Maybe a bottle of Jim? Yeah, that sounded good.

Bottles never let me down.

Like women, like Phoenix, like Luca, Frank, hell I came out of retirement to help them save The Family not put it in more danger and wave a red flag in front of the Feds.

Nixon walked into the room with Trace close behind him,

they were laughing about something and then he pulled her into his embrace and kissed her mouth.

I looked away as knives of jealously surged through my body. I'd never wanted Trace, yeah she was beautiful, but it had always been Mo.

The same girl who was not but an hour ago wrapped up in enemy territory with stars in her eyes.

That girl had no idea the lengths Tex would go—I did. I knew. I knew that in the end you could deny your blood all you wanted, but it still flowed through your veins, a daily reminder of the person you were destined to be.

He was a killer.

The enemy.

So the way I saw it, we were putting our lives in the hands of two of the most messed up people in the world. Tex and Phoenix.

That bottle of Jim Beam was looking better and better.

"...Maybe he needs a girl." Trace whispered.

My head jolted up. "You guys talking about me?"

"Never." Nixon smirked. "You okay, man?"

"Nothing a bottle or two can't fix."

Nixon winced, his eyes taking in my bouncing knee and inability to focus on anything for more than three seconds before looking back at the bottle.

"Trace?" Nixon turned to her. "Why don't you go see what Mil's doing? And tell Chase I need him."

"Yes, master." Trace rolled her eyes. "Where's the please?"

I coughed to hide my laugh as Nixon clenched his jaw tight. "Please."

"Better." She grinned and skipped away down the hall.

"Someone's got your balls in the palm of her hand."

"Let's leave my balls and her hands out of this." Nixon grabbed the bottle from me and retrieved two glasses. "Mind telling me why you look like shit?"

"It's a new style I'm trying." I pulled at my long hair and winced. "Jared Leto meets Sicily."

"Try harder." Chase said strolling into the room. "Or at least put eyeliner on."

"Right, that'll make associates quake in their boots. Long hair and eyeliner." I rolled my eyes. "Why hadn't I thought of that?"

"I got the brains in the family." Chase grinned. "Simple." He angled his head. "Mind telling me why you look like shit?"

I groaned into my hands.

"Great minds." Nixon elbowed Chase.

"No sleep?" I offered. "It takes a toll."

"So does sex, but I look awesome." Chase popped his knuckles. "What do you know, man? It's better to tell us."

"Can't," I snapped. "Just be prepared for Tex to be different when he gets back, that's... that's all."

"Where is he?" Nixon pushed away from the table and looked around. "Shouldn't everyone be sleeping anyway?"

"Out," I seethed. "Drinking and whoring? How am I supposed to know?"

Nixon's eyes narrowed in on me. "Frank and Luca?"

"Sleeping." I shrugged. "They're old."

"I'm old." Chase groaned. "My knees cracked today... it was sad."

"Vitamins." I snapped my fingers. "Like Centrum Silver?"

"I said they cracked not that they needed replacements, you ass." Chase got up from his chair. "So, what's the plan for tomorrow?"

"Other than surviving?" I grinned.

Nixon stared hard at me, making my comfort level basically dissipate into thin air. "People start arriving tomorrow, we'll make them as comfortable as possible... actually." He grinned. "I think a good old fashioned family dinner is in order."

"Please tell me you're drunk." I rubbed my face with my hands.

"I'll cook." Chase rubbed his hands together. "Besides it's only a few of Luca's men and The Alferos that will be here that early."

"Fantastic. What? Do we pat them down at the door?"

"What's a family dinner without a little gunfire?" Nixon slapped my back and stood. "You worry too much."

No sooner did the words leave his mouth then Tex barreled through the door looking a hell of a lot worse for the wear and ready to shoot anyone in the face who as much as breathed in his direction.

"Rough night?" Chase piped up.

Tex's eyes narrowed in on Chase, without saying a word he stomped towards him, punched him in the face and then spat on him as Chase tumbled to the floor. To be fair, it was a total sucker punch, unlike Tex.

"What the hell?" Chase roared from the ground.

"You dare talk to me like that?" Tex sneered. "I have more blood in my pinky finger—more freaking royalty then you do in your entire body. Next time you address me as Sir or I shoot you. Understood?"

Chase's face twisted in rage, his eyes narrowing into tiny slits as he clenched his fist at his side. Any minute the guy was going to launch himself at Tex and try to break his jaw in half.

Nixon reached for his gun, but I grabbed his hand and shook my head.

The girls came charging into the room. Mil went immediately to Chase's side, calming him down, which was a necessity since a pissed Chase was a violent Chase. "Are you okay?"

"Peachy." Chase growled.

Trace looked between us and Tex. An expression of worry crossed her features as she saw Nixon's hand on the gun and my hand on his.

And lastly there was Mo.

Shit, this wasn't going to begin or end well. I fought the urge to groan as I watched her face twist with concern.

"Tex?" Her voice was soft, dripping with sensitivity that Tex didn't deserve nor want. "What are you—"

"Stop talking." His teeth clenched so tight the muscles to his jaw strained with the need to release. "Now."

Mo crossed her arms. "This is my house and—"

"It's Nixon's house." Tex shrugged, though it did nothing to relax his shoulders; hell they were up by his ears he was wound so tight. "Now get out of my way before I physically remove you."

"You wouldn't—"

Without a word he picked her up off the floor and set her roughly against Nixon before stomping off to his room.

"And so it begins." I whispered under my breath.

Tears filled Mo's eyes as she ran towards her room and slammed the door.

"Someone mind telling me what the hell that was?" Chase rose from the floor and touched his swollen cheek.

"That—" I lifted my glass into the air. "—was Vito Campisi Jr. I suggest you sleep with a gun under your pillow." I was sure going to.

Standing, I slowly made my way down the hall and knocked lightly on Mo's room. Without waiting for her to answer, I let myself in, closed the door and sighed.

"He didn't mean it, he didn't—" She fell into a fit of sobs against the bed.

My heart strained and twisted with rage.

"He's just not himself and—"

"He's exactly," I said softly, " "himself, and that's been the problem all along. When you finally accept who you are— the old you is gone only to be replaced with the one true thing in life."

"Blood," she whispered.

"Blood," I agreed sitting on her bed. "For what it's worth, I'm sorry, Mo. Sorry this didn't turn out the way you wanted."

"Are you going to hit on me now? Kiss me and make it better? Hug me and pat my hand then just wait for my heart to heal itself so you can marry me and give me fake promises of a fake future?"

I licked my lips and offered her my hand. "Absolutely not. I'm just going to hold your hand."

"Oh."

I squeezed her fingers. "I'll be here... if you let me... I'll be here."

"I don't know what I want." She clenched my hand tighter.

"That's okay too." I lie down next to her, holding her hand but not touching her. "Sometimes it's okay just to... be."

CHAPTER FORTY-THREE

When you marry the man, you marry the mob. Nobody ever tells you that... until it's too late.

Mo

SERGIO'S HAND SQUEEZED mine tight, so tightly that I swear I lost feeling. I think in his own weird way he was trying to comfort me—but the thing about comfort? It only works if it's the right person, and yeah, he was the opposite of right. He'd always been.

Wrong for me.

Bad timing, bad memories, just all around bad decisions surrounded me and Sergio's weird relationship.

Tex, I wanted Tex, but he didn't return. No, the man that just picked me up and freaking sat me against my brother like a toddler? That wasn't the man I loved that was someone else entirely. I had to believe it was an act, a way to push us away because of what he was planning to do. After all, people can't just stop being themselves, can they?

"You're thinking awfully hard for someone who should be sleeping." Sergio yawned and turned to me. His dark silky hair fell across a strong jaw with a bit of scruff. He really was pretty to look at.

But I didn't want pretty.

I wanted bad for me.

I wanted dirty, dangerous. I craved stormy blue eyes, Sergio's were too green for my taste.

"Did I pass?" He smirked, his white teeth flashing in the darkness.

"Pass what?"

"Inspection?"

I smiled and looked away.

"Ouch." Sergio sighed. "Guess not."

"It's not you—"

"It's not you, it's me..." he sang. "Heard it once, heard it a thousand times. Mo, against my own better judgment I'm in here with you. I know who owns your heart, I'm not going to try to pull you from the dark side. Comfort, that's why I'm here, so stop staring at me like I'm going to try to take off your shirt or kiss you."

"Sorry." I croaked, immediately feeling guilty for thinking that exact thing of him.

"Sleep." Sergio kissed my head. "I'll stay until you fall asleep and shoot anyone who comes through that door."

"Even Nixon?" I yawned and turned on my side.

"Especially Nixon. That guy's had it coming for a while. Don't worry your pretty little head though—I'll just graze him."

"Wow, great bedtime story, Sergio, really, you should teach children or something."

"Damn, are you saying I missed my calling?"

"That's exactly what I'm saying."

His warm chuckle calmed me down, not enough to actually relax, but enough to not want to scream or cry or rip my own hair out or Tex's for that matter.

"Sleep."

"Bossy."

"Sleep," he whispered, this time more harsh. "If you don't close your eyes I'll sing, and I have a shit voice."

"Believe me, I know. I used to sit next to you during Mass."

Sergio laughed softly. "Guys aren't meant to sing, we're meant to shoot things."

"Again, you're like walking wisdom."

"Goodnight, Mafia princess."

"Night." I sighed and succumbed to the heaviness in my body, as my eyelids got heavy the last vision I had was of Tex's mouth right before he kissed me.

CHAPTER FORTY-FOUR

The Mafia is an organization, it's planning, it's strategy, but most of all it's Family. People rarely understand how loyal the Mafia is, that is until it's too late and that loyalty is tested. Most of those people end up dead.

Tex

I SLEPT LIKE ABSOLUTE crap. Correction, I slept like the crap that feeds on the crap that your goldfish craps out when it has the craps—hell yeah, you're in a bad place if you compare your life to goldfish poop.

It probably had to do with all the plans Phoenix and I had gone over. Right, that was the worst possible thing to think about before going to bed. I tried to think about Mo but every time I did, my stomach rolled with sickness and worry. I'd been a complete ass to her and to Chase, but like Phoenix said... everything from here on out depended on my ability to fully step into the role.

No regrets.

He'd made me swear it on not just my life, but my sister's and Mo's.

And I took my vows seriously—all of them.

By the time five a.m. rolled around, I knew I wasn't going to get any more sleep so I threw on a pair of running shoes and grabbed my phone.

Two hours later, I had sweat pouring down my entire body and still felt like that damn goldfish, all belly up and sick. Things were going to get worse before they got better, which was probably why I was having trouble dealing.

When you know there's a storm coming you do everything you can to prepare yourself, but when you're the storm? When you're the one causing all that damage? It sucks. People talk about the after effects of the storm, but they never talk about the before... the before is worse. After all, anticipation is always worse than the actual outcome.

I had to believe that there was a light at the end of the tunnel and if there wasn't, well I was screwed.

Whistling, I pulled open the door to the house and walked into the kitchen. Chase was standing there shirtless, sweat pouring down his chest as he devoured a cinnamon roll and cup of coffee. My stomach growled at the smell of fresh rolls.

"I made the rolls." Chase's eyes narrowed over his steaming cup of coffee. "After I punched a bag with your face on it."

"How'd my face turn out?" I asked, genuinely curious.

"Wouldn't know." Chase shrugged. "I got tired of punching and eventually pulled out my gun. I'll buy Nixon another punching bag tomorrow."

"Hmm, got a little rage, Chase?"

"I don't know Tex, care to sucker punch me again and find out?"

"Ladies." Nixon stormed into the room. "Tuck those ovaries back into your pants and grow some balls—nobody's punching anyone."

"Says who?" I snorted bracing my hands on the counter top.

"Says the guy who's going to put a bullet in your head if you as much as hint as disrespecting me in my own home." Nixon yawned and reached for a cup, then offered me one. "Coffee?"

"Probably time to retire when threatening your friends over coffee seems normal, Nixon." I took the cup. "Just saying."

"Probably time to take Xanax if you're punching your best friend in the face for breathing." Chase lifted his cup mockingly into the air. "Just sayin'."

"Fair." I seriously had to fight the urge to laugh as Chase's bruised cheek flashed under the kitchen lights. Phoenix had said to change the tables, be unpredictable. Punching Chase was the only way I could think to shake things up without actually shooting someone. It raised suspicion, but still kept me in the house until it was time.

"I hate mornings." Trace shuffled into the kitchen, her hair in a ponytail and eyes barely open. "Coffee me."

Chase handed her his own cup and got another one for himself. "Sleep well?"

"I'm sorry, are you actually talking to me right now? Before I even take a sip?" Her eyes widened as she leaned in towards Chase.

Note to self, coffee first, chat later.

Chase grinned patronizingly and patted her head. "Aw, you're so feisty, like a little... mouse."

"Name calling gets you nowhere," Trace fired back.

Chase smirked. "That's not what Mil says."

"Mil says her husband needs to stop picking fights with people smaller than him." Mil announced walking into the room.

Chase's entire face lit up.

I looked away. I didn't want to see everyone happy and together, not when my own freaking life was such a mess. Not when I had to do what I was going to do. Damn, I couldn't even look into their eyes without feeling guilt slice through me.

I grabbed the newspaper just as the entire room fell silent and tense as hell. I knew it was Mo. I could tell from the way the air shifted, from the way my body heated by just having her near. With slow movements I lifted my head over the paper and stared.

What I saw had me reaching for my gun.

Sergio was whispering something in her ear as he poured her a cup of coffee. Holy shit, I was going to break his hand.

He snaked his other arm around her and touched her shoulder. Just kidding I was going to break both his hands and stuff them into his mouth.

Mo smiled at him.

I gripped the table with my left hand, my fingers digging into the wood.

"Easy," Nixon whispered from next to me. "We don't want to have to buy a new one."

"A new Sergio or a new table?" I said through clenched teeth.

"One's irreplaceable."

"What?" I looked down. "This is an antique?"

Nixon smirked. "I mean Sergio, you jackass."

I shrugged and went back to my paper and read, you know if reading meant I stared at the same sentence while trying to eavesdrop on Mo and Sergio's conversation.

"Family dinner." Chase announced sitting down next to me. I scooted away towards Nixon and crossed my arms.

Pissed. I had to look pissed.

And ready to kill them.

All of them.

"Family dinner." Nixon repeated, leaning back in his chair. "I'll have Luca and Frank let everyone know. Most the Alferos are in town, The Nicolasis just flew in this morning, so we'll plan for something around five."

Chase cracked his knuckles. "I'll have Mil help me cook."

"You sure about that?" Phoenix stumbled into the kitchen took one look at me and glanced away—no recognition. No emotion. Damn he was good. "Last time I ate something she cooked, I got food poisoning."

"I was five." Mil rolled her eyes. "And it was cookie dough, I blame the raw egg."

"Note she said raw." Phoenix plopped down on his chair. "I'll be helping Luca and Frank today."

"Great." Nixon sniffed and stole part of my paper. "Just make sure nobody shoots anyone on the way here."

"Can't make any promises," Phoenix said blandly. "But I'll give them all the talk."

"The talk?" Trace asked in a quiet voice, though she seemed a lot less hostile than earlier.

"Yeah." Phoenix didn't make eye contact. I wasn't sure if he felt guilty over what had happened or what was going to happen, either way his eyes averted to the wood table as he shrugged and answered, "The whole, a bullet for a bullet, a punch for a punch, you kill my Family I obliterate yours, you know... The Talk."

"Yeah." Trace squinted. "They don't teach that in school."

"Speaking of school." Mo finally spoke up. Her voice made my entire body tense... I wasn't sure if it was from addiction, yearning, or fear. Maybe all three. "I want to enroll for Winter classes."

All eyes fell to her.

Trace cleared her throat. "I should probably join you."

"Me too." Mil nodded slowly. "I have a year to finish anyway."

"Wait." Nixon held up his hand. "You guys want to go back to Eagle Elite?"

"Why not?" Trace shrugged. "It's not as if someone's going to murder us in the iron gates."

Nixon glanced at me, I looked down, my eyes were guilty. It had been my suggestion. I couldn't believe Mo was actually listening to me. Then again, maybe I could.

She was moving on.

And it hurt like hell.

Part of me wanted her to fight, a giant part of me wanted her to push every boundary I set in place. Instead, she listened to me. She was fulfilling her promises and for once in my life I really wished she wouldn't.

Sergio reached across the table and touched Mo's hand to gain her attention. I gripped one of the butter knives in my fingers in anticipation of cutting his off.

"Great idea, Mo." He winked at me. "I can always go with you girls when you enroll. The new Dean is a close friend."

"That's true," Nixon said slowly. "Okay, but not until Winter classes start, alright?"

"Great." Mo took a drink of coffee then looked directly at me. The smile that was originally on her face transformed into something I never thought, in all my years I'd see directed at me.

Fear.

CHAPTER FORTY-FIVE

Life always presents opportunities for redemption.

Phoenix

"NIXON?" I CLEARED my throat. "A minute?"

With a swift nod, Nixon stood, kissed Trace on the head and led me into his office shutting the door behind him. "What's going on?"

"Nothing." I braced my hands behind my head and sighed. "I just... I hit a snag."

He pursed his lips together. "What type of snag?"

"The female kind."

"She pregnant?"

"What?" I gasped, horrified. "No, what? Is who pregnant?"

"Easy." Nixon grinned. "I was kidding and I don't even know who you're talking about."

Swear sweat started to pour from my temples. My body demanded I pace back and forth to get rid of all the tension and anxiety building inside of me. "Bee." I cleared my throat. "Tex's sister."

"Tell me she's not dead."

"She's not dead." Right, the woman would be the death of me, not the other way around. "She's just making things difficult on those I left in charge. I think it might be good to bring her to dinner and introduce her to family. Alfonso's been appeased for the moment."

"How?" Nixon licked his lips.

"Luca had me deal with the situation." I tilted my head and narrowed in my gaze, basically challenging him to doubt me.

"So... problem solved? Just like that?" He crossed his arms.

"For now..." I said slowly. "Yes, just like that."

"Do I want to know how?"

"No." I said honestly. "And even if you did, I wouldn't tell you."

"Damn." Nixon sighed. "Luca really did a number on you, didn't he?"

I shrugged. "So, Bee?"

"Won't that be like waving a flag in front of the Campisi clan?"

"Why yes." I smiled. "Yes it will."

"We have your boss and his sister and mean to do what? Go to war?"

"Not war." I stuffed my hands in my front pockets. "Besides, Alfonso's been appeased, he never wanted her anyway. In fact, the minute I infiltrated the family he couldn't get rid of her fast enough, she has a... wild streak."

"Wild as in, she's cranky?"

"Wild as in she shot me in the arm." I coughed. "Wild."

"Ah, so you've met your match."

I felt my entire face pale as my body went rigid as a statue. "No, I don't... I mean... I haven't been with a girl. Look, is it okay or not?"

"Phoenix—"

"I'm asking permission."

"Bring her." He snapped. "And Phoenix, if you need to talk to someone or —"

"I'm straight," I fired back and grabbed the handle to the door. "See you tonight."

"Be safe." He called.

"I'll try." I lied. Because safe wasn't a word I would use to describe what I was around Bee. Try… tortured. And now that I'd slipped information to Tex, now that I was playing both sides hoping that the end result would be worth it, my entire life depended on the trust of Tex and his sister as well as Nixon.

My phone buzzed in my pocket. I looked down at the screen.

T: She's all yours. Bitch bit me.

Hell, it was going to be a long ass night.

CHAPTER FORTY-SIX

Sicilian Mafia Rule #5: Never look at the wives of friends. Ever.

Mo

TEX DISAPPEARED FOR MOST of the morning and afternoon. By the time the scents of dinner started floating through the house I was ready to lock the door to my room and stay there.

My plan had been simple; cause him to react in any way possible. He'd reacted all right, just not the way I suspected. He almost ripped the table apart with his bare hands and I'm pretty sure at one point contemplated stabbing Sergio with a butter knife. But that was it.

I let out a breath and slouched in my big chair, staring at myself in the mirror.

It was time for plan two.

Make him want.

Wearing that white bikini was out of the question, but maybe wearing a short dress wasn't? I knew we'd said our goodbyes but part of me wondered what would happen if I just fought for him? What if I fought for us? I had to try right? Isn't that what wives do for their husbands? They fight until they have nothing left. And I was going to do the same thing.

If only I could convince him that I'd follow him anywhere, do anything to be with him. Even if it meant moving back to Sicily, even if it meant leaving my blood.

A loud knock interrupted my thoughts as two heads poked around the door. Trace and Mil.

They both wore wide grins.

"What?" My eyes narrowed as I crossed my arms. "You guys look suspicious."

Laughing they tumbled into my room. Not a care in the world those girls, either that or they hid their fear well. The dinner wasn't going to be pleasant.

"So." Mil fluffed her hair in the mirror while Trace walked over to the bed and sat. "We're going to make you look amazing."

"You mean I don't look amazing now?" I gasped pulling at my New York Giants t-shirt.

"Tex hates the Giants." Mil laughed.

"I know." Grinning I looked down. "Thought he might enjoy a little teasing this morning."

"Yeah, and that ended well." Trace said from the bed.

"Hey!" I threw a pillow at her. "When Nixon was mean to you, who helped you?"

"Um, not you?" She caught the pillow. "On account that you had five billion secrets and refused to tell me any of them."

I waved her off. "Excuses."

"He's an ass." Mil pointed out. "You still want him?"

I licked my lips and looked down at my clenched hands. "He gave me one hour..." My shoulders tensed. "Then another two to say goodbye... we slept together and that was it."

"Bastard," Mil hissed, while Trace's eyes watered with tears on my behalf.

"It's fine." I lied. "He's only doing what he thinks is right."

"Which is probably wrong." Mil's eyebrows arched. "You know, since he's male and all."

"So very, very, true," Trace agreed.

"So." Mil rubbed her hands together. "We're going to put you in a sexy black dress, stiletto heels, and bust out the bright red stripper lipstick that Chase never lets me wear on account that I remind him of strippers."

"Takes one to know one." Trace held up her hand for a high five.

"I'll take that." Mil slapped it.

I rolled my eyes and stayed put. "I don't really feel like getting all dressed up only to get rejected in front of my family."

"Chin up." Mil smiled. "Chase does it every day."

As both girls started walking toward me I knew I had no option but to concede and let them help.

Maybe, just maybe it would work.

An hour later, and I was pretty sure Mil was under the impression that hair spray was used to keep *everything* in place, not just hair. I was like a walking dome of aerosol as I straightened my dress in the mirror and looked at my kohl-lined eyes.

They'd given me bright red lipstick, a smoky eye, and teased my hair until it begged for mercy. Yeah strippers had nothing on me right now.

My dress was officially so short I was afraid to pick up something off the floor lest I give one of the older associates a stroke, and my Michael Kors heels made me almost six feet tall, a relative giant.

A knock.

It was the girls. They said they'd come back for me, more like threatened that if I tried to sneak through the window they'd just track me down and bring me back. I knew they would too. It was Mil and Trace.

"Ready?" Mil peeked around the door and grinned saucily. "Damn girl, you clean up well."

Trace winked and pushed the door open wider. Both of them had tight cocktail dresses on that weren't nearly as short as mine. Mil's was a strapless plain dress in navy blue, paired with taupe heels and Trace wore a white halter dress with red heels.

Apparently I was the only Vegas stripper in the group. Fantastic.

"Come on." Mil held out her hand. "Family's already starting to arrive, and Chase is in the kitchen freaking out over the shrimp."

"Of course he is." I gripped her hand and followed both girls down the hall towards the laughter and smells.

Chase was in the kitchen, chugging wine from one hand and stirring something with the other. His apron was splattered with something yellow and he looked a little drunk.

"Chase?" Mil came up behind him. "Did you save the shrimp?"

"I hate shrimp," he muttered. "Yeah I saved them after the butter freaking sprayed all over my apron and—" He stopped talking when his eyes scanned me from head to toe. "Tex is going to shit a brick."

"Tex?" Nixon walked into the room and glanced at me, did a double take, then stalked towards me. "No, turn around, change."

"I'm not a kid." I crossed my arms making my boobs look bigger in the strapless sweetheart dress. I knew they looked bigger because the dress was so low it was entirely possible they were going to fall out at any minute.

"Damn it, Mo!" Nixon smacked Chase, probably because he was convenient, and reached for the wine bottle. "This isn't open for argument, you will change. Now."

"No she won't," Trace challenged. "Because that's my dress, and I believe you told me that if I didn't buy it, you'd just go back to the store and get it."

Nixon's eyes flashed. "For *you*."

"So why can't Mo borrow my clothes?"

"Yeah," Chase piped up, his smile wide. "Why can't Mo wear your wife's clothes?"

Nixon closed his eyes and pinched the bridge of his nose. "Mo..." He swallowed, his Adam's apple bobbing up and down. "Please? Tex is going to lose it, I can't... he can't lose it in this type of environment."

"Tex is a big boy." I uncrossed my arms. "A very big boy."

"Didn't need to know that." Nixon coughed behind his hand and looked helplessly at Chase, who offered him a wine glass and a pat on the back.

"It will be fine," I lied, knowing full well it wasn't going to be fine when Tex saw me, his reaction would probably be worse than Nixon's was, and Nixon was currently finishing off half a bottle and staring at me like lightning was going to strike any minute.

"Nixon." Sergio walked into the room, texting on his phone. "Nicolasi clan just pulled up—they're going to want wine." He glanced up in my direction and swore his entire jaw going slack. "Damn it, Nixon, do something!"

"About what?" I sauntered by him and snagged a glass of wine off the table. "World hunger?"

"You know damn well what I'm talking about." Sergio's nostrils flared.

"She's an adult." Nixon croaked, right my bet was that he almost choked on the word adult. "She can wear what she wants."

Sergio shook his head a few times before muttering more curses under his breath and walking out of the kitchen.

The girls and I helped Chase get the appetizers out along

with the wine, men poured into the house, some our age, but most of them three times our age and watching us with the type of curiosity I wasn't comfortable with. It had been years since the Nicolasi family had decided to visit and we weren't exactly on great terms after my father all but kicked them out of the country.

One of the elders walked by and spat on the ground. Right, my point exactly. I quickly stepped over the spit, offered the grumpy man some wine and continued my search for Tex.

It wasn't until an hour into the guests arriving that I knew Tex had walked in the room.

All talking ceased.

All eyes were behind me. Slowly I turned to see Tex in gray slacks and a tight white button up. He looked good enough to eat with his stormy blue eyes taking in every single inch of the room.

I waited for those eyes to fall on me.

And when they did, I took a step back, as the blue raged from storm to hurricane within a second.

"Campisi." The man who had spit on our floor nodded his head. "It is good to see you, yes?"

"That depends." Tex took a step towards the crowd and tilted his head. "Are we going to have trouble this evening?"

Holy crap. I quickly looked at Nixon, but he was watching with mild amusement. What the heck! Sweating, I nervously licked my lips and waited for someone to say something.

The man chuckled. "Ah, to be young again."

"That's what I always say." Luca stepped up and joined in laughter then turned briefly to Tex, giving him the coldest look I'd ever seen in my entire life.

Frank, Trace's Grandpa nodded once then went to Tex and led him into the room. "A few men you should meet... trustworthy men who despised your father."

"A friend of my father is my enemy." Tex snorted. "An enemy of my father is my friend." He held out his hand and began conversing, and I watched in horror as every single man in that room straightened their ties and focused in on Tex as if he was the *Cappo* already.

He walked into the room and demanded their allegiance.

And they freely gave it.

Because of blood.

A choking sensation washed over me as I looked down at my dress. What was I trying to prove? My fighting for Tex wouldn't save us.

Not when he'd already jumped in with both feet.

"Mo?" Sergio said from behind me. I jumped a foot and turned.

"Hmm?"

"You okay?" His eyebrows drew together in concern as he looked from Tex to me.

"Fine." I waved him off. "Just a bit stressed, lots of guns in the room and all that."

"Guns are tools, try not to think of them as weapons. After all, people kill people, guns are merely the object they use in order to carry out the sentence."

"Comforting." I snorted.

"You need a drink." His fingers gripped my elbow as he led me out of the room and into the kitchen.

"Yeah," I sighed. "I really do."

CHAPTER FORTY-SEVEN

Things look better when you've spent time apart from someone or something you care about. Said no one. Ever.

Phoenix

"GET OUT OF THE DAMN CAR." I gritted my teeth. "Now."

"No." Bee crossed her arms and examined her nails.

Groaning, I closed my eyes and imagined myself banging my head against the door in frustration. "Bee," I tried again. "Your brother, the one you've never met, is inside, I need you to get your ass out of that seat and say hi."

"You left." Her voice wavered.

Good Lord I deserved this, all of this, her, the drama, the fighting. I deserved it, but I didn't have to enjoy it.

"I had to save your brother's life." My teeth snapped together. "Apparently I have a hero complex."

She snorted, then smiled, a row of white teeth flashed before biting on her soft pink lips and looking down at her feet again. From where I was standing I was safe. I wouldn't be able to smell her vanilla perfume or look into her crazy deep blue eyes. They were like staring at the ocean and I really didn't need that type of distraction. Not now. Not ever. She tossed her auburn hair. I damn near whimpered as the vanilla scent floated out the open window and landed on my body, threatening to overtake all logic.

"Bee." I opened the door to the car and leaned in. "I'm sorry I left you, but I'm here now and I won't leave until you're safe. You have my word."

Her eyes fluttered closed. "You promise?"

"I swear it." After all I was probably going to die soon anyway.

She took a deep breath and straightened her black cocktail dress. It had capped sleeves and was freaking glued to her body. I had to look away as she pointed those long legs out of the car and stood.

They went on for miles those legs, I would know, she kicked me with them twice. Apparently the woman had me confused with a soccer ball, it was the only explanation to the bruising on both my calves and thighs.

"Fine." She stood, her head nearly kissing my chin. "But only for an hour, and then I want to do something fun."

"Fun." I clenched my teeth. "Fine, I'll let you watch a Disney movie."

She pushed against my chest. "Phoenix, I think we both know I'm not a little girl."

Wrong thing to say. My eyes immediately took in her curvy figure. No, she was a nineteen-year-old bombshell with the ability to flatten me on my ass.

"Let's go," I snapped slamming the door behind her. Her heels were a little higher than she normally wore, forcing her to walk slower than a turtle with hemorrhoids. "Sometime this year, please."

She rolled those blue eyes and flipped her damn hair again then waltzed into the house like she owned the joint.

I followed, wincing as the smell of food hit my nose. I hadn't had much of an appetite since my meeting with Tex and the closer The Commission got, the sicker I felt.

"Who's this?" Mo was the first to see us, her smile was bright, fake, but bright.

"Bee," I said as Tex's sister opened her mouth. "This is Tex's sister."

"Bee?" Mo tilted her head.

"It's my nickname." Bee elbowed me in the ribs. "From this one."

"I like it." Mo smiled and shook Bee's hand, "Why don't I introduce you to some of the girls?"

"No." Bee snatched back her hand. "I mean, no thank you. I really, um, I would really like to see my brother."

"Oh." Mo's face lost some of its color. "Well he's in the living room talking with some—"

"Phoenix?" Tex stalked towards me. "Is this?"

Bee launched herself into Tex's arms. "You look like me!"

Tex's face broke out into a smile as he returned the hug then set her away from him. "Yeah well, I think that means we're related."

Bee laughed, the first time I'd actually heard her laugh, and it was Tex who got it out of her. Of course.

"We should talk." Bee's face was so animated it hurt to look at her. "I mean, later, I know you have lots going on and—"

"I'll make time," Tex interrupted. "For you I'll make time, it's good to see you healthy and happy?"

She nodded slowly.

"Phoenix kept his hands to himself?" Tex leveled me with a glare.

Bee shook her head. "No he kissed me like fifteen times." She leaned up and whispered loudly. "With tongue."

"No!" I held up my hands. "She's lying, she tends to exaggerate."

She let out a little laugh and crossed her arms while Tex's frozen glare never left my face.

"Shit." I gulped and looked away. "I swear man, I didn't

touch her, I don't touch girls, you know that."

"You're gay?" Bee gasped.

Moaning I just shook my head and walked into the kitchen. She was his problem now, not mine.

The minute I poured myself a glass of wine I felt a hand on my shoulder. When I turned it was to see Tex chest to chest with me. Great.

"I need you to watch her."

"I'm more of a delivery type of service." I tried to side step him. "I don't babysit."

"Please." Tex's eyes pleaded. "These men... I don't trust them, not yet, and I need to be able to focus. You know I do. I'm having a hard enough time focusing with Mo in that damn dress."

Dress? What dress?

I shrugged. "Fine, I'll watch her for the night then I'm done, she can move in with Luca for all I care."

Tex snorted. "That would be the day."

"Don't knock it till you try it." I threw back the glass and set it on the table. "Now if you'll excuse me I'm going to go put on a cup... last time I wasn't prepared for the kicks."

"Kicks?"

"You really don't want to know."

I walked off down the hall with the sound of male laughter behind me, yeah he laughs now. Just wait. Bee was a freaking force to be reckoned with. I couldn't wait to rid myself of her.

Right, just keep telling yourself that.

CHAPTER FORTY-EIGHT

Sicilian Mafia rule number 8: When asked for any information, the answer must be the truth.

Tex

BLACK, BLACK, BLACK, BLACK, damn it! People were talking to me, touching me, offering me cigars, time at their vacation homes, their freaking daughters and all I could think about was Mo.

In that black dress.

Officially my favorite color of all time.

On her, and only her.

Being impassive when she was in the room was like denying the sun was shining. Deny it all you want, but at the end of the day you're still going to get burnt if you don't have sunscreen.

She was searing me.

"More wine?" Speak of the damn devil. Mo carried a bottle in one hand and a little tray of shrimp in the other.

"Lovely." Frank Alfero winked at Mo. "You read my mind."

"I try." She smiled and offered us all food.

"My daughter." One of the men whose name escaped me began chomping on the shrimp. "She is very beautiful." He nodded. "Would make a good wife."

"He's married," Mo said through clenched teeth.

"Oh…" The man held up his hand. "I meant no offense."

"Of course." Her smile was syrupy sweet.

"Mo." Sergio walked up to her and wrapped his arm around her shoulders. "Why don't you go put that down and get some food in your stomach."

"Oh." Her brows furrowed. "Okay."

"I'll take it." Sergio sent her on her way and elbowed me while nobody looked. Bastard.

"An attentive spouse is hard to find." The man lifted his cup to Sergio. Hell. No.

"Isn't it though?" He tilted his head and walked off, which probably saved his life considering I was contemplating about a thousand different ways to strangle him with my bare hands.

"The Commission." Frank cleared his throat. "Should be good for us old men to discuss the new bosses."

"It should."

They continued to talk, boring me to tears, I tried to appear interested. When the conversation shifted to the Nicolasi family I excused myself and went into the kitchen.

Mo was sitting on one of the barstools laughing while Sergio lifted a grape to her lips.

Was he freaking kidding me?

"Eat," he commanded.

Mo rolled her eyes and took the grape from his hand popping it into her mouth. Good girl.

She reached for another one, her hand colliding with his. Bad girl, bad, bad, girl. Jolting back, she apologized.

"Never apologize for holding my hand," he said sternly.

She wasn't holding your hand jackass, she was reaching for a grape!

"You're beautiful."

What right did he have to tell her that? My blood boiled as he tucked a piece of hair, my hair, behind her ear and leaned in.

"Sergio," I said in clipped tones. "Frank needs you."

"You're sure?"

"Go." I barked.

Slowly, Sergio pulled away from Mo and walked by me, but not before bumping my chest with his shoulder. Yeah keep that up dude, we'll see who ends up dead by morning.

Mo got up from the stool and started collecting dishes. Her dress hugged every angle of her body like a second skin. Then she bent over the counter, nearly sending me into a fit of hysterics as the dress rose to her ass.

"Mo," I groaned. "You need to go change."

Her hand hovered over some of the dishes, I could see every muscle in her body tense before she turned and shrugged a shoulder. "I like my dress."

"That—" I pointed. "—is not a dress and you know it."

"Oh yeah?" She turned fully to me, propping her hands on her hips. "What else would it be?"

"Lingerie?" I offered. "I mean if your goal's to get every guy in this room salivating over you while I watch, then by all means go for it, but don't come crying to me when one of them corners you and tries to rip that sorry excuse for a piece of clothing from your body."

With a gasp she put her hands over her mouth, tears filled her eyes.

"Mo—" My voice cracked. "I won't ask again. It looks... desperate." Lies, all lies, she looked beautiful, and I couldn't be in the same room with her, couldn't even concentrate on breathing in and out if she was going to keep walking around like that. I was ready to murder any guy who looked at her, even the ones I knew that were half blind because of age.

"You should go." Her voice shook. "Now."

"Mo—"

"Please."

I took a step towards her and another, and another, until I was inches from her face.

Make it real! Phoenix's voice blared in my head. "You have to make them believe it or you're sentencing them all to death."

"Fine," I seethed, baring my teeth. "Wear whatever you want it's not like I care anyways. You were just a little crush... something to..." I grinned, hating myself. "Pass the time with. But now that I've had you... hell, who cares if they all want to try a sample."

With a cry she slapped me across the face once then backhanded me. I let her. Better she hate me, better she believe me, better she be alive.

"I hate you."

I leaned in until our lips almost touched. "Good."

She stormed past me in tears. I leaned against the counter, letting my head fall slack as my stomach churned with anger and sadness.

"Ouch," Phoenix said behind me. "I didn't say to destroy her, just to make her believe it."

"Not now." I snapped.

"Bee's hanging out with Trace and Mil. You better hope they don't get their claws too deep. Oh, and Nixon wanted me to tell you it's time for dinner. The men want you to say the prayer."

I snorted. Right, I was going to talk to God in front of the men I was supposed to kill; that wasn't sacrilegious, no, not at all.

"May God have mercy on my soul," I muttered.

"He better..." Phoenix followed me out of the room. "Because I've done way worse than you and I'm still hopeful that I won't rot in Hell."

"Aren't we all?" I breathed taking in each of the faces I

was going to eventually betray. "Aren't we all?"

CHAPTER FORTY-NINE

*The Cosa Nostra asks only two things, loyalty and silence. How
appropriate considering one would die without both.*

Tex

I WENT INTO THE DINING room expecting to sit next to Nixon,
not to my horror, to be seated at the head of the table. Damn,
but they were already grooming me; preparing me for the role
I never asked for but had no choice to take.

With confidence that felt so fake I wanted to roar, I made
my way to the head of the table and stood, taking time to
glance at every face. Around forty people were seated at the
table. From made men in the Nicolasi clan to associates, to the
Alferos.

And they were all looking to me—even Nixon. Though
his gaze could be considered more of a mild curiosity than
anything. Damn, but I would have loved for him to bust my
ass and boss me around at that point, but he'd been right
earlier. They all had. Stepping up was the only choice to keep
everyone safe, so he wasn't interfering, and I both hated and
loved him for it.

"Omerta, my men of honor." I lifted my wine glass. "It is

humbling to sit before you, to take my birthright back from the grips of insanity, to claim what's been rightfully mine for over twenty years. I pledge my loyalty, will you also toast to yours?"

Every glass lifted.

Sealed.

Done.

Even Mo, with shaking hands had lifted her glass, and it freaking killed me inside to watch her toast to something so menacing. It was like cheering for the dark side knowing damn well the story wasn't going to have a happily ever after.

"*Salud!*" The men cheered.

I sat as plates were passed around. My gaze couldn't help but flicker to Mo, but each time I looked at her, she was drawn into herself.

That is until Sergio made her laugh. Again.

Then touched her leg. Once, twice, a third time.

I gripped my fork.

"You alright?" Luca whispered from my left. "If I was a suspicious man I'd say you were... jealous?"

"Luca." I turned to him, my eyes cold as death. "Shut the hell up before I stab you with my steak knife."

His grin was wide and unwavering. "Campsi's, so blood thirsty."

"Nicolasi's, so... strategic," I hinted.

His hand paused mid-air, his wine lifted to his lips but he didn't sip. "If you mean to accuse me of something, speak plainly."

I shrugged. "Just... observing."

"And what do you see? Hmm?"

Phoenix said we could trust Luca... I hated that he was probably right, because I really didn't like the guy. In fact, I wouldn't shed a tear if he suffered a stroke, heartless or not, the guy was... slick.

"I see an alternate ending," I said quietly. "One I control."

"And if you lose that control?"

"Then we all lose."

"And if you win?" His eyes took on a dark hue as he leaned forward, his dark hair in direct contrast to his bright eyes. "What happens then?"

"Your plan succeeds."

He threw his head back and laughed. "Bravo."

"Luca?" Frank asked from across the table.

"Lovely wine, just... the perfect amount of spice, don't you think gentleman?"

I lifted my glass and stole another glance at Mo. Sergio was touching her hair—again.

And then he wiped something from her face.

I let out a growl and threw my napkin onto the table.

Nobody paid attention to me, but Mo saw the movement, so did Sergio.

I couldn't make a scene, but I was about to. I was three seconds away from ruining everything because the bastard couldn't keep his hands to himself.

The hour went by like slow torture, every laugh from their side of the table had me dreaming about murder, every touch drove me to the edge of insanity, and every time she looked at me with those hurt eyes, was like getting shot in the heart with acid soaked bullets.

"Gentleman." Nixon stood. "Whiskey and Cigars are waiting in the billiards room."

Everyone stood; myself included, and began filtering out the door towards the billiards room. When Sergio made his way around the table, I grabbed him by the hand, squeezing and whispered, "Make a sound and I'll break your fingers, starting with your pinky."

He rolled his eyes but didn't say anything. You know something's wrong when threatening a guy inflicts irritation rather than fear.

The girls all walked by in oblivion—all except Mo.

"Sergio?" Damn the girl was observant.

"Is none of your concern," I said smoothly. "We just need to have a little… chat. Man to man."

Mo looked down at our hands and the awkward twisting I was inflicting on Sergio's. She reached out as if to stop me and whispered, "Tex don't hurt—"

I gently pushed her away and dragged Sergio down the hall where no one could hear the sounds of bones snapping.

"Tex!" Mo charged after me, her scent wrapped around my head making me fuzzy. Kill, I wanted to kill him for touching her, this was no warning, I would end his life if any part of his body grazed hers again.

"You do not touch her." I spat in his face and landed a blow to his liver, not hard enough to kill him, just enough to make him hurt worse than if I'd just released a bullet into his skin. "You do not look at her." I slammed him against the hallway wall and punched him in the jaw. With a curse he toppled over, spitting out blood. I picked him up by the shirt and lifted him against the wall again, this time, my knee met his stomach with a sharp jab. "You do not breathe her same air. She isn't yours to take care of."

Sergio grinned, his smile bloody. "What?" Blood spewed from his mouth. "And she's yours?"

I dropped him to the ground and stabbed my finger in his chest, "Damn right she is!"

"No!" Mo shoved me from behind. "Leave him alone! At least he's trying to comfort me when all you've done is make me cry!" She pounded at my back with her fists. "I hate you! Do you hear me? I hate you!"

Sergio held up his hands, his lips twisting with contempt, before storming off. Mo continued her assault on my back. Once the hitting stopped, she started kicking me with her heels.

With a curse I turned around and picked her off the floor. I was going to lock her in her room until she calmed down, the last thing either of us needed was for any of the Family to see her or me in our current state of rage.

"I hate you!" She wailed, still trying to kick anything she could with those spiky heels.

When I kicked the bedroom door behind me and set her on her feet she charged towards me again, fists flying.

"Mo!" I ducked and grabbed her wrists. "Stop it!"

"No!" She jerked against me, tears streamed down her face ruining her makeup. "You don't get a say anymore! Not when you walk away! Not when you give up without a fight! You're weak! And I hate you for it! I hate you!"

My heart surged with anger at her words. Didn't she see I was saving her? Protecting her? With a roar I released her hands and picked her up again, tossing her against the bed, she bounced up once and wrapped her arms around me, maybe trying to choke me out, I wasn't sure. We fell to the ground in a heap. I tried to get up, but she climbed onto my back and kept hitting.

"Damn it, Mo!" I finally pried her free.

Huffing with exertion she bent over.

And I freaking lost my mind.

It was the only way to explain why, instead of running, I charged towards her and slammed her tight body against the wall hard enough for pictures to crash onto the floor. Her mouth was already open for my kiss when I began devouring her. My hands pinned her wrists hard above her head—it wasn't enough. With a growl I lifted her off the ground, she gripped my hair with both hands for balance and moaned as my teeth ripped at the front of her dress.

Everything inside of me snapped as my mouth watered at the taste of her—like an animal, I ripped the front of her dress down and set her on her feet only long enough to tug the infuriating piece of clothing away from her body.

She stumbled out of the dress and slapped me across the face.

I rubbed my jaw and smirked. "Do that again, I dare you."

Her eyes heated as I gripped her wrist and jerked her against me, our mouths molded together, hot and needy. I reached for her bra and unsnapped it, Mo reared back, bearing her teeth.

"Bite me, and I'll just enjoy it more." I kicked her bra away from us and waited, my chest heaving with unchecked desire.

Mo's eyes flashed and then her nails were digging into my neck, she scratched down to the collar of my shirt and with a rip tore it open, buttons went flying. I couldn't have cared less. The woman freaking drew blood with those nails as my shirt was flung to the floor.

Her hands dipped into the waist band of my pants, tugging me closer to her. With at tilt of her head, our mouths collided again, this time slower, more tortuous. She licked my lips with slow languid movements; swear the woman was mimicking sex with her mouth. With her hands she was doing things at my waist, the feathery touch of her fingers trailing along my skin left scorching heat in their wake.

For the first time in days I felt—I felt everything.

All it once it was like an explosion ringing in my ears, I wanted to close my eyes to the feeling of it all—I'd been numb after meeting with Phoenix, and now I was alive—bleeding and alive.

Mo pulled back, and I realized she'd unfastened my pants. With a feral glaze in her eyes, she jerked them downward, flinging them to the floor. I stepped out of them nearly stumbling as I pulled her into my arms again, my hands digging into her hair and pulling so tight she winced.

Her head fell back, exposing her neck, and I took full advantage, sucking her skin all the way down to her collarbone—one of my favorite places.

Her breasts teased my chest and her nipples hardened to

rigid pebbles.

My hands hooked around her hips and lifted her into the air tossing her onto the bed.

As I slid off my boxers, I crawled slowly up her body, licking, tasting, and biting my way up her leg until my head was next to her thigh. Shivering she arched her back and let out a little moan.

And I lost it, for the second, third, maybe fifth time that night.

Making her scream was my only goal.

Damn I was going to go to Hell for walking away after this—but I couldn't... she was my drug—my sweet addiction—and I needed a fix more than I needed another breath of air.

"Tex!" It was the first time she'd spoken to me since I'd scolded her. Eyes wide open she pushed against my chest. "I still hate you for what you're doing."

"Good." I kissed inside her thigh and reached up to tug her body closer to mine. "Hate me in a few minutes—love me now."

Her eyes took on a dark hue before flashing again as I gently slapped her leg and smirked.

The woman reared up and bit my lip.

Damn if I didn't love that.

"Scream for me," I whispered against her mouth tasting blood. "Only me, not him... not anyone else. You're mine. Make me believe it."

With a cry I thrust into her while simultaneously jerking her body down by her shoulders, staking my claim once and for all. She took me in and then tightened her muscles, squeezing herself around me, gripping me in the most intimate way I'd ever experienced. The abrupt sensation had me arching backwards, my body unsure if I wanted more or less.

She moved underneath me, rocked her hips a little.

More, definitely more.

Sharp nails dug into my back, beckoning me to pump harder and harder until I was out of breath, until all I saw was Mo—until she was my whole world—my existence.

Her muscles constricted around me, so tight it was all I could feel, her entire body taut. With a cry she pulled me down to her, our mouths meeting somewhere in the middle as her tongue tangled with mine.

And then she moaned, gently, in my ear.

And I was done—so done.

Finished.

The end.

We looked at each other—both of us naked and panting and I said the one thing I knew no guy who actually loved someone should ever say. "We can't do that again."

CHAPTER FIFTY

A woman scorned is a woman no man — Mafia or not — wants to deal with.

Phoenix

I SIPPED THE WHISKEY and winced. You know something's very wrong when you're unable to drink the pain away — when you feel so numb that the alcohol may as well be water dripping down your throat. I set the glass on the table and got up to stretch.

The men were in deep conversation about The Commission — something I really wanted to stop hearing about, all things considering.

"I'm going to go check on Bee," I whispered to Luca and slapped him on the back.

He nodded once and returned to his conversation. Funny, Luca was the last guy on this planet I thought I'd align with. He'd tried to kill me when he'd first met me, weird how my murderer turned out to be my savior — more of a father figure than my own.

I scratched the back of my head and walked into the living room where the girls were having wine.

Bee was sitting in the corner, listening politely. Every few seconds she'd tilt her head and sigh, I knew that look. Insecurity at its finest, she wasn't sure how to act or what to do. She crossed and then uncrossed her legs, took a sip of water, and looked down at her hands.

"Bee," I called. "Come here."

She jolted from her seat and walked towards me. I ignored the sway of her hips just like I ignored the vanilla swirling around my nose. "Are you okay?"

"Why?" She crossed her arms. "Are you going to take me away now?"

"No."

"I'm bored."

I pressed my lips together in annoyance. "I'm not your entertainment."

Bee gave me a one sided shoulder shrug and looked up through half-lidded eyes. "Do you want to be."

"Stop." I swallowed convulsively.

Her eyebrows pinched together in mock innocence as she reached out and touched my arm. I jerked away. "Stop what?"

"You know exactly what I'm talking about." We'd had this discussion numerous times. I didn't do girls, I didn't fall prey to her pouty lips or her swaying hips, no matter how many times she tried. I wasn't a toy for her to toss around just because she wasn't getting her way.

With a pout she crossed her arms. "Come on, you have to be curious. All those long nights watching me sleep..." Her hand reached out, fingers tickled my forearm as she caressed. "Did you ever wonder what face I saw in my dreams?"

My teeth clenched together as I looked away. "No. Now stop. I'm not taking you home yet, not when Tex still wants to talk with you."

"You're a bastard," She hissed.

"Thank you." I stepped back.

With balled fists she let out a low growl and stomped on

my foot with her giant-ass heel then marched past me.

Instant agony radiated up the top of my foot to my ankle. I forced a smile through the throbbing torture. My toe was probably broken; somehow Bee had managed to wedge her stiletto on top of my big toe rather than between my toes. Great. Just add a limp to the rest of the drama going on in my life.

"You okay?" Trace came up beside me and put her hand on my arm.

I tensed, hyperaware of every single finger that was pressed into my skin. Everything about her reminded me of what I was, what I'd done. Bile rose in my throat as I let out a small groan of irritation at my own weakness. I couldn't control my mind as images of her broken body flashed through my head. I was worse than the devil—I *was* the devil.

She dropped her hand and looked down. "That looks painful."

"That's not pain," I whispered looking down the hall were Bee had disappeared. "Real pain isn't getting shot, or stepped on, or kicked, or punched. Real pain isn't something tangible, you can't see it, can only feel it as it wraps it's hands around your neck and slowly chokes you to death, it follows you everywhere tortures you with every waking moment, giving you no peace. Pain is allowing yourself to feel guilt, shame, sadness, and even love. Trace, that's what hurts a person. My foot? That's nothing compared to hearing girls screams every night I go to bed." I looked into her eyes. "Or seeing your face every damn day. That's real pain."

Trace's brown eyes welled with tears, long lashes blinked trying to hold the water in as her gaze stayed focused on mine.

She couldn't fix it—I didn't want her to, but at least she knew I was sorry, more sorry than I'd ever be, so sorry that to stand by her was the worst pain of all because it was a constant reminder of the sickness that had stained my soul and taken control of my actions.

"I'm sorry." I shoved my hands awkwardly in my pockets. "That was uncalled for."

"No." She shook her head slowly. "I think it was the right thing to say."

I licked my lips and nodded, feeling my cheeks stain with embarrassment at what I'd just shared.

"Hey." Chase appeared and slapped me on the shoulder. "Either of you two seen Tex? Some of the guys are leaving and wanted to say goodbye."

Trace angled her head. "Last I saw he was pushing Sergio down the hallway."

"Oh good." Chase nodded. "Another body I'll get to bury."

Trace winced.

"He's kidding." I rolled my eyes. "Just saw Sergio, he looks like shit, I haven't seen Tex though."

"Maybe he's in his room…" Chase looked behind him.

"Or Mo's." I grit my teeth at the possibility. He'd better not be anywhere near her, unless he was making her believe he was a disinterested bastard with a heart of stone.

Chase grinned. "Horny little bastard. Alright, I'll go check."

He ran off leaving me alone with Trace again.

"Wine?" She held out her hand.

I wanted to take it; instead I stared at it for what it was, a peace offering, one I didn't deserve.

"It's just a hand Phoenix."

"No." I grasped her fingers. "We both know it's really not."

CHAPTER FIFTY-ONE

You may as well have killed me.

Mo

MY HANDS TIGHTENED into tiny fists. Without warning him, I sent off a right hook, slamming Tex in the cheek. His body moved to the side, barely. Blinking a few times he looked down and sighed. "I deserved that."

"You deserve a swift kick to the nuts."

"For having sex with you?"

"For leaving afterwards."

"Mo, I never promised—"

Another punch, my knuckles started to bleed as I wailed on him a third time. Finally he gripped my wrists above my head.

"Stop!" he growled.

I bucked against him, wrapping my arms around his waist. With a moan he lowered his head to mine. "Do that again and you're just going to get more pissed with my next actions."

"Go," I whispered hoarsely, injecting all the venom of my hatred for what he'd become into the one word. "Before I pull out my gun and give you a better reason."

Swallowing, Tex nodded and kissed me softly on the forehead. I nearly burst into tears, probably would have, if the door hadn't been flung open.

"Son of a bitch!" Chase yelled, slamming the door behind him and charging towards Tex.

Tex stumbled away from me as I pulled the bed blankets up to cover my nakedness.

"You're lucky I'm not Nixon," Chase seethed pushing against Tex's muscled chest. "He'd put a bullet in your head."

"And what are you going to do?" Tex took a step towards him. "I'm the freaking godfather, killing me is like writing your own death sentence."

I gasped at the truth of his words. What type of monster was Tex turning into? To say that to his best friend? To challenge him in such a way?

Chase chuckled. "Who the hell said anything about killing?" He moved so fast my eyes almost didn't track him. Tex was on his back in seconds. Chase hovering over him, delivering blow after blow to Tex's face. When Tex raised his arm to ward off the blows, Chase went in on Tex's ribs, right left, right left.

And Tex let him.

"Chase, stop!" I wailed. "You're going to kill him!"

"No." Chase drove his fist into Tex's side. "I won't."

"Chase!"

The door burst open again; this time it was Phoenix. With a curse he ran to the guys and pulled Chase from Tex's bloody body. Chase still tried to lunge for Tex but Phoenix had his arms pinned behind his back.

Tex pushed up to a sitting position, blood tricking from a cut to his left cheek. One eye was already beginning to swell shut. "That all you got, Chase?"

With a roar Chase elbowed Phoenix in the stomach, twisting his arms out of his grip and dove for Tex, this time

ELICIT

jumping into the air as his fist landed against Tex's temple.

He crumpled to the floor.

He hadn't even defended himself, and Tex was a relative giant; he could have, easily.

But that hadn't been a Campisi taking the hits, that was Tex, *my* Tex. He'd felt guilty, and he'd needed to feel the pain as a reminder. I knew that about him, knew he was taking physical punishment for the emotional damage.

"Enough!" Phoenix roared. "Chase, leave."

"No." Chase heaved, wiping his hands on his shirt. "Not until—"

Phoenix sighed, reaching to the small of his back and withdrawing his gun then pointing it at Chase. "I said leave."

Cursing, Chase stomped out of the room while Phoenix put his gun away and slowly walked over to Tex.

"Is he okay?" I squeaked.

"I hope it was worth it." Phoenix ignored my question.

I reared back. "Worth it?"

"Sleeping with him. I hope it was good, because he's going to have a hell of a headache and most likely two bruised ribs."

I choked on a sob, covering my face with my hands. "Nothing's worth him getting hurt over."

"Then stop." Phoenix's voice was hoarse. "Stop hurting him, Mo. Stop making him turn into something he can't be. Stop dreaming he's going to come back and save you. There is no white horse, there is no happy ending in this story, alright? You aren't one of the lucky ones and I'm sorry that I have to be the one to tell you that. But in no way is that man." He pointed at Tex. "Going to say screw it to his own family in order to marry you."

"He could though." I fought the doubt in my head. "I could stay married to him, I could help align the families, like before. You said—"

"Forget what I said," Phoenix snapped. "This isn't a

253

game, Mo! People's lives are at stake. What if I told you it was Chase or your brother, would you pay attention then? Hmm?"

I shook my head in an effort to fight the truth. "You're lying."

"Am I?" Phoenix threw his hands up into the air. "What could I possibly gain from a lie? When the truth is so damning!" He bit down on his lip and placed his hands on his hips. "Mo, you need to stay out of it. Let him go, if you don't..."

"If I don't?"

Phoenix turned away from me, his face like ash. "Imagine a world where a husband is forced to kill his wife. Imagine a world where a brother is forced to watch his sister get raped. That's the world you live in, Mo. That's the world his father—" He jutted his finger towards Tex. "—created. It's his legacy, that's what Tex has to fix. That's what he has to protect everyone from. If he fails to gain the allegiance of Alfonso's men, if he fails in any way to gain the allegiance of the other families, if he shows weakness, that's the legacy you'll be allowing to live, and if for some reason he fails... we're all going to die."

Tex stirred with a moan.

Phoenix knelt down to his side and shook his head. "I won't tell you again, Mo. Leave him alone. Go get dressed, I won't watch. Let me know when you leave and I'll go about getting him cleaned up."

Slowly, I rose from the bed and quickly slipped on a pair of yoga pants and a sweatshirt.

"Also." Phoenix didn't turn around. "I need you to get Nixon."

"But—"

"Mo." Phoenix's voice was harsh, edgy. "Get Nixon."

Getting Nixon meant he'd know what happened and I knew I looked like I'd just been with someone, the room smelt like us, I smelt like him. Tears threatened as I walked down the hall and into the Billiards room.

"Nixon?" I pasted a fake smile on my face. "Can I talk to you?"

He flashed a smile. "Of course."

That same smile stayed firmly in place until he reached the door, his fingers dug into my arm as we walked swiftly down the hall.

"What's going on?" he asked smoothly, as muscle ticking in his jaw as his teeth clenched harder.

"Chase almost killed Tex."

Sighing, Nixon looked up at the ceiling and crossed his arms. "For the hell of it, or was there good reason?"

"Oh, there was a reason." Chase stumbled out of the bathroom, his hands a bloody mess. "He slept with Mo."

I took a step back as Nixon took a menacing step forward.

I jutted my chin forward in defiance as I challenged him with a glare. "He's my husband."

"Funny you should say that." Chase crossed his arms. "Because when you were both busy ripping each other's clothes off, the deal was just getting signed."

"Deal?" Fear spread through my body like ice. "What deal?"

"An alliance," Chase scoffed. "What? He didn't mention it to you?"

"What type of alliance?" I asked knowing I probably didn't want to know the answer.

"The most powerful family in Sicily is the Campisi clan... the second most powerful, Nicolasi."

"So?"

Chase shook his head. "So do the math."

"Nixon?" I pleaded.

"He's going to marry into Nicolasi; it's been decided. I told them how I altered the marriage records between you two to protect him from the hit. Luca's drawing up the new contract later this evening—they want it a done deal so they have a joined front at The Commission."

My heart dropped to my knees. Nixon kept speaking but I couldn't make out any words, just white noise. Tex knew. He'd known the whole time and he still did what he did... he knew my heart would be broken but he broke it anyways. He broke it with the full knowledge that I'd never forgive him, never be able to come back from this moment. We all have those instances in our lives, where something big happens, where we have a choice to react and let that something big define us or mold us. I had no idea what I was going to do. All I knew was that I couldn't envision myself ten years from now healed. I didn't see a future anymore. All I saw was black—all I felt was fear.

Gasping I put my hands over my mouth and let out a little sob. The pieces fell into place, why he'd said goodbye, why he was cutting off all communication. And finally, why he'd let Chase almost kill him.

Shaking, I tried to move away from Nixon but my feet wouldn't budge, instead my knees knocked together as I bit down on my tongue until I tasted blood.

"Mo." Nixon grasped my elbow. I jerked away from him, my eyes downcast, focusing on the hardwood floors.

"Is everything okay?" Luca's accented voice pierced the haze of shock.

"Fine." Nixon answered just as a noise sounded from the end of the hall. Phoenix walked slowly around the corner, Tex's heavy body leaning on him as they made their way towards us.

It all happened at once. Nixon reaching for me, Chase doing the same, Luca touching my other arm.

With a hoarse cry I pushed at Nixon and pulled the gun from its holster strapped to his chest, inside his jacket.

With shaky movements I pointed the gun at Tex and screamed, "You bastard!"

Phoenix froze as Tex lifted his head, his face a mask of confusion and blood. "Mo…"

"No!" My hand trembled as I pressed the barrel of the gun to his muscled chest. "How could you?"

"Mo this isn't the place to—"

He flinched and licked his lips as I jammed the gun harder against his body. "What? Air out our dirty laundry? Tell everyone that about fifteen minutes ago we were naked? Oh, I'm sorry, when would be the right time? How about after I find out you're marrying a Nicolasi bitch just to align the families!"

Tex paled, his mouth dropped open, then closed, then opened again. "Mo, it wasn't a sure thing. I didn't—"

"Shut up!" I wailed, shaking the gun harder against him. "You don't get to talk. You don't get the satisfaction of apologizing, and I'm sure as hell not forgiving you, not now, not ever. We. Are. Done." I wanted to pull the trigger. I wanted him to hurt as bad as he hurt me, but I couldn't. No matter how much I hated him, I still loved him. My heart wouldn't let my finger squeeze. So instead, the gun fell from my hands and clattered to the floor. "Move."

Tex and Phoenix stepped apart. I walked through them, head held high. Screw him, screw all of them! I was done, so done.

CHAPTER FIFTY-TWO

Violence breeds more violence. Always.

Phoenix

EVERY MUSCLE IN TEX'S body was taut, waiting to spring into action. It took every ounce of strength I had, to hold him in place and keep him from running after her.

I hated that everything was working out so well almost as much as I feared the opposite.

"Well." Luca's eyebrows shot up in surprise. "That was interesting."

"Sorry." Tex muttered.

Chase swore, shaking his head in disgust. "I'm not."

"Tex." Luca barked. "You should say goodbye to the men. Nixon, as the host you should leave with him and Chase, you look like hell, don't come out."

"Wouldn't even if I had to." Chase glared. "Besides, you're not my boss."

"I think I speak for bosses everywhere when I say... thank God." Luca hissed.

Chase rolled his eyes and went in the opposite direction. I pushed Tex forward. Nixon put his arm around Tex's shoulders and gripped his head, jerking it towards him as he spoke in hushed tones. Yeah, Tex was a dead man walking.

"So..." Luca pulled out a cigar and rolled it between his fingers. "Game." He stuck the cigar in his mouth. "Set."

"Match?" I offered him a matchbook.

Luca took the matches and grinned, cigar still sticking out. "I knew I could count on you."

"What's done is done."

"Not yet." His smile fell. "Not yet."

CHAPTER FIFTY-THREE

*Even if you're heartless — one still beats inside your chest. Irritating,
to say the least.*

Tex

I WENT THROUGH THE MOTIONS. I said goodbye to the men, I
shook hands, I accepted the cigars and drinks, I laughed like I
didn't have a care in the world and talked to them as if I truly
cared whether or not they all got shot at The Commission.

It was all a lie.

Because my heart wasn't in it.

My heart didn't even exist anymore. I'd already given it
away. I promised myself I'd make it real, and I'd done exactly
that. Only the joke was on me. I gave her everything, knowing
there was no turning back. Knowing that in that moment, in
her room, I was finally allowing myself to feel one last time,
what it was like to be loved.

I knew the minute we were done that it was over.

I knew the future wouldn't include the love of my life,
but an arranged marriage with a strange woman who would
bring the Campisi family back into trusted circles.

Power, it was all about power. Being a part of the Mafia

was like being in a chess game where you had no idea if you were the queen or a pawn, until it was too late, until you lost the entire game or until you won.

I wasn't sure if I would win.

But I sure had to try.

"Hey." Bee walked up to my side and touched my arm. "Think we can talk?"

"Yeah." I said hoarsely. "Let's go out back."

I gripped her hand in mine and led her to the backyard. It was a chilly evening, but Nixon had turned the outside heaters on just in case the men wanted to go outside and smoke.

"So." She stood beneath the heater, arms crossed. "You're my brother."

My smile felt forced. I had no connection to this woman, no memory of her, she was a stranger, yet I'd die for her. The absolute madness that washed over me at keeping her safe wasn't even logical. I just knew I'd kill for her, without a second thought.

"That I am."

"You're tall."

"I ate a lot of spinach growing up," I joked.

She snapped her fingers. "Right, I was never one for vegetables, always fed them to the dog."

"Which is why you're smaller than me."

She grinned. "Yeah it has nothing to do with me being a girl."

"Woman," I corrected. "You're all grown up."

"Do you... ?" She chewed her lower lip and took a tentative step forward, her heels clicking on the wood. "Do you remember me at all?"

I sighed, scratching the back of my head. "By the time you were born I was long gone, Bee. I'm sorry."

Her brows furrowed for a minute. "Yeah, me too. It would have been nice to have someone to talk to."

Uncomfortable, I cleared my throat. "Well, I'm sure you

had friends, right?"

Her look was incredulous. "Friends? Brother dear, I had to look up the definition of that word when I was six and saw a TV show about a sleep over. Dad never took me anywhere. I'm pretty sure the only reason I lived was because Mom was so fiercely protective, didn't want to lose another child and all that."

Pain pierced through my chest. What would it have been like to have had a parent care so desperately for you? I didn't know. Would never know that kind of love.

A brief image of Mo flashed across my mind.

That was a different kind of love, and it was no more.

"Have you heard from her?"

Bee shook her head. "After Phoenix took me into his protection I was cut off from the entire family... Phoenix was afraid Alfonso would try to use me as a way to get to you."

"Smart." I sighed. "I guess I owe Phoenix a lot. He um, he never touched you, right?"

Bee snorted with laughter. "You kidding? Swear, I asked him if he was gay every single day he was with me."

Yeah I bet Phoenix had hated that. "So, he didn't?"

Bee's cheeks stained pink. "He doesn't even see me."

Yeah, I highly doubted that. Phoenix may have been to Hell and back but he was still a man and my sister wasn't a child. Hell, I was having a hard enough time letting her wear a cocktail dress in public.

Clearing my throat, I looked away. "You'll stay here."

"Here?" She repeated "In Chicago?"

"Here." I licked my lips. "With me and the Abandonato's until I take my place."

Bee's shoulders slumped as she examined her nails, almost trying to appear indifferent about the whole thing. "So, is that what you're going to do? Follow in Daddio's footsteps and damn us all to Hell?"

"No," I snapped. "I'm going to fix it."

"But—"

"Leave it at that," I warned. "I'll keep you safe and I'll fix everything—all of it."

"So, you're Superman now?" Another step towards me and then finally she laid her head on my shoulder. "I always was fond of the cape."

"No..." I wrapped my arm around her. "Superman would find a better way to do what I have to do."

"And what's that?"

"Kill a lot of people."

"Oh." She didn't cringe at all instead she pressed closer to my side. "Just do me a favor?"

"Anything."

"Don't kill Phoenix."

At that I laughed. "Can't kill what the devil don't want."

She tensed.

"Did I say something wrong?"

"He's been good to me, even though he says I'm a pain in the ass, and maybe I am, but I just... I swear I'll kill you myself if you tell him this but..."

"Spit it out Bee..."

"He's the only friend I've ever had."

My heart shook with injustice as my arm clenched her tighter to me. Sad, when the killer becomes your friend, when the very devil is the only one keeping you company at night. What type of life is that? What type of childhood? When the darkness is your only comfort, your only warmth.

"I won't," I answered finally. "I won't kill him."

"Thanks," she breathed. "I mean if anyone should get the honor it's me, did you know he made fun of my shoes?"

"The absolute nerve."

"Right?"

"I'm surprised he's still walking."

"I did stomp on his foot."

"Mature."

"I thought so."

"Bee?"

"Yeah?"

"I don't know you well yet—but I'll protect you until I die, you know that right?"

She sighed. "Yeah, Tex. I know."

CHAPTER FIFTY-FOUR

Waking up alone is a very cold feeling even when sunlight burns your skin.

Mo

SUNLIGHT PIERCED THROUGH the curtains in my dark room. It felt warm, protective. I could almost believe I wasn't dead inside. I could almost imagine a world where Tex was lying next to me.

A world where the Mafia didn't exist.

And marriage wasn't used politically. Who was I kidding? I'd done the same thing in order to protect him. The only difference had been I loved him. I still loved him. Though hate was making a huge play at trying to trump that love. I never could quite understand how he could say he could never hate me as much as he loved me—he was doing a really good job of proving the opposite of that.

A knock sounded at the door.

Ignoring it, I put the pillow across my face and groaned.

"Mo." Mil stepped into the room. I could hear footsteps, ah she probably brought Trace with her. Fabulous. Both of them present to witness my inability to lift my head high enough to eat breakfast or walk down the hall.

"Get up!" Mil slapped my butt.

Trace sat on the other side of the bed and gave me a concerned look. "You need to shower."

"I'll shower when I'm ready." Which was never, but they didn't need to know that. I still had his smell on me, I wanted to keep it that way. Visions of us together plagued my sleep until finally I just gave up and stared at the ceiling as images of Tex's smile flashed through my mind.

Trace sighed and lay down next to me. "Remember when I first came to Eagle Elite?"

I almost laughed out loud. Yeah I remembered, she was an absolute train wreck that girl. "Nixon was a complete ass to you, and I'm pretty sure Tex and Phoenix flipped you off to say hello, and don't even get me started on Chase."

"Chase was the nicest," Trace defended. "Good job catching that one, Mil."

"He's my prize bass." Mil lay down on my other side.

"I'm sure he'd be happy to be compared to an ugly fish." I said dryly, knowing Chase was way more vain than any of them gave him credit for, then again, it was for good reason. Not that I would admit that out loud. My eyes had always been for Tex.

No more.

"You saved me," Trace whispered. "I remember thinking you were insane." She chuckled. "But you were so strong, I mean you even stood up to Nixon, all I kept thinking was that I admired the person you were, wanted to have that type of confidence, you know?"

I fought the tears clogging my throat, making it impossible to breathe normally.

Trace kept talking. "When the guys bullied me, you made them stop, when Nixon fed me tofu, you got after him, and when I found out all the dirty little secrets you were never afraid, just accepted things and moved on with your head held high."

"I was a different girl then," I whispered hoarsely.

"Don't be." Trace reached for my hand and held it tight. "Don't let others change the person you've always been. So your heart's broken…"

I snorted wanting the conversation to end.

"So your life's a mess." Mil added.

"Are you guys trying to make me suicidal?"

Trace sighed. "So Tex is an ass."

"Truth." Mil agreed.

"So." Trace squeezed my hand tighter. "What's Mo Abandonato gonna do about it?"

"Lie in bed until I die alone?" I offered.

"Try again." Trace pinched me.

"Ouch!" I pulled away. "That hurt!"

"What are you going to do about it?" Her voice was stern as her eyes flashed. "When have you ever let the guys tell you how to live your life or what to do? Didn't you have enough of that with your dad?"

I reared back as if slapped. The woman knew too much. "This is different."

"The hell it is." Mil pushed up from the bed and crossed her arms. "I'm the head of a Family too. Tex is allowing them to pull the strings on purpose… haven't you been watching? Sergio's reaction to Tex? Phoenix's reaction to Sergio? Luca? Something isn't right."

"So what? We go all spy on their asses?" My eyes started to water with tears. "Guys, I'm done. I'm exhausted, my heart hurts… this is bigger than us. We can't just go all Harriet the Spy on them and then solve the War of the Families."

Trace tilted her head in amusement. "We aren't solving anything."

"Guys, thanks for stopping by but I think I'll stay right here."

"Tell her." Trace nodded to Mil.

Mil pulled out her phone and pressed play. Tex's voice immediately came into focus. "We stage a coup. We overthrow, make a big scene in front of The Commission." He paused. "You're talking about suicide, does anyone even know about this?"

"Luca invited Alfonso," Phoenix whispered. "You have to shoot him, there has to be a body count and it has to be bloody."

"I can do bloody."

"You'll have to hurt those you love... push them away for now, it will make it easier, you can't hesitate, it has to be real, Tex, do you get what I'm saying?"

"Does Luca know about this?"

"You know about this, I know about this, Luca and Sergio..." Phoenix swore. "Either they set me up to fail or they're testing me, not that it matters, I'm doing the right thing. This time, I'm doing the right thing."

"Horrible." Tex sighed. "When death is the only way to do right."

"Memorize the names, memorize the photos, you won't have a lot of time to react Tex. Remember, this is life or death."

The recording stopped.

Dumbfounded I stared at Mil and then Trace. "What does that mean?"

"We have a few theories." Mil cleared her throat. "I haven't shared it with anyone. I mean, I'm not an idiot. I love my brother, but my trust? It doesn't stretch that far, I've been tailing him, or my men have been tailing him. I just... I don't know Mo, when I told Trace, she said I should come to you. It's possible that things with Tex, aren't exactly what they seem."

"And if they are?" I asked the question they both were too afraid to whisper out loud, knowing that if it was true, he was lost to me for forever.

"Then," Mil said, shrugging, "he really does kill

everyone, turns to the dark side, marries some Nicolasi bitch with a giant hairy mole on her face and buck teeth, and we order a hit on her and make it look like an accident."

I laughed. Laughed for the first time in what felt like forever as Mil looked at me as if she was dead serious. I loved that girl. Just... loved her. "You get scarier the longer you're married to Chase."

"He's a really bad influence." Mil nodded, eyes wide. "So much violence in one body, impressive really."

"Gross." Trace held up her hands. "No more details." She turned to me. "So you gonna sit and pout all day or can we lure you out of the bedroom with talks of coffee and homemade cinnamon rolls?"

I perked up. "Chase baked this morning?"

"Chase bakes when he's stressed." Mil nodded. "Or not getting any."

Trace groaned in her hands.

Mil threw up her arms. "I was tired! Last night was draining, I said no, sue me, at least you get rolls out of it."

"We all win." I nodded triumphantly. "Thank you for your sacrifice, Mil."

"Welcome." She grinned and pulled me in for a hug. Trace wrapped her arms around both of us.

"It will be okay," Trace said. "I promise."

"I hope you're right." I frowned. "I really do."

CHAPTER FIFTY-FIVE

When you don't get your way… tail a person and find out the truth.

Sergio

I TRIED TO HIDE the surprise on my face when Mo walked into the kitchen smiling. Chase's mouth dropped open; apparently I wasn't the only one shocked. Nixon kicked him under the table.

We all stared at the table, me at my coffee and then back up at Mo as she took a roll from the pan Chase just pulled from the oven, and stuffed it in her mouth.

Tex marched into the kitchen.

I shifted uncomfortably. Damn it was like watching a TV show. He stepped around Mo, careful not to touch her, poured himself a cup of coffee then came over and sat with us at the table.

Bee soon followed.

And then Phoenix.

I almost choked on my own roll when in silence, everyone continued eating their meal as if last night hadn't been complete and utter chaos.

"Next week is Christmas," Nixon announced not looking

up from his paper. "Chase you making Lasagna?"

"You know it." Chase lifted his roll into the air and took a large bite out of it, moaning as he chewed.

"Tex, you wanna help put up decorations, I think you should still be here... or are they shipping you off to Sicily right after The Commission?"

Nixon was officially fishing for information in the most upfront way I'd ever seen a man fish.

I leaned forward, noting how Phoenix did the same thing, both of us waiting for Tex's answer, both for different reasons. I was told to let the chips fall and I hated that I was putting faith in two men I really didn't like all that much.

Tex gave a non-committal shrug "Like they could ever tell me when or how I should leave." He smirked. "I can easily decorate your giant ass house Nixon... eyes closed."

Nixon chuckled and held up his coffee. "Well I would hate to break tradition. You know how Chase likes to pretend he's helping when really he's freezing his nuts off."

"It's masculine," Chase piped up. "Nailing shit to the house."

Mil rolled her eyes.

"So it's settled." Nixon set his coffee down, it clattered against the table. "The Family will all be together for Christmas. Breathing, alive, celebrating?" His eyes met Tex's.

Without as much as a flinch, Tex lifted his coffee into the air and smiled. "Of course, wouldn't have it any other way."

I almost groaned and dropped my head to the table allowing it to bang a few times just so I felt the pain.

What. The. Hell. Was Luca thinking? We'd be lucky to survive that long.

Four more days until The Commission and things weren't looking better. Campisi's clan would be there, not just Alfonso but all of them, Luca had made sure of it with his ridiculous invitation through Phoenix, which meant only one thing.

Either Alfonso survived or Tex survived.

Either way one of them would have to make an example out of the rest of the families in order to stay in power. The *Cappo di Cappo* didn't do small and if Tex truly wanted to see another Christmas, he was going to have to put on the show of a lifetime.

Luca had said to trust them.

I trusted no one but myself.

I had no choice but to drink my coffee and pretend to be ignorant of every side of the situation.

The girls easily fell into conversation with each other — everyone but Mo.

"So?" Bee directed her attention to Mo. "You think you can help me?"

"I'm sorry, what?" Mo licked her lips and shook her head. "Sorry, I'm tired."

"Shooting." Bee grinned happily. "Trace and Mil said they'd teach me, can you help?"

"Uh… sure." Mo set her coffee down. "That would be fun." When she reached for her coffee again it was at the exact moment Tex reached for another roll.

Their hands collided.

Awkward would be an understatement.

I decided to make it worse. Mainly because I could, and because after looking at the way Mo stared at Tex, I knew. She'd never be for me. I wasn't him, it was as simple as that.

Didn't mean I couldn't at least get in a good jab so he realized what a complete and utter ass he was. "So the girl you're going to shack up with." I cleared my throat. "You see her picture yet? Rumor has it Nicolasi girls are really… bendy."

Mo's face paled as Tex pushed back his seat and stood. "I couldn't care less."

"Well," I kept poking, "You are going to marry her, I mean the contract's been drawn up, and you'd be an idiot not to take the protection of the only family still in Sicily… right?"

He closed his eyes briefly before a cruel smile plastered across his face. Phoenix nodded his head to Tex and returned his attention to the paper.

"It only makes sense." Tex puffed out his chest. "The *Cappo di Cappo* marrying the Nicolasi clan, just think… we'd be unstoppable. Hell, the Alferos, De Langes, and Abandonatos combined couldn't out buy us, out weapon us, or stop us. I'm thinking…" He nodded and offered another smirk around the table as he walked into the kitchen. "I'm thinking it sounds good. Damn good, after all what type of leader would I be if I wasn't fully invested in all that power?"

Nixon clenched his teeth while Chase gripped his coffee cup so hard it almost splintered into his hands.

Phoenix, however, appeared indifferent.

"Good call," I finally said. "Abandoning the family that raised you in order to join the devil… how… typical of a Campisi."

Tex froze and then slowly turned his murderous gaze on me. I had the sudden urge to jump out of my seat and run. Like a complete coward. "They say a boss always has to order a first hit, Sergio. Don't make me an enemy, you don't want to know the pain I could bring you. The suffering, the absolute entertainment I'd feel at strangling you with my bare hands."

With that he walked off.

Chase let out a whistle and set down the paper. "Happy Sunday."

"God's day." Nixon added.

"I've got some prayer beads if you need them, Sergio." Chase nodded. "You know, just in case."

I rolled my eyes and leaned back in my chair.

What was Tex doing?

And why was Phoenix okay with it?

Hell, even if I did end up dead, I'd be okay with the situation as long as it was handled in a way that protected the family. What a completely morbid thought.

CHAPTER FIFTY-SIX

The Mafia by definition should say. "Happy Endings die here."

Tex

I HAD TO ADMIT, watching Sergio's shit-eating grin fall from his face as he turned the color of a ghost was probably the highlight of my week, maybe even my month.

With a grunt I punched the bag harder. I needed a way to get out my aggression, and sitting at the table with Mo, pretending not to care when she was staring into her coffee like it held the secrets to the world? Hardest damn thing I'd ever done.

Damn contract. I barreled my fist into the punching bag.

Damn Luca. Two roundhouse kicks. Another punch.

Sweat was pouring down my face.

"Did you get the text?" Phoenix scared the hell out of me as he walked into the weight room and held the bag. I continued punching.

"You mean the text with all the pictures?"

Phoenix nodded slowly.

"You know I have a good memory, man. Six of Alfonso's men are going to be dead by my hand come this Thursday."

"And the other fourteen?"

I paused, allowing myself to catch my breath before landing a right hook then a left to the bag. "They're all old."

Phoenix sighed. "Kind of the point, Tex."

I stopped punching and hung my head. "You're asking me to cleanse the old to make way for the new."

Phoenix released the bag. "How do you suck out poison? Fast or slow?"

"Why are we sucking poison?"

His eyes flashed. "Answer the question."

"Fast, you have to get as much out as you can otherwise the person loses time."

"So you shoot fast... you suck out the poison. The slower you go about it the more dangerous it becomes. Kill them all, Tex. Not one lives. That list, if it ever gets back to you, to me, to us?" he cursed and ran his hands through his hair. "It's almost like treason, you know?"

"Yeah." I chewed my lower lip. "I'm well aware of what we're doing."

"That's why they can't know." Phoenix grabbed the back with his hands. "Now hit."

Right, left, right, left, I hit until I was completely spent. Until sweat poured down my face into my eyes.

"Good." Phoenix stepped back. "Some of the targets will be out tonight. I'll text you the address. Watch them, memorize their movements, their mannerisms, even drunk they'll show you their tells. But don't let them see you."

"Got it."

"And Tex?" Phoenix stopped halfway to the door.

"Yeah?" I wiped my face with a towel. "If I'm in the line of fire... I won't hate you... just know. I would never hate you. Rather I die than any one of those bastards live."

I swallowed. "Phoenix... were they a part of it? I have to know."

"It's not a personal vendetta, Tex." Phoenix swore and

slammed the wall with his hand. "If it was I'd be the one doing the shooting. Just know... those men... they were with my father and with yours. If they don't die... that prostitution ring stays open. If they don't die, those weapons keep coming up from Columbia. If they don't die, it will be our heads. They won't stop until they've hunted us all down."

"I wish there were another way."

Phoenix let out a large exhale. "Don't we all?"

"One more thing."

"Dude..." Phoenix hung his head. "I'm tired."

"What would you do?"

He turned, his eyes pensive. "What would I do?"

"If you knew you only had four days to live."

Red stained his cheeks before he cleared his throat and rocked back on his heels. "Whatever I'd miss the most, I'd do every damn day until it was time."

"Even if it was twirling like a ballerina?" I joked.

"Right." Phoenix barked with laughter. "Especially if it was that, I could dance circles around you, don't make me prove it."

I held up my hands. "Nobody needs to see that."

He chuckled.

"I'm glad you're not dead, man."

His face turned serious. "Say that after Thursday."

I was quiet as he left the room. Only then did I whisper, "I will. I swear it."

CHAPTER FIFTY-SEVEN

And when you fall down... you pick yourself up... and try again.

Mo

I WASN'T USED TO LYING to people that I loved. Usually I only lied to people I didn't know. Decision made, I gripped the knives in my hand and strapped them to the inside of my thigh. I slid my black knit dress over my head and grabbed my over–the-knee Chanel boots. They'd always had a bit of space on the top so it was easy to sneak weapons. I'm sure clothes whores everywhere were proud of my accomplishment, slipping another two knives into the top, just in case.

I grabbed my black leather jacket and shrugged it over my shoulders, then cracked my neck.

My .45 was lying on the bed. With determination I pulled the gun into my hands and loaded it then pulled back the safety. I needed to be ready for anything.

Lastly, I looked in the mirror.

I didn't really recognize the girl staring back at me. She seemed afraid and I refused to feel afraid.

Inhaling deeply, I closed my eyes and focused on my own mission. If the guys were going to play blind to what was going on that left me and only me.

Regardless of where tonight led me, even if it meant I was stepping into my own grave, or maybe into the realization that Tex had never been mine to begin with? I'd at least have answers, I'd have peace knowing I had done every single thing I could in order to secure my happiness, my family's safety, and maybe even Tex's.

When my eyes opened.

I saw.

Me.

Mo Abandonato, twin to one of the most powerful mob bosses in the country, in love with the freaking Godfather, daughter to a slain bastard and best friend to the De Langes, I popped my neck, the Alferos, and the Nicolasis. God help me.

I would do my job.

After all, a made man is made by his first few kills, by his ability to pull the trigger without hesitating.

I was finally at that moment.

And it felt good. It felt freeing to let go of all the drama, all the heartache, and focus in on the bigger picture.

The Commission and Tex's sudden shift, along with his and Phoenix's plans.

I sent a quick group text to everyone telling them I was going out for a run and opened my window, jumping out onto the grass with a small thud.

Tex was getting ready to leave, that much I was sure of. I'd lied to the girls about shooting, knowing I would miss my chance to tail him if I stayed.

I ran over to the black Mercedes and jumped in. It was newer, not familiar to Tex who always saw me drive the Range Rover, even though the Mercedes was actually my car.

I quickly pulled out of our lot and drove around back so nobody would see me, then inched through the gate and waited at the end of our property, by the cows.

Within minutes Tex sped by in the Range Rover,

sunglasses on and attention totally focused in on everything straight ahead.

I smiled as one more thing clicked into place. I'd been counting on him driving the Range Rover. My plans would have been totally shot had he not driven that car.

A moment of pure genius had washed over me as I realized that the same tracker stupid Phoenix had injected into me was amongst all the gear Nixon had in the gun room, as I liked to call it. It was only too easy to slip one between the backseat of the SUV and download the app on my phone.

I waited a good five minutes before taking off.

And what do you know? Tex had stopped around fifteen miles later at a pretty upscale restaurant and bar called, Tapas.

I parked across the street a few cars back and waited. It was now or never and I had all the time in the world.

CHAPTER FIFTY-EIGHT

Too many men involved meant one thing. Elimination.

Tex

I WAS GOING TO OFFICIALLY kill Phoenix. The men I was supposed to be tailing? Complete and utter fools. No, really. They poured in and out of the restaurant, drinking, sucking down cigars like they didn't cause cancer and laughing loudly.

Each of them was too involved in conversation to even look down the street. Did they really think they were safe here? I didn't recognize any faces, though Alfonso did make an appearance once when he came outside to smoke a cigar and talk to the circle of men.

They were all in their late fifties to early sixties. It made me sick to think of what they were involved in.

It didn't bother me in the least that I'd be the one introducing them to the Devil. After all, they'd been in charge of one of the worst prostitution rings known to the Cosa Nostra.

It had started with the De Langes and I thought it had ended the night I killed my father.

I was wrong.

As Phoenix so nicely pointed out by way of Luca.

Two men were constantly reaching behind their heads, scratching at their upper backs, twitchy. Meaning, they were used to distracting with their hands while they used the other hand to pull out a gun. I made a note of it on the photographs I'd brought with me.

Another man's eyes were downcast as he tossed dice in the air, up and down up and down, waiting, ever so patiently. He'd be the first to pull a gun, the last to die. His movements were smooth, fluid.

Another man found everything hilarious—he was most likely drunk, stumbling all over the place and hitting people on the back, a slight limp made him an easy kill. Probably had a broken kneecap at one point in his life.

I continued watching, memorizing their movements like a musician would memorize music. That's what it was to me, watching people was an art, it was studying each breath, each step, each slouch. People were easy to read. They were my antelope and I was the lion.

Finally, most of them shuffled in after about two hours of constantly walking in and out of the restaurant. They'd most likely drink red wine, toast to what I'm sure they assumed was a new era for the Campisi family underneath Alfonso. After all, everything fell into place. They scared me into hiding—or so they thought, after threatening me and Mo, and by doing so, secured themselves an invitation with the rest of the American Mafia.

To them, it was finally a homecoming.

To me? It was a really fancy funeral.

Time to go.

I started the car and looked in my rearview mirror.

"Well shit." I licked my lips and slammed the steering wheel as I watched Mo. She was looking at my car and at the restaurant. My body shook with terror. She had no idea the danger she'd put herself in, or the absolute chaos that would happen if she were caught. Everything Phoenix and I worked for? Gone. Done.

I needed to draw her away from the restaurant.

With another curse I pulled out and started speeding towards my bar.

Mo followed at a fast pace but stayed a few cars back.

The minute I pulled up to the restaurant I peeled around the parking lot and parked out back, dust shot up from my sudden acceleration. Turning off the car with a jerk, I ran around the building and watched as she pulled in and looked around.

"Gotcha."

CHAPTER FIFTY-NINE

If you try to sneak up on a boss… make sure he isn't aware of it.

Mo

WHERE HAD HE GONE? I licked my lips and leaned over the steering wheel. His car could be parked out back, but that meant he was probably going inside the building.

I could go home.

But facing him sounded like a better idea.

So I swallowed the anxiety building inside of me and reached for the door handle, slowly pushing it open.

Until it was jerked out of my grasp.

And a menacing Tex was filling the space between me and the outside world.

"Have fun on your little stakeout?" he asked calmly.

"Did you?" I retorted.

He leaned his muscled arms against the top of the car and bore down on me. "Oh, I'm about to."

Before I could move or scream or do anything he jerked me away from the car and tossed me over his shoulder. I tried to reach for my gun but it was impossible with the way he was carrying me.

"Put me down!" I snarled.

Tex ignored me as he waltzed into the noisy bar and carried me through the main area towards the back.

"Everything okay, boss?" The bartender asked.

"Perfect." Tex's grip on my body tightened. "I may be a while."

Oh, hell.

I squirmed against him but it was impossible to move. I needed to wait until he set me down before I reached for anything.

Remembering all the training the guys had given me—specifically Tex, I let my body go limp in his arms.

With a grunt his grip released just as we stepped into a dark room, the door slammed behind us. I kept my body relaxed.

Tex's grip loosened even more as he set me on the floor, trying to steady me with his hands so I didn't fall over. I teetered towards him like I was going to pass out, then as fast as I could, I knelt and jerked two blades from each boot.

The lights were off as moonlight filtered through the only tiny window in the corner of the room. I could see Tex's teeth but nothing else. I backed away and held up the knives.

"Mo." Tex's gravelly voice sounded exhausted. "Put the knives down."

They flickered in the moonlight as he approached until I was almost back against the wall, the only place where the light was shining enough for me to see him and him me.

"You'll have to take them from me first," I sneered.

Tex's solid face cracked into a grin. "Oh sweetheart, I would love nothing more."

He moved so fast I almost didn't get out of the way fast enough as his hands came for mine. I fell down to the floor and sliced his jeans with each knife then rolled away. Dust caked my legs and boots.

Cursing, Tex looked down. "Mo, these were my favorite

jeans," he said in a sarcastic tone filled with mock hurt.

"I think I improved the look."

Tex lunged for me, gripping my hands and jolting one knife free while I held the other in my right. I twisted into him and used all my strength to hit the inside of his ribs. Grunting he stumbled back only enough for me to move a foot before he gripped my leather jacket in his hands. I twisted out of it, and reached for my gun with my left hand.

Tex threw the leather jacket to the ground and smiled. "Fine, you wanna play? You want to beat the shit out of me? Will that make it better, Mo? What the hell can I do that will convince you how much I loathe you?" His eyes flashed. "We don't exist anymore, Mo. Sorry but that's the world we live in. You think I wouldn't hesitate to kill you? You think I care if you hate me? So what? Hate me. So what? Shoot me. But at least make it a fair fight. Drop the gun, drop the knife, we both know I helped train you. Come on, Mo..." The more he taunted the more pissed I became, but I knew what he was doing, egging me on, using that as a tactic to get me to snap and spring at him so he could display my weakness.

Instead, I calmly put the safety back on the gun held it out in front of me and dropped it. It clattered to the ground along with my knife.

"Scared?" I asked holding up my hands.

"Girls with fists terrify me." Tex bared his teeth in a predatory smile. "Plus I hate tickle fights... you know this."

"I'll try to keep your balls attached, but I can't make any promises, Tex."

"Aw, can't have sex with me so you don't want anyone else to either?"

"Please." I snorted. "Like you could perform without my help."

He laughed and took a step toward me, raising his hands in a boxing stance. "Don't be pissed if I break your nose, Mo, but look on the bright side, you always wanted a nose job, right? Think of it as a step in the right direction… say it with me, plastic surgery."

"Never mind, the balls go." I shrugged. "Hope you're not too attached."

"Aw, baby, I think you're the one attached." He swung lazily in my direction, taunting me as we began dancing around each other.

"It's cute." I swung with my left then tried a knee to his ribs, he deflected with his hands, pushing me away.

"What is?"

"You're attachment to your manhood." I ducked as he swung at me again and landed a side kick to his right thigh. He winced but said nothing. I knew it hurt.

"Most men are, Mo. Most women are too, but hey, I got no complaints."

"Wanna hear 'em now?" I hit with my right fist and tried an upper hook, deflected at every turn, I tried a front kick then spun into a roundhouse.

He gripped my leg and flipped me on my back, hovering over me. "You're too slow."

"Am I?" I twisted my legs around his waist and flipped him onto his back, as I landed a blow to his cheek.

His head barely moved as a smile curved across his lips. "So what? I let you beat me and you feel better about being abandoned?"

"Why are you tailing those men?" I punched him again, my knuckles starting to hurt.

He grinned. "I'd die before telling you."

"So die." I grit my teeth and landed another blow to his temple before he gripped me by the waist and lifted me into the air, slamming me onto the cement then pulling me up like I weighed nothing.

"Why can't you just be a normal girl?" he raged pushing me against the wall, trapping me with his body. "Why can't you go cry and spend money and drink wine? Throw darts at my face. Why can't you be normal?"

I tilted my chin towards him and whispered. "You wouldn't love a normal girl."

His eyes shifted, his breathing ragged as his warm body pressed me harder against the wall. "I can't protect you if you keep following me."

"Who said I need protection?"

"Those men would rape you." Tex pounded his hand into the wall next to my head. "They would rip you apart limb by limb for as much as breathing their same air, you wanna keep tailing me? Fine, just don't expect me to be able to save you when they sell your body to the highest bidder."

Air whooshed out of my lungs. "Alfonso's men?"

Tex froze.

I quickly did the calculations. "Will they be there Thursday?"

"Mo." Tex shook his head. "Go home. Go to bed. This is done. I don't know how else to tell you without freaking losing my mind. We are done." His voice wavered. "We are nothing."

I stood on my tiptoes and gripped his face with my hands. "Liar."

His mouth opened.

And I kissed him.

CHAPTER SIXTY

Kissing the enemy is always a rush. It's why people do it.

Tex

MY MIND ONLY REGISTERED her kiss; nothing else existed, nothing else mattered. I gripped her elbows with my hands and slid her up the wall. I had nothing left, no control. There was nobody there to stop me, nobody there to tell me what to do.

And that's when it clicked.

I don't know how or why.

But by doing things Phoenix's way, I was still allowing myself to be a puppet. Used in order to put an end to something horrible.

But what if... I moaned as Mo's grip tightened around my neck, her hands dug into my hair. What if I trusted someone?

What if I trusted her enough?

What if I loved her enough?

"Mo." I gasped.

"If you say we can't do that again, I'm shooting you, Tex. I'm dead serious."

I laughed. I couldn't help it.

"Are you laughing at me? Swear I'll do it, Campisi."

"Cool your jets Abandonato." I set her on her feet and took a step back. The woman wouldn't stop. I'd done everything I could short of injuring her to get her to understand that we couldn't be together.

And here she was.

Nixon hadn't tailed me.

Neither had anyone else.

Mo. Leave it to Mo.

"So." She crossed her arms. "You ready to tell me why you're being such a jackass to everyone and going all storm trooper while everyone else is Jedi?"

"Admit it, I'd look like hell in white, Mo." I leaned back against the table and crossed my arms.

"Ah." She stepped forward and mimicked my movement, crossing her arms. "So this is about the Family color? No one's gonna be mad if you wear black, Tex."

I hung my head, my smile growing to epic proportions. "Yeah, I've really been losing sleep over it."

"Just think... all those sleepless nights, solved by one fight with me."

"Right." I swallowed. "Mo Abandonato, the answer to everything."

My eyes widened at the sudden idea popping into my head.

"What's up crazy eyes?"

I opened my mouth then closed it. "What if?"

"What if... what? The earth was flat?"

"You're a genius." I rushed towards her and grabbed her face, kissing her mouth so hard I felt her wince.

"Huh?" She almost tripped when I released her.

"Make it real." I laughed out loud. "Well damn, Phoenix, you could have just spelled it out for me."

"I'm Mo." She waved in front of me.

"Can Trace and Mil keep a secret?" I asked.

"Yeah." Her eyes narrowed. "I can too, you know."

"No secrets from you. Well, I mean one secret, but what I need to know, is this… how good of an actress are you?"

She put her hands on her hips. "I once convinced Nixon I saw dead people, and he believed it for two years."

"Good girl." I held out my hand. "Now, I need you to listen very carefully."

CHAPTER SIXTY-ONE
And the lies continue...

Mo

"ARE YOU READY?" Tex asked once we pulled up to the house. It was dark and I knew that Nixon was going to be pissed I'd been out so long. I'd texted him that I'd taken a drive after my run but I knew he was still going to unleash on me.

I popped my knuckles. "Yup, I can do this."

Tex laughed. "Right, more like you're going to really enjoy it."

"That too." I smiled. "Think of it as payback for breaking my heart."

"You know." He nodded. "If we weren't sworn enemies I'd totally love you."

"Aw." I elbowed him hard in the ribs. "I'd still hate you."

"Fine." He grinned.

"Fine." I chewed my lower lip.

With a curse he pulled me into the shadows and kissed me soundly, his mouth dancing with mine like it was meant for me, like he was meant for me. My heart hammered in my chest as he kissed each cheek and then kissed me on the mouth again, his tongue sliding past my lower lip only to retreat as he stepped back. "Yeah, good thing we're enemies."

I straightened my leather jacket. "Until the end."

He held out his hand and enclosed it around mine. "I'll hate you until the end."

I nodded. "Try not to cry."

Wincing, Tex stepped back. "I want to have kids someday, remember that, Mo."

"Can't make any promises," I sang. "Now let's go."

I walked in the house, fury etched in my every movement as the door slammed in Tex's face.

"Mo! Get back here! Now!"

"No!" I roared turning on my heel. "You sick bastard! How could you!"

Silverware clattered to the ground as every head around the dinner table was focused in on us. It seemed even Luca and Frank were visiting for a nice calm normal dinner.

Too bad, so sad.

Tex reached for my arm and pulled me roughly against him, I turned around and slapped his face so hard my hand stung. "Don't you dare touch me!"

"I'll touch whatever the hell I want." He grinned crudely. "You keep forgetting... I could own you if I want."

Out of the corner of my eye I saw Nixon stand.

"Aw, baby." I angled my head and threw a right hook to his face. He staggered to the side. "You wish."

Tex rubbed his jaw. "Well now I don't, hell you never brought that type of violence into the bedroom. I had no idea Mo... I could have totally tied you up—"

I slapped him again.

He gripped my hands. "Do it again, regardless, you're nothing to me. You, you're family, in a few days I'll be a distant memory."

I smiled sweetly. "Not if I kill you first."

"I'll sleep with one eye open."

"And one finger on the trigger, lover." I kneed him in the balls for good measure then stormed into the kitchen and poured myself a glass of wine. When Tex was done cursing I slowly made my way to the freezer and pulled out one solid ice cube. "I know it's kind of big considering what you got down there." I tossed it at his face. "But try to make it work, Campisi."

"You're lucky I don't shoot you for your disrespect," he sneered, batting the ice out of the air with his free hand.

"To kill me you'd have to kill Nixon, and Chase, and Sergio, probably Phoenix, definitely Luca, wow, bringing down all the families on yourself. That your big bad plan, Godfather? Make everyone hate you?"

"If I have to." He stood to his full height. "Besides, what's a few more deaths on my hands after Thursday? Hmm?"

With that he walked out of the room leaving me scowling in his direction.

Nixon was the first to speak. "Mind telling me what that was about?"

"Mind telling me why you didn't shoot him?" I fired back.

Nixon rolled his eyes. "Shooting Tex wouldn't help the rage, Mo, plus regardless of how awful he's being, I kind of need him to live for at least three more days."

"And after?" I asked.

"We'll pick straws." Nixon grinned.

Chase snorted. "Dibs on the short one."

"You cannot kill him." Luca slammed his hands onto the table, and stood. "He is the key to everything. You kill him and you sign your own death sentence."

Frank stared straight ahead, his mind appearing to work a thousand miles a minute.

Phoenix met my gaze, his eyes piercing, knowing. I rolled my eyes at him and gave him the finger. Let the countdown begin.

CHAPTER SIXTY-TWO

There is no truth, only suspicion.

Phoenix

"YOU DIDN'T FIND that weird?" I asked again. "Not weird at all?"

Sergio took a long sip of his wine and stared out the living room window. "Mo's always been a passionate girl and Tex, well, he's coming into his own. After Thursday..."

"You mean after everyone dies..."

"Right." Sergio shrugged. "Things will fall back into place."

I rolled my eyes at his back and walked off. He was too calm. If anything, that irritated me even more. He reminded me way too much of Luca, calm, cold, calculating.

I'd officially had enough drama for the evening. With a yawn I made my way to the guest room and stepped inside.

Bee was sitting on my bed reading.

"What the hell are you doing?"

She didn't look up, just turned the page. "Reading. Why what's it look like I'm doing?"

"You're in my bed."

"It's Nixon's house, Nixon's bed," she said in a bored tone. "Did you know that Edward's a vampire!"

Dear God, deliver me. This was my penance for being a bastard, torture by Twilight. Not okay. "You've been sheltered entirely too much, who gave you the book?" Name and social security number, if you please. I had someone to murder.

"Trace."

I held back a groan. There went that plan. "How... kind of her."

"He's so hot."

"You can't see him."

Bee looked up from the book. "In my head I totally can."

Rolling my eyes seemed childish but it was exactly what I wanted to do. "Please don't describe him. I'm tired and the last thing I want to talk about is fake vampires."

She sighed. "Your loss, man."

Man? What? Like we were bros hanging out now?

"Bee." I licked my lips and tried a different tactic, one that didn't have me sobbing and begging for her to get out of my room. "I really need to get some sleep."

She lifted a shoulder. "So sleep."

"In my bed."

She scooted over. Her vanilla perfume hit me full force with that simple movement. Clenching my fists, I took a few deep breaths. It didn't help.

Sweating, I croaked. "Bee, I sleep alone."

Finally, she put the book on the nightstand and crossed her arms, making her body look that much... better, if that was even possible, in her tiny tank top and shorts. "But when you protected me you stayed with me."

"To keep you alive." I clenched my jaw until it popped. "Trust me, you're safe here."

Her eyes welled with tears. "Please, Phoenix?"

Tears. I did not work well with tears and she knew it.

Sighing, I reached back and peeled off my shirt then

walked over to my dresser, pulling it open to grab a pair of track pants then slamming it shut. Without another word, I dropped my jeans to the floor and put on the pants then turned off the light.

"Thanks." Bee whispered. "I just—thanks."

She had no idea that her version of safe was deranged... almost sick. She was lying next to a rapist, next to a murderer, next to an absolute monster and yet, that was how she found peace at night. While, me? I found none. None at all. Not when I heard her finally succumb to sleep, or when her arm reached for my body, or when she curled next to me and sighed.

It was Hell.

And I knew she might sleep like the dead.

But I was a live wire. Staring wide eyed at the ceiling, telling my body it wasn't responding. Forcing my breathing to even out. And lying to myself once again that I felt nothing for that vanilla scented beauty asleep in my arms.

CHAPTER SIXTY-THREE

Waiting for death—not the best way to spend a sunny day.

Sergio

BY THE TIME WEDNESDAY night rolled around, I was ready to take a gun to Tex—or maybe even Mo. The fighting had gotten worse. How was that even possible? If anything Tex had turned from a cocky disrespectful little shit into a rage-oholic with a serious god complex.

When nobody poured him a cup of coffee he yelled at Mo to fix him something on account of women should serve their men—the bosses.

That earned him a punch to the gut and a threat with a knife. Swear Nixon almost unleashed on him, but we all knew, until Thursday there was nothing we could do, until things played out.

Tex was untouchable.

So I did nothing while he cleaned his guns in front of me then threatened to engrave my name on each bullet just to be sure.

Every time I approached Luca, he told me to leave it. Right, leaving it meant we were all dead, but I'd done everything Luca had asked me to. I'd done right by The Family. In the end, it probably wouldn't be enough.

Fighting erupted in the kitchen, groaning, I jumped up from my comfortable seat in the living room and made my way towards the yelling.

When I turned the corner I almost walked back to my spot, maybe if I ignored the problem it wouldn't be a problem?

"You son of a bitch!" Mo held Tex at knife point. "How could you even say that about us? About your family? We practically raised you!"

"Raised me?" Tex roared, his face contorting with rage. "I was your puppet! Nothing more than a pawn in a bigger game! You protected me so you could use me, just like you're using me tomorrow!"

"Tex." Nixon looked ready to snap as he took a tentative step forward pushing Mo to the side. "This isn't you, whoever keeps starting these fights, yelling, attacking Mo. This isn't the kid I grew up with. You forget, we were raised together."

"By your sick father." Tex scowled.

Nixon's teeth clenched as Chase slowly approached the group. "Actually my sick father, but details." He waved his hand in the air. "Tex, tomorrow, you end it. Tonight... can't we just imagine a world where you aren't pushing us away in order to distract us from the bigger picture?"

"What?" Tex hissed.

Chase and Nixon shared a look.

Damn, things just got interesting. And here I thought Nixon and Chase were just agreeing to Luca's terms because they had no choice. Leaning against the wall I crossed my arms and waited.

Tex's chest heaved with exertion as Nixon tilted his head, his eyes calculating. "You'll always choose Family, Tex. And that's fine, blood wins out, pretty sure we already had that conversation. But you should know one thing."

Tex rolled his eyes.

"We're brothers," Chase said in a low voice. "Blood does always win, but we've shared blood." He held up his palm. "All four of us." Phoenix flinched from his spot near the other doorway. "And that means that regardless of the choices you make tomorrow—you aren't joining the enemy—you're defeating him, because the minute you take your spot, you'll finally be home. But that doesn't mean we aren't still here, living, breathing, fighting for you."

Nixon slapped Chase on the back and zeroed in on Tex. "Fight all you want man, but we'll stick by your side until the end. Even if the end means our deaths. We aren't stupid. It's possible you'll have a choice to make tomorrow and if there's anything we've learned about Phoenix's situation, an honorable death is a good death.

"Nixon!" Trace half pleaded. While Mil stared at the hardwood beneath her feet, Mo had moved around the kitchen and was standing by the girls.

Tex seemed to be weighing his options as he looked around the kitchen and then a smile curved his lips as his gaze met Nixon's cold stare. With swift movements he walked until his nose was almost touching Nixon's. The tension was so thick I wasn't sure if I should intervene or just let things play out. I glanced at Phoenix out of the corner of my eye, his fists were clenched tightly at his sides, if there was going to be a fight... I'd have to save Tex, damn but that felt wrong. I had to keep him alive, at all costs.

Nixon's breathing was ragged as his eyes narrowed into tiny slits.

Tex grinned smugly then whispered, "*Volpe.*"

Not what I was expecting.

Nixon's eyes went wild as they darted back and forth and then with a cruel smile he reared back and punched Tex in the face.

Tex staggered backwards, blood streaming down his chin. He nodded his head once and sauntered down the hall cursing the Abandonato family the entire way.

I scratched my head in confusion. "Did he just call you a fox?"

Chase met Nixon's stare, they both turned to look at Phoenix who had gone completely still.

"What the hell am I missing?" I asked calmly.

Nixon sighed and then turned around. "Nothing worth discussing. The Commission is tomorrow, I suggest everyone get some sleep."

Too confused and tired to even prod further I threw my hands in the air and walked down the hall to my guest room. The minute the door closed I pulled out my cell and texted Luca:

Me: *Tomorrow's the day we find out what Tex is made of... Phoenix too.*

Luca: *Trust the plan.*

Me: *That's the problem, I don't trust anyone.*

Luca: *Maybe, it's time, you start. Have a good night's sleep, things will work out, they always do.*

Scowling, I typed back: *Absolute power corrupts, absolutely.*

Luca: *Absolute power corrupts, absolutely, only when we allow it. There is always a choice, Sergio. Never forget that.*

Too frustrated to respond I threw my phone against the bed and sunk low into the mattress, my head in my hands. I went through every strategy, every outcome, every plan I'd help Phoenix, Luca, and Frank formulate since the beginning. I'd done the best I could. I'd come out of hiding in order to make sure that the Family was secure, the only issue was, I felt like I had lost my humanity in the process.

I guess that was what happened when you're a death dealer.

With a grunt I lie back down on the pillow and tried to concentrate on a simpler time, when we were all kids, when war games were something we heard the adults discuss in hushed tones. When battles between families meant nothing to us, when power and greed were abominable.

That time was long gone.

And now, I was tired.

Nothing. I had nothing left.

I tugged out the piece of paper in my pocket and stared at it. My last will and testament. I sealed the paper in the envelope waiting for me on my desk. The most pathetic part was, I had no family to address it to. My own father didn't want me living, most my uncles were in prison, and I was stuck between wanting to keep the law, and having to break it. I had no name to put on that blank envelope, and it killed me inside that that was most likely my future. Lonely and blank. Never to be remembered. Some legacy.

CHAPTER SIXTY-FOUR

Risk… is always worth it. Or is it?

Tex

I HAD TO HAND it to Mo, she'd done a hell of a job. I only hoped it was enough for the guys. I was stuck between needing them to react tomorrow and also needing them to keep me alive.

It was a tug of war of sorts, treat them like absolute shit but drop the hint that there was a reason behind it.

A very solid, life altering reason.

Phoenix had said to make it real and I knew now, I knew why. I needed every reaction from them to be real, I was already risking too much with Mo knowing, but I hadn't been able to do it. Lie to her face again and again and again. It didn't help that I was absolute crap at hiding my feelings from her, each time she kissed me I reacted like she'd just set my body on fire. So it was impossible.

Funny, it had been her idea to drop the *volpe* hint. Damn, that woman was brilliant. My stomach clenched… now if only there was a way out of that contract with Nicolasi. Mo knew I couldn't back out, just like she knew I was going to have to hurt her in order to prove to the men I meant business.

A knock sounded at the window. I jumped out of bed and grabbed my gun.

Mo was grinning from the other side of the glass.

When I rolled my eyes, she held up a stuffed fox and pouted, her lower lip sticking out.

My smile grew and grew and grew, finally I opened the window and leaned out. "What up, Romeo you trying to romance me?"

"Yeah but you didn't have a balcony."

"So you brought a fox?" I nodded towards the stuffed animal. "A stuffed fox that's missing an eye?"

"Tragic washing machine accident."

"Ah." I took the animal. "I see."

"Can I come in?" Mo shivered and pulled her leather jacket closer to her body.

I stepped back and licked my lips. "They say keep your friends close and your enemies closer, so yeah, hop on in." I backed away more so she could pull herself up and into my room. She landed with a thud, turned and closed the window, followed by the blinds.

"Planning on killing me or something?" I pointed to the blinds and tossed the fox onto the bed. My bones ached, my heart ached. Every damn thing ached when I thought about it. There was no way I was going to get any sleep.

"Tex?" Mo whispered, her fingers grasped mine lightly. I led her to the bed and sat, patting the spot next to me.

"Yeah?"

"I have an idea."

I glanced sideways and frowned. "Okay."

"Shoot me."

My face froze in shock. "You want me to… shoot you?"

"Yeah." She nodded, her eyebrows pinching together like she was thinking too hard. "You have to make an example, right?"

I wasn't comfortable with where this was going. "Mo, I

can make an example without shooting you."

"Well you don't have to kill me!" Her words rushed out. "Just hurt me a little, I mean you were planning on slapping me, which is fine and all."

I groaned, officially the worst conversation in the world.

"But—" She licked her lips. "—I just think, it would make a bigger impact if you shot me, make it a shoulder shot, or even in the leg, I mean it didn't hurt that bad, and it's not like I died, right?"

My eyes closed tightly until they burned. "Mo, you're asking me to shoot you."

"I'm your enemy."

"Until the end," I whispered.

"Right." She gripped my hand. "Just... think about it, but don't tell me if you're going to do it, just do it... I don't want to know it's coming. My reaction has to be real, but Tex, you can't take on five heads, you can't take on that many men and survive, I think you should tell Nixon and Chase."

"Can't," I said hoarsely. "If anything gets back to them... it's their heads that roll. I can't handle that, Mo. It's bad enough that Phoenix, Luca, Frank, and even Sergio will be in trouble if it gets out. The plan was to keep The Abandonato family clean. The one family powerful enough to keep everything together if things get... bad."

Mo swallowed. "You should shoot Nixon too."

I groaned. "Are you insane?"

"Think about it!" She hit me in the shoulder. "You can huff and puff all you want, but in the end, if you don't harm the powerful ones closest to you—all you are is a murderer. A boss who cleansed out the bad, but nobody will fear you. They may take you seriously but you have to actually hurt people."

"That was the original plan." I exhaled. "But I told Phoenix I couldn't do it."

"I never thought I'd utter these words." Mo sighed heavily. "But Phoenix is right."

"Damn him." I fell back against the bed and sighed. Mo followed, resting her hand on my chest.

We laid there in silence for a few minutes before she moved closer and kissed my neck. "Try to live."

Her voice was shaky with emotion. I tried to ignore the pang in my heart but it was impossible.

"Mo." I swallowed a few times, my throat clogging with tears, "If I had a choice—"

"I know—"

"No!" I pulled away abruptly. "You don't."

"Tex, it's okay you don't have to do this." Her eyes blinked rapidly like she was holding back tears. "We already said goodbye, remember?"

"If I didn't have a sister." I whispered.

Mo leaned her head against mine. "If you weren't son to a dead *Cappo di Cappo.*"

"If his legacy wasn't still alive." My voice trailed.

"If you didn't need the help of the Nicolasi family."

I cursed then crushed my mouth against hers. She moaned as I flipped her on her back and deepened the kiss.

"Mo." I pulled back and gripped her hand placing it on my chest. "Know this... my heart will always beat for you and you alone, my friend, my lover, my enemy, my soul."

Tears dripped down her face as she nodded and tugged my head to hers, her mouth meeting mine in a frenzy. "I'm proud of you."

"Don't be."

"Can't help it." She sighed, her lips lingering across mine, brushing feather light kisses across my skin.

We kissed for a while, not talking, memorizing, saying goodbye for the second time in two weeks. I glanced up at the clock and it was nearing midnight.

"Mo—"

"You don't have to say it." She moved from underneath me and stood to her feet. "Keep the fox."

I chuckled. "A one eyed fox for good luck? What could go wrong?"

"Don't be an ass," Mo taunted. "He protected me from monsters, maybe he'll protect you from yours."

"Mo." I shook my head. "Tomorrow I become that monster."

"No." She licked her lips and pressed a kiss to my cheek. "Tomorrow, you become our savior."

CHAPTER SIXTY-FIVE

Sleeping is for the dead.

Phoenix

I SLEPT LIKE CRAP.

So many lives hung in the balance, mine included, but I didn't really value my own life, especially when measured against theirs.

In an hour we would leave for The Commission. My stomach was in knots. I closed my eyes and brushed my fingers across the tree where the guys and I had etched in our names... the names of the Elect. The place where we swore we wouldn't become our fathers.

Damn, but I'd become him without even knowing it.

I felt for Tex, I really did, because I knew better than anyone else what it was like to have ugliness as a legacy. I understood it because I lived with it every damn day, no escape, nothing.

The wind picked up causing a chill to reverberate through the air as the cool air bit through my jacket.

"Crazy," Nixon said suddenly from behind me.

I didn't turn around. "What is?"

Chase answered from my left as Nixon stood to my right. "It doesn't even seem real that we were kids."

I shook my head. "Childhood? Did we even get one?"

"No." A fourth voice answered. Tex. "Pretty sure we skipped that part."

"I would have loved to have had a fort." Chase stuffed his hands in his pockets.

"At least a treehouse." Nixon added.

"Or a bad ass lawnmower to ride." Tex chuckled.

We fell silent, nothing but the wind whistling through the trees and the tension dripping off every one of us.

"How deep does blood go?" Tex asked breaking the silence.

"To the death." I croaked. "Until the last breath leaves my body."

Chase lifted his palm to the inscriptions on the tree and pressed his hand firmly against it. *"Sangue in assenza."* Blood in no out.

Nixon placed his hand over Chase's. *"Con la morte a trovare la tu libertà, ma è la vita dove si è veramente liberi."*

I closed my eyes as the truth of his statement poured over me. "In death you find your freedom, but it is life where you are truly free." My shaking hand went over Nixon's. I didn't expect Tex to join us, after all, he had to stay numb to the emotions if he was going to follow through.

I was shocked when his hand pushed across mine, he whispered gruffly, *"Se il mio sangue, non sia vana."* He repeated it in English. "If my blood spills, let it not be in vain."

"Amen." Nixon whispered.

"Amen." We joined removing our hands.

The back door slammed, jolting us out of our moment, possibly the last moment the four of us would have together alive.

"We should go." Sergio called from the back porch. "Now."

Tex walked away first, then Chase, and finally Nixon.

I watched as my three best friends held their heads high, no fear visible on their faces, and I had to wonder. Was I leading them to their deaths? Or had I done enough to save them? By telling Tex, had I saved more lives, or just added to the body count?

I made a quick cross with my hands and kissed my knuckles. "May God be with us."

CHAPTER SIXTY-SIX

A corrupt heart elicits all that is bad within us...

Mo

I WAITED FOR THE GUYS to leave before taking off after them. Tex had already given me instructions on where to go. I was about to start the car when I heard a knocking on the window.

Trace stood, arms crossed, glaring.

I hit the down button. "What's up?"

"You're going to The Commission aren't you?"

"No."

"Yes you are."

"No I'm not."

"You're a crap liar." Trace opened the door and pulled out her gun, making sure the chamber was loaded.

I groaned.

"Don't worry, I'll wait in the car but I'm not letting my best friend go there without backup."

"And what?" I laughed. "You don't even know what's going on, Trace. It's best that way."

"Mil's there." Trace swallowed. "You're going and Nixon may die. I'm going to be there, in the car, but I'll be there. If I hear gunshots I won't run in the line of fire, Nixon's already threatened me, but if I'm the only one not injured I can at least drive everyone straight to Stephens's hospital and make sure nobody dies."

I closed my eyes and nodded. "Fine."

"You're going to help him aren't you?" She stuffed the gun back in her purse and cocked her head towards me. "Tex, I mean."

I shifted uncomfortably and turned on the car. "Maybe... if I can."

"You're going to just waltz right in there?"

"I'm Nixon's twin." I grinned. "I have just as much right to be there as he does. After all, I'm a Mafia princess, the guys will be pissed but it's not like they won't have bigger issues, plus I have a great excuse."

"What? Insanity?" Trace rolled her eyes.

"No, of course not." I slipped Nixon's phone out of my pocket. "He has my phone instead of his, damn iPhones, can't tell which is which."

"Scary brilliant." She nodded approvingly, her lips pressed together. "Try not to die, okay?"

"Say a prayer that I don't."

"Been saying a lot of those recently."

"I believe it." I pulled out of the driveway and made my way down to the warehouse. The thing about The Commission... there were going to be too many people in one place to actually meet at a hotel besides the whole possible gunfire thing was kind of an issue. So we were meeting at one the Abandonato family dealerships. The warehouse behind the dealership was normally used for packing and merchandising but it worked and it was extremely clean, plus it helped that when it was built the windows were double enforced along with the fact that there were video cameras everywhere.

We controlled the environment, but we sure as hell didn't control the outcome. My hands were sweating by the time we made it to the property. It was only twenty minutes from the house, but I felt each one of those minutes as the time slowly ticked by.

"So—" "Trace clasped her hands together. " —here we are."

"Yeah." I licked my dry lips. "Here we are."

The parking lot was littered with Mercedes' and black SUVs were parked outside.

"I'll get in the driver's seat so we have a fast getaway."

"Right." I snorted. "Like in the movies."

Trace smiled sadly. "Yeah."

"Love you." I hugged her quickly and hopped out of the car as she whispered, "Love you."

My boots clicked against the pavement as I made my way towards the door. With a deep breath I pushed against the metal handle and let myself inside. No going back now.

It sounded like a hive of bees as the talking buzzed around me. I walked further into the room. Long rectangular tables were lined in a large U. Coffee and tea sat in pots on each table. Black cloths were blanketed over everything. If I wasn't in a warehouse I'd think we were in a restaurant.

I cleared my throat. The talking ceased as all eyes fell to me.

I offered a simple shrug and walked up to Nixon holding out his phone. "Figured you may need this."

He frowned taking the phone from my hands. "I wouldn't have answered my phone anyway, Mo, you know that."

"Yeah, but I'm your sister." I smacked him upside the head for effect. "I worry."

A few of the men chuckled while others whispered, "Women."

Nixon didn't miss a beat he took in my dark clothing and glanced down at my tall boots, a flicker of silver must have caught his eye as he froze and then met my gaze. "What game are you playing at, sister?"

"My favorite," I whispered. "Hunters and foxes."

He nodded once then turned. "Gentleman, I'll be sure she leaves before the meeting starts."

They waved him off while I walked over to one of the tables and poured myself some coffee.

A hand shot out to touch mine. "My, my, look how you cleaned up."

Alfonso's voice made my blood run cold. I jerked away from his grasp and sneered, "Looks like they invited everyone to this party hmm?"

"Only the important ones were invited, the filth just arrived." He lit his cigar and leaned back in his chair. I seriously almost punched him across the face, instead I rolled my eyes and grabbed my full cup and moved back towards Nixon. Lifting the cup to my lips, I scanned the room, taking in each solid detail. The Campisi's were seated at the head of the table; Tex was standing near them, but wasn't speaking. The Nicolasi clan was to the right of The Campisi Family and the other three, Alferos, De Langes, and my family were to the left. Nixon and Chase were talking in hushed tones while the men all laughed and pretended like the world wasn't ending.

Any minute now, Tex.

Any minute.

He had to strike before the meeting. But he also had to get them scattered better, at this point he'd have to kill by going down a line of men which meant he'd be shot before he got to man number two.

Crap. I set my coffee on a nearby table and shrugged out of my jacket. I was prepared for the worst. With a yawn I stretched my arms above my head and then popped my neck gaining some of the attention from the men in front. When I reached for my coffee, I clumsily dropped it to the floor. It shattered on contact, with a curse I knelt down low, my top dipped giving every man in front of me an adequate view of my breasts.

Chairs slid back and in an instant I had several associates helping me pick up the pieces of my broken cup.

"Careful." One of the men helped me back to my feet. "We wouldn't want to get blood on your clothes."

"It *is* hard to get out." I nodded innocently.

"Yes, it is." He said gruffly his eyes scanning me from head to toe. "It really is." Gross, he was over twice my age and balding. I offered a sweet smile. "Thank you so much, all of you for helping, I'm so sorry, I feel stupid."

"No, no." Another man's hand shot out and gripped my wrist. "It is no problem." His accent was thick, almost thicker than Alfonso's. If my count was right, I'd pulled at least three of the Campisi targets away from Tex. It had to be enough. Dear God let it be enough.

Something slammed against one of the tables. I looked up into Tex's eyes as he leaned over menacingly. "I'd like to call this meeting to order."

Alfonso sputtered, turned red, then pushed away from his table. "Only the *Cappo Di Cappo* can call the meeting to order."

Tex's lips pulled into a predatory smile. "I just did."

Alfonso's eyes narrowed. "It has not yet been decided."

"So let's decide now." Tex strolled around the tables then took center stage, holding his hands in the air. "After all, not only did you try to kidnap me, and murder me and Nixon's sister, but you put ten million freaking dollars on my head." He threw his head back and laughed. "The family's worth five times that, if not more." He grinned tauntingly. "Which means only one thing... you don't have access to the funds because my father never named you in the first place. You're here because I allow it, you breathe, because I allow it, you live because I allow it."

The bosses stood... Luca, Nixon, Mil, Frank and started pacing.

"You," Alfonso spat pointing his finger at Tex. "Are cursed, an abomination, you should have never been born!"

"Yet." Tex sighed and lifted his hands into the air. "Here I am."

"You're too young."

"And you're too ugly, yet you don't see me yelling that from the rooftops. I'm it. I'm your maker, your creator, your death dealer, your freaking salvation. Take it or leave it."

"And if we vote and you lose?" Alfonso shrugged. "Will you back down?"

A muscle clenched in Tex's jaw. He had to do something, the men were starting to talk amongst themselves. I knew what they would say. Tex was young, he wasn't a sure thing, he wasn't sane.

"Your own father thought you cursed!" Alfonso spat. "It is a fact, a fact you know all too well. He sent you away, what type of father does that to his only son? He never even came for you." Alfonso laughed to himself and held up his hands to the men around him. "You deem to put your trust in a mere child who's own father didn't even want him? Let us not forget... Tex killed the boss of all bosses, killed him in cold blood."

"He had help." Luca's teeth clenched.

"Guilty." Alfonso shrugged. "Anyone who helped him would be guilty. Death is the only solution. You kill the *Cappo di Cappo*, you will be killed. You helped formulate a plan to kill him? Your death is mine."

The Campisis all stood nodding their heads.

Tex's shoulders straightened.

And I knew, he'd made up his mind. He was going to make an example of strength.

"The Abandonatos don't want me, the Nicolasis fear me, the Campisis don't know what to do with me, and the De Langes and Alferos want to stay out of it. So what's a guy to do?"

Alfonso folded his hands in front of him. "He could die, honorably and allow the families to reign in peace."

Tex winced and shook his head. "See uncle, that's the problem, why create peace, when war is so much fun. Does peace bring you more money? No. And I think in the end where the money is, The Family will be. You talk of peace, you preach of honor, yet you still run prostitution rings out of Sicily, pulling girls from their families and offering protection at a price. You say I'm too young, but I say you're too old, too old to realize the ancient ways no longer work. Fear breeds more fear, manipulate too much and you show your weakness. Peace? Hell no, I aim to bring down the fires of Hell on The Five Arms—and I'm going to start with you."

Part Three: The Cleansing
CHAPTER SIXTY-SIX

Blood cleanses all that is evil within us.

Tex

I NEEDED MO TO move a little to the right, but I had no way to tell her that. I also needed a few of the men to get away from Nixon but I couldn't tell him that either. Instead, I continued threatening Alfonso, forcing him to react. But he was smooth, so good at twisting words.

Mo was right.

It was time for action.

"You're a stupid, stupid child." Alfonso's eyes blazed while the men fell silent again.

I grinned. "My father said something similar, before I put three bullets in his head."

A resounding gasp was heard as the men started shouting amongst themselves. I held up my hand for silence.

Alfonso clenched his fists at his sides.

"He called me cursed and in the end, I think he was the one who was cursed, after all, he was already running from me. Already fearful of the truth he saw in my eyes, that I would end him. That I would be the death of him. I think he saw it when I was born. I think he knew it in his bones, that I would come for him."

I closed my eyes as I allowed the bitterness and resentment to fill me, I was going to use it, I was going to use that darkness for good, even if it killed me. I thought of my father, of being abandoned, of being cursed. When my eyes opened, rage consumed me as I looked around the building. A sea of familiar faces stared right through me. It was as if the past twenty-five years of my life had held no meaning at all.

Had I been nothing to them?

Nothing but a joke?

The reality of my situation hit me full force, I stifled a groan as I fought to suck in long, even breaths of the stale dusty air.

"It is your choice." The voice said in an even steady tone, piercing the air with its finality.

"Wrong." I stared at the cement floor; the muted color of grey was stained with spots of blood. "If I really had a choice, I would have chosen to die in the womb. I would have drowned myself when I was three. I would have shot myself when I had the chance. You've given me no damn choice, and you know it."

"You do not fear death?" The voice mocked.

Slowly, I raised my head, locked eyes with Mo, and whispered, "It's life. Life scares the hell out of me."

A single tear fell from her chin, and in that moment I knew what I had to do. After all, life was about choices. And I was about to make mine. Without hesitation, I grabbed the gun from the waistband at my back, pointed it at Mo and pulled the trigger.

With a gasp she fell to the ground. A bullet grazed my shoulder as I knelt taking time to reach for the semiautomatic on the concrete. When I stood, I let loose a string of ammo; the sound it hitting cement, brick, bodies, chairs, and anything else in the line of fire filled me with more peace than I'd had in a lifetime of war.

I stalked towards him, the man I was going to kill, the man who had made me feel like my existence meant nothing. I held the gun to his chest and squeezed the trigger one last time. When he collapsed in front of me, it was with a smile on his face, his eyes still open in amusement.

Chaos reigned around me and then suddenly, everything stopped.

When I turned it was to see at least twenty dead, and Nixon staring at me like he didn't know me at all—but maybe he never had. And wasn't that a bitch?

He took a step forward his hand in the air. "Tex—"

"No," I said, smirking. "Not Tex. To you?" I pointed the gun and pulled the trigger. "I'm the *Cappo*."

Nixon flinched but didn't move, as the bullet whizzed by his head hitting the man behind him—the one that had been pointing a gun directly at the back of his head.

I turned slowly, seventeen of my targets were dead, three still living, and three innocents caught in the crossfire.

"What the hell are you doing?" someone yelled.

"Sucking out the poison." I pulled the trigger, killing the guy who'd asked the question. Two more to go.

The last two that had been with Alfonso looked at each other, then at me, they both dropped their guns and held up their hands.

"I'm your judge, your jury, your executioner," I spat. "I own you, all of you," I shouted, turning around so that each head of the family could see my eyes. Mo got up from the ground and calmly walked to Nixon's side. I'd barely grazed her shoulder but it probably still burned like hell. "Do you think I wouldn't hesitate to kill my best friends?" I nodded to Phoenix and then to Nixon. "I'm a Campisi, I am your leader, double cross me, and nothing will save you. Nothing will redeem you in my eyes. I won't hesitate to kill you where you stand. You're either with me or against me."

Nixon was the first to step forward, dropping his gun onto the ground. "We're with you."

Chase followed, then Mil, Luca, Frank, the rest of the associates nodded their affirmation.

Tension released from my shoulders. "No more." My voice was hoarse. "Vito Campisi is dead, his legacy dies with his men, it died with Alfonso, I stand before The Commission demanding a new era. One filled with pride, not secrets or deception. One that brings powers back to the family." I locked eyes with Phoenix. "Instead of shame."

The men nodded their agreement.

The two Campisi targets stood in front of me, their heads bowed. I didn't want to kill anymore, I was already numb with guilt, anger, sadness… I had done what had to be done and I would have to live with it for the rest of my life.

Swallowing I pointed my gun at the first one. "Will you return with me as a witness, or do I end you here? Lie and it will be the last thing to cross your lips."

"I return." The man trembled. "With pride, I return with the *Cappo di Cappo*."

Nodding, I moved the gun to the other man. He lifted his head and sneered. "Rot in—"

I pulled the trigger, just once, as he fell to the ground.

With a grimace I turned. "Anyone else?"

The room was silent. Luca was pale as he made his way towards me, it didn't register that he was limping. With a grimace he reached for my face and kissed me on either cheek. "May God bless the new *Cappi Di Cappo*, may he protect our families until the end."

The men repeated. "Until the end."

"Amen." Luca whispered, a single tear rolled down his face. I gripped his arms as he slumped against me. With a curse I pulled him to the floor looking for injuries.

When I ripped his jacket open, it was already too late.

Two bullets had torn into his stomach. His eyes closed.

Luca Nicolasi, boss to the second most powerful Family in Sicily had just died in my arms—after blessing me as the new leader of the five families.

CHAPTER SIXTY-EIGHT

When a boss dies, his legacy dies with him, the men... they are lost.

Phoenix

I FOUGHT TEARS as I watched the life leave Luca's body. What had I done wrong? I'd tried to protect him, pushed him out of the way, instead I must have pushed him in the line of fire. Guilt swarmed my every thought as I tried to take a breath only to need another and another. On legs heavier than lead, I walked over to the body and slumped to my knees. The man who had been closer to me than a father, the man who had saved my life, possibly my soul, had just died.

And to mourn him showed our connection.

So I kept quiet while my insides screamed with injustice. It should have been me. Men like Luca, you never knew if they were good or bad. One minute they were spouting such wise nonsense that you had to respect them, the next moment their words were lethal.

For the last month Luca had been my only friend. The only person who saw me for me and didn't turn away.

I'd just lost everything.

And I couldn't even cry.

Frank wrapped his arm around me and squeezed. He knew. Frank knew. I lifted my gaze to Sergio, he'd been standing near the Abandonato family during the fight. His face was pale as he bit down hard on his lower lip.

I'd done everything right.

And someone had still died by my hand. It had been my plan after all, make them fear Tex. Luca had said to invite the Alfonso and his men as a way to make for a way to make peace with Tex, he wanted them to discuss logically what should happen and who should take the place as head of the family.

And I'd gone against that, telling Tex to do the opposite, knowing this was a situation where words wouldn't work.

"Not your fault, son." Frank whispered. "He trusted you, this was his plan all along."

Tex's eyes flashed.

I swallowed the giant knot of guilt in my throat. "To die?"

Frank smiled sadly. "For you to live."

We didn't rush as the bosses all shook hands and made arrangements with each other. Numb, I watched as each boss kissed Tex's right hand. We'd done the right thing. In the end, order had been restored.

At the cost of Luca's life.

CHAPTER SIXTY-NINE

Maybe, just maybe, the ending isn't all bad. Which isn't to say it's happy... but perhaps not being bad is all we're given.

Tex

SHOCK COURSED THROUGH me as I rode home with Mo. She gripped my hand and said nothing. It terrified me that she'd witnessed that side of me, yet I was comforted that she was alive, breathing, okay.

We all decided to let the associates go back to the hotel while the bosses met. It was only four now. It should have been five.

I sent Mil and some of the De Langes to take care of the body, knowing full well that because of their interesting background, they'd be able to keep it on ice while we planned the funeral.

When I walked into the house it was to find Nixon beating the shit out of a wall.

Chase pushed Nixon towards a chair and yelled. "Calm down, man."

Nixon pushed Chase away and jerked out the chair, sitting in it and crossing his arms.

Sergio and Phoenix were discussing amongst themselves, Frank stood near the kitchen.

"Enough," I said softly.

All eyes fell to me. Mo squeezed my hand and walked down the hall.

"That was your plan all along," Nixon whispered. "Why?"

"It was my fault," Phoenix said. "Luca, Frank, and I... we knew that Tex had to make a stand, we knew it had to be in front of the entire family." His shoulders slumped. "Luca wanted to use words. Sergio slipped me an invitation to Alfonso and his men. They thought they were coming to The Commission to celebrate gaining control of The Family—officially."

Sergio groaned. "Actually..." He coughed and looked around. "Luca knew talking wouldn't work."

"What?" Phoenix hissed.

With a curse, Sergio slumped into one of the chairs and spoke in a wooden voice. "He knew Phoenix needed to prove himself again, in order to gain back the self-respect he lost. He knew you—" Sergio glanced quickly at Phoenix. "Knew that you wouldn't like the idea of Tex walking into a room only to most likely be shot... along with the rest of the Family. Luca discovered that Alfonso meant to make an example out of Nixon, Chase, the wives, Frank..." His voice broke. "So he gave Phoenix the choice, do the job you've been told, or make the call, only the call a boss could make."

Phoenix paled. "But, what if I hadn't told Tex?"

"Then we wouldn't be here," Sergio said quietly. "He trusted that in the end you'd do the right thing, redeem yourself, find your soul, and finally find peace. He knew it was a risk, he knew he may die in the process, knew that we'd all die if Tex didn't do *something*. He knew *you*, Phoenix, better than you knew yourself."

Nixon exhaled loudly and leaned back in his chair. "Why

not tell us?"

"If things ended badly," I said finally. "It would get traced to everyone but you..." I swallowed. "The Abandonatos are the most powerful family in America, we needed you guys clean, alive, and in the dark."

"You shouldn't have made that call," Chase said.

"We did what was best," Frank said. "You're family has taken the brunt of things for the past twenty years, it was time we protected you, it was time to do the right thing."

Shaking, I finally sat down. "What happens now, do I move back to Sicily, run the Family from here, make a second in command?" I groaned. "Marry into the Nicolasi family still?"

Frank hesitated briefly before drumming his fingers across the table. "Well, that all depends..."

"On what?" I barked, my patience was officially gone.

"On Phoenix."

All eyes turned to Phoenix, his eyebrows knit together in confusion. "What do you mean, it depends on me?"

Frank stood, with shaking hands he pulled a piece of paper from his pocket and read. "On the terms of my last will and testament, I leave all of my earthly possessions, listed in detail within my will, to Phoenix De Lange."

My mouth dropped open as Phoenix made a noise that sounded a hell of a lot like a whimper.

"I understand that The Nicolasi family will be in need of a leader, I also understand that in rare times it is allowed to choose someone who is not blood, someone who has within them the heart of a warrior, the loyalty of a true family member. Blood does not always win. After all blood is a part of the human heart, and I deem this heart ready to lead. I name the next boss of the Nicolasi family: Phoenix De Lange."

Frank set down the paper and wiped his face with a cloth. "So, as I said, I guess it all depends on, Phoenix, what will be your first act as Boss?"

Phoenix had grown so quiet I was afraid he'd died of a heart attack, or at least shock.

His face had gone completely pale. "But I'm not his son, I'm not—"

"You were more his son..." Frank's voice shook. "Than you will ever know."

"I..." Phoenix's voice cracked. "I need... some time."

"And a drink." Nixon exhaled loudly and knocked on the table. "Someone get him a drink."

"He doesn't drink anymore." I took my eyes off Phoenix and made eye contact with Nixon. "But I'm pretty sure now would be a good time to pick up the habit again."

"No drinks." Phoenix held up his hand. "Time, I need time."

CHAPTER SEVENTY

The Mafia is where broken hearts go to die…

Mo

THREE HOURS.

I waited three hours for Tex to knock on my door. I willed him to enter into the room and at least tell me that things were going to be okay.

My arm was a little bit sore but it was barely scratched and hadn't bled all that much, I took some painkillers anyway and tried to read a book.

But how do you read a freaking romance novel after surviving a gunfight? I mean seriously. It was almost laughable… almost. My stomach clenched at the sight of Luca slumping to the ground. I'd never fully trusted him, but he was good—in the end, he was good and he'd died. It was unfair, but then again, nobody ever said the Mafia was the place to go when you wanted fairness and equality.

Even though I'd been waiting for it, the soft knock on the door startled me. I opened my mouth to say "come in," but Tex had already pushed the door nearly off the hinges. He slammed it behind him and stalked towards me, his face intense, serious.

I gulped. "Things not go well?"

"Marry me." He kissed my mouth, hard, so hard I fell back against the bed with a huff.

"What?"

"Again, for real, marry me." His lips collided with mine as his tongue entered my mouth. My breathing picked up as his hands moved to the skin of my stomach. "Please, please don't say no. I won't survive it, I won't, Mo."

"But..."

Tex's mouth assaulted mine again, stealing my words.

"But, the contract."

"Void." He teased my lower lip with his tongue. "Ripped up."

"What?" I gently pushed against his chest. "How? Why?"

Tex sighed and leaned back. "It's a long story."

"So tell me."

"Say yes first."

I grinned at his hopeful look, he was too beautiful, even after seeing all the death and destruction, I could look at him and see beauty, I could see goodness, love, desire. His blue eyes flashed with hunger as he leaned in, the roughness of jaw brushing against my cheek. "Say yes."

"What was the question again?"

Tex pulled back and stood in front of me, gripping both my hands, then as if having second thoughts, bent down on one knee. "Marry me, not because you're forced at gun point, not because you have to, not because there is no choice, or a damn contract signed in blood. Marry me because I love you. I love Monroe Abandonato with every bone in my body, I love you. Marry me, because you want to, because I can't survive without you, because I don't want to imagine a world where we aren't together. Marry me, because I can't stand the thought of waking up next to anyone one else but you, for as long as God allows me to live, I want to wake up to your face, your lips, your smile, you. I just want you. God knows Mo, if I were given one wish in this world, I'd ask for you. Every time. I'd ask for you."

Tears streamed down my face as I nodded. "Yes, yes I'll marry you."

His mouth crashed into mine as he pushed me back onto the bed, hovering over me as he searched my eyes. Then with a soft moan, he tracked kisses over my lips, down my neck, back up to my chin... I groaned with delight as he lifted my shirt, his mouth moving across my stomach, caressing every inch of my skin until my body burned for him.

"Wait." I gasped pushing at his hard body. "How?"

He stopped kissing me and rested his head against my chest. "Does it matter?"

"How did the contract get destroyed?"

Tex slowly lifted his head. "Phoenix."

"Can he do that?"

"He's the new boss of the Nicolasi family. He can do whatever the hell he wants, from ripping contracts to lighting his pants on fire." He slowly inched his way up the bed until our mouths met. "Now, can we please make love? I'm tired of making war, Mo. I'm finally tired of making war."

"Yeah," I croaked. "We can make love."

He kissed me soundly on the mouth. I arched up to meet him as a frenzy took a hold of me. Free! We were finally free to be together. I gave myself up to him with a cry as he pulled my shirt over my head and kissed me gently on the chin.

"Three hours?" I teased.

Tex's breathing was ragged as he reared back and spoke in reverence. "Every hour." He kissed my forehead. "Every day." His kiss moved to my right cheek, then my left. "For as long as we both shall live."

"Wow," I breathed. "That's a lot of hours."

"Promise me forever—I'll give you eternity." His lips caressed mine. "I'll give you everything."

"Good." I tugged on his hair as he let out a slight groan. "Enemies?"

"Always…" I teased as my arms wrapped around his neck. "Until the end?"

He chuckled and then peeled off his own shirt. "Damn right, until the end."

CHAPTER SEVENTY-ONE

And so it begins... a legacy nobody wanted, dropped into a killers lap.

Phoenix

MY HANDS SHOOK as I stared at the stack of papers in front of me. A year ago I wouldn't have been intimidated by black and white ink, by signatures and dotted lines.

But I was absolutely terrified.

My mind wouldn't allow me to register the fact that Luca had planned the entire thing, that he'd pre-determined that I was worthy when he wasn't even sure I would be.

Faith that I really didn't deserve and a type of love I never really got to know—until it was too late.

Frank had the papers in his car—in his damn car! Like Luca knew he was marching off to his death!

After reading through the first paragraph my knees buckled and I fell to the ground, groaning, screaming— mourning.

It took Tex, Nixon, and Chase to finally pull me to my feet and take me into the office. Even then, I was so raw, so alive that I was afraid if anyone touched me I would scream in agony from the pain of the emotions swirling through me.

"Do you need me to read it?" Nixon had asked once I'd calmed down enough to breath and keep from passing out.

I nodded, biting down on my fist as I stared at the wall.

Nixon read, I heard nothing.

Two hours into it I finally told them to leave me alone... everyone left but Tex. I knew what he wanted, could see it in his eyes, tension and anticipation had wrapped itself so tightly around him that the guy hadn't stopped clenching his fists.

"Phoenix." Tex licked his lips and took a seat across from me. "I don't know if threatening you will do anything. But I'll threaten you if I have to." His eyes flickered towards mine before staring back at the floor again. "If you'd rather I cry, I can do that too."

I sighed, hunching my shoulders, trying to crawl into myself.

He cleared his throat. "If you want me to get on my knees, fine." With a grunt, he dropped, his knees hitting the dark wood floors with a thunk. "I'll get on my damn knees, I'll beg and I'll plead until my voice is hoarse... don't make me marry someone I don't love. Don't allow that contract to go through. Make your first act as boss a positive one, for me, for Mo, for The Family." His tone turned desperate as he reached for his hair and tugged tightly, his teeth clenched as a hoarse cry escaped his lips. "I love her so much. I can't breathe man, I can't freaking breathe without that woman, I can't—" A tear fell down his cheek before he could stop it. "I can't do this life without her by my side. The darkness... it's so cold, but it's inviting, you know? Like I could lose my damn soul and it would be okay—she pulls me from that, she's the only one that can, the only one that makes that hole not feel so big." His hands shook as he rocked back and forth. "Please..." His voice cracked. "Please, Phoenix, please give me this one thing. I'm begging you, man to man, friend to friend, boss to boss, please give me Monroe Abandonato."

I didn't deserve his begging.

I would have had said yes had he decided to punch me in the face and laugh afterwards—I owed him that much. Besides, something told me that I would need a favor from him someday, one of epic proportions.

But it wasn't the driving force behind my decision. I thought back to Luca, the type of man he was. In that moment, he would have looked stern, possibly pissed, but he would have done the right thing. He always did the right thing, so to honor his memory, I did the right thing for the second time in my life, I did the right damn thing.

"Tex." I fought like hell, I fought the emotions coursing through my veins, I fought the anger, the fear, the humility. "You didn't even have to ask."

Blinking rapidly, he looked into my eyes, his own full of unshed tears. "What?"

I stood and held out my hand. He gripped it as I pulled him to his feet. "I want my first act as boss to be a good one, a pure one, God knows not all decisions will be as easy as this." I pulled him in for a hug. His arms tightened around me as I whispered. "Be happy, brother." Because that's what he was, a brother, and I vowed in that moment to never, ever let my brothers down again. Not Nixon, not Chase, not Tex.

Minutes later when he walked out of the room, I broke down and cried. I cried because I'd finally been given what I'd wanted my entire life—but the cost had been too great.

The man undeserving.

How did people survive this? Tears poured down my face as the realization that I would never be able to earn what Luca had given me, but I sure as hell was going to try.

CHAPTER SEVENTY-TWO

Maybe blood doesn't always win out — maybe sometimes love can trump blood.

Mo

I WOKE UP WITH a smile on my face—I tried really hard to look cool about it too. I'm lying next to the sexiest man on earth and he's all mine, no biggie, right? Right?

No. I glanced to my left. That would be a hell no.

His arm was thrown above his head and the blanket had fallen down to his waist revealing his tight golden abs and part of his hip bone. My breathing picked up speed as I kept looking.

Tex's hand shot out and gripped my wrist. Laughing, I tried to pull back, but eyes closed he lifted me effortlessly onto his body and placed his hands on my hips.

One eye opened, then two, as a smirk crossed his face. "Morning beautiful."

"Don't you mean good morning?" I leaned down and kissed his mouth softly.

"Freaking great morning." He returned my kiss with fervor. "Best morning of my life. You?"

"Ah." I pulled back and shrugged. "I'd give it a seven or eight."

Tex bucked underneath me, tossing me against him and then flipped me onto my back as he kissed down my neck. "Yeah, yeah, keep talking."

I arched beneath his touch. "Talking's overrated."

"Yeah." He ripped the blankets from the bed and devoured me with his deep blue eyes. "It really is."

When we joined everyone for breakfast an hour later, things appeared normal, well as normal as our family got. Nixon was cleaning guns, Chase was arguing with Mil about chickens—I didn't want to ask. Trace was pouring herself a third or possibly fourth cup of coffee. Sergio was staring at the wall, probably pondering ways to kill things and cereal was everywhere.

Arguing burst out between Trace and Chase the minute I sat down, again with the chickens.

I grinned and poured myself a cup of coffee, briefly meeting Tex's gaze. He yawned and then said loudly. "So Nixon, I slept with your sister last night."

All talking ceased.

A vein on the side of Nixon's temple pulsed, he calmly set down his gun, still pointing it in Tex's direction and leaned forward. "And by sleep you mean, you were guarding her virtue or taking it?"

Tex winked at me. "I took it."

Nixon stood.

Tex laughed and crossed his arms. "Three times?" He scratched his head. "Or was it four? Mo?"

Chase burst out laughing making everyone else erupt into laughter as well.

Nixon sat down and groaned into his hands.

"Chin up!" Tex grinned. "We're just trying to make you an Uncle, what's the harm in that?"

"I'm seriously too young for this type of stress."

"Gray hair." Trace coughed and pointed at Nixon.

His eyes widened in absolute horror.

"Kidding." Trace leaned over and kissed his cheek. "You, silver fox, you."

"I miss years ago when you guys were scared to tease me." Nixon rolled his eyes towards the ceiling. "Now it's like I point and shoot and you look at me like, what? That all you got?"

Tex raised his hand.

"Not now, Tex," Nixon snapped, though he was smiling.

Phoenix wandered into the room and sat in one of the empty chairs. He looked horrible but also... at peace.

"You good?" Nixon hit his back twice.

"Yeah." Phoenix reached for a coffee mug and grabbed the coffee. "I really think I am."

"How bad ass is this?" Swear Tex couldn't wipe the grin from his face if he tried.

"What?" Chase asked.

"The four of us." Tex's eyes were clear as he looked at each guy. "The Elect... together again... bosses."

Nixon sat back, his face one of awe.

Phoenix grinned, probably for the first time since he'd died and come back to life. And Chase nodded his head in amusement.

"Just so you guys are aware." Mil held up her hand. "This doesn't mean you get to build a tree fort and put capes on. You're men, no more carving names in trees and running around in your underwear."

"Didn't mind it last night," Chase muttered.

"Chase!" Phoenix and Nixon said in unison both covering their years.

"Like I said." Tex lifted his coffee cup. "It's good. It's really good."

"Yeah." Nixon met his gaze. "It is."

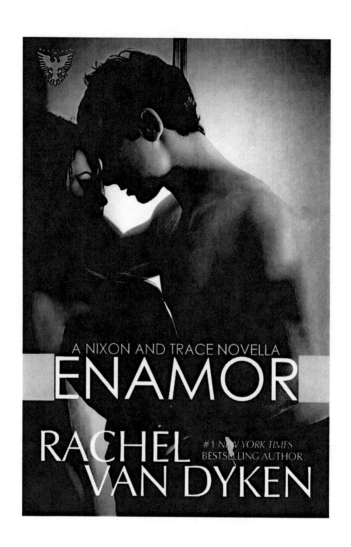

A NIXON AND TRACE NOVELLA

ENAMOR

RACHEL VAN DYKEN

#1 NEW YORK TIMES
BESTSELLING AUTHOR

Enamor
A Nixon and Trace Novella

Enamor: Infatuated or in love with. To be smitten or besotted, literally ensorcelled by.

CHAPTER ONE

Nixon

I STARED UP at the ceiling and memorized each of Trace's breaths, still debating what to do, how to return everything to normal. It had happened so slowly, the downward spiral into madness and now I knew more than anything that I couldn't give her what she needed, not by myself. I could love her, but eventually if she didn't have a life of her own, she'd resent me, and I cared about her too much to put that type of weight on her shoulders.

With a sigh, I rubbed my hands against my face and turned on my side. Dark hair spilled around her pillow like a crown encircling her head. Damn but she was beautiful. Every day I spent with her was like another slam to the heart, I cared too much for her and it terrified me. Terrified me that one day my enemies would discover my weakness—my wife—and take her from me.

"Nixon." She groaned and lifted her right hand to cup my face. Blinking her eyes open she smiled. "Are you having nightmares again?"

"No." I leaned in and kissed her nose, needing to touch her, needing to be closer. The obsession I had over her was ridiculous but telling myself that didn't really work, it just was. Fighting it only made me tired; pushing her away had only hurt us both in the end, which was why I was having such a hard time right now.

"Do you need water or something?" She closed her eyes briefly then opened them, probably trying not to fall back to sleep. "What can I do?"

I licked my lips, my lip ring gave off a metallic taste as I self-consciously licked against the dryness again, damn why was I so nervous? She was my wife!

Her eyebrows arched as she pushed up to a sitting position. "Okay, so now you're freaking me out, what's going on?"

"Everything." I scooted up and wrapped my arms around her body, her head fell against my chest. "I want you to be normal."

"As opposed to crazy?"

"As opposed to getting shot at." I cursed the fact that I couldn't say that in a calm voice, couldn't even think about it without shaking with complete and utter rage. I'd like to think I'd come a long way with my anger, but thinking about anyone hurting Trace was my tipping point, it always would be.

"School." I cleared my throat. "It was what your grandma wanted."

"This..." She pulled away to look at me. "The reason you look like someone died is because you want me to go to school?"

"We talked about it a few weeks ago but then everything happened, and I just... I want to make sure you girls actually do it. I need you to do it."

"So you can shoot things in my absence?" She teased.

"Not funny and I only pull out my gun for very serious reasons, violence shouldn't be the first answer."

"Whoa there, preacher, didn't you shoot Tex in the shoulder a few weeks back? In the kitchen of all places?"

"Entirely valid circumstances," I argued. "And you know it."

"Normal would be punching him."

"I have rage issues," I defended. "So back to the school topic..."

With a smirk, Trace fell back against my chest and gave me a few pats. "I'll go to school... if."

"Oh wow, bargaining with the boss... tell me how that goes." I scolded.

"Oh wow bossing your wife around, let me know when you want to have sex again."

"I'm listening." I growled, irritated that she bested me, again.

"I want to learn how to fight."

I took a deep breath. "That's it? Okay fine, you can take a kickboxing class."

"Not kickboxing," she said proudly. "Israeli hand-to-hand combat."

I clenched my jaw so tight it damn near popped. "That's not my specialty..."

"I know that."

"That's Chase's and Tex's..."

"And Phoenix."

"Hell, no."

"Trust him."

"No."

"Nixon…" Trace tiled my chin towards her face. "Think of it as a small step. Let him train me, I'll go to school and you guys can build back up that fragile relationship."

"He attacked you!" I roared pushing away from her. "And now you want him to touch you? To teach you how to defend against monsters like him? Sadistic freaks who think it's okay to overpower a woman?" My chest heaved with exertion as I clenched my fists and managed—only slightly—not to punch the hell out of the headboard until my knuckles bled.

"See?" Trace didn't react, at least not outwardly. "You're still upset, and I think I need this, Nixon… to get over things, I think we all do."

"Not if I kill him."

"He's a boss now." Trace pointed out, slowly drawing lazy circles on my chest with her fingers. "You can't."

I snapped my teeth. "Watch me." I was ready to get in the car and freaking drive to Sergio's house, put a bullet between his eyes and never look back, the rage was so menacing, so dark, it was hard to stay calm, hard to even think about him touching her, using the same tactics he'd used before. I closed my eyes and pinched the bridge of my nose against the memories, against the trauma.

"Nixon." Trace gripped my hands in hers. "You trust me, now it's time to trust him, time to forgive. You say you forgave him, but right now says something else, you say you want me to be happy, let me be happy. Let me do this, let me heal, let me stop being afraid, let him stop torturing himself. Let us live."

I groaned, touching my forehead to hers. "I'm dangerously close to tying you to the bed right now so you can't tell anyone this plan."

"Please." She snorted. "Like I'd stay tied, you always give up once you can't take it anymore."

"I'm immobile," I taunted. "Like a stone or a statue or a—"

Her hands moved down my naked torso, she tucked her thumbs into my boxers and tilted her head. "Oh yeah, just like stone, Nixon."

"I've created a monster."

"Yup."

"I don't like this plan."

"So… make the call, boss." She kissed my mouth, hard, her lips pressing against mine, as her tongue slipped past my lip ring, flicking it once, twice.

Groaning, I pulled back. "Damn it, you know I love that."

"So?"

"Fine." My heart hammered against my chest. "But if anything goes wrong, and I do mean anything, you tell me, you run out of the workout room and tell me."

"Then you have a deal." She held out her hand. I stared at it and smirked patronizingly. "What?"

"Sorry sweetheart, that's not how we seal the deal in the bedroom. At least not in my house."

"Oh, your house?"

"My house." I bit down on my lower lip then kissed her neck. "My wife." I grabbed her shoulders and ran my hands lightly down her arms, my hands rested on her hips. "Mine, mine, mine, just in case you were wondering. This." I tugged her body against mine. "All mine, so sweetheart, don't you think we can do better…" I trialed open mouth kisses down her collarbone until I met her breasts. "Than a hand shake?"

"Y-yes."

"Yes what?" I teased.

"Yes sir." She smacked me on the shoulder then stopped talking all together as I showed her exactly why it was important to seal the deal my way—not hers.

CHAPTER TWO

Trace

I WAS NERVOUS. Not like, first-day-of-school nervous where you imagine yourself completely naked and people pointing and laughing, but throw-up nervous. As in, I really shouldn't have tried so hard to convince Nixon to let me do this when I wasn't even sure I wanted me to do this.

I clenched then unclenched my fists as I waited in the gym. The old clock on the wall mocked me as I leaned against the wall. A practice mat was set out on the middle of the floor. Pretty sure my butt was going to be spending a lot of time on that particular mat in a few minutes.

Nixon refused to tell me about his conversation with Phoenix but I couldn't imagine it being a pleasant one. Nixon had truly come a long way with the whole anger thing but when it came to Phoenix, he still lost all control.

My answer came a minute later when Phoenix pushed open the door to the workout room and briefly glanced in my direction. He set down his water bottle and a white towel then faced me.

A swollen lip and the beginning of a bruised cheek was

the only evidence I had that he'd talked to Nixon, or better yet, that Nixon's fist had talked to Phoenix's face. I still wasn't sure if it was because Phoenix had originally said no and Nixon had convinced him, or because he'd said yes and Nixon was threatening him.

Phoenix took a deep breath and walked to the middle of the mat. He hadn't always been a monster to me. In the beginning he'd been one of untouchable Elect, perfect, good looking, funny and then after my attack he'd morphed into this monster. I think even in my dreams I imagined him as this sinister beast. Not the broken man in front of me with shadows under his eyes and secrets behind his lips.

No the man I was looking at, wasn't the same man. Which was why I could do this, which was why I needed to do this as much for me as for him.

"Should we start?" He asked softly.

I licked my lips and nodded, meeting him in the middle of the floor, my fists were still clenched at my sides.

Phoenix sighed heavily then looked directly at me, his eyes finally meeting mine in such a piercing gaze I wanted to run out of the room. So much pain was hidden behind those eyes, why had I never seen it before? Had he truly been that good at putting on masks? At covering what he really was? Raw—every emotion was readable on his face, this was killing him, ripping him to shreds. I almost backed out right then and there but again, we needed this, to heal, to make things better.

"*Krav Maga*," he spoke with authority, "is basically hand-to-hand combat, it's deflection, it's attacking with so much thought it seems almost thoughtless. Whether you're pushing away a gun, a knife, or just gouging someone's eyes out in order to run, the point is never to engage long enough to get hurt, but long enough to be able to escape, do you understand?"

I swallowed and nodded. My throat was already dry, my heartbeat picked up as he took a step forward. "The proper stance is similar to a boxing stance, feet shoulder width apart, and your dominant leg first."

I bit my lip and looked down at my left foot then my right. "How do I know which is dominate?"

"Which foot do you lead with while snowboarding?" he asked.

I shrugged. "Never been."

Without any warning he pushed me roughly against the shoulders. I staggered back on my right foot.

He nodded his approval. "Right foot in front, left foot towards the back but not far enough to look like your about to kick someone's ass."

I positioned myself somewhat to the side.

He shook his head. "No, you look like you're about to punch me, all you need to do is wind up your arm and you've just given yourself away, space your legs a little closer together." His hand moved to my hip adjusting my stance and then moved to my hands. "Keep your hands loose, no clenching, you haven't been attacked yet, you have no idea if you need to throw a punch or a kick."

"Right." Information swirled around my head as I tried to keep my focus on him and not the fear that was already starting to course through me at the fact that he'd just touched my hips, and then my hands. I was seriously losing it.

"Hit me," he ordered.

"Um?" I licked my lips. "Is this part of the training?"

"Hit me."

"Phoenix."

"Hit me dammit or I'm going to hit you, do you want to be hit first?"

I hit him.

Not hard.

It was more of a light slap across the cheek. He cursed and staggered to the left rubbing his cheek. "You slapped me."

"You said to hit you!"

"Hit." He nodded slowly, fighting a grin. "Not slap."

"I was confused." I chewed my lower lip and put my hands on my hips. "Plus aren't they interchangeable?"

His eyebrows shot up. "Hit me again and I'll tell you."

"In the face?"

"Would you rather hit me in the balls?"

"Am I supposed to answer that?"

He looked away from me and then down at the floor. "Make a fist, hit me, however Nixon trained you, however Frank taught you, hit me that way, in the face, right now."

"But—"

He moved so fast I didn't have time to prepare. One minute he was in front of me, the next minute I was on my back and he was standing over me.

"That," he said offering me his hand, "is how fast an attack happens. I think we're both aware that hesitation gets you nowhere. When I say hit, I mean hit, you don't hesitate. When you're in a situation, you act out of impulse out of necessity out of habit, not out of hesitation, got it?"

"Yeah." I rubbed my hands together. "Got it."

"Hit me."

Yeah, I officially hated training.

"Fine." I answered raising my fist.

In an instant he'd deflected my fist and reached for my throat softly pushing me back. "What did I do just now?"

He could have hurt me, could have bruised my trachea, instead it had been done so softly it almost tickled. "When I went to hit you, you saw it coming, I think you used my momentum to push me to the side and counter attacked."

His grin was so beautiful I think my mouth dropped open.

Let it be known that I'd never, in my entire life, seen a real honest to God smile from Phoenix. Sure, I'd seen him laugh but it had always been sinister, even when I first met him there was darkness lurking.

This was sunlight.

I actually looked away like a total coward, not sure I wanted to see the light, not sure I was ready to feel the humanity I knew he possessed again.

"Well done." He clapped twice. "So most attackers go for easy, they grab a girl's hoodie or her ponytail."

"Or her book bag." I added, not recalling for a moment that was exactly what he'd done to me.

His smile fell.

His entire demeanor darkened.

I took a step back.

He took another step forward.

Hot and cold washed over me, should I run? Was that too far? Had I pushed him? Woken the beast? I was just getting ready to bolt when he whispered, "Right, or a book bag, purse, anything that can tug the person' body close enough to where you have leverage."

I gave a quick nod.

"So, the minute that happens, you need a plan. Already you're stuck against the person's body, and a guy can easily overpower you, so the idea is to give yourself some time to use his body weight against him or surprise him. Depending on the situation."

I gulped and then nodded slowly. "I'm ready. Show me."

His eyes widened a bit before he took another step forward. "Just tell me, tell me..." his voice cracked. "...if I scare you, say..." He closed his eyes again. "Saying stop would bring back too much, can we think of a word that isn't..." he didn't finish just stared at the ground, his face pale.

"Moo." I nodded. "I'll say moo if I'm freaked."

A smile broke out on his face. "You're going to moo?"

"Like a total cow."

He barked out a laugh and nodded his head. "Alright, if you moo I'll back off, just make it loud."

"It's really the only way to Moo, Phoenix." I winked and

then got in the ready position.

CHAPTER THREE

Nixon

"WOW. ALL YOU NEED is a set of binoculars and a creepy van and you'd be a relative stalker. Hitting up the local playground later?" Chase slapped me hard on the back and laughed.

"Hilarious." I didn't turn around, didn't acknowledge his teasing, just watched the screen in front of me and winced every damn time Phoenix put his hands on her.

I was in the security room, doing my job, which was to protect Trace. She'd see me if I looked through the window outside, so this was the next best thing. Watching their training like live TV. "How'd you find me?"

Chase sat down in the chair next to me and leaned back. "Easy, I saw Phoenix in the gym with Trace and put two and two together. She'd see you through the window so—"

"Sometimes it terrifies me how much we think alike."

Chase cursed. "Don't I know it."

"Are we starting a spy club?" Tex's booming voice sounded behind me. I groaned into my hands ignoring the hard slap on my back.

"Nixon's monitoring," Chase answered for me, nodding reassuringly.

Tex scratched his head. "Don't you have, oh, I don't know… a family to protect? People to kill? Torture? Threaten?" He put his feet on the table in front of me and leaned back in his chair like Chase did.

"It's Saturday." I said gruffly.

"Right." Chase nodded. "I forgot we don't kill things on Saturday, it's why I set that bad ass spider free this morning… no blood on God's day, oh wait, no that's Sunday…"

"Where's Mil?" I changed the subject. "Shouldn't you go check on her or something?"

Chase chuckled. "Because she's five and in need of a babysitter?"

"Shopping." Tex licked his lips and watched the screen in front of me. "She and Mo wanted to make appetizers for New Year's."

"Shit." I jumped out of my seat. "Today's New Year's Eve?"

"Calendar app." Chase shook his head. "On your phone, use it, set an alarm or something."

I sat back down and groaned. Trace had begged me to get sparklers for tonight and I'd totally forgotten.

"I need a favor."

Both guys stood abruptly and ran to the door.

"Not that kind of favor you bastards." I rolled my eyes. "I need sparklers for tonight, and some fireworks."

"Aren't those illegal?" Tex tapped his chin. "I mean I think the city of Chicago has this weird thing about fireworks within its limits and we did have a drought."

Chase put an arm around Tex's shoulders and nodded solemnly. "One should never take chances with fire safety."

"Agreed." Tex grinned.

I looked back at the screen to make sure Trace was okay and then back at them. "Fireworks, consider it your job."

"It'll cost you." Tex exhaled loudly.

"Extortion." I cursed. "Nice."

"Let's say we get these fireworks." Chase crossed his arms and leaned against the wall. "What will you do for us?"

"I won't kill you," I answered honestly. "Happy New Year."

"You know I'm really glad he's taking those anger management classes," Tex said to Chase. "Vast improvement since last Christmas when he tried to set the tree on fire because you looked at Trace cross eyed."

Chase grimaced. "To be fair I was trying to lighten the mood."

"Yeah this isn't memory lane and I'm not the ghost of Christmas past," I said gruffly. "Fireworks…" I cleared my throat and looked heavenward. "Please?"

"Say with a cherry on top," Tex whispered. "Say it, say it, say it."

Chase clapped.

I leaned forward to bang my head against the desk and grumbled, "With a cherry on top."

They laughed and walked out of the room while I lifted my head to the screen again. Phoenix had Trace in a type of headlock. I almost bolted out the door when she stepped on his foot, elbowed him in the ribs and twisted out of the hold.

Furious, I knew I couldn't do anything except watch, and trust both of them, something that was getting harder and harder every damn time he put his hands on her body.

CHAPTER FOUR

Trace

I WAS JUST about to Moo when Phoenix released me, his breathing labored, he took a step back and nodded. "Good job."

"Thanks." I huffed, sweat was starting to fall down my temples. I was desperately trying to get my shaking under control, but it was harder than I thought it would be.

"Are you okay?" Phoenix glanced briefly at my hands, his eyes narrowing. "If I pushed you too hard—"

"Totally fine!" I said in a high pitched lame voice. "I'm just tired and I didn't expect the fighting to be so…"

"Personal." Phoenix nodded curtly. "It's always personal, Trace. Just like killing, whenever your body is in contact with someone else's, whether it's negative or positive, an exchange takes place, it either drains you or inspires you, the choice is always yours."

My mouth would have dropped open in shock had the gym door not burst open with a loud thud. "You guys finished?" Nixon's eyes searched wildly over my body, from head to toe his eyes memorized every single inch of me, probably trying to find a hair out of place so he could put a gun to Phoenix's head.

"Yup!" I jogged over to him and threw my arms around his neck, kissing his cheek. "And I did good!"

Nixon's jaw flexed as his arms braced me, holding me so tight I almost let out a little squeak. "Of course you did."

"Same time tomorrow?" Phoenix called over his shoulder as he made his way to the door.

"Yup." I licked my lips, not breaking eye contact with Nixon. "That'll be great, thanks Phoenix."

"Yeah." The door slammed shut behind him, leaving me and Nixon staring at one another.

"Tell me the truth." His teeth ground together, his face was pale as if he was three seconds away from either passing out or all the blood had rushed to his hands so he could pummel Phoenix. "Did he hurt you? Scare you? Make you feel anything less than secure?"

"No, no, and no." I sighed against Nixon's chest, my cheek finding comfort in his soft black vintage t-shirt. "I was a bit scared once, but it was weird, like he could sense it, he stepped back, he never took anything further than I wanted and well we came up with a type of safe word."

Nixon's grip on my body loosened. "A safe word?"

"Yeah." I grinned up at him. "Moo."

His stern expression turned into a smile, and then a full out laugh as he tugged me tighter against him and kissed my forehead. "Leave it to you to Moo when you're getting attacked."

"What?" I pulled away and swatted him playfully. "I was being clever."

"Right." His crystal blue eyes narrowed. "That's the word I was thinking... clever."

"Liar." I pointed at him. "Hey want me to show you what I learned today?"

After a severely long patronizing look Nixon took a

stance in front of me, one that said, I'd like to see you try.

I walked up to him and shrugged, then ran my tongue along the bottom part of his lip. With a groan he lifted me into his arms—that's when I struck. I kicked the inside of his knee causing him to fumble since he wasn't expecting it and then elbowed him in the ribs followed by a front push kick to his thigh, he stumbled down a bit and then looked up at me. "That was cheating."

"That," I said, dusting my hands together, "was winning, but I understand how you'd be confused, since it's so rare that it happens to you."

"Run."

"Nixon—"

"Run."

I turned, but not fast enough, he tackled me to the ground, rolling me onto my back then straddled me with his hips, pushing me against the mat. "I think I won."

I wiggled beneath him a bit then threw my head back and let out a tiny moan. His mouth dropped open as he lost complete control and started kissing down my neck.

"No," I whispered wiggling again as he started reaching for my t-shirt. "I think I did."

"We both win." He said gruffly, peeling my t shirt off then following with his. "It's a tie, now keep moving exactly like that." The cold lip ring had me almost screaming as it came into contact with my bare stomach.

"This thing on?" Someone came on over the intercom. "As much as I love a free show and all that, we're out of popcorn and somehow this feels like I just caught my parents having sex, so if you could please bring this to the bedroom we'd all be really thankful."

Tex.

I felt myself blush.

"Cameras." Nixon cursed and moved away from me then gave the middle finger to the camera on the side of the wall.

"Sorry, I forgot I left Tex in there."

I tugged the back of Nixon's neck and kissed him hard across the mouth then glanced at the camera. "Don't like what you see, Tex? Close your eyes."

"Sorry Trace. Continue." Tex said over the intercom.

"Your eyes better be covered, bastard."

Tex's deep laughter boomed over the intercom. "I did one better, I turned off the monitor, now if only we could turn down the sound. Real world problems and all that…"

"Just leave, Tex!" Nixon roared when I started peeling off his jeans as fast as my hands would let me.

"Hey did she hurt you?" Tex asked. "I heard you yell?"

"Tex! I will shoot you!" Nixon yelled and then hissed when I tugged on his lip with my teeth scratching down his chest. "Damn, that feels good."

"You felt me caressing the screen?" Tex asked.

"Tex!" This time I yelled. "Go away!"

"Fine, fine." The buzz of the intercom turned off but I was too distracted to ask if he was still there, watching. Who cared? I was with my husband and I wanted him—desperately.

"We really doing this here?" Nixon mumbled against my lips, his tongue diving in before I could even answer yes or no.

Apparently we were, because he was already pushing me against one of the walls and stripping down my yoga shorts until I was in nothing but my sports bra and under armor. "I'm sweaty."

"Good." Nixon licked down my neck and then moved his tongue towards the indentation of my hips, I lurched forward, catching myself with his head. "I like a little salt."

With a groan I gripped him by the hair tilting his head up so I could stare into his eyes, those same crystal eyes that held me captive the very first day at Elite, the same eyes that used to cause fear, were now the object of absolute undying, unrelenting love.

Slowly, Nixon rose to his feet, pushing me back against the wall, his hands on either side of my face as his forehead touched mine. "I love you. More than anything in this godforsaken world—I love you."

It transported me back—back to our first time back to the moment I gave him not just my heart but my soul. At the time I wasn't even nervous, the idea to be nervous hadn't even crossed my mind. All I knew was that he'd looked so lost, so desperate, I wanted the darkness to go away so bad and I wanted to be the one to make it go away. I wanted to be his savior—for once in my life I wanted to do the rescuing. So when his hands moved to my hips, when he gently pushed me back onto the bed, when he didn't use any words, but his hands to convey the absolute horror of our situation, the danger, the fear. I let him, without hesitation. I opened up my body, my heart, my soul to everything that was in him, knowing it was possible that it would be the last time. Of course, I didn't know Nixon would fake his own death—I didn't think him that crazy, but something was wrong.

My body shuddered as his fingertips had caressed my bare skin, danced along my collarbone, then moved down to remove the rest of my clothing.

Every inch of me wanted to feel every inch of him, I almost cried out before we'd even started—knowing I would be a wreck when we were done, unable to pull myself away from him, even if he pushed me away, even if it's what was best.

"I love you," he'd whispered in my ear, over and over again as his mouth unlocked every secret I'd kept, touched places I'd never touched. "I love you," he whispered with conviction when he made me his, when the pieces of the puzzle that was our relationship finally settled into place, when the sensations of having a man who loved me so desperately, washed over me, moved within me, against me, and then with me again. I squeezed my eyes shut then opened them, hands gripping his shoulders as I let go—and gave him everything.

I watched as he opened his eyes, locked them with mine, and took all.

In hindsight, it was stupid to think that I could ever erase the marks he'd made on me—but when death surrounds you, something desperate claws within to be released. I thought I was going to go crazy and there was Chase. The guy who really didn't deserve the hell and torture I put him through.

"Be present." Nixon kissed my mouth, his breath hot on my neck. "Be here, with me now, not in the past, not in the future. Here." He lifted me against the wall, his hips rocking into mine. "Be here, Trace."

I sighed, running my hands through his dark hair. "For you..." I hooked my feet behind his back. "I'm always present." I felt my eyes well with tears. "Right here, forever."

"I'm never leaving you, Trace." He vowed his eyes darting back and forth between my lips and my gaze. "Ever. We're forever... you and me. Not being with you would be absolute death. I love you." He shuddered. "I love you so damn much."

Our mouths met in the same frenzy as before, only this time, I ignored the fact that I was sweaty, that we were in a gym, that I'd just learned how to fight from the one guy that tried to take the fight out of me. Nixon slid off the under armor as I fumbled with the rest of his jeans, sliding them as far as I needed before he slammed me back against the wall and reminded me again and again how much he really did love me.

CHAPTER FIVE

Nixon

I ALWAYS THOUGHT I would die alone—I mean, Mafia boss doesn't really scream marriage with kids, but that's what I wanted with Trace, she made me crave normal, she made me believe it was possible. She inspired me to pull away from the blood and darkness to want something more for myself, for my family. I leaned my head against hers, my breathing ragged as her body was still wrapped tightly around mine.

I didn't want to move.

Wasn't sure it was even possible.

Funny, I'd always been a really careful type of person, every decision I made was made with strategy, with thought, with absolute control over every single player in the game.

And I'd totally dropped the ball. I would have laughed but I wasn't sure if Trace was going to be freaked out and slap me or just shrug. I never knew with Trace, she was about as unpredictable as a bomb. So when I looked at her flushed face, and finally pulled my body away from the warmth of hers. I wasn't sure what to say.

"Nixon?"

"Shit." I buttoned my jeans and helped her set herself to rights. "Trace, I swear we'll be more careful next time, I think I was too upset with Phoenix and then I lost control and—"

"Careful?" She squinted. "You didn't hurt me, plus I'm pretty sure I can kick your ass now."

"No, not that." I sucked in my lip ring waiting for her to put two and two together. Then again, it was Trace, innocent, I-grew-up-on-a-farm, Trace. I'd have to spell it out for her, fantastic. "We um... just had unprotected sex and I know we're a forever thing but you know..." I swallowed, shit was I sweating? "Sometimes accidents happen and," I rubbed my forehead, while Trace gave me a blank-as-hell look. "And kids are probably a long way off and I don't want you to freak out, just don't cry, it will be fine, I mean it's probably—"

Trace burst out laughing. "Wow I can't wait to sit in on that particular conversation when we have kids, you uh see son when you love a girl and..." She covered her mouth, laughing even harder.

I about choked on my tongue. "Kids?"

"Right." She nodded slowly. "Usually the product of too much hot and crazy sex with your Mafia boss husband who can't seem to keep it in his pants long enough to protect his wife from what I'm only assuming is pregnancy." She winked. "Good talk, Nixon, and if I'm pregnant I probably will cry, but it will be the good kind. I promise. Now stop being so still. It's freaking me out."

"You don't mind?" I blurted.

"Having the best sex in the world? With you?" She looked around. "Trick question, right?"

"No." I couldn't help but puff up my chest a bit. "I mean bringing a kid into all of this."

Trace cupped my cheek with her hand. "The way I figure... we get a do over... your parents messed you up so badly, why not start a new legacy? One we control — turn the bad into good. Besides, I would love to have little boys that

362

look exactly like their dad running around the house tying Tex's shoelaces together. Priceless."

I barked out a hoarse laugh and jerked her against my chest. "Have I told you I loved you today?"

"Say it again."

"I love you..." I whispered in her hair. "Today, yesterday, tomorrow, forever. I can't wait... to start a family with you and that's the truth."

"Well that's a relief." Trace sighed. "You know all things considering."

I wrapped my arm around her and led her to the door.

"Oh and we should probably go to the security room, make sure there isn't a tape Tex or Chase can use as bribery."

"Another reason I love you." I pushed the door open. "You think like a boss."

"Can't help it. I'm sleeping with him."

"Yes." I growled. "You are."

CHAPTER SIX

Trace

I TRAINED WITH PHOENIX for five days, each day was more grueling than the next, by the time day six came around I was sore everywhere and he was relentless in pushing my every limit, hitting my every nerve.

Yawning, I waited for him to arrive at the gym. Normally he was right on time, but he was already five minutes late.

The lights went off.

I looked around, blinking as my eyes adjusted to the darkness. It was really early in the morning so it wasn't necessarily sunlight flickering in the window.

"Concentrate," Phoenix said softly. "I'm going to attack you from behind, this is the only warning you'll get."

My mouth went completely dry and then watered as I tried to swallow, tried to gain my bearings. Suddenly his arms were around me, and I freaked like lost my mind. I screamed and just slumped against him.

"What the hell are you doing?" He pulled me tighter against his chest.

"I'm... I don't know, I'm scared."

"No," he said quietly. "Fear causes your senses to be heightened, your smell, taste, sight, use the fear, rather than let it cripple you, what are you going to do, how are you going to save yourself? You have five seconds to make it to the door before you die. What. Do. You. Do?"

With a roar all the training came back slamming into my brain as I flipped him over me, hitting him in the chin, the nose, and then pulling a knee to his ribs as I ran towards the door like a woman insane.

When I reached the door, the lights flickered on.

"Told you she could do it." Phoenix said from the ground as Nixon stood on the opposite end of the room, arms crossed, gaze murderous.

"I did," I huffed. "I did it."

Nixon's nostrils flared as he moved toward Phoenix.

"No!" I yelled, then ran, not thinking about anything but making sure Nixon didn't do something he would regret. I moved in front of Phoenix just as Nixon's fist came back. He paused mid-air, his jaw cracking.

"Move, Trace."

"No." I reached behind me to help Phoenix up. "He didn't do anything wrong. He's training me, and he's doing a good job. I trust him."

Phoenix collapsed out of my hands slumping to the floor in a heap. I turned around thinking maybe he was bleeding or something but he was just staring at the ground, his eyes watery.

Nixon looked between us then with a quick nod stormed out of the room.

It was quiet, except for my heart slamming against my chest and Phoenix's heavy breathing.

Not knowing what else to do I sat down next to him.

We sat in silence for five minutes.

"You should have let him hit me."

"That wouldn't have made you feel better, Phoenix."

"Yeah," he whispered hoarsely. "I know."

More silence. What was I supposed to do? How do you comfort someone you aren't even sure you aren't still pissed at? Or scared of?

"I have nightmares." Phoenix finally said. "Of that afternoon, almost every night. It's like this horror movie on repeat and the part that really sucks is every time, every damn time, I scream at myself to make a different choice. I watch myself hurt—" His voice cracked. "I watch myself hurt you, I watch myself turn into this monster and every time I can't help but think, if only I could stop it this time, it will be okay. If only I could stop—" Phoenix shuddered, closing his eyes as he rocked back and forth. "I hate the dreams, Trace, but not as much as I hate myself."

Slowly, I inched my hand across the mat until my fingers collided with his. It's funny, I thought his hand would be cold, lifeless, I thought his touch would scare me.

Instead, his fingers were warm, his hand rough but strong. He gripped my fingers so tightly I almost winced, he gripped them like I was the only thing keeping him above the water.

"Trace—"

"Phoenix," I interrupted. "Maybe we should just start over, I don't know this guy, this one you are right now. I never had the privilege of meeting him." I elbowed him in the ribs. "And the thing is, he's kind of great."

"Yeah?" He licked his lips and glanced up at me through long eyelashes. "You really think so?"

"I know so."

He lunged for me, enveloping me in such a tight hug it stole my breath away. "I would like that, a lot."

I hugged him back just as tight. "Me too."

CHAPTER SEVEN

Nixon

"DUDE, TURN UP THE SOUND." Chase moved around me and started playing with the monitor.

"Stop." I smacked his hand. "They need privacy."

Tex and Chase just stared like I'd lost my mind.

"Did you hear that?" Tex tilted his head while the gum dropped completely out of Chase's mouth. "Privacy? Did he say privacy?"

Chase still wasn't speaking. I could tell he was fighting a losing war in his head. He'd been just as pissed if not more when everything happened with Phoenix and then marrying Mil had helped alter his view a bit of what had happened to Phoenix as a kid to make him the way he was, but I think, just like me, he had this uncontrollable rage, this need to shoot the guy for everything he put us through.

"Chase?" Tex nudged him. "You alright?"

"I'm thinking about it," Chase finally answered, stretching his arms above his head and letting loose a string of curse words. "Trusting him is hard, Nixon."

"So is dying," I said honestly. "Our lives are hard.

Everything about what we do is hard, Chase."

We all fell silent.

Tex was the next to speak. "I know you guys know this, but Phoenix basically saved us all, he's proven again and again we can trust him and the guy just hugged Trace like she was on her death bed. I know we've forgiven him, I know it's water under the bridge, I know it still sucks, for everyone, just because the pain is still there doesn't mean we can't move away from it, learn from it."

I smirked. "When did you get so smart?"

"I married your sister." Tex winked. "Oh and *I'm* kind of the *Cappo* so yeah there's that too."

"There he is." Chase coughed.

"Did I pass?" Another voice interrupted. I nearly fell out of my chair trying to stand to my feet while Chase and Tex moved out of the way.

Phoenix was leaning against the door, his face impassive as if he knew the whole time we'd been spying on him.

"Yeah, Nixon." Chase turned to me. "Did he pass?"

Tex grinned, facing me too, the bastard.

I rose from my seat and shrugged. "It was never a test."

Phoenix nodded once. "She knows the basics so we'll probably only train three times a week now to get her to pro level."

"Pro level?" Chase asked.

Phoenix smiled. "Yeah Chase, pro as in, good enough to kick your sorry ass."

Tex held up his hand for a high five from Phoenix while Chase scowled. "You aren't supposed to make her better than me."

"Like that's hard." I laughed.

Chase lunged for me, I ducked just as he tried to punch me in the jaw, then grabbed him by the waist pushing him against the wall.

Tex swore then jumped in followed by Phoenix.

"What the hell!" I yelled. "No biting!" I elbowed Chase in the chin while Phoenix pulled Tex away from Chase.

"Boys." Trace said from the door. "They never change."

"We have fun parts." Tex felt the need to point out. "Like you really want us to change, that."

I let out a low growl. "Talk about parts again in front of my wife and you'll be the recipient of shiny new ones, *capiche*?"

Tex grinned, lifting his hands into the air while I approached Trace and kissed her across the forehead. "You sure you're okay?"

"Sure I am." She grinned then peered around me. "I'm going to be able to kick Chase's ass finally!"

"A little too early to celebrate." Chase said from behind me. "But dance if you must."

She wiggled a bit in front of me. Rolling my eyes I lifted her into my arms and helped her wrap her legs around me. "How about we take that dance elsewhere."

"Yes." Chase coughed. "For the love of God, take it elsewhere."

"Like he should talk," Tex murmured. "Oh and PS you made our lamp fall down last night."

"Earthquake." Chase called. "They happen in Chicago."

Phoenix was standing silently by the door, his look pensive. "She hurt you or something?" I kept my voice light, but I could tell it wasn't helping his mood. Instead he shoved away from the wall, his expression indifferent.

"Phoenix?"

"Just tired," he finally said, pulling his phone from his pocket, when he looked at the screen he paled.

"What?" I still had Trace in my arms, but I was ready to jump into action if I needed to. "What's wrong?"

"Oh nothing…" His eyes flashed. "Just babysitting duty."

"You got a kid we don't know about?" Tex teased.

Phoenix blushed. "Yeah, something like that. I'll catch

you guys later, and Trace..." he paused in the doorway. "Good job today."

"Thanks." She beamed.

Phoenix nodded to us and walked briskly out of the room.

"So." Chase coughed. "Not weird at all, what's stuck up his ass?"

"Sure as hell isn't a woman," Tex commented. "The guys like a monk these days, won't drink, rarely swears, and I'm pretty sure he actually said a prayer before eating yesterday."

"Someone should." I rolled my eyes. "Bye guys, I've got official..." I hefted Trace higher. "Business to attend to."

"Nice." Chase laughed. "Good wording, that's not suggestive at all, be careful we don't need any kids up in here."

Trace sighed and looked directly into my eyes. It felt like we were sharing a giant secret, one that probably would happen sometime in the near future and for once it didn't scare me, but it sure as hell made me walk a lot faster down the hall towards our bedroom. After all, what kind of boss would I be if I wasn't thorough? What kind of husband... if I wasn't seeking to constantly please my wife.

I slammed the door behind me and dropped Trace to the floor.

"So about those kids..." she teased then lifted her shirt over her head.

"Keep talking." I commanded, not caring that the guys knew exactly what was going on... as far as I was concerned it was none of their business, and she? She was finally, finally, all mine.

EMBER
Eagle Elite Book 5

Ember: A small piece of burning coal. **Origin:** Old English, Germanic. Example: All it takes is a one tiny piece of Ember to start a flame, one small flame to burst forth into a fire. One spark, and a man's world may implode from the inside out.

PROLOGUE

Phoenix

"DO IT," MY FATHER spat. "Or I will."

I looked at the girl at my feet and back at my father. "No."

He lifted his hand above my head, I knew what was coming, knew it would hurt like hell but had no way to fight back—he'd already starved me of my food for the past three days for arguing, for trying to save the girl.

His fist hit my temple so hard that I fell to the ground with a cry. The click of his boots against the cement gave me the only warning I'd have as he reared back and kicked me in the ribs; over and over again he kicked. The girl screamed, but I stayed silent. Screaming didn't help, nothing did.

I waited until he was done—I prayed that he would kill me this time. I prayed so hard that I was convinced God was finally going to hear me and take me away from my hell. Anything was better than living, anything.

"You worthless—" Another kick to the head. "Piece of shit!" A kick to my gut. "You will never be boss, not if you cry every time you must do the hard thing!" Finally blessed darkness enveloped my line of vision.

I woke up from the nightmare screaming, not even realizing that I was safe, in my own bed. With a curse I checked the clock.

Three a.m.

Well, at least I'd only had one nightmare—that I'd remembered. I'd been living with Sergio for the past week, his house was so big that I basically took the East Wing and he took the West, said he'd hated living alone anyways. I wasn't stupid, I knew the guy wasn't exactly a big fan, but it worked, I needed to stay in the States while I figured shit out.

And I wasn't ready to leave. Not when I needed to learn all I could from Nixon. Not when I had responsibility.

"Hey!" Bee barged into my room.

"Damn it!" I pulled the blankets over my naked body, my heart picking up speed at her tousled hair and bedroom eyes. Tex's sister, Tex's sister. My body wasn't accepting that— physically it wasn't accepting any information other than she was beautiful.

And it was dark.

I looked away scowling.

"I heard screaming." Bee took a step forward, her perfume floating off of her body like an aphrodisiac or drug, making me calm, making me want something I had no business wanting.

"Yeah well." I gave her a cold glance. "Clearly I'm fine, so you should go. Actually, why are you here? You know you live with Tex right?"

She shrugged and sat on my bed. I clenched my fists around the blankets to keep from reaching out to her.

"He's with Mo, and they need privacy, I'm not stupid, so I asked Sergio if I could move in for a while."

"You did what?" I asked in a deadly tone.

She grinned. "I'm your new roomie!" Bee bounced on the bed and gave me a shy look beneath her dark lashes. "Admit it, you miss our slumber parties."

Forget the nightmare—I was looking at it.

CHAPTER ONE

Phoenix

IF THAT GIRL TEXTED me another picture of herself one more time I was going to lose my damn mind.

I drove like an insane asylum escapee back to Sergio's then speeded to a stop right in front of the gate, waiting impatiently for it to open, tapping my fingers harshly against the leather steering wheel of my Mercedes C class coupe. Another gift from Luca... I would have rather had his life, than the new car every guy on the planet was salivating over.

I wanted a lot of things.

But want didn't really belong in my vocabulary anymore.

The gate opened, slower than I would have liked since I was pissed off. I sped through the minute I saw an opening, not caring that I could possibly scratch the ridiculously expensive car and pulled to a stop right before hitting Bee.

"Damn it!" I threw open the door and slammed it as hard as I could. "What the hell are you doing?"

"You curse more now." Bee's eyebrows furrowed. "You know that?"

Yeah I was picking up bad habits where she was

concerned, really, freaking awful bad habits. "What do you want, Bee? And didn't we talk about the pictures? I don't have time to respond to pictures of goats and sheep and ugly dogs. I have a business to run, a family to protect..." My voice trailed as her face scrunched up with hurt.

"I just..." She shrugged. "Thought they would cheer you up."

"How is a turtle making it through traffic then causing a ten car pileup cheerful?" I challenged.

She smiled wide, hitting me square in the chest. "Because the turtle made it!" She danced around in front of me and clapped, then paused and arched her eyebrows in my direction.

"I'm not clapping."

"It's worth clapping for."

"Turtle power," I said through clenched teeth. "Now, was there anything else? You said something about an emergency?"

"Oh." She waved me off. "I need help picking out my first day of school outfit."

"Call a girl," I snapped, walking past her.

I felt warm fingers on my arm, and before I could jerk away, I was rendered completely paralyzed by her tender grasp. Shaking, I swallowed the terror and gave her a pointed look.

Her face fell but she didn't remove her hand. "I just... I heard they wear uniforms at Elite I just don't want to look stupid, I only have a few choices, I mean it's not a big deal, I just..."

Well, damn me to Hell. I sighed and hung my head. "Fine." I'll just try to ignore the way that the clothes hugged her body then when she was done twirling in front of me, I'd go puke in the bathroom and run ten miles to get the image out of my head. Sounded like the time of my life. Bring it on. After all, I deserved that type of torture, didn't I?

"Yay!" She clapped again then looped her arm in mine. "Thanks, Phoenix, I knew I could count on you."

Funny she should say that… after all, I wasn't that guy. The trustworthy one, the accountable one, the mature one. I may as well be a body without a soul. It's what I felt like most days and she did nothing but remind me… that I'd once had it all and lost it.

"Hey." Bee nudged me. "You look like you've seen a ghost."

"Every day in the mirror, Bee, every day."

"What?" Her smile fell.

I forced my own. "Nothing, let's go pick out shoes."

"Awesome!"

Bang Bang

PROLOGUE

Amy

"AX?" I KNOCKED on his bedroom window and waited.

Nothing.

Fear gave into panic as I knocked harder this time. The sound of glass breaking made my palms sweat. I could still hear my parents fighting. It was always the same with them, my father wanted to be more than just an associate... A made man, that was his dream. A made man for the De Lange family. One of the worst families in the American mafia. They didn't play by the rules anymore and my dad wanted to be a part of their game, rules or no rules.

I knocked harder. "Ax, please, it's Amy."

The screaming got louder. I fought the urge to cover my ears as I glanced back at the house. Slinking further into the shadows I wrapped my arms around myself and shivered. I hated Chicago. As soon as I was eighteen I was going to move.

I wanted to be warm.

The chill of fear and death surrounded me—choked me from birth until now. I was seventeen. I only had one more year, one more year and I was running away. Ax said he'd help me, though I wasn't sure what he could do since he was nothing but a mechanic.

Teeth chattering, I knocked one last time and prayed he was home. I'd already tried his cell but it had gone straight to voicemail.

Finally, I saw a shadow move in the window.

And then I saw his face.

It was always like the first time with Ax. He had sharp defined cheekbones, a strong jaw, full lips meant for kissing, though it's not like I would know, I was his friend, nothing more. He was beautiful. Like the prince from a story book. I'd always thought of him as my own personal prince and he'd laughed it off saying princes in the stories never worked on cars and had grease on their faces.

"Amy?" He jerked open the window, his shirtless body stole my breath away as his muscles flexed to push the last part of the window up. "What's wrong? Are you okay? Why the hell do you have a bruise on your cheek?"

"Too many questions." I forced a watery smile, "Can I stay here tonight?"

He sighed, his shoulders slumping over with sadness, guilt, pity? Who knew. "Amy, this has to stop, why don't you just move in?"

"Right." I laughed, "Move in next door with the enemy."

He rolled his eyes, "Just because I'm related to the Abandonato family does not make me the enemy, I'm not in the business, neither is pops, you know that."

"Help?" I held up my arms.

Laughing, he reached over the ledge and hauled me into his room. His warm chest was all I needed, he was all I needed.

"Same fight?" He released me onto my feet, I fought the urge to sway into his arms, to lie and say I tripped. Just being in his embrace made me forget about the pain on my cheek... and the accompanied pain in my chest at the fact that my dad had hit me, again.

Ax steadied my shoulders with his hands, then softly grazed his fingers tips over my face as he reached up and touched the bruise. "I'll kill him."

"With a wrench?" I teased pulling away from Ax even though it was the exact opposite of what I wanted.

"Ames..." Ax swore and ran his fingers through his messy dark brown hair, "Hitting you is not okay, it's never okay for a man to touch you in a violent way. I don't care if you yell in hise face, I don't care if you kick him in the junk and pull a freaking gun on him — it's never okay for a father to touch his daughter in a way that isn't an expression of pure love and devotion."

"Nice words..." I bit down on my lip to keep myself from bursting into tears, "They sound pretty... a little too pretty for someone like me."

"Amy," Ax gripped my chin with his hand, "You deserve more than nights crawling into a losers house just because you have to escape your dad."

I jerked away, "You're not a loser."

"I'm not exactly a winner either." He smirked, "But I'm glad I'd get your vote for Homecoming King if it came down to it."

I rolled my eyes. "Hows work?"

"It's work." He said in a serious tone, something flashed in his eyes before he looked away and pointed to the bed, "Right or left?"

"Middle?"

Rolling his eyes he asked again, "Right or left?"

"Middle."

"I can do this all night, Ames."

"Funny, me too." I crossed my arms and smirked.

He burst out laughing, "Fine, you can have part of the middle and I"ll just try not to fall on the floor, but no promises."

I moved towards the bed, "If I hear a loud thunk I promise not to scream."

"Right, it's just my head shaking hands with the nighstand, no big." He winked and pulled the covers back. "Need something to sleep in?"

"Uh, yeah." I looked down at my jeans and white t-shirt. Self consciously pulling it over my stomach. My dad yelled at me for wearing skanky clothes but it wasn't for lack of trying to wear normal clothes. We had no money, and I didn't exactly have funds to keep shopping. How was it my fault I hit a growth spurt?

I hoped Ax didn't notice the blush on my face. I was ashamed that I couldn't even afford to go to Wal Mart.

I was even more ashamed that my father blamed me for his inability to stop gambling.

"He a made man yet." Ax asked once we were settled into bed.

"No." I wrapped my arm around his chest, my usual position when I spent the night. "And it's not like things would get better even if he was, but you aren't supposed to know any of that. It's not like the mafia smiles on people who know their business."

He snorted, his body tensed. "Right."

"I mean it, Ax. I can't lose you."

"I'm a mechanic, hardly a threat." He kissed the top of my head, "Now try to sleep."

I closed my eyes and took a relaxing breath just as a loud gunshot rang my ears, jolting me awake.

"Stay down." Ax pushed me against the bed, his body hovering over mine. His entire face changed from calm to rage in that instant. His muscles flexed as he reached into the nightstand and pulled out a .45.

"Ax?" I whispered, "Why do you have a gun?"

"Shh." He held the gun to his lips. "I need you to be quiet."

I nodded. Tears already pooling in my eyes.

Another gun shot rang out and then his bedroom door flew open. It was his older brother Sergio. "Time to go, covers blown."

The door slammed shut behind him.

I stared at Ax.

He stared right back.

More gun shots.

More bursts of light.

And then Sergio was back in our room, slamming the door behind him. "So we have to go to plan B, they're pissed we've been spying on them, we have to go, now!"

Cursing, Ax flew off of me grabbed another gun out of his nightstand and started packing stuff into a duffle bag.

"She comes with us." Ax barked.

"She's a De Lange." Sergio spat, "She sure as hell is not coming with us."

"She's not like them..." He argued, "He hits her, she needs to come."

The sound of male voices yelling had me running into Ax's arms. He kissed my forehead just as I was jerked away from his arms.

"No." Sergio said in a stern voice.

"Yes!" Ax pulled me back, "We're not leaving here. She stays I stay."

The bedroom door burst open and everything happened in slow motion as a man held up a gun and pointed it towards Ax.

"Bang." The gunshot rang out.

Ax stumbled, "Take her Sergio, protect her, I'll cover you, just take her."

With a curse Sergio pushed me out of the window then followed.

"Ax!" I screamed, but Sergio covered my mouth.

Just as another bang rang out, lighting up the once dark bedroom.

Sergio pulled out his cell, "Pick up at The Spot, thanks Nixon... I owe you."

"What about Ax?" I tried to fight against Sergio.

"Either he's dead or he's going to be." Sergio pushed me down the alleyway, keeping to the shadows, "And it's your fault. Never forget, it's your fault my brother's dead. But what should I expect from the De Lange blood line? You were born to kill... born to die."

My world shattered that day.

I lost my best friend.

I lost my heart.

My shield.

My soul.

And buried it right along with his body. The boy who wasn't who he said he was — the boy who protected me from my own family.

The boy who took two bullets for me and paid with his life.

Bang, Bang. Was the new soundtrack to my life.

Welcome to the Mafia.

ELITE
Eagle Elite Book 1

PROLOGUE

WHOEVER TOLD ME life was easy—lied. It's hard. It sucks. The crazy thing is—nobody has the guts to admit the truth. Everyone, and I mean everyone, has a secret. Everyone has a story that needs to be told. Hurt is everywhere; as humans we practically drown in its essence, yet we all pretend like it doesn't exist. We make believe that everything is fine, when really, everything within us screams in outrage. Our soul pleads for us to be honest at least once in our lives. It begs of us to tell one person. It forces us to become vulnerable to that one person, and the very second that we do, everything seems better.

For a moment, life isn't as hard as it seems. Effortless. It's effortless, and then the gauntlet falls.

When I met Nixon I had no idea what life had in store for me. In my wildest dreams, I could have never imagined this.

"Everything..." He swallowed and looked away for a brief second before grabbing my hand and kissing it. "Everything is about to change."

CHAPTER ONE

"I CAN FEEL YOU breathing down my neck, Trace." Grandpa gripped the steering wheel and gave me a weak smile before he reached back and patted my hand.

Yup, patted my hand.

As if that's going to make me feel any less nervous.

I closed my eyes and took a few deep breaths, trying to concentrate on the excitement of my situation, not the fear. I refused to be scared just because it was new.

I mean, sure, I'd never ridden in an airplane before last night, but it wasn't as if I was freaking out...yet.

I missed my dogs and everything about our ranch in Wyoming. When my ailing grandma suggested I enter the contest, I obeyed to make her happy — anything to distract me from her illness. Besides, it's everyone's dream to go to Eagle Elite, but your chances of getting in are slim to none. One company did a study and said your chances were only slightly higher than that of your body morphing into the body of a whale.

Guess that made me a big, giant, fat whale, because I got in. I'm pretty sure the company did it as a joke, but still.

Out of millions of applicants, they drew my number, my name. So fear... it really wasn't an option at this point. Going to Eagle for my freshman year of college meant that I was basically set for life. I would be placed in a career, provided for in every way possible. Given opportunities people dreamt of.

Sadly, in this world, it's all about who you know, and my grandpa, bless his heart—all he knows is the ranch and being a good grandpa. So I'm doing this. I'm doing it for me and I'm doing it for him.

"Is that it?" Grandpa pointed, snapping me out of my internal pep talk. I rolled down my window and peered out.

"It...uh, it says E.E. on the gate," I mumbled, knowing full well that I was staring at a steel gate that would have made any prison proud. A man stepped out of the small booth near the entrance and waved us down. As he leaned over the car I noticed a gun hidden under his jacket. Why did they need guns?

"Name," he demanded.

Grandpa smiled. He would smile. I shook my head as he proceeded to give the guard the speech, the same one he'd been giving all our neighbors for the past few months. "You see my granddaughter, Trace." He pointed at me. I bit my lip to keep myself from smiling. "She got into this fancy school, won the annual Elite lottery! Can you believe it? So I'm here to drop her off." How did Grandpa always stay so completely at ease all the time? Maybe it was because he was always packing a gun, too, but still. He and Grandma were the coolest grandparents a girl could ask for.

I swallowed the tears burning at the back of my throat. It should have been him and Grandma here with me, but she died of cancer about six months ago, a week after I found out about the school.

They were my world, Grandpa and Grandma. Being raised by your grandparents isn't all that bad, not when you have or had grandparents like mine. Grandpa taught me how to ride horses and milk cows, and Grandma could bake the best apple pie in the state. She won at every state fair using the exact same recipe.

My parents died in a car crash when I was really young. I don't remember much except that the night they died was also the night I met my grandparents for the first time. I was six. Grandpa was dressed in a suit. He knelt down and said something in Italian, and he and Grandma took me away in their black Mercedes. They moved their whole lives for me, saying it wasn't good for a little girl to live in the city. Chicago hadn't seemed that bad to me, at least from what I remember. Which wasn't much.

I gave Grandpa a watery smile as he reached across the console and grasped my hand within his large worn one. He'd sacrificed everything for me, so I was going to do this for him, for Grandma. It may sound silly, but as an only child I felt this immense need to take care of him now that Grandma was gone, and the only way I could see myself doing that was getting a good job and making him proud. I wasn't sure about his retirement, or about anything, and I wanted to be. I wanted to take care of him, like he took care of me. He was my rock, and now it was my turn to be his.

Grandpa winked and squeezed my hand again. He was always so perceptive. I could tell he knew I was thinking about Grandma because he nodded his head and pointed at his own heart, and then pointed at mine as if to say, She's in your heart. She's in mine. We'll be okay.

"You aren't from around here, are you?" The man interrupted our exchange and directed the question at me.

"No, sir."

He laughed. "'Sir'? Hmm... I have to say I like the sound of that. All right, you check out. Drive straight down the road for one-point-five miles. Parking is on the right and the dorms will be directly in front of the parking lot. You can drop her off there."

He slapped the top of the car and the gate suddenly opened in front of us.

My heart was in my throat. Large trees lined the driveway as Grandpa drove the rental toward the dorms.

Nothing in my life had prepared me for what I was seeing. The buildings were huge. Everything was built in old stone and brick. I mean, I'd seen pictures, but they did not even come close to reality. The dorms looked like ritzy hotels.

Another security guard approached the car and motioned for Grandpa to turn it off. My mouth gaped open as I stepped out of the car and leaned my head way back so I could look up at the twelve-story building.

"New girl's here," came a voice from behind me. I flipped around and my mouth dropped open again.

"So squeaky clean and innocent. Like a little lamb. Right, Chase?" The guy tilted his head. Dark wavy hair fell across his forehead; he had a lip piercing and he was dressed in ripped jeans and a tight t-shirt.

I backed away, like the little lamb/whale that I was.

My grandpa stepped forward protectively, reaching inside his jacket, probably for the gun that was usually present. I'm sure he was just trying to freak the guys out. "A welcoming committee? This place sure is nice." Anyone could see the guys standing in front of us were not here to welcome us and certainly weren't part of any committee, but Grandpa was making a point, marking me as his to protect. I stepped behind him and swallowed at the dryness in my throat.

"Is there a problem?" Grandpa asked, rolling back his sleeves. Whoa. Was my seventy-two-year-old grandpa going to get in a rumble or something?

The guy with the lip ring stepped forward and then squinted his eyes in Grandpa's direction. "Do I know you?"

Grandpa laughed. "Know many farmers out in Wyoming?"

The guy scratched his head, giving me a lovely view of

his golden tanned abs as his hand reached above his head. I swallowed and grabbed my grandpa's arm.

The guy named Chase smirked and hit the other guy on the back. He glared in my direction and then stepped right up to me, reaching out to lift my chin, closing my gaping mouth.

"Much better," he whispered. "We'd hate for our charity case to choke on an insect on her first day." His eyes flicked to Grandpa's and then back to mine before he walked away.

His friend joined him and they disappeared behind the dorm. I could feel my face was heated with embarrassment. I didn't have much experience with guys. Okay, it was safe to say my first and only kiss had been with Chad Thomson and it had been awful. But still: something about those guys warned me they weren't good news.

"I don't like those boys. They remind me of... Well, that doesn't matter." Grandpa scratched his head then went to the trunk of the car to pull out my few things. I was still trying to get over the fact that I had embarrassed myself when someone walked up to us with a clipboard.

"No parents allowed in the dorms. Sorry. Rules." She popped her gum and winked at my grandpa. Was she flirting with him? What the hell kind of school was this? The guys had piercings and treated people like dirt, and the girls flirted with old men?

My grandpa shot me a concerned look and sighed, placing his hands against the rental car as if trying to brace himself for the emotional turmoil of the day. "You sure you'll be okay here?"

I sighed heavily and looked up at the intimidating building. I needed to do this for him, for us. It was why I had applied.

Taking a deep breath, I stepped away from him and gave them both my most confident smile. "I'll be fine, Grandpa, but I'll miss you so much." Warm tears streamed rapidly down my face as I stepped into his embrace.

"I have some things for you. I know..." Grandpa coughed and wiped at a few of his own stray tears. "I know she would have liked you to have them, Trace."

Wordlessly, he walked away from me and pulled a small box from the back of the car, then returned and handed it to me. "Don't open it until you're in your dorm. Oh, sweetheart, I'm going to miss you so much."

I hugged him again and closed my eyes, memorizing the way his spicy scent filled my nostrils with all the comforts of home. "I'll miss you more."

"Not possible," he said with a hoarse voice. "Not possible, sweetheart."

He released me and folded some cash into my hand. I looked down into my clenched fist, where a few hundred dollar bills were rolled with a rubber band. "I can't take this." I tried to give it back, but he put his hands up and chuckled.

"Nope, your grandma would roll over in her grave if she knew I was dropping you off at some fancy school without an emergency fund. You keep it. You hide it in your pillow or something, okay?"

"Grandpa, we don't live in the Depression anymore. I don't need to go hiding money under my mattress or in my pillowcase."

He narrowed his eyes and laughed. "Just keep it safe."

I hugged Grandpa one last time. He sighed heavily into my shoulder. "Be safe, Grandpa. Don't let the cows out and keep milking the goats. I really will miss you."

"And I you... Just, do me a favor." He pulled away and looked into my eyes as I nodded. "Be careful. There are people out there who..." He cursed. Grandpa rarely cursed.

"What is it?" Okay, he was starting to scare me.

He looked behind me and pressed his lips together in frustration. "Nothing. Never mind. Just be careful, okay, sweetheart?"

"Okay." I kissed his cheek.

Grandpa grinned and got into the car. I waved as he drove off, then turned back toward the girl with the clipboard.

"Okay." I took a soothing breath and faced my future. "So where to?"

"Name?" she asked, sounding bored.

"Trace Rooks."

The girl smirked and shook her head as if my name was the most amusing thing she'd heard all day. Was everyone rude here?

"It's your lucky day," she announced, motioning toward the building. "You are in the United States."

I looked around just to make sure I wasn't getting punked. "Um, yeah, I know. I'm American."

"Gee." She put the pen in her mouth and sighed heavily. "I didn't know that. You seemed foreign to me. Where did you say you were from? Wyoming? Do they even have electricity there?"

I opened my mouth to defend myself, but she interrupted me... again.

"I know where we are, New Girl. Rooms are themed based on countries. Don't ask me why; it's just how it's done. Your room is the United States Room. Go make yourself at home. Oh, and welcome to Elite." She eyed me from head to toe twice before finally spinning around and returning to the building.

How was I supposed to get all my stuff in the building? Wasn't there some sort of welcome packet or directions or something?

I vaguely remembered some information that had come in the mail the week before. It had my student ID card, amongst other things. I rummaged through my purse and found the packet and quickly began scanning it for the schedule.

"Are you lost?" a deep voice asked from behind me. I turned around and quickly came face to face with the same guy I'd seen before. Only this time he had three friends with him, not one. Lucky me.

"Nope. Apparently I live in the United States." I gave him my best smile and tried to lift my heavy suitcase with my free hand. It didn't budge and I almost fell over. Awesome.

"I'm Nixon." He moved to stand in front of me. His icy stare did weird things to my body. I'm pretty sure what I was experiencing was called a panic attack. Every part of my body felt hot and then cold, as if I was going to explode any minute.

"Tracey, but everyone calls me Trace." I held out my hand.

He stared at it like I was diseased.

I quickly pulled it back and wiped it on my jeans.

"Rules."

"What?" I took a step back.

The guy from before named Chase left the waiting group and approached us. "He's right. As cute as you are, Farm Girl, someone needs to tell you the rules."

"Can it be fast?" I asked with an overwhelming sense of irritation. I was tired, jet-lagged, and about five seconds away from crying again. I'd never done public school, let alone a private Elite school where the guys were tattooed, pierced, and better looking than Abercrombie models.

"You hear that, Chase?" Nixon laughed. "She likes it fast."

"Pity." Chase winked. "I'd love to give it to her slow."

I gulped. The two guys behind them laughed hysterically and high-fived one another.

"The rules." Chase began circling me slowly, making me feel like one of those carcasses vultures feed on. Fantastic.

"No speaking to the Elect, unless you've been asked to speak to them."

"Who are the—"

"Nope. You've already broken a rule. I'm speaking, New Girl." Chase smirked. "Geez, Nixon, this one's going to be hard to break in."

"They always are," Nixon replied, lifting my chin with his hand. "But I think I'll enjoy this one."

Okay. It was clear someone had just dropped me into a horror movie where I was going to be offed at any minute.

"If an Elect talks to you, never make eye contact. Because, technically, you don't exist. You're just a pathetic excuse for a human being, and at this school, you're a real tragedy. You see, while one of the Elect is out running for president and basically ruling the free world, you'll be lucky to be working for one of our companies. You follow the rules, and maybe we'll throw you a bone."

Furious, I glared at him, ignoring their second rule. "Is that all?"

"No," Nixon answered for Chase. This time his touch was smooth as he caressed my arm. I tried to jerk away. His face lit up with a smile, and honestly, it was like staring at a fallen angel. Nixon was gorgeous. He was an ass, but he was a gorgeous ass. "You feel this?" His hand continued moving up my arm until he reached my shoulder, and then his hand moved to my neck and his thumb grazed my trembling lips. "Memorize it now, because as of this moment, you can't touch us. We are untouchable. If you as much as sneeze in our direction, if you as much as breathe the same air in my atmosphere, I will make your life hell. This touch, what you feel against your skin, will be the only time you feel another human being as powerful as me near you. So like I said, feel it, remember it, and maybe one day, your brain will do you the supreme favor of forgetting what it felt like to have someone like me touching you. Then, and only then, will you be able to be happy with some mediocre boyfriend and pathetic life."

A few tears slipped down my cheek before I could stop them. I knew I needed to appear strong in front of Nixon and Chase. I just… I didn't have it in me, not when he would say such cruel things. I choked back a sob and stared them down, willing the rest of the tears to stay in. I didn't care who these guys were. They had no right to treat me like this, though it still stung. I so desperately wanted to fit in.

He jerked his hand away from my face. "Pathetic. Are you going to cry? Really?" Nixon scowled and held out his hand to Chase. Chase handed him some Purell.

"Don't want to get farm on my hands, you understand." Nixon smiled such a mean smile that I literally had to clench my hands at my sides to keep from punching him in the face and getting expelled.

"Don't even think about it, New Girl. You touch me, I tell the dean, who just so happens to be Phoenix's dad. We control the teachers because, guess what? My dad pays for everything. Now, if you have any questions about what we talked about here, please direct them to Tex and Phoenix, 'kay?"

The two guys who had been standing back from us waved and then flipped me off.

"That's how they say hello," Nixon explained. "All right, Chase, it seems our job here is done. Oh, and Farm Girl, don't forget. Classes start tomorrow. Welcome to Hell."

Eagle Elite Series Reading Order and Release Dates
Elite
Elect
Entice
Elicit
Bang Bang (novella September 2014)
Enforce (Elite from Nixon and Chase's POV December)
Ember (Phoenix's story 2015)

OTHER BOOKS BY RACHEL VAN DYKEN

The Bet Series
The Bet (Forever Romance)
The Wager (Forever Romance)
The Dare

Eagle Elite
Elite (Forever Romance)
Elect (Forever Romance)
Entice
Elicit

Seaside Series
Tear
Pull
Shatter
Forever
Fall
Strung

Wallflower Trilogy
Waltzing with the Wallflower
Beguiling Bridget
Taming Wilde

London Fairy Tales
Upon a Midnight Dream
Whispered Music
The Wolf's Pursuit

Renwick House
The Ugly Duckling Debutante
The Seduction of Sebastian St. James
The Redemption of Lord Rawlings

An Unlikely Alliance
The Devil Duke Takes a Bride

Ruin Series
Ruin
Toxic
Fearless
Shame (October 6, 2014)

Other Titles
The Parting Gift
Compromising Kessen
Savage Winter
Divine Uprising
Every Girl Does It

About the Author

Rachel Van Dyken is the *New York Times, Wall Street Journal,* and *USA Today* bestselling author of over 29 books. She is obsessed with all things Starbucks and makes her home in Idaho with her husband and two snoring boxers.

CPSIA information can be obtained at www.ICGtesting.com
Printed in the USA
LVOW07s1913241115

464028LV00006B/576/P